All rights reserved

The characters and events portrayed in this book are fictitious. Any similarity to real persons, living or dead, is coincidental and not intended by the author.

No part of this book may be reproduced, or stored in a retrieval system, or transmitted in any form or by any means, electronic, mechanical, photocopying, recording, or otherwise, without express written permission of the publisher.

ISBN: 9798333415523

Cover design by: Tracy Morand
Editing by: Jo Morand

Printed in the United States of America

This book is dedicated to those who believe in everyday magic, the glory of God and His Majesty. All gifts come from Him.

S.G.MORAND

TO TURN THE TIDES OF WAR

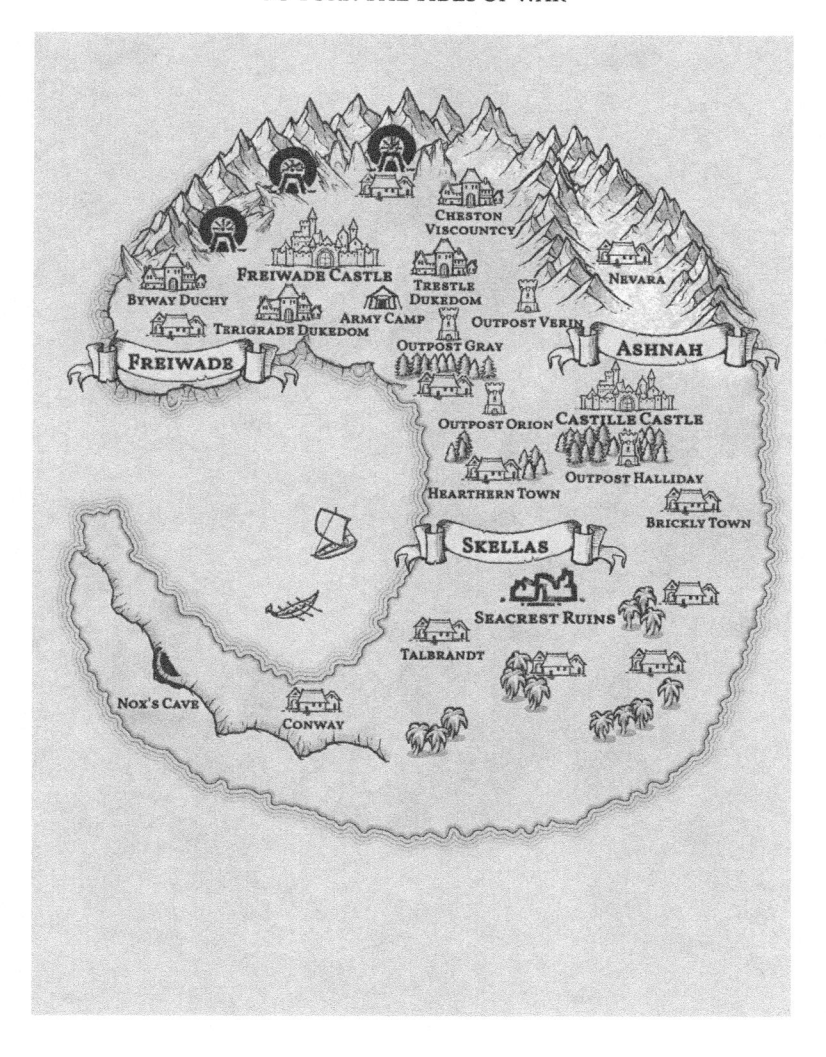

S.G.MORAND

TO TURN THE TIDES OF WAR

S. G. Morand

S.G.MORAND

PROLOGUE

The cave was dark... dark and damp.
Its depths were never-ending, fathomless, lifeless.
It was as if it were a portal into another world, one few had dared to cross. Those who did cross over always left... different, changed. They were altered in a way that could never be reversed. Maybe it was for that reason or maybe for one even more sinister that the cave and its secrets had been buried for so long. Such secrets were often lost or buried. The very history of the world had been forgotten because of conquerors and destruction. The past had long been overwritten by the painful present. The secrets of this cave were another of those casualties. The only knowledge of the power contained deep within the jagged stone fortress was found in an old, wind and salt-weathered parchment that by fate, or maybe misfortune, had found its way into Brion's hands.
The ocean mist stung Brion's face. Pellets of salty water hit his cheeks like the lashing of a whip. He pulled his cloak tighter in a vain attempt to block out the bitter cold. It was winter in Skellas and winter, like every other season, meant cold and damp. It was

a type of cold that sank into Brion's ribs and nestled there unwilling to leave. It was a type of dampness that made his limbs feel like rusty hinges, creaking with every step he took. It was an unbearably *human* feeling.

All of that would change soon enough.

Once he entered that cave, he would not be the same. He would no longer be weak and powerless. He would no longer be a bystander in a war that had sucked the life out of his people. The kingdom of Freiwade's efforts to overpower the neighboring land of Ashnah had bled Skellas dry. All of the yield of Skellas's labor and industry had been sent on to the powerful but land-locked and infertile nation that held control of them. Their resources were taken to fund and feed the unnecessary war that was driven by the Freiwade royal family's need for power.

Brion had suffered and watched his kingdom suffer for too long, unable to do anything to stop it. He knew he was a rarity. The pittance of magic ability that ran through his veins was unheard of outside of Ashnah where a single mage had changed the tide of the past war. Brion's parents, long dead now, had prayed to Ashnah's God for a miracle for their fallen kingdom. They were another oddity in Skellas, believing in a God that few others did. When Brion was born and his power discovered, they didn't see it as the miracle they had asked for but a curse instead. They'd cast him out onto the streets to fend for himself. Skellas was known for its closely-knit communities. Even orphans were cared for by the entire town. They never feared hunger or cold. But Brion's town had abandoned him in an instant.

He'd found another town, hidden his ability, and lived, despite the rejection that carved a hole in his withering heart. Brion wasn't sure where his abilities came from but if they did come from Ashnah's God then he was about to make them his own.

Brion's power was nowhere near strong enough to win a war. But that was what Skellas needed. They needed an end to the war. If he presented himself to Freiwade as a living weapon, if he destroyed Ashnah and won the war, maybe, just maybe, Skellas would be able to thrive again. Despite the rejection of his parents, Brion loved Skellas. It was the only home he'd known. And when he kept his powers hidden, he was treated well. To win the war for Skellas, Brion needed power unlike anything anyone had seen before. He needed the ability to overpower Ashnah's current mage and cause their substantial army to cower. He needed the strength to avoid becoming a puppet of Freiwade. He couldn't just be their weapon. He had to be a threat to them as well as Ashnah. Then, when the war was over and he had proven himself an invaluable asset, he could make his demands. The king would have no choice but to oblige.

Brion tried to remind himself that it would all be worth it in the end as he looked into the gaping maw of the cave, threatening to swallow him whole. The darkness was all-consuming. Once he stepped inside, there would be no turning back. Brion took one last look at the dreary, gray sky, listened once more to the waves crashing against the rocks, and then took a deep breath and plunged into the darkness.

The change was instantaneous. The great black nothingness enveloped him in a suffocating embrace.

The temperature dropped another ten degrees, sending shivers down his spine. Brion's footsteps echoed as he walked through the water that dripped down from above. The droplets landed on his bare head, dripping from his curls onto his nose. The wind howled outside and waves from the nearby coast could still be heard. But they sounded different now, muted as if Brion wasn't hearing them from the cave entrance but from a great distance, locked behind impenetrable walls. Before long, even that muted sound faded. It was replaced by the constant nerve-wracking drip...drip...drip of the water from above and the even greater sound of Brion's own ragged breathing.

There was no light from the entrance, though Brion was sure it was only a few feet behind him. Black nothingness stretched out before him and behind him. He had a feeling there was still a long way to go. He tried not to succumb to the sensation of the walls closing in around him but the cave itself was narrowing. He stretched his arms out to the sides and felt the rough, pillar-like basalt rock, damp and covered with barnacles.

Panic gripped Brion's heart in its icy fist. Maybe he should turn back. Could he turn back? The entrance to the cave had disappeared completely, leaving no trace that it had ever been there. Brion reminded himself that he needed this power. Skellas needed this power. He'd come too far and waited too long to turn back now.

He'd found the parchment by chance. After a particularly rough day, mending nets and trying to ignore the growing ache in the pit of his stomach, he'd ventured to his favorite beach, a remote outlet that was difficult to access. It was the perfect place for privacy and Brion had always felt a sense of peace there. He often only had time to visit the beach during high tide but that day he had escaped from his work early and found the beach stretching further away, the ocean a speck in the distance. He took the opportunity to explore the beach as he never had before. He walked further out across the sandy terrain, barefoot and content. That was when he discovered the cave. It was hidden in a crevasse against the rock. When the water was high, the entrance was perfectly inaccessible. Brion felt that he had found a hidden treasure. He was eager to explore but as he approached the entrance to the cave, he could feel a chilling presence emanating from its mouth. It was unusually dark and foreboding. Outside the cave was a small crack and within that crack was a box. The wood was decayed from saltwater. Its metal hinges were covered in brine and rust. However, inside the box was a parchment nearly intact. That parchment changed the world as Brion knew it.

    He was a mage. He finally understood the oddities about himself. The parchment made it so painfully clear. He knew about the mage of Ashnah but in opposition to what the king of Freiwade declared, the parchment insisted that magic was not a curse but a gift and that gift could be amplified. The cave was the key. But that power came with sacrifice. The parchment warned any mage who found it to destroy the cave instead of accepting the treacherous power within. But that power was exactly what Brion had been seeking. Still, it took a long time to commit to such a lofty decision.

Now, he was fully invested. He could not turn back. He could only move forward.

The darkness was the worst part. Brion knew he would lose his nerve if he was kept in the shadows much longer. He tried to summon a light with his magic. It was one of the only bits of magic he could use. The only knowledge he had of his power came from the parchment and the strange accidents which had followed him from childhood. There was a spark in the palm of his hand. The light flickered once like a dying candle then vanished before it could fully form. He cursed his lack of ability. His determination to enhance his power only increased. He would continue in the darkness for now.

The shadows were so complete that Brion couldn't see his hand in front of his face. He stumbled as he walked against the oppressive dark, parting it with each step like a veil. Then, so gradually he hardly noticed it, there was light. It was unlike any light he had seen before. It was an unearthly light; red in tint, and pulsating like a heartbeat. There was a sound too, a sound like breathing. It was a deep, rasping breath that grew louder and louder the closer he approached.

Brion's own heart pounded along with the strange, staccato rhythm. His breath synched with that of the *entity* before him. He could see it. He could see the thing that he had worked so hard and come so far to discover. The pool of power written and warned of in the parchment. Its red light illuminated the small chamber and cast everything in an eerie, otherworldly glow. Brion removed his cloak. He was no longer cold. He moved trancelike towards the pool. The rasping breaths grew loud, unpleasantly so. Then, as Brion leaned forward to look into the glowing depths, the sound stopped completely. Silence stretched through the cave. His distorted reflection stared back at him cast in the red glow. There was a strange look on his face, and something about the reflection did not look like him. He noticed vaguely that the stalactites hanging from the ceiling of the cave did not appear reflected in the pool. There was only Brion and the strange glow.

He had arrived at his destination. There was only one more step to reach completion. He would drink of the pond and then Ademar's three kingdoms: Skellas, Freiwade, and Ashnah would be balanced again. His power would bring an end to the war. His sacrifice would save them all. Reaching into the satchel that hung at his side, Brion retrieved a goblet.

He bent, cautiously, and touched the cup's rim to the glowing substance. He couldn't call it water. He watched as the red, glowing liquid filled the cup, retaining its light even as it shifted from pool to goblet. Brion studied it with a sense of dread. If only there was another way. Numbness crept over him. As he drank the sweet liquid from the goblet, everything went dark. The pool lost its glow and the chamber was cast into shadows. A deeper, more intense darkness crept into Brion. It sunk its fangs into his throat, its arms wrapped around him in a suffocating embrace, it crept down his spine and melted into his bones. Brion's life bled out, replaced by *something else.*

It was dark. So, dark.

Brion was weak. Brion was a child. Brion was a fool.

Brion was gone.
Now, there was only *Nox.*

CHAPTER 1

Sir Eamon Burke of the Nevara Barony Battle School had a saying, "Strength, bravery, and determination are the true virtues of a knight."

Corin Faye knew he was none of those things. He had a weak build and was barely strong enough to lift a sword. He was slow, clumsy, and as his comrades often said, "pathetically naïve." He was not fearless by any means. He had known true fear all his life and instead of gaining an immunity to it, he had come to realize that he was right to be afraid. The world was a treacherous place and Corin knew that better than most. There was only one of Sir Burke's qualities that Corin possessed and it was perhaps the only reason he had made it so far in life. He had determination and plenty of it.

Unfortunately, determination could only get a person so far. In Corin's case that determination led to trouble more often than not.

"He doesn't know when to quit," his companions said of him.

"Sometimes I fear you'll find yourself in an early grave, Corin," Sir Burke had said on more than one occasion.

Determination was only a good thing if there were skills, talent, or potential to back it up. Corin might have the one value but in most other areas, he was dreadfully lacking. He was of average height but still much shorter than the other squires. He was a good strategist but he refused to make a sacrifice that weighed the needs of the many over the lives of a few. He struggled to plan mock conflicts especially in knowing that he didn't have the strength to fight in any battles he might plan. It seemed to Corin that everything he did, and in every area he excelled, it was still never enough. Unlike the others, he had no natural talent, unless getting in trouble was considered a talent.

Somehow, he had managed to carry on regardless. It was a wonder he had made it to the position of squire. Well, less a wonder and more Sir Burke's kindness and pity. Nevara, being a small barony in the cold, blustery north, did things a little differently. The baron of Nevara had established a school for would-be knights run by one of the kingdom's finest and a native of Nevara himself, Sir Eamon Burke. The school had started as a way to train young Nevaran men as squires before sending them off to other baronies, dukedoms, and even the capital of Castille to be knighted. However, Sir Burke's renown and reputation for training up successful knights had attracted neighboring nobles to send their sons to remote Nevara for training. Corin's background as an orphan without a single drop of noble blood in him made his presence at the battle school nothing short of a miracle.

However, it was not a miracle that he had kept

his spot at the school. Corin had one characteristic that set him apart from his peers. He was willing to do anything, even the most unpleasant, disgusting, and demeaning of jobs, in order for his presence to be tolerated. If he was dismissed from the school, he had nothing else waiting for him. He had no home, no family, and no future. If he could fight for the king and be something other than a weak, pitiful orphan, then he didn't care what unpleasantries he had to overcome in the process.

To Corin, it wasn't a question of *if* he would become a knight, only a question of *when.* If his accident-prone nature had a say in the matter, he would be waiting a very, very long time. As Burke put it, Corin had, "a knack for getting into trouble." Corin did his best to make up for it. When the practice dummies started leaking sand after Corin walked past them, he was the first to volunteer to patch them up. When he somehow caused all of the lanterns to go out during a watch just by sneezing, he offered to take the midnight watch for the next two weeks. And when he accidentally set his wooden practice sword on fire, he still wasn't sure how he'd done that, he cleaned the lavatories by himself without being asked.

So, when he headed for training after a particularly rough night's sleep, interspersed with the snoring of the other squires and a few horrible dreams of shadows creeping through the darkness and grabbing hold of him, Corin could only pray that nothing would go wrong that day. He was tired, sore, and all-around miserable but he wasn't going to complain. The moment he picked up his sword, he accepted that it was going to be a rough day. Hours later, when he had run through the same drill for the better half of the morning making no progress whatsoever, he started to wonder if he should just crawl back to bed. His sword was heavy in his hands as he hacked away at a target, again and again, unable to master the combination of strikes.

"That's enough," Sir Burke said with a sigh.

Poor, long-suffering Burke. The knight was Corin's hero and he knew he made the man's life very difficult. Burke was supposed to be training knights, not dealing with a weakling who had no business holding a sword. Burke didn't show his frustration often, though the gray hairs in his head and the circles under his eyes conveyed his stress well enough. Sometimes Corin wondered why Burke hadn't kicked him out of the school long ago. He knew, if he didn't improve soon, the knight would have little choice but to do so. Corin was nearing the age where men were either knighted or made their living elsewhere. Corin waited for Burke to correct whatever he was doing wrong but the man didn't seem to have the energy.

"Just… keep working on it later," Burke said. He waved for another squire. "Practice combat, keep with the wood swords. We don't want to be dragging any bodies away when you're done."

Corin winced. Something had changed with Burke lately. Corin wasn't sure exactly when it had happened but there was undeniably a new tension in the air among Burke and his trainees. The training had become more serious and Burke's patience seemed stretched thin. Corin knew he needed to improve soon; time was running out.

He squared up to his opponent, feeling a rush

of shame as he did so. Phineas York was a new squire but he still fared better in a fight than Corin did. Then again, Phineas was the son of a viscount. He was destined to train as a knight before he was even born. Corin shrugged his shoulders a few times to loosen up and waited for Phineas to make the first move. His best chance would be to dodge Phineas's strikes until he saw an opening. Phineas had already gained a reputation for being a careless fighter, making rash decisions and not taking time to study his foe before attacking. Corin knew he would have to exploit that weakness if he had any hope of besting York. Corin didn't have to wait long before Phineas lunged forward, sword poised to strike.

Corin stepped to the side, barely dodging the attack. Phineas might be rash but he was also fast and strong. Corin had barely registered that thought when another strike came his way. It took the space of six seconds for Phineas to knock Corin down. Even then, Corin wasn't finished. He rolled back to his feet. His hands stung from bracing against the hard-packed dirt. Corin scrambled for his sword and then went on the offensive. Phineas deflected his strikes easily.

"Come on street rat," Phineas taunted. "Is that all you've got?"

Corin felt his strikes grow more frenzied as he tried to match his opponent's quick pace. He tried to calm himself and push aside the unbidden swell of anger at York's words. He'd been called worse. He was constantly being reminded that he was a nobody among nobility. He should be used to the snide comments but, somehow, they still stung. He didn't have long to think over the words before Phineas had disarmed him again.

Corin growled in frustration but tried to keep himself focused as he retrieved his sword once again. He had to keep fighting. The other boys had stopped to watch him and Phineas, eager as always to see Corin fail. They laughed and jeered. Taunts of, "weak", "pathetic", and "disgrace" filled the air, each singeing Corin like the sparks of a raging fire. Corin's exhaustion from the previous sleepless night only added to the white-hot fury growing in his chest. Why was it always him? The nobles could scent out an outsider like ravenous predators. They turned on Corin like a blood-thirsty pack of wolves.

Phineas made small jabs with his sword, toying with Corin. Phineas, the squires, Sir Burke, and Corin all knew who would win the fight. Corin was so, so tired of constantly losing.

"It's a pity really," Phineas remarked almost casually. There wasn't so much as a bead of sweat on his forehead. This fight was easy for him. Phineas's voice dropped down so only Corin could hear it, "It's not fair of Burke to lead you on like this. You have no hope of being a knight. He should have dismissed you long ago."

Corin dared to glance at Sir Burke. There was a painful expression on his face. Corin had seen it many times before. He had seen it as a child on the faces of passersby when he sat in the streets begging for food or work, anything to get by. It was all the more painful to see it on Burke's face. Pity. It was the reason Corin had been allowed into the battle school. It was the reason he had lasted so long despite his lack of progress. He hated it. He hated that Phineas York, a privileged nobleman, could see it too.

"I won't lose!" Corin spat out through gritted teeth.

"You will," Phineas said. "You always do."

Phineas raised his sword in an overhead strike that Corin knew would end the fight. Corin let loose an animalistic snarl and raised his own wooden blade to block. The weapons clashed together with a resounding clunk. Phineas pressed down, pushing Corin to the ground. Corin gritted his teeth in agonizing frustration as his knee bent and then made contact with the ground. He refused to cave to Phineas' raw force. He would not lose again! Corin's arms shook and he knew in an instant his strength would give out.

Keep fighting! His mind screamed at him but his body would not obey.

Phineas pushed harder and Corin's arms wavered as his enemy's sword inched closer and closer to his straining face. It would all be over soon.

"I won't lose again!" Corin cried out.

Corin felt like his heart was bursting out of his chest. A lump of anguish seized his throat in a chokehold. Even his limbs felt heavy with the anger, desperation, frustration, and disappointment that filled every inch of him. He felt like he would die if he didn't let go of the feeling. Corin screamed, every emotion surging through his body contained in that single cry, and with that release came a feeling unlike anything Corin had experienced before. It was painful and wonderful at the same time. The ground shook beneath him and his heart pounded urgently, trying to escape through his chest. There was a fire inside him that grew and grew until it was burning him, consuming him. Corin gasped with pain but it was like a part of him that he had never realized he possessed had awakened. It was *glorious*!

His arms stopped shaking and slowly, so slowly, he pushed back against Phineas's sword. The tables had turned. Corin felt powerful and he knew he was going to win. Phineas's eyes went wide as he realized the same thing.

"What?" Phineas gasped, suddenly struggling to fight back against Corin.

The pain was growing. It felt like something living was trying to claw free of Corin. He couldn't contain it. He blinked and, in an instant, it burst from him.

Someone was screaming. Was it Corin? Was it Phineas? A light, brighter than anything Corin had seen before, blasted out like a shockwave. Corin was at the center of it. The light was like a powerful wind, buffeting everything in its path with an indescribable force. Phineas flew across the courtyard. Corin fell to his knees. His hands connected with the ground, steadying himself. A thud accompanied the motion and Corin wasn't sure if it was his heart settling back in his chest or something else. A shiver ran over his body and then he was shaking all over. A tingling feeling washed over him and he sucked in deep breaths of air while he waited for the sensation to dissipate.

When Corin finally mustered the strength to look up, he found the rest of the squires staring at him. Their expressions were filled with a mixture of shock and outright fear. Sir Burke, his hero, backed away from Corin in what looked like horror. Corin studied his hands with incomprehension. What had happened? Had he done this? The subtle glow still emanating from his palms seemed to prove that he had.

Everyone slowly broke out of their stupors. Some ran over to Phineas who lay unmoving on the ground. Some of the squires drew their swords, staring at Corin as if he might attack them next. How was Corin supposed to fix this? He didn't even know what had happened. Corin looked around at the destruction he had caused and, with his heart pounding so fast he feared it would burst, he pushed himself to his feet and he ran. Whatever had happened, he knew it would be the last straw. He would be dismissed from the school without hesitation. There was no place for him now.

CHAPTER 2

Corin had never been well-liked before. He certainly hadn't expected that things would change for the better after the accident. That was all he could think to call it, "the accident." Corin still wasn't sure what had happened and he had a feeling Sir Burke and the other squires were in a similar situation. They avoided Corin like he had grown horns and a tail or caught the plague.

Although Corin had run, he'd quickly reigned in his nerves and regained some composure. He couldn't run. Where would he even run to? He realized that the strange and piercing pain that had come earlier had dissipated as soon as his fight with Phineas was over. It was replaced with a surge of adrenalin that made Corin feel energized and giddy. He recognized the feeling from his many runs around the barracks. Sir Burke referred to the sensation as a "runner's high." That "high" did nothing to alleviate Corin's growing worry. However, his fear and confusion took a step back as a new determination to discover what had happened appeared.

He returned to the courtyard where many of the squires were still gathered. They worked together with a physician to lift a prone figure onto a cot. Corin was horrified at Phineas's state. Was he dead? A moment later Phineas twitched almost imperceptibly and released a low groan. Corin felt a surge of relief. He wanted to go and question the squires and physician and offer his help and apologies but he knew he wouldn't be welcomed. He hung back instead and scanned the courtyard. Sir Burke was gone. Corin knew where he would be though. Determined to find out the truth and apologize for anything he might have done wrong, Corin hurried to Burke's office.

A young squire who hadn't been in the courtyard earlier was waiting outside the door. "Corin?" the boy asked.

Corin nodded.

"Sir Burke can't see you right now," the boy said. "He wants you to wait in the barracks. He'll send for you. In the meantime, you're not to attend training and your meals will be brought to you."

"What!" Corin objected. "Am I under house arrest? I don't even know what I did wrong. Just let me speak to Burke. I can explain. We... we can sort this out."

The boy shook his head and said nothing more.

Corin stared longingly at the door to Burke's office. He knew he could force his way past the boy and demand to talk to Burke but he also didn't want to make things worse. He had no idea what had happened but he had the sinking suspicion that he was at least partially responsible. So, he returned to the barracks as Burke had instructed and he waited... and waited for Burke to summon him.

It was immediately obvious that Burke had

emptied Corin's barracks, moving the boys who had shared the space with Corin to another room. They didn't stop by to check on him either. Patrick, Jeffrey, Hal, and Westley were all gone. They left behind no trace of their presence. It was as if they were ghosts. Corin was all alone. A week passed, or at least Corin suspected it was a week. It was easy to lose track of time when his days were only punctuated by the delivery of meals and mundane hours spent in solitude. A small part of Corin was nearly overcome with the urge to run. He was sure he had done nothing wrong. He had done nothing to deserve such treatment. And what would come next? Would he stay imprisoned in the barracks forever? Would he be expelled from the school? Or worse? Corin wasn't sure of anything except the fact that the waiting was slowly driving him insane. He couldn't take much more of it. The suspense was the worst part. He hadn't heard a word from Sir Burke and he was starting to fear the worst. All day he waited for word and at night his sleep was plagued with dreams of a noose tightening slowly around his neck.

Perhaps worst of all was being trapped alone with his thoughts. A week passed, giving Corin a significant amount of time to think things through. What had he done? Why hadn't he been banished from the school or worse? Was Phineas alright? Corin tried to gather information about his fellow squire but the only contact he had with another human was a knock at his door that informed him his meal was waiting outside. Corin would yell through the door, demanding answers. But silence was the only response. He could only pray that Phineas was alive and well.

Corin wasn't great at praying. Burke had instilled in all of them a belief and fear of God. They'd been instructed in the truths of the Bible from the moment they stepped into the battle school. Corin found it difficult at times to believe in God when he had seen so much suffering and abandonment throughout his life. However, he'd seen the belief that Burke expressed and Corin wanted the joy and kindness that was so ingrained in his mentor's life. He tried to gain a better understanding of God and, in his moment of personal crisis, prayer was the only place he could turn.

Before long, Corin's thoughts shifted and a sinister fear crept into his chest. Was he a monster? He had caused that explosion, hadn't he? What if it happened again? Corin could still feel a phantom of that adrenalin-filled feeling lingering just beneath the surface. He forced himself to remember the pain he had felt and the destruction that had been caused. He couldn't help waiting, as tense as a spring, in anticipation of something going wrong.

By the end of the week, Corin had sorted out the issue entirely. He wasn't responsible for what had happened. It was impossible. It must have been some freak accident. The only question was, what could have caused it and why did Corin have to be caught in the middle of it?

Why did misfortune always follow no matter where his life led him? Corin had never taken his position at the school for granted. He wasn't a nobleman's son, and he wasn't talented with a sword or lance. His first memories were from the playroom of an orphanage where he had stayed until he turned thirteen. Then he was cast out, deemed old enough to look after himself and seek a trade. Corin had taken odd jobs for two years after that, doing whatever he had to in order to eat. Sometimes he was given lodging as part of his payment but, more often than not, he spent his nights on the streets. The town of Nevara was peaceful. There was little to no crime and the townspeople were kind even to him. But it was cold, so terribly cold. The winters were long and harsh. The summers were short and cool. Snow piled high and lasted until late spring. The mountains surrounding the town made for blustery winds and little sunshine. The farming season was shorter than in many areas of Ashnah which created even fewer work opportunities for a thirteen-year-old boy. It was a miracle Corin had survived as long as he had. He was certain if he'd been left to his own devices much longer, he would have either starved or frozen to death.

Sir Burke had pulled Corin off of the streets and given him a chance first as a page then as a squire and eventually as a knight if Corin could prove himself. Burke had either seen something in Corin that no one else had or taken pity on him. Either way, it had saved Corin. He didn't know what he would do if he was kicked out of the school now. He suspected he would find out soon.

There was a knock at the door to the barracks but Corin didn't call for information. He'd given up on trying to get an answer. He wondered how he had so thoroughly lost track of time. He felt like breakfast had only been delivered an hour before. He got his answer when the voice behind the door finally spoke.

"Sir Burke wants to speak to you in his office right away."

Corin leaped from the cot he'd been sitting on and raced to the door but he hesitated before stepping into the corridor. What would happen now? Would Burke finally get rid of him once and for all? Corin wasn't sure what Burke wanted from him but he was sure it would be the end of his future aspirations of being a knight. The squire outside the door was gone by the time Corin mustered up the courage to step into the hall, leaving Corin to find his way to Burke's office on his own. As he walked, he tried to remember every detail of the accident. He tried not to focus on the fact that it could be the last time he walked the battle school halls. He hoped he would always remember the way the floor creaked and the dull smell of sweat hanging in the air. He'd suspected for some time that he would leave the school not as a knight but as an outcast. Still, it hurt to have to leave everything behind, especially because of something he couldn't have possibly been responsible for.

Corin passed the courtyard as he walked and noticed a large crack running the length of the cobblestone field. There was even a depression in the wall where Phineas had crashed. Corin knew Phineas's body couldn't have caused the damage. Something else, the same force that had sent Phineas flying, must have crushed the stones. Corin paused and stared at the phenomenon. His certainty solidified. He couldn't be responsible for what had happened.

But how could he prove his innocence?

The door to Sir Burke's office loomed ahead of Corin, large and foreboding. Behind that door lay

Corin's future. When he stepped inside that office, he'd be expelled from the school and everything would change. He would deny any involvement in what had happened but he doubted he would be believed. After all, this was not only a horrific accident, it was a perfect excuse to finally be rid of Corin. He might as well get things over with. Corin raised his hand, took a deep breath, then knocked.

"Come in," Burke's voice called from inside.

Corin took another bracing breath before pushing open the door. He stuck his head around the corner slowly, worried that Burke would yell at him to get out of his sight or possibly even throw something at Corin's head. But Burke sat calmly behind his desk, more at peace than Corin could have possibly suspected. It was a sight Corin had seen more times than he could count. Burke was sitting peaceably at his desk, papers strewn before him, a look of immense concentration on his face. The only difference this time was that Burke was not alone.

A white-haired man sat in one of two chairs in front of Burke's desk. The man turned to study Corin as he stepped into the room. The stranger's light blue eyes seemed to bore through Corin and he quickly turned his attention to Burke instead.

"You wanted to see me, sir," Corin said with a slight tremor in his voice.

"Yes, of course. Have a seat," Burke gestured to the empty chair.

Well, at least he didn't seem scared of Corin like he had right after the accident. He did seem wary though, on edge, as if he were waiting for Corin to attack. Corin didn't understand why. Burke knew as well as Corin did that he was no threat to anyone, except maybe himself. Corin lowered himself into the chair, trying to ignore the feeling of the white-haired man staring at him. He had no idea why the stranger was there. It didn't matter. Corin's meeting with Burke would likely be over quickly.

"Corin, this is Clifton Eaves," Burke said, gesturing to the stranger.

Corin bowed his head awkwardly in greeting. Clifton smiled and offered his hand. Corin reluctantly reached to shake it but Clifton seized Corin's wrist and pulled him closer to stare intently at his face. Corin tried to yank his hand away but Clifton's grip was too strong.

Clifton murmured something under his breath. It sounded like, "Is he the one?"

Corin looked worriedly to Sir Burke but his mentor was watching the exchange with a confused and curious expression.

"Yes," Clifton muttered. "Yes, you were right to contact me, Sir Burke."

Corin tried to refrain from shaking as Clifton finally released his hand. Burke cleared his throat to break the tension.

"You're certain?" He asked Clifton.

The strange man nodded solemnly. "Yes. I can't explain how but I know."

Burke shifted in his seat and then straightened as if donning a mask. He turned to Corin. "Firstly, I have to apologize for the way you've been treated, Corin. You see, I had to contact the castle and I didn't want to take any chances with anyone's safety, yours or the other squires. If I'm being honest, I didn't know how to handle the situation," Burke explained.

"You did everything right," Clifton consoled him. "It's good that you contacted us and I do apologize for the delay. The roads are treacherous this time of year and… I got a little held up before leaving the capital."

"What's going on?" Corin asked, growing increasingly unsettled and confused.

Why had Burke contacted the castle? Why had someone journeyed to Nevara all the way from the capital? Surely it couldn't be to discipline Corin.

Burke opened his mouth to explain but Corin realized there was something else more pressing that he wanted to ask first.

"Sir, what happened to Phineas York? Is he alright?"

Burke coughed, "Right, I expected you would want to know."

If Burke was expecting the question, then why did he seem so unnerved by it? Corin felt a chill seep into him.

"York has been moved to his family estate in Cheston where it is hoped he will make a full recovery from the injuries he sustained."

Corin caught onto the word "hoped" with dread.

"Then his injuries were severe?"

Burke looked away and his answer was quiet, "Yes, very."

Silence filled the office. Corin felt sick. Whatever had happened, Phineas had paid the price. Corin had never liked Phineas but he hated to hear of him being hurt. He was grateful that the other boy was at least alive and with his family. Things could have gone worse.

"The Castille family will of course cover any expenses of his recovery and compensate him and his family for the trouble they've faced," Clifton put in.

Corin stared at the man in shock. "Why would the king cover the expenses?"

Burke cut in before anyone could say anything further, "Let's stop skirting around the obvious reason you're here, Corin. Something very strange happened a few days ago when you were fighting against Phineas York."

Corin's mind was still whirling but he snapped out of his daze enough to realize that he needed to pay close attention to whatever happened next. His future depended on it. Corin could feel a lump forming in his throat. This was it. It was time for him to be asked to leave and never return. Maybe he should just accept his fate. But Corin couldn't resist making one last defense.

"Sir, I don't know what happened, but surely you realize that it couldn't have been me that caused it."

Burke sighed and rubbed his temples. "Corin," he said softly, waiting until Corin met his eyes to continue, "we both know that you've never really fit in here."

The words pierced Corin like a sword, swift and fatal. He knew it was the truth. He'd always known it. But hearing Burke say it so plainly was more devastating than any punishment that might be inflicted on him. Corin's ears rang as he focused his gaze resolutely on Burke's desk. The wooden surface was ancient. It wasn't the first time Corin had noticed the beautiful steadfastness of it. But it would be the last time.

Burke pressed on, unaware of Corin's despair. "Nevertheless, you've worked harder than all of the other squires to amount to something. You came from nothing and you understand that if you want to earn something in life it cannot be handed to you, you must work hard for it. It's a lesson I wish many of the others could comprehend. You've struggled and you've persevered but your time at the battle school has come to an end."

Corin sucked in a breath. He felt like he was choking on his tongue. It lay like a stone in his mouth, unable to form words to defend himself. He glanced at the door. He needed to escape the office before he completely lost control of his emotions. However, he knew he had to wait to be dismissed and he refused to spend his last few moments at the school in tears. Why did his humiliation have to be in front of the stranger though? Didn't he deserve to face this loss with some privacy?

Burke wasn't finished. Corin tried to listen to what his mentor said next. "You will be greatly missed here, Corin. If not by the others, then at least by me. You... you were always special among the group. I don't regret for an instant allowing you to train. I only regret that I won't be able to finish your training. There is a reason you've never quite fit the mold of a knight and, in a way, it's a relief to know that God's purpose for you has finally been unearthed. You will amount to great things, Corin, just not here, not as a knight. You belong with Clifton at Castille Castle, training to be a mage."

The simple word rang through the air, terrible and wondrous.

"A mage!" Corin cried, jerking his head up in shock.

"Yes, Corin Faye. Burke has told me about these "accidents" you've become accustomed to," Clifton put in. "They were not mere accidents, but the result of uncontrolled and suppressed magic."

Suddenly it all hit Corin like a ton of bricks. Mage? *He* was a mage. Impossible! Mages were more legend than fact. Only two mages had appeared within written history. The first was Neos Loch, the war hero whose name was revered and feared throughout Ashnah, Freiwade, and Skellas. He appeared in the heat of the greatest war the kingdoms had ever faced and turned the tide of battle, giving Ashnah the victory against Freiwade. Then there was the other mage. Corin swung his gaze back to Clifton. He pushed back his chair to put some distance between him and the strange, white-haired man.

"M...mage," Corin stammered, eyes wide.

Clifton winced and raised his hands placatingly, "Yes, yes but there's no reason to be nervous, Corin."

There was something about hearing his name on the mage's lips that made Corin's skin crawl. Clifton, *the* Clifton Eaves. He was the only known mage in existence. Clifton's fine clothes denoted influence but there was nothing inherently powerful or menacing about the man. Despite the white hair, Clifton didn't seem much older than Sir Burke. However, his eyes were solemn and ancient. The way he studied Corin made the hairs at the back of his neck prickle with unease. No, there was definitely an underlying power in Clifton. It was hidden by a calm, nonthreatening exterior but there was no doubting that the man sitting next to Corin was indeed Ashnah's mage.

Why had Clifton been sent to Nevara? There was no way that Corin could be a mage. He wasn't powerful. He wasn't special in any way. He was just an orphan from the streets of an isolated northern town. Besides, he didn't want to be a mage. Mages were cursed. Rumors abounded that their power was unnatural and that God had turned His back on them.

Corin looked to Burke, the devout man of God, "Sir, I'm not a mage. I can't be a mage. I'm not a monster. You know me."

Clifton flinched but Corin didn't take notice of it. He was frantic, pleading for Burke to understand. He couldn't stomach the thought of his mentor fearing him or thinking of him as cursed.

Burke's expression softened. He leaned across the desk. "Mages are not the monsters that the rumors would lead us to believe, Corin. I'll admit that I did hesitate to report the incident to the castle. I have fallen victim to a few rumors myself. But that is all they are, hurtful rumors. The truth is that this kingdom would not be here if not for a mage. Towns like Nevara thrive on rumors and ghost stories but I've been to the capital, Corin. It's not the case there. Mages are not cursed, they are gifted."

"It's true," Clifton added. "Long ago, knowledge abounded but now Ashnah possesses the few remaining ancient texts, a Bible, and a scroll that offers some of the only written history of magic. Mages are simply individuals who have been gifted abilities by God. The powers are rare and should be used in service to others which is why Neos Loch and I served Ashnah as protectors of the kingdom. It is a lofty calling to be chosen as a mage, Corin. It is not a curse but a blessing."

Corin couldn't accept that. The last thing he wanted was to be pulled away from his training as a squire. It wasn't a blessing to be different and to have to leave behind everything he knew and valued.

"I'm not a mage," Corin insisted. "The accidents are just that, accidents, nothing more."

"I see you don't believe us," Clifton said. "I don't blame you. I had the same reaction when I discovered my abilities. I couldn't believe that it was real. I doubted everything. But I wouldn't be here telling you this if I was not certain of your power, Corin. I can see the traces of the magic still emanating from you. It was a powerful burst of magic that escaped during your fight with Squire York. It was painful and terrifying, I imagine. Something similar happened to me the first time my magic truly surfaced. That's why it is so important to learn to control the abilities you were gifted with. If not, you or someone else might get hurt. You must be trained, Corin. You will join me at Castille Castle, it's your duty."

Something inside Corin snapped. He felt a wave of dizziness wash over him. This couldn't be real. He must be dreaming. His hands were shaking and he felt a bead of sweat drip down his cheek, or maybe that was a tear. An unbearable panic settled inside him, squeezing his chest in a vicelike grip.

"I think he's in shock," Burke said. Corin barely heard his voice over the pounding of his heart.

In a way, it almost made sense if he was a mage. He'd been prone to strange accidents since before he could remember. The incidents only grew stranger the older he became. He remembered his practice sword catching fire without a flame in sight, extinguishing the lanterns with a single sneeze, all the other incidents, and of course, what had happened during his fight with Phineas York. Corin had always assumed bad luck just followed him wherever he went but maybe, just maybe, it was something more than that. Surely the castle wouldn't have sent their only mage to remote Nevara if they weren't convinced Corin was a mage. Surely Sir Burke, the best tactician and smartest man Corin knew, wouldn't believe it if it weren't true. Still, how could it be? If Corin was a mage, everything he knew about himself and the world around him was suddenly called into question. He felt a hand on his shoulder and looked up to see Burke standing in front of him.

"Breathe, Corin. It'll be alright."

Corin did as he was told and sucked in several deep breaths. The oxygen didn't quite reach his lungs but Burke seemed pleased. The hand on his shoulder was like an anchor keeping Corin in the present moment. Slowly he stopped shaking and his breathing calmed.

"Good. Are you alright?" Burke asked him gently.

Corin nodded, although at that moment he felt anything but all right.

"I know this is overwhelming, Corin, but I promise it will start to make sense," Clifton reassured him.

Corin wasn't so sure but he nodded anyway.

"I'm sure you have many questions," Clifton said, "but for now I think it would be best for you to take a few moments to process things. We will leave as soon as you're ready. I assume you'll need some time to gather your possessions. I'll be waiting for you outside."

Clifton stood and straightened his long overcoat. Corin and Sir Burke exchanged glances. They both knew that Corin had only a spare set of clothes to his name. The battle school had provided everything else he had.

The strange figure of Clifton Eaves disappeared through the door, leaving Corin and Sir Burke alone. Corin felt his breath start to hitch again as all that he had been told flooded his mind, each thought fighting for dominance amongst the others.

Sir Burke cleared his throat and reached behind his desk for something. "I suppose you won't be needing it now, but it never hurts to be prepared," he said as he handed Corin a long, leather-wrapped package.

Corin took it carefully, trying to focus on the package and ignore the ache of despair in his chest. His fingers fumbled as he pulled aside the leather covering, revealing a sword. It was plain and unembellished but his heart lifted as he looked at it. He could see his haggard reflection in the blade and, touching his finger to the edge, he was delighted as a small pinprick of blood appeared on his fingertip, demonstrating the blade's razor-sharp edge. He looked up at Sir Burke, expecting the man to tell him that this was some kind of joke. Burke grinned at him.

"Be careful, this one's real," he said lightly.

Corin looked down at the blade in his hands again with a sense of awe. He noticed something else as he turned the weapon from side to side, surveying it better. The initials *C.F.* were engraved on the hilt. Corin Faye. A lump formed in Corin's throat. He fought back tears. This was no mere sword. It was made for *him*. An engraving took time and forethought. Burke had prepared this blade for Corin.

"As you know, all squires graduating onto knighthood are bestowed a standard-issue long sword. Although you're not technically graduating, you are moving forward in life and I believe you've earned this. I'll tell you what I tell all the graduates, 'Take care of this sword as if your life depended on it because someday it just might'."

Corin couldn't take his eyes off the gleaming blade. Somehow, despite all the odds against him, Sir Burke had anticipated Corin graduating from the battle school. He'd spent the time and resources to have a sword crafted specifically for Corin. He'd believed in him. Corin closed his eyes, the thought painful and touching at the same time. This would be the hardest part. It wasn't leaving the battle school or saying goodbye to his dreams of knighthood that would hurt the most. The real pain would come from having to say goodbye to Sir Burke. The man had been the closest thing to a father Corin had ever had. He'd treated Corin with more respect and kindness than anyone else and he had believed in Corin even when Corin could not believe in himself.

"Thank you, sir, for everything," Corin said, fighting past the lump in his throat.

"Well, I guess this is farewell, Corin Faye. Keep working hard and don't lose sight of who you are. My prayers go with you. Remember first and foremost to look to God for guidance and follow His path for your life. He has great plans for you, Corin, don't forget that."

Burke patted him on the shoulder and Corin raised himself shakily to his feet. He moved numbly to the barracks to retrieve his few possessions, taking a long moment to remember everything about the battle school, knowing he would likely never step foot in its walls again. He kept the sword clutched in his hand, its weight seeming unnaturally light and comforting. It was the last reminder of what his life had been.

It wasn't until he stepped into the carriage waiting outside and took a seat across from Clifton that he truly processed what he was leaving behind. Burke's grim face peered at him from the great oak doors of the battle school. The carriage jostled to a start and, with a blink, everything Corin knew and loved was gone.

CHAPTER 3

King Histen Corpin II of Freiwade had the custom of taking court surrounded by all eight of his sons. It was an unorthodox tradition and one that was frowned upon by the king's advisors and most of all his general, Sir Havoc. However, the king would not be dissuaded from his decision. There was no questioning the fact that some of his sons were more suited to the task than others. They all shared the Corpin family resemblance: tall, dark-haired, and with bright hazel eyes. Well, all of them except for Dane, the youngest. Dane was different in many ways from his brothers and not merely in appearance. Although his darker skin and curled hair stood in sharp contrast to the others, it was arguably his gentle demeanor that set him apart the most.

Dane was well aware that his presence in the castle was an accident. His entire life was an accident. He was constantly reminded of this fact by his father's advisors, his brothers, his father, and most of all the queen. It was partially for that reason that Dane so detested standing at court beside his father and brothers. The action put him on full display like some kind of curiosity or freak. It seemed he was the only one who disliked the experience so greatly. His brothers either relished in the attention or tolerated it.

Warson, the eldest, was eager for a chance to show himself in a kingly position. He was the most brutal of Dane's siblings, having had years to perfect his sinister nature and fiery temper in order to impress their father. He valued strength above all things and was the shining star of the Corpin family. However, much to Warson's displeasure, his future as king wasn't set in stone. Their father had yet to choose an heir from his sons. Dane suspected it was to spread discord and distrust between them. It was the type of game their father liked to play. Dane was only grateful that he posed no threat to his brothers. He had no desire to be king and he certainly did not want to attract any more negative attention from his siblings.

However, it was not Warson who unnerved and unsettled Dane the most. That honor was solely Claude's. Dane's second-eldest brother stood at their father's right side, watching the affairs of the court closely, silent and calculating. His dark attire caused him to stand out the least among the brothers. He was a shadow. Dane suspected it was intentional. Claude was not the type to draw attention to himself. Dane had been around Claude all his life but he was no closer to understanding his motives. He wondered at times if Claude would vie against Warson for the throne or if perhaps he would seek a cozy position as chief advisor to the new king. Dane disagreed with many of his father's decisions as king of Freiwade and he feared what life would be like if Warson took the throne but, most of all, he dreaded the uncertainty of what might happen if Claude ruled. Dane had never been sure of what Claude wanted.

His other brothers were less overtly threatening. Their personalities ranged from the flamboyant Thorin who enjoyed all sorts of revelry and drunkenness to Dion whose only desire was to maintain his noble status and the delicacies that it afforded. Horace was a truly unlikeable and bitter person, sickly and full of jealousy for all his brothers' good fortunes or pleasures. Scythe was proud and slightly delusional in seeking the throne for himself. And finally, there was Acedio who had long given up on power and life in general, instead lounging about in his chambers and only venturing outside when it was demanded of him. Dane tried to avoid them at all costs, making himself a ghost in the castle, unseen and unheard. It was only the court gatherings that forced him into the open. At the current meeting, he was pressed against the wall behind his father's throne, attempting to sink into the shadows completely. Acedio leaned heavily against the wall to Dane's left, his eyes drifting closed even as their father addressed his subjects. In all fairness, it had been a dull meeting.

Despite Freiwade's preparations for war, the court gatherings lately had been filled with complaints from nobility desiring greater variety in their meals than the standard seafood imported from Skellas. The fare had grown less varied recently as the king prepared stores that would last throughout what would likely be a long war. Ashnah's plentiful harvests had supported the rocky land of Freiwade for as long as Dane could remember but, if the king got his way, then clams, oysters, and white fish from Skellas would have to suffice. There were also pleas from the commoners who demanded reduced hours working in the mines. It was grueling work and dangerous too. They argued that their reduced rations made the long hours of work unrealistic. The king listened to all of the arguments, complaints, and queries but in the end each and every caller was sent away as the king would "consider" their requests. With the looming war, Dane doubted either the nobles or the commoners would be satisfied with the king's decisions.

They were at least nearing the end of the hearings. Dane was glad of that. He'd gotten very little sleep the previous night. Horace had locked him out of his room somehow, leaving a note reading: *Such fine quarters are not fitting for a mutt, go sleep in the kennels instead.* Dane still wasn't sure how his brother had done it but after attempting to get into the bedroom for close to an hour, he'd given up and slept in an unfurnished guest room instead. There was an ache in his lower back from lying on the floor. He tried to rub at it without drawing attention. Despite his best efforts, he heard Horace snicker from a few feet away. The sound was followed by a sickly cough. Dane forced his glower away and maintained the pleasant, unaffected expression on his face. He could retaliate somehow but he wouldn't. He never did.

"Your Majesty," the peasant in front of the throne spoke softly, "I hail from Skellas."

There was an audible grumble throughout the room and looks of distaste were cast toward the humble man at the foot of the dais. The man either didn't hear the derogatory remarks of the gathering, which was unlikely given their volume, or he was used to such treatment. The king sighed in boredom and waved for the man to get on with it.

"Your Majesty," the man continued, "I come on behalf of my people, pleading for time. We need more time before the next required export of supplies. Our ships must be fortified for the coming winter months. Our sails need to be repaired and our nets mended."

The king leaned forward on his throne, a dark expression crossing his face, "Who are you, exactly, to speak for your people?"

The question caught Dane off guard. He would have expected a quick refusal or another vague dismissal that promised consideration that would never happen. However, King Corpin seemed *interested* in this newcomer, this Skellan. Why?

The man stuttered, "I am only a sailor, your majesty, a simpleton really. I have a family, two boys who sail alongside me, and a wife and daughter at home. I come on behalf of them and others. Our ship is damaged. There is a breach in the hull and the sail has a tear that will only grow with continued use. We haven't had time to repair the damage while keeping up with our quotas. We'll manage the load faster if we can mend our vessel."

The king's nose wrinkled as if he were smelling something foul. He fixed a terrible look on the commoner, a look that made Dane shrink further against the wall. "Skellas is under Freiwade's command," the king's voice thundered. "Do you not think my rule is sufficient? It is Freiwade who will determine when ships are to be repaired and quotas reduced. It is Freiwade who gives you work and can take it away. Who are you to question my rule and my decisions?"

The sailor cowered, raising his hands in defense. "Please, Your Majesty, I meant no offense."

The man might have said more but at that moment there came a great rumbling and ruckus from outside the courtroom. The doors at the back of the room burst open and five soldiers rushed into the room, taking up defensive positions. The occupants of the courtroom cried out with panic and fear.

The king rose from his throne with outrage, "What is the meaning of this!"

He received his answer soon enough. A dark figure, intimidating in a complete and indescribable way, swept into the room. The figure took no heed of the soldiers with their spears leveled against him. Dane knew the soldiers, the king, the advisors, and everyone else in the room would be powerless to stand against this unknown entity. A dark energy, unseen but present like smoke or shadow billowed out behind the newcomer. It seemed to be emanating from within him. A chill of unnatural, uncontrollable fear pierced Dane's heart. He felt sweat form on his forehead and the palms of his hands. His knees wobbled unsteadily and his breath gasped unevenly.

The man, if he could even be called a man, approached the throne. The soldiers backed away, making no attempts to stop him. One of them dropped his spear. It clattered on the ground, breaking the silence as the soldier fled from the room. Everyone else seemed frozen in some sort of trance. They were unable to leave, unable to speak, unable to even properly think through what was happening.

"S... stop! Come no closer!" The king demanded, his voice wavering in a manner Dane had never heard before.

The powerful stranger took a single, rebellious step closer. A mocking expression crossed his face, daring the king to act against him. Dane saw his father's throat bob as he swallowed. His regal stature faltered as he took a half-step in retreat and the back of his knees bumped against his throne.

The stranger gave a mocking half-bow. His eyes never lowered as he fixed all those in the room with a keen, calculating look. "Your Majesty," he said. His voice was coarse and absolute.

"Who are you?" the king questioned.

The man offered a short, staccato laugh. "I am your secret weapon to defeat Ashnah and bring glory to Freiwade. You may call me Nox."

The name felt like ice in Dane's veins. He shuddered.

"*What* are you?" Claude asked, stepping forward.

Nox turned his attention to the second Corpin son. He nodded almost respectfully at the question. "I am a mage."

A ripple of surprise swept over the crowd. A mage? Freiwade had never possessed such a weapon. The only two mages in existence had served the kingdom of Ashnah. They had fought against Freiwade, not for it. The power of a mage was unrivaled. The power was blasphemous, corrupting, and dangerous. The man standing before them seemed to prove all those things as accurate. More than that, Nox was clearly not an average mage.

Though Dane had never personally seen or met a mage before, he could tell, he could *feel*, that Nox was not fully human. There was something dark and evil within the mage.

Dane wasn't the only one who could sense it. Everyone in the courtroom from the generals, advisors, and nobles, to Dane's brothers and the king himself were all consumed by fear... terror.

Dane looked to his father, the king. The ability that Nox possessed was undeniable but Histen Corpin II was still ruler of Freiwade. He held the power in his hand to either accept Nox's offer of service to the crown or demand the heretic's swift execution. It was no simple decision. Despite his lack of experience and as his brothers called it, "Naïve Compassion," even Dane could see that if his father accepted Nox's service, the mage would prove to be a problem in the future.

The king studied the newcomer with intensity but it was Claude's piercing gaze that made Dane look away, keeping his focus entirely on the mage. Dane knew what the answer would be. He knew the king would do anything to win the upcoming war. Freiwade was, and maybe had always been, desperate for control. And the king of Freiwade was no fool. The kingdom could not afford a prolonged battle, not when so much of its resources came from Ashnah's bountiful harvests. Skellas's imports were stretched thin enough as it was. Freiwade needed more power before they invaded Ashnah. They needed all the strength they could get. They had been fighting fruitless skirmishes for years, decades even. The only reason the war hadn't come sooner was because

Freiwade lacked the power necessary to fight it. They couldn't refuse such an offer. A mage could be the advantage they so desperately needed.

Nox cleared his throat, "I am no mere mage, Your Majesty. My power is greater than that of Ashnah's pet. His talents are only natural, and limited. My power knows no bounds and has no limitations. I can not only lead your kingdom to victory but defeat Ashnah's beloved mage."

Dane swallowed past a sudden lump of fear in his throat. He had heard stories all his life about the power of Ashnah's mages. Although the kingdom of Freiwade detested them, they also recognized the threat they posed and feared them. Now, this strange man claimed he could best Ashnah's mage. It should be impossible. Yet, somehow Dane knew Nox was telling the truth.

Apparently, the king knew as well. "Freiwade will accept your service in the war. You appear to be a powerful asset."

A shadow passed over Nox's face. His mild expression soured into a disgusted look.

"I will not be your *asset*," he objected. "I know your methods, o mighty king. I will not be a pawn in your war. You will make me head over your army and give me the honor of leading the charge against Ashnah or I will not fight for you at all."

Again, the king hesitated. It was a lofty request and one that Dane knew would outrage his father's generals. He dared a glance at General Havoc who wore a snarl that could curdle milk on his brutish face.

"Do you doubt my power?" Nox asked.

Dane felt a tugging sensation starting in his

chest and creeping along his body, immobilizing his limbs and yanking him forward. It happened so suddenly that he was powerless to react against it. His heart pounded with terror. He felt the terrible temptation to scream. Below the surface rose another feeling, defiance. He struggled against the invisible bonds that pulled him towards the mage. There was no stopping the power. Dane found himself beside Nox. The man's cold hand clasped the back of Dane's neck, holding him in position like a rebellious child. Dane knew at that moment that he would die at the hands of this wicked mage. He could see the excitement in his brothers' eyes. Even Acedio had leaned away from the wall, eagerly anticipating Dane's end. Thorin watched with one eyebrow raised and Dion was grinning like a child being offered a sweet.

Dane looked to his father. He could only hope the king would put an end to this. He could demand Nox to release him. He could accept the mage's terms and save Dane from his grasp. He knew his hopes were fruitless when he saw his father's indifference. It didn't matter that Dane was at death's door. It was only an unexpected turn of events. It would not change the outcome of the king's decision one way or another.

Nox's scoff echoed in Dane's ears. The mage leaned down. His breath was icy instead of warm as he whispered in Dane's ear. "The king and his sons are even more wicked than I am it seems. Are they so willing to sacrifice you, boy?"

Dane stayed silent. He wouldn't grace the mage's comments with an answer, despite how truthful they might be.

Nox tightened his hand around Dane's neck. His short nails bit into flesh, causing Dane to wince. He closed his eyes. What would death be like? At least his death would be memorable. He wouldn't find his end from a poisoned meal or a dagger in his chest as he lay sleeping. But the painful demise Dane expected never came. Instead, Nox released him. Dane was shoved aside like the useless leverage he was. He tripped and nearly fell but quickly steadied himself and raced to the nearest wall, putting as much distance between himself and Nox as possible.

"I will accept your condition," the king said. "It is reasonable enough that you should lead the army. However, I'm sure you'll understand I can't simply dismiss my generals so you can replace them. You'll have to work alongside them. Use them as an outlet to instruct the soldiers, if you will."

Nox shrugged, returning to his earlier nonchalance.

The king cleared his throat and shifted on the throne. "With that decided, one of my soldiers will ensure you're comfortable until finalizations are made."

Nox inclined his head mockingly to the king before striding purposefully towards the door. A miserable-looking soldier followed after him. As soon as the mage was out of sight, Dane slumped against the wall. A weight seemed to leave the room with Nox and the crowd released a collective gasp of relief. Dane tried to steady his heart but he felt that he would never catch up to it.

On the dais, the king had leaned over to speak to General Havoc. Dane could not hear the exchange but he knew his father well enough to suspect he was instructing his chief general to keep an eye on the mage. Histen Corpin II was no stranger to utilizing spies. Neither was Claude who was issuing his own orders to his lackeys standing by. One way or another they would be receiving a full report of Nox's action and whereabouts. The general leaned away from the king; his objection was obvious but he would still follow orders. In Freiwade, the king's word was final.

Horace and Scythe passed by Dane as they headed for the door, eager to escape the dreadful atmosphere that lingered even after Nox's departure. As they left, Dane could hear Scythe's snide remark clearly, "It would have been better if the mage had killed him."

Horace's joking reply came a moment later, "It would have saved us the trouble."

Dane leaned further into the shadows, filled with a dread he couldn't explain.

CHAPTER 4

The ride to Castille Castle was long and it gave Corin plenty of time to think.

Corin had been doing a lot of thinking lately, more than he cared to. He had always been more of an act-first, think-later, type of person. Thoughts were dangerous. It was much easier to keep busy instead. The mage, Clifton, remained quiet. He probably sensed Corin's inner turmoil. Corin had never been so confused and lost. It still didn't seem real. He felt numb as he stared out of the carriage window and watched miles upon miles of countryside roll by.

"What's the capital like?" Corin asked, needing to break the silence somehow.

"Big," Clifton answered. "You get used to it after a time. I also came from a small town. Brickly, in the pasturelands. It took some time to adjust but I've come to enjoy the castle, though I don't venture into the town often."

"Why not?"

Clifton hesitated. "I'm kept busy in the castle. A mage's work is never done." He laughed nervously. "I expect the main difference for you will be the weather. I never realized how cold Nevara was."

Corin shrugged. "You get used to it when it's all you know." He huffed in amusement. "It's a matter of pride for Nevarans that we're made of tougher stuff than the rest."

"Well, you certainly seem to be, from what I've heard from Burke."

Corin turned to the window again. Just what had Clifton heard from Burke? Corin's past was not a glorious one and he wasn't exactly comfortable discussing it with a stranger. Besides, how had he ended up talking with Clifton so casually? The man was a powerful mage and he had come to Nevara to take Corin away from everything he knew. He didn't want to let his guard down.

He wondered if he'd ever return to Nevara. For some reason, he wasn't sad to see it go. The town itself held no fond memories for Corin. It was only Burke whom he would miss. He studied the snow outside piled alongside the rough road. The carriage hit a dip in the road and jostled roughly. His eyes shifted back to Clifton who was looking out his own window. Corin still couldn't believe he was sitting across from a mage, the only mage in existence, unless what they said about Corin was actually true. Clifton seemed normal enough. His eyes weren't glowing, he spoke normally, he wasn't emanating strange light. Maybe Corin shouldn't have listened to the town gossip so much. He was pretty sure none of the people in Nevara had met a mage before but they certainly had plenty to say about them. He wasn't sure what he should believe anymore. He hated going into his new life so in the dark.

He had more questions than he could count but

he couldn't find the right words to phrase them. There was one question chief among the others that, try as he might, he couldn't quell. Eventually, it burst out of him despite his best efforts to pass the ride in silence.

"How is it possible that *I'm* a mage?"

Clifton jerked his head towards Corin, surprised at the outburst. He smiled softly. "You're still doubting yourself I see."

Corin threw up his hands in exasperation. "I'm not powerful. I'm not wise. I've spent all my life failing even the simplest tasks and disappointing everyone I've grown close to. Mages are almost unheard of. They possess indescribable power. I'm just an orphan who can't properly hold a sword."

Clifton's expression turned serious. "Why are you so determined to think so little of yourself, Corin? You're right that you're not worthy of such power. No one is. You didn't earn this because of anything you did. You were chosen. This gift of power comes from God. He gave you your abilities. The Bible says, 'It is by grace you have been saved, through faith – and this is not from yourselves, it is the gift of God – not by works, so that no one can boast.' If you don't have to earn salvation, what makes you think you need to earn the gifts God gave you? Another verse, one of my favorites, states, 'For many are invited, but few are chosen'. You were chosen, Corin. You've done nothing to earn it. It is what you do from this point forth, how you choose to use your gift, that matters."

"But how do you know this gift is from God? I've always heard that mages were cursed, that they were forsaken by God."

"There are accounts in the pages of the Bible

that talk of men healing the sick, calling fire or rain down from heaven, parting seas, and surviving a stoning. All of those gifts were bestowed on chosen individuals by God. They were blessed and they used their abilities to serve the kingdom of heaven. Those gifts are what we today refer to as magic. We get the word magic from a scroll that was brought to our kingdom of Ashnah during the Great War. It was rescued from a burning library and brought to Castille for safekeeping. The scroll is the only known document containing an in-depth study of magic and its uses. It describes magic as something unusual, removed from the everyday, a unique ability. Some might call the abilities you and I possess gifts but the scroll gave us a unique title."

"Mages," Corin muttered.

Clifton nodded. "My mentor Neos Loch, and I have both dedicated our lives to studying magic and trying to determine its uses and its limitations. Evidence suggests that many individuals used to possess such gifts. Loch, before his death, and I, now, have tried to determine why so few possess magic. I fear it is because so few believe in the living God. All of Ademar has drifted away from the truth. Wicked human nature has driven many away from God."

"But why me?" Corin asked. "I… I believe in God but I'm not as good of a follower as someone like Sir Burke or even many of the other squires."

"I wondered the same thing when I discovered my abilities. I didn't know at the time that they were gifts but when I presented myself to Neos Loch, he showed me the truth of my power. I didn't even believe in God at the time. I think God is gracious and

He wants to give everyone gifts and abilities. He chose me, though I still don't understand why. I have to believe it was because He knew I could have an impact on the world around me because of my gifts. Or maybe it was simply to be here to train you, Corin. All I know is that God's ways are greater than my own. The important thing is to turn to Him now more than ever before and to recognize the truth of these gifts, that they come from God. They are a blessing, not a curse and we should use them to glorify Him."

Corin again looked out the window, feeling overwhelmed by the deluge of information he'd just received.

"The history of magic and how it is used is a complicated thing to study but there is still time," Clifton reassured him.

Corin knew he would need a lot of time to learn what was required of him. He doubted he could do it at all. He knew so little of the history of his kingdom, of the Bible, and of life in general. The battle school took in mostly nobles who had already received extensive schooling in all areas of history, writing, and mathematics. Corin's teaching was limited. The orphanage had given him basic reading and writing skills and Burke had taught him all about strategy and geography. However, his historical teachings were mostly related to battles and treaties. He knew nothing about magic, its origin, and its uses. He felt immeasurably behind.

He closed his eyes for a moment to pray. *God, I know I haven't sought You as much as I should have. I've had my doubts, I still do, to be honest. But if what Clifton says is true, if You really have gifted me with this power, help me. I don't know how else to ask it. I'm not the right person for this. Why would You choose me?*

Corin felt a little silly with his prayer. He wasn't sure if God had even heard it. But he would take any help he could get. He wanted to pray for the ability to be taken away. He didn't want it. He didn't want power, or privilege, or any gift. He just wanted to go back to training as a knight. But he had a feeling that type of prayer would only go unanswered.

"You will understand these things, Corin. Don't think you have to comprehend all of it at once. It's overwhelming, I know."

Overwhelming didn't begin to describe the feeling in Corin's chest. Silence stretched between Corin and Clifton. Corin was grateful for the pause in conversation. He continued to look out the window but he didn't take in any of the scenery. It wasn't until Clifton pointed out a swift river coursing through the fields that Corin realized the cold, snowy landscape of Nevara had faded away. It was warmer inside the carriage, growing so warm that Corin rolled up the sleeves of his shirt to his elbows. Excitement surged inside him. He'd never been outside of Nevara before. He'd grown so used to the gray skies and snow-covered ground that he felt like he was in some far-off land when he noticed the changing atmosphere. The sun shone down on everything, illuminating it in a brilliant light. The sun was treasured in Nevara because it rarely peeked through the thick clouds to make an appearance. Now the warm light was everywhere, shining on everything unabashedly. He could feel the warmth of it on his face through the window and it filled him with memories of curling up around the orphanage's warm fire with the other children. Its warmth filled him like the hearty feast that was held at the battle school for each graduating group of squires before they left to take up positions as knights.

    Corin felt himself start to smile. He abruptly stopped. He wasn't supposed to be happy. He was leaving everything behind. He was leaving his home behind. And he couldn't shake the feeling that he was being lied to about everything. The memories were just that, memories. He would never again feel that warmth of companionship or brotherhood. He'd never again eat a feast with the knights in training. He'd never again experience the safety and carefree attitude of childhood. He had no idea what awaited him in Castille. Above all, he doubted it would last for long. Maybe it was true that he was a mage but Corin had messed up everything else in his life, what made this any different? He would be out on the streets before the end of the month. And then what?

    Even with the dire thoughts filling his mind, he was amazed by the beauty all around him. The fields stretched on for what felt like an eternity. Mountains towered all around, snow covering their peaks. Blue rocks and gigantic, green trees painted a picture unlike any Corin had seen before. Farmlands, rich with the upcoming harvest, were interspersed with woodlands and pastures filled with grazing cattle and sheep. Everywhere there were signs of plentiful life. Ashnah was flourishing beyond anything Corin could have imagined far in the north of Nevara. It was peaceful. Magical. The sun warmed his skin and before Corin knew it, he was dozing off into a peaceful sleep.

He wasn't sure how long he slept but sometime later Clifton woke him. Corin blinked back to consciousness. A brief jolt of panic laced through him when he couldn't remember where he was. He was frightened at Clifton's presence until he remembered everything that had happened. Then the fear and uncertainty were replaced by deep sadness. He could see that the sky had darkened outside the carriage. Shadows stretched menacingly across the land. He'd been more tired than he had realized.

Corin rubbed the sleep from his eyes and released a yawn. Clifton chuckled and Corin ducked his head in embarrassment. He wondered how pathetic he must appear to the mage. Clifton was important, valued, and he had been sent to Nevara to fetch Corin, a mere boy. Corin could feel Clifton's eyes on him but when he looked up, Clifton had turned away.

"We're here." Clifton murmured.

Corin crinkled his brow in confusion. "Where?"

"The castle."

CHAPTER 5

Castille Castle was magnificent. There was no better word to describe it. Corin stood with his mouth agape as he took it in. He'd never seen any structure like the castle before. In Nevara, there were no such buildings. The largest structure was the battle school and it was a single, spread-out story. The church and its orphanage were the most beautiful buildings in Nevara but they paled in comparison to the castle. It towered above with soaring turrets and four imposing towers. Stones larger than Corin was tall constructed the breathtaking structure. The exterior walls were so expansive that the castle blocked the setting sun. Lights flickered from nearly all of the windows, lighting up the dimming sky. Corin glanced over his shoulder and took in ornate, iron gates that separated the castle grounds from the town beyond. He could just make out the grouping of buildings in the distance. The houses and shops were more plentiful and larger than those in Nevara. As the sun started to set, the town seemed quiet and peaceful. In the other direction was open land where sheep and cattle were no doubt sent to graze.

"Welcome to Castille Castle, Mage Corin,"

Clifton said.

Mage. The sound was foreign, especially directed toward Corin. He didn't like the title and he knew it would take a long time to grow accustomed to it.

"I thought it best to walk into the courtyard. It's only fair to give you a moment to take everything in before the chaos of introductions begins."

Corin was surprised by the thoughtful gesture and he was grateful for it. The shocks of the last few days had come in quick succession. Now, standing so close to the castle, everything felt overwhelming and new. He'd never experienced such grandiosity. It was nice to have a second to immerse himself in it.

"Thank you," Corin said.

"We'll proceed when you're ready. Everyone's eagerly waiting for you."

Corin peered at the arched entrance to the courtyard. Clifton had ordered the carriage to stop at a bend in the path between the gate and courtyard, hidden from the view of those waiting at the foot of the castle. At the moment, no one would know he'd arrived. It was tempting to take the opportunity to flee before it was too late. Corin forced himself forward instead. As Clifton had said, everyone was waiting for him. The notion of so much attention was unsettling. He didn't want to inconvenience them by keeping them waiting. He felt a thrill of panic and tried to think of anything besides what might be waiting in the courtyard. He settled on studying the intricate arch above him as he stepped under it.

He heard murmurs immediately rushing over him like a mudslide. It was too late to back away now. The arched entrance disappeared, replaced by a darkening sky. Corin slowly forced himself to lower his gaze until he was studying the courtyard itself. And the people. There were so, many people. As soon as Corin had stepped into the courtyard, knights moved into position, forming ranks on either side of the path leading to the castle entrance. Their immaculate armor was the ceremonial type. The formation they had taken was the kind that Corin had been trained to exhibit in the presence of nobility, diplomats, and even royalty. Corin couldn't take his eyes off of them, wondering what it would be like to stand among their ranks. He craved the experience and wondered if he ever could have reached the level of mastery required of the capital's knights.

"Corin," Clifton said, gently nudging him.

Corin pulled his eyes away from the knights and followed Clifton's gaze to the foot of the castle. There stood the king. Corin swallowed hard. He never thought he'd see the king in person. The most he had hoped for as a knight would be to serve some remote barony or lordship. He'd never expected to be welcomed at the castle as someone of importance, a mage. The king was surrounded by men and women in fine dress. They were likely nobility, advisors, and other important officials. However, it was clear who among them was King Rupert Castille. It was not only the crown resting atop his head that declared his position. He stood with regality and composure. His broad shoulders were set with dignity that only a royal could possess. Even from a distance, his gaze was locked on Corin.

Corin dropped his stare, focusing on the

cobblestones at his feet. He couldn't do this. How was he supposed to greet a king? He didn't know the proper ways to address the monarch. He'd rarely even been around nobility during his time with Sir Burke. The young men he'd been training with were noblemen but in the battle school they were all on the same footing. Now, Corin realized he would be thrust into a world filled with nobles and finery, courtly etiquette and niceties. He felt sick.

"Eyes up," Clifton reminded him. "You're a mage, be proud of it."

It was immeasurably difficult to do as Clifton asked but Corin forced himself to straighten his posture and focus ahead. However, it was impossible to look at the king. Corin turned his attention to the knights on either side of him. Behind them stood nobility, inspecting Corin with a mixture of amazement and apprehension. They looked like they couldn't decide if he was to be revered or reviled. Corin felt his joints stiffen as their stares pierced into him like arrows. Each step forward towards the castle entrance came with greater difficulty until Corin felt like he was trudging through a swampy mire. Only Clifton at his back kept him moving forward.

The stairs grew closer until Corin had reached the bottom step and was looking up at the figures looming above. Corin was forced to face the king. He fought past the unexplainable fear overwhelming him and looked to King Rupert Castille of Ashnah. From a distance, the king had appeared an entirely foreboding figure, regal and broad. Now that he was closer, Corin could see the king's face clearly. He was surprised at what he found among the lines.

The corners of the king's mouth were crinkled with smile lines. His tawny, brown hair, lined with silver, didn't seem as carefully put together as Corin would have expected of a king. A somewhat unkempt beard trimmed the king's face, giving him a jovial, fatherly look. If he had been wearing common clothes, Corin might have taken him for a knight or lord, nothing more. But his garments could only belong to royalty. The cape hanging from his shoulders was trimmed with golden rope, jewels festooned at its base. The robe underneath was a rich burgundy lined tastefully with fur. Puffed sleeves were gathered at the wrists with golden cuffs. Underneath it all, the king wore a gleaming breastplate and a ceremonial scabbard hung from his waist. The clothes alone were more extravagant than anything Corin had previously seen. The only gold he'd seen in the past was a thin band on Sir Burke's ceremonial scabbard. The knight had always used a plain leather one for training and rarely brought out the sheath gifted to him upon his knighthood. Yet the king wore gold from the crown atop his head to the toes of his boots.

With Clifton at his heels, Corin was forced to take the first step up the stairs and then the next. The king and his companions waited patiently until Corin was standing before them. Corin felt small, insignificant, and wholly unprepared as he presented himself. Eyes were riveted on him from all directions. He felt like prey being hunted. Nothing in that moment seemed real. Corin felt as if he were floating outside his body, a mere spectator of what was happening. Then the king spoke, addressing Corin directly.

"Welcome, young mage," the king said. "We are honored to meet you and welcome you wholeheartedly to Castille Castle."

Corin thought he might faint. An unbidden blush of embarrassment and mortification crept up his neck and flushed his cheeks. No one had ever been honored to meet him before, least of all a king. He bowed quickly and with a complete lack of grace. He bowed a second time for good measure.

"Let us all welcome this young man who has been blessed with such a mighty gift," the king addressed the crowd.

Cheers, some eager, some reluctant, rang through the courtyard. Corin felt the flush disappear from his face, replaced by a deathly pallor. He reached out for something to hold onto so he didn't fall over. He couldn't collapse in front of the king and all these people. His hand found Clifton's arm and, although Corin hardly knew the man and was horrified that he had to resort to such measures, he clutched Clifton like a buoy keeping him afloat. Clifton offered him a faint smile and patted Corin's hand reassuringly. The cheers faded away and the king spoke again, addressing the crowd.

"This is a fine day for our kingdom. God has bestowed on Ashnah a great gift."

The king continued to speak but Corin couldn't pay attention to the words. He turned his attention instead to the others gathered at the top of the stairs. On the king's right-hand side was a man in full armor. Corin knew instinctively who the knight must be and his knees quaked at the sight of him. It had to be Sir Gregori Hayes. Hayes was the battle master of the king's forces and head of Ashnah's knightly order. He was the man to whom even Sir Burke reported and the hero of every knight and knight-in-training in Ashnah. Corin's mentor had spoken of Hayes with the utmost respect and Burke did not praise lightly. Corin was surprised at Sir Hayes's youth. The man couldn't have been more than forty and even that seemed a stretch. Corin had heard legends about Hayes. There were stories of his bravery, ingenuity, and strength. He was said to be braver than any of his men. He'd fought alongside the other knights in great battles and skirmishes. Despite Ashnah's long period of peace, there were still battles to be fought on the borders and Hayes had led them all. The scar cutting along his cheek and upper lip was supposedly earned from defending one of his men, a mere foot soldier, during a skirmish. Corin was awed to be in the presence of such a revered hero, a man Burke had once said he was honored to call a friend.

Hayes caught Corin's stare for a brief instant. Corin felt his eyes widen and he tore his attention away. Next to Hayes was an even younger man, not too much older than Corin. He stood in the shadows of the doorway out of sight of the crowd and just barely in Corin's view. His eyes were focused not on the king as he spoke, nor on the crowd standing below. With a piercing stare, he looked at Corin as if peering into his soul. With a shiver, Corin quickly looked away.

On the other side of the king stood... Corin's mind faltered. The young woman standing at the king's side was beautiful. Her honey-colored hair reflected the sunset. The bouncing curls trailed down her shoulders, stray hairs framing her soft face. Her gown was an olive color, patterned on the edges with leaves and flowers and embroidered at the shoulders with creeping golden vines. Corin's eyes explored her face. A soft, warm smile stood out but, when she caught Corin staring, her lips quirked at the corner as if she were sharing a joke with him that no one else understood. Corin blushed fiercely and focused again on the king.

The king finished his speech and was met by another round of applause. Then he turned his attention back to Corin.

"Now, for introductions. This is my most talented and loyal knight, Sir Hayes. He's in charge of the garrison at the castle and heads Ashnah's knightly order."

Corin bowed to the knight but Sir Hayes extended a hand and Corin, feeling warmth pool in his chest, took the offered gesture. As he shook Hayes's hand, he was glad for the first time to be at the castle and offered such an opportunity.

"I...it's an honor, sir," Corin stuttered. "My mentor, Sir Eamon Burke, speaks highly of you."

A hint of a smile crossed Hayes's face. "I would hope he does; I've fought at his back more times than I can count. If you were one of Burke's prodigies, I'm sure you'll accomplish great things here, Corin. Welcome to Castille. My knights and I are at your service."

Corin felt light-headed with the praise from such a great man. He might have kept on shaking Hayes's hand like a fool if the king hadn't swept in again.

"This," King Rupert said, gesturing to the

beautiful young lady, "is my niece, Ruena."

The girl bowed her head to Corin, a bright smile illuminating her face and causing Corin's heart to flutter. He bowed to her awkwardly, very aware that he could never hope to match her grace. He knew he should have expected no different but he was mildly disappointed to find out she was the king's niece. A lady of such high status was the type who couldn't be seen associating with someone as low as Corin. He felt a pang of sadness at the forced distance that would be between them.

"Welcome," the girl greeted. Her silken voice was just as elegant as she was.

"I trust that your journey went well?" The king cut in again.

"He slept nearly all the way here," Clifton answered.

Corin felt his cheeks heat again. He dropped his gaze from the nobles surrounding him, focusing on the tip of his boot which had gained a smudge of dust, though he didn't know when.

"You must be tired from your journey. You'll be shown to your room before long, but first, a great feast has been prepared in your honor."

Corin felt only dread at the idea. He'd hardly eaten that day but the idea of sitting through a feast where all attention would be directed at him was sickening. He'd much rather go to bed and pretend that everything that had happened was just a dream.

The king gestured to a servant who had been standing beside Ruena. The girl stepped forward and held out her hands expectantly. Something about her was vaguely unsettling. Corin didn't have to look at her face to feel the intensity of her prying, inquisitive stare. It felt like she was reading him like a book that she didn't particularly enjoy. He felt as if all his secrets were laid bare. *She's just as aware of how little I belong here as I am,* Corin thought.

"She'll take your belongings to your room," Clifton told him, explaining the girl's outstretched arms.

Corin pulled himself from his daze. He wasn't carrying his satchel; it was still in the carriage. He was about to say so to Clifton when he realized that the girl wasn't waiting for his satchel at all. His fingers brushed the sheathed sword at his waist. He'd worn it all the way from Nevara, unwilling to let it out of his sight for even a moment. The last thing he wanted to do was allow this judging servant to take it from him. However, he knew it would only draw more attention to him if he refused. He reluctantly unbuckled the scabbard and relinquished it to the girl. The girl bowed slightly then turned and disappeared inside. Corin watched her and the sword go with trepidation.

"Now, let's eat," the king said.

Clifton cleared his throat and Corin glanced at him with confusion. Clifton was looking at him with a pointed gaze that took Corin a moment to comprehend. He realized that he was expected to say something, probably wise and insightful. All of this was in honor of him, after all. Corin had never been good at speeches. He'd never had much occasion for them. He fought for something, anything to say but his mind was a complete blank. Finally, he managed to stumble out a few stuttering syllables.

"Thank you, sir," Corin mumbled then realized

that 'sir' wasn't the right way to address a king. He cringed.

Clifton clamped a hand on Corin's shoulder, shaking his head slightly. The pity in the gesture was obvious. Corin was accustomed to pitying looks from Sir Burke but Clifton's pity uniquely unsettled him.

The king accepted the gratitude without commenting on Corin's poor etiquette. He turned and led the way into the castle. Corin followed behind, feeling numb and awkward. It wasn't until he passed the strange young man in the shadows on his way into the castle that Corin realized he hadn't been introduced. Everyone acted as if the man was invisible. Corin couldn't help but glance at him but before long he was out of view and Corin was inside the castle.

CHAPTER 6

Inside the castle was just as beautiful as its exterior. The walls were covered in tapestries depicting historical scenes of both times of peace and war. The colored threads blurred as Corin walked past them, trying to take everything in as he went. Sconces were spaced every few feet, brightly illuminating the long hallway. Corridors led off on either side of him, leading deeper into a maze of stone. The high walls might have seemed suffocating to some but, after years in the tight battle school barracks, Corin found the place spacious and expansive. If anything, it felt mazelike. The walls seemed to stretch on indefinitely and Corin knew he was only being shown a small portion of the castle. Corin wondered if he would ever be able to find his way out if the need arose.

He trailed after the king as the man led the way through the twisting corridors until he stopped in front of a large set of double doors that Corin assumed must lead to the great hall.

"There's an antechamber to your right where you can freshen up before joining us," the king said. "Please, take as much time as you need."

The king, Ruena, and Sir Hayes proceeded into

the great hall. Corin watched the door open and then close behind them. He couldn't shake the sense of amazement that he was in the castle and that he had met not only the great Sir Hayes but the king of Ashnah as well. And Ruena. Corin noticed after a moment that the young man who hadn't been introduced was lingering in the hallway. He was still watching Corin, surveying him from head to toe. Corin caught his stare and swallowed hard but he forced himself not to look away. Whatever the man was looking for, he appeared satisfied and he left to join the others in the great hall.

"I can wait for you here if you'd like," Clifton offered.

Corin shrugged off Clifton's obvious concern. He needed a moment alone. He had a feeling the small antechamber would be the only chance he'd get for privacy.

"I'll be okay," Corin said. He didn't wait for Clifton to leave before opening the door and stepping inside.

When he caught a glimpse of himself in the mirror, he hardly recognized the figure staring back. A wave of nausea rushed over him. He'd met the king like that? Sir Hayes too. His curly brown hair was sticking up on one side from his nap during the carriage ride. Dark circles lined his hazel eyes making him look half-dead. His simple clothes, the inelegant tunic and pants he'd worn throughout his training with Sir Burke, were wrinkled and dusty. Worst of all, Corin was pretty sure he smelled like horses.

He must have been quite the sight for the nobles. He looked like he'd been dragged from the streets. Technically he had been. Burke had ingrained in him the importance of first impressions. Corin had been so distraught and confused over everything happening that he'd let the entire castle see him looking like a vagabond. He swallowed hard and set to work.

He wetted his hands in the washbasin and tried to slick back his unruly hair. He feared he was making the situation worse when his reflection hinted at a cow licking his head. Frustrated, Corin ruffled his hands through the mess, trying to at least make it appear purposeful. It was horrible but it would have to manage. He brushed his hands over his clothes, emitting a cloud of dust that made him cough. How had Clifton still seemed so put together after the journey? The wrinkles refused to disappear no matter how many times Corin yanked and pulled at the fabric. He hated the idea of going out in front of everyone in his current state but it couldn't be helped. They were all waiting for him.

The nausea crept over him again, so fast that Corin gagged and had to fight against the urge to be sick. How had he gotten himself into this mess? How was this happening to him? He was in the castle about to have dinner with the king and countless members of the nobility. Only a week ago he'd been doing his best just to avoid being kicked out of the battle school. Only that morning he'd learned he wasn't going to receive a death sentence for the accident with Phineas York.

Corin faced the mirror and didn't recognize the face peering back at him. It was true that he was unused to mirrors but even so, he could tell something had been irrevocably changed within him. The pale face reflected back looked a little green and unbearably young. He was so inexperienced in everything. How could he possibly be the mage they were all excited to welcome? He couldn't do this.

Corin grabbed hold of the edge of the counter, gripping it until his fingers ached. Dizzy. He was so dizzy. Was he going to pass out? It had happened before when he overexerted himself in training. But he hadn't been training now.

How was he going to do this?

Corin closed his eyes and bent until his forehead was pressed to the cool, marble countertop. He sucked in a deep breath while his stomach churned. *God,* he prayed, *how am I going to do this? I can't do this.*

Corin received no answer but the roiling nausea in his gut settled and the dizziness faded. His breathing evened out and the sound was calming. For a moment he wasn't in the castle. He wasn't hiding from the great hall and the people waiting for him. He wasn't even back at the battle school. He was nowhere and he had nothing to worry about. When he finally opened his eyes and lifted his head, he was ready. At least, as ready as he would ever be.

Before he could change his mind, Corin yanked open the door and stepped into the hall. The minute he caught sight of the imposing oak doors of the great hall, his composure fled. The dizziness returned in a rush and he had to brace his hand against the doorframe of the antechamber to steady himself. He was tempted to rush back inside and really be sick. He forced himself to take another deep breath and then strode purposefully to the foreboding double doors ahead. They towered over him like the gates to hell. It took an immeasurable surge of strength for Corin to push them open.

What waited inside struck him with a terrifying invisible force. There must have been at least three hundred people gathered at the tables around the room. As the doors opened, they all turned to stare directly at Corin. Corin's eyes darted around the room in a panic, looking for some escape. He stood frozen. His joints refused to move. All he wanted to do was run.

"Corin!" Clifton called out. The mage rushed across the room until he was standing in front of him. "This way."

Clifton took Corin's arm and led or, more accurately, dragged him further into the room. There was a raised dais at the end of the long stretch of tables. Corin could make out the figure of the king sitting there along with Hayes, Ruena, and others. Corin looked down, focusing on the floor as Clifton led him forward. Everyone's eyes bored into him like hot embers. He felt the stares crawling over him. Corin's shoulders lifted as if they were a shield protecting him from those penetrating eyes. Murmurs filled the room. The voices were indistinct and blended into a never-ending buzz. Corin could only catch a word or phrase occasionally. "Mage" was the most common but "strange", "unnatural", and "cursed" were also prevalent. Time blurred and Corin wasn't sure if it was seconds or minutes until his toes touched the bottom step leading up to the head table. Clifton released his arm and Corin realized he had to fend for himself. He forced his stiff legs to climb the steps and looked up just long enough to see the king gesturing to the seat beside him. Corin stumbled to the seat, wedging himself between the king and Clifton. The stares continued. Everyone was fixated on him and him alone. He sunk into his chair, wishing he could disappear. He was accustomed to large groups from the mess hall at the battle school but he had always been virtually invisible there. He'd never had to sit at the front of the room.

"Mage Corin, are you ill?" Ruena's sweet voice forced Corin to emerge from the depths of his thoughts.

He cleared his throat and forced himself to sit up a little straighter. "I'm alright."

Her relieved smile made Corin feel a little guilty for his behavior. He tried to pay attention to the meal and ignore everyone around him. He glanced at the king and saw that the man was no longer wearing the gleaming breastplate from before.

"Where's your breastplate?" Corin asked, then immediately blushed at his blunt, impolite words.

The king laughed. "I couldn't bear to wear it any longer. It's dreadfully hot. I couldn't wait to get out of it. Besides, metal doesn't expand well to a full stomach."

Across the table, Hayes rolled his eyes. "It's a shoddy and impractical spectacle, nothing more. A real knight wouldn't be caught dead weighed down by such a gaudy decoration."

Corin pressed himself into his seat, surprised at the words spoken so casually to the king. However, King Rupert nearly choked on his drink trying to quell his snort of amusement. "I dreamed of being a knight once but I suppose it's good for all involved that dream didn't come to fruition."

Corin was grateful he didn't have to respond because at that moment plates of food were brought to the table and placed in front of Corin and the others. Roast lamb, potatoes, vegetables, fresh bread with jams, and meat pies were distributed. Corin had never seen such a feast. The gatherings Sir Burke put on for graduating squires were no small affairs but this was unlike anything Corin had experienced.

Last of all a goblet of rich, dark wine was placed in front of Corin. A feeling of mortification settled over him. He'd never drunk alcohol before. Burke had prohibited it at the battle school claiming that a knight must be clear-headed at all times. "I've seen many a warrior reduced to a babbling fool over a single glass of strong liquor," Burke had stated on more than one occasion.

Corin subtly pushed the goblet away. He hoped it wouldn't be a common occurrence at meals. He dreaded the idea of having to ask for something else. He'd go thirsty that night and hope for water in the morning.

"Come now, Your Majesty," Hayes's voice cut in among the murmurings of the waitstaff. "Not everyone has a taste for strong drink. Surely, the mage would prefer something more refreshing after such a long journey. Besides, if I know Burke, then I suspect young Corin has never touched ale or any other similar drink."

Corin hunched over as the king's gaze settled on him and then on the drink that had been nudged aside.

"Oh, of course," the king said. He gestured for a servant and Corin overheard talk of cider instead.

He was horrified at the attention but when he finally looked up, he saw that Hayes and Ruena also had glasses of something different in front of them. The meal continued with no more setbacks after that. Despite the twisting of his stomach, Corin found the food incredible. It was rich and savory but tastefully so. He had to force himself to eat slowly to not overwhelm his already nervous stomach. Each bite allowed Corin a moment of silence from the continuing stares and whispers.

The king offered a steady flow of conversation, asking Corin about Nevara and the battle school. It was difficult for Corin to respond. It felt foreign and strange to be speaking to the king. Even sitting in his presence felt like a dream. He worried he would stumble over his words or say something foolish like he had earlier. What was the proper etiquette he should use? Should he look at the king or keep his eyes lowered? He knew he couldn't stay silent, so he forced out responses to the king's questions. He spoke highly of the battle school and especially of Sir Burke.

"He gave me a chance even though I had nothing to offer," Corin said. "He's a strict teacher and wants to ensure that the squires he trains are more than prepared to step into their roles as knights."

"We need more capable fighters," Hayes grumbled. "Too many young nobles come to the castle expecting a position that they've done nothing to earn."

"Now, Hayes, we all know not all of the knights are like that. After all, you wouldn't let them step foot into the castle without proving themselves."

Hayes huffed. "Maybe, but it's not only the newer recruits that we have to worry about. There are plenty of men who are supposed to be leaders who could easily be replaced by more capable men who are half their age. Yet, they think they deserve their positions because they've served for so long. It's not age or experience that matters most but honor, courage, and the capacity to be a good leader. That's what's lacking in so many of the warriors now."

Corin had the feeling this was an ongoing conversation and one that could become unpleasant quickly. The king glowered at Hayes and Hayes likewise glared at the plate of food in front of him.

"What is Nevara like?" Ruena asked. Corin suspected it was an effort to break the uncomfortable silence. "I've heard it's terribly cold in the winter."

"It's cold all the time," Corin answered, equally grateful for a change of subject. "But during the winter it gets so frigid that men grow icicles on their beards and women's hair freezes into thick strands."

Ruena smiled and, now that he was sitting across from her, Corin noticed her deep blue eyes. They were like the night sky. The reflections from the candles spread across the table reflected in their depths like twinkling stars. Corin realized he was staring and quickly looked away.

There were other nobles seated at the high table but they only talked amongst themselves and stared at Corin with a mixture of wonder and unease. Their furtive glances punctuated their muted conversations. Corin noticed that the young man from before was missing from the group. He considered asking about the stranger but couldn't bring up the courage to do so.

Only one other man seemed confident enough to address Corin outright. He was introduced as Duke Heirson who was visiting from Trestle, his estate on the border. At the man's left side sat a towering young man, Dresden Heirson, the duke's son. The duke welcomed Corin to the castle formally but with no kindness. Corin was grateful that the man didn't ask any questions, his piercing stares were difficult enough to stomach.

"How do your parents feel about all of this?" Hayes asked Corin. "They must be in disbelief finding out you're a mage."

Corin looked down. He'd just started enjoying the sensation of conversation. He'd never been around people who wanted to know about him and cared what he had to say. But this was a question he was far from comfortable answering. Clifton spoke for him.

"Corin's an orphan," Clifton explained. "Sir Burke found him after he'd left an orphanage and invited him to train as a page and then a squire at the battle school."

Corin was grateful for Clifton's delicate phrasing. He didn't want someone he respected as much as Hayes to know the full truth. He wasn't proud of his days on the street and being rescued wasn't as flattering as being invited.

"You must have noble blood then?" Hayes asked.

This time Clifton looked to Corin, also expecting an answer.

Corin shook his head. "No. Or at least, I don't think so. I don't know anything about my parents. Sir

Burke didn't care about my heritage. He allowed me to train regardless, despite how unorthodox that is."

Hayes smiled. "That sounds like Burke. He's never been one to hold to such trivial traditions."

"You know, both Neos Loch and myself also came from humble upbringings," Clifton said. "It seems to be a connection of sorts."

"Perhaps God chooses those who know the meaning of humility to ensure such great power is appreciated and not abused," the king suggested.

The thought stayed at the center of Corin's mind throughout the meal. The feast was long and filling and, when the king finally suggested that Corin be shown to his room to get some sleep, Corin felt his eyes droop in exhaustion.

A young boy, probably about twelve, was brought to the table.

"This is Will," the king explained. "He'll be your personal helper, Corin."

The wide-eyed boy shifted nervously and nodded respectfully to Corin. His uncertainty was obvious but Corin was grateful to not see any fear in the boy's expression.

"Will has been assisting me as a secretary of sorts," Clifton explained. "He's the castle scribe's apprentice."

"Old Murdoch refuses to leave the library even for an occasion such as this," Hayes commented with a laugh.

"Will has been personally selected to assist you however he can, Corin," King Rupert explained.

The boy smiled at Corin awkwardly and bowed his head in greeting. Corin stood and bowed to the table, uncertain what kind of farewell was appropriate. Fortunately, many of the people gathered around the room had already retired and the walk to the hallway was far less intimidating. Will led the way and Corin numbly followed. It quickly became clear why Corin had been led to an antechamber to prepare instead of his room. Will led him up through a long corridor, taking several turns along the way. Will pointed things out as they walked: paintings, tapestries, corridors that led to more corridors, windows out of which Corin could only see his reflection against the dark sky beyond. And then they arrived at a seemingly endless staircase. Corin wondered if his room was in one of the towers. He dragged himself up each step, feeling the exhaustion from the day weighing down on him with an unbearable force. Will chattered in a way that seemed more nervous than excited as they walked.

Corin filtered out the words, unable to process any more information after the overload he'd already experienced throughout the day. Finally, when he worried his feet wouldn't hold him up any longer, Corin reached his room.

"Mage Clifton's room is right across the hall," Will explained, pointing out a door identical to Corin's.

The boy opened the door to Corin's room and Corin stumbled inside. He glanced around briefly, amazed at the luxury of the place but not really taking any details in. He did see with relief that his sword and satchel were carefully laid out on a desk near the only window in the room.

"Can I help you with anything else?" Will asked.

Corin could only shake his head in answer. "Thank you," he said quietly. "I'd like to be alone."

The boy left without another word and Corin strode purposefully towards the bed. He collapsed into its unbelievably soft depths and let out a sigh of satisfaction. Corin didn't bother to undress. He was too tired to change into the nightclothes laid out on the bed. He simply kicked off his boots, removed his belt, and slipped under the covers.

If tonight was anything to go by, he would have a long day ahead of him tomorrow. For now, he would get all the sleep he could and hope that when he woke up he would discover that this had all been a dream.

CHAPTER 7

The castle was dark at night. An eerie emptiness filled the corridors. Though it was loud and bustling throughout the day and evening, at night it was silent and empty. The nobles had all gone to sleep, returning to their guest rooms either drunk from indulgence or simply good company. Occasionally the tall, sturdy shape of a knight could be seen standing in a corner, sword hanging from his side, spear clutched in hand, at guard against any unforeseen threats. The only sounds in the quiet were the shifting of tired legs to maintain vigilance at such a late hour. Shadows crept along the narrow hallways. The only light came from the soft illumination of the moon outside. It was a small moon that night and offered little in the way of brightness. A few torches were lit beside the guards, standing out like beacons on a stormy sea.

A lone figure, ghostly in the shadowy dark, crept through the abandoned corridors with a purpose and destination in mind. Cal moved in silence. The darkness was more a comfort than an obstacle to his progress. He was just another shadow creeping along the walls. He didn't need light to guide him. He knew exactly where he was going. But first, he had to make a little detour along the way.

He passed a knight and they exchanged subtle nods of recognition. Cal was just another noble finally heading off to bed after an exciting evening. He belonged. His casual stroll, relaxed posture, and nod were proof enough of that. Besides, Cal's face was a common one around the castle. He didn't stand out but he was just recognizable enough to be considered a permanent installment among the nobles, knights, archers, and royals. His steps slowed as he rounded a corner. He was careful with each step to maintain complete and utter silence. He wished he could assign Lark to this job. Her small stature, light weight, and knack for avoiding attention would make her much better suited. Even Dusk would be better at this. Cal was more suited to direct approaches. But Lark had another assignment and Dusk was… busy staying out of sight of the visiting nobility for the next few days. Not that Dusk would risk this particular job anyway.

Before long, the door was in front of him and Cal leaned against its corresponding wall, pressing himself flat against the smooth, stone surface. To a passerby, he'd appear just another noble who'd had a bit too much to drink and needed a moment to steady himself before he continued to his room. He slumped a little, furthering his ruse. However, the movement served a secondary purpose. His head tilted down, ever so slightly closer to the keyhole. Through the tiny opening, Cal could just hear the murmur of voices. He shifted himself a little lower, bending his knees as if he couldn't fully support his weight. The sounds cleared.

Duke Heirson's disgruntled voice filtered

through the door and Cal was grateful for once for the man's loud, grating tone. It made him easier to hear.

"Treated like commoners," Heirson complained. "Ridiculous that we're expected to share a room. I know for a fact that the king has plenty of space to accommodate larger crowds than this. It's pure disrespect for my position."

Cal had to restrain his snicker. If only the duke knew the truth. It was true that the king could have afforded to give the duke and his son separate rooms. They'd been put together not out of disrespect but to make Cal's job easier.

"But we were invited at least," the duke's son, Dresden, said. The young man's voice was quieter than his father's but still contained a hint of displeasure.

"It's to be expected that we were," the duke responded. "Despite the king's best efforts to disgrace us, our position does afford us some privileges."

There was the shifting sound of someone sitting down and a stretch of silence before the duke spoke again.

"This is all pathetic," he said with a huff. "This mage business is just a distraction. The king is hiding the true state of things from his people. He doesn't want anyone to know how incompetent he is or how Freiwade is quite literally on this kingdom's doorstep."

Cal grimaced at the harsh words. They were true of course. However, he didn't like the idea of the duke possessing such knowledge. The Heirson Dukedom, Trestle, bordered Freiwade, so it made sense that the duke knew the truth of the precarious situation Ashnah was in. It was a risk that Cal had tried to warn the king about. He feared the duke wouldn't keep the matter to himself and it wouldn't do to raise a panic.

"War is brewing, Dresden, and try as the king might to ignore it, it won't be covered up by the appearance of a boy mage for long. It's only a matter of time before the truth is out and the people panic. The distrust in Ashnah's royal family and the unrest that it causes is something that the king himself is laying the groundwork for. He's soft, just like his brother was."

"But the mage isn't just a distraction. He's a real mage. What if he's the secret weapon Ashnah needs to triumph over Freiwade?" Dresden asked. "If Ashnah wins the battle…"

"That slip of a boy won't be the war hero they're hoping for. He's no Neos Loch, that's for certain."

"But…"

"That's enough," the duke cut off his son. "As long as King Rupert sits on the throne, Ashnah has no chance of winning the war. The king cannot comprehend the threat Ashnah faces. The era of peace has gone on for too long. Ashnah has become complacent and no one so much as the king. Rupert never should have become king. Once, I thought his brother would be a powerful ruler, just what our kingdom needed, but the man was a fool, running off with a peasant woman and getting himself killed. Rupert wasn't trained for the position of king, he's a second son, incapable of filling the role of the first."

Cal sensed an uncomfortable silence fill the room. Dresden himself was a second son with a brother long since dead.

The duke continued, either uncaring or maybe

unaware of the impact of his hurtful words. "When the war comes, and it will come, the king will be caught unprepared. No mage or any other ally will save him. And after that, someone will have to step up and fill that gap of power to ensure that Ashnah has a capable ruler sitting on the throne."

Treacherous words. Words that could send any average man to the stockades. But the duke was no average man. His dukedom held a powerful position for Ashnah's defenses and his family line stretched past the great war to a time when even written records were lost. The Heirson family was respected, revered, and of such an important lineage that even the king had to treat them with the utmost esteem. Unless the duke spoke such words in a very public setting, he was allowed his opinions. In the privacy of his rooms with supposedly his son as the only witness, this conversation might as well have never happened.

"There is the matter of the girl though," Dresden said.

The duke's scoff reached Cal even through the door.

"She's hardly a definite heir. As far as Ashnah is concerned, at least a good majority of its nobles, her father abandoned any claim to the throne when he married that commoner and ran off to the countryside. She might as well share as much Castille blood as we do. Besides, no one will accept a woman ruler in a time of war and a girl even less. She wouldn't pose a problem. Either way, do not concern yourself about the matter, I have a plan for Ruena."

The words made Cal's blood boil in a way that

none of the other vile the duke had spat did. He clenched his hands into fists and forced himself to keep his breathing quiet. The worst part was the subtle truth in the duke's comments. Many in the court didn't see Ruena as a viable heir to the throne. Still, Cal would be caught dead before he allowed the duke to claim his relation to the king's second cousin through marriage as a reason to sit on the throne.

"Even so, I still think you could be underestimating the mage," Dresden pressed. "Mage Clifton might be getting old but the boy could have potential. I just... I don't," he lapsed into silence.

The duke sighed heavily. "If you were truly a duke's son, you wouldn't be so concerned about what a mage could or could not do. You should be more concerned about your role in the matter. You're not as well suited to your position as you should be. I suppose that is partially my fault. If you'd been trained from youth, you would have been more than ready to step into the role of a ruler. You wouldn't be nearly so flighty at least. If only the young men these days, the rulers no less, would grow backbones. Real nobility does whatever it takes to ensure their lands and lineages endure."

Cal could practically hear Dresden's wince. He had to fight against his own. The duke's words were brutal and unyielding.

"That boy mage is ill-prepared for a fight. He could hardly lift his eyes from the floor during the banquet, much less stand up against Freiwade's forces. The kingdom is slipping. It's up to the nobility to ensure that Ashnah doesn't fall. The mage may not be able to stand against Freiwade but I assure you the

Heirson line will endure no matter the threat. Our dukedom has faced greater threats from the inside than any that Freiwade or a mage could pose."

Silence stretched long in the room and Cal could practically feel the tension between the duke and his son, though he wasn't entirely sure why. Finally, Dresden spoke.

"Maybe it would do us well to question whether the cost of preserving our name is worth the price we've paid to do so."

"You act as if we're betraying the kingdom, Dresden. We are doing what we can to serve Ashnah. The name Heirson does not just come with land and a title, it also comes with duty."

"You know that's not what I mean."

Silence filled the room again and Cal thought perhaps they had gone off to their separate sleeping rooms but then the duke spoke again, his tone callous.

"Go to bed. I believe you've had too much to drink tonight."

The sound of shifting filtered through the door and Cal took that as a cue to leave as well. He'd heard all that he was going to. As usual, it was frustratingly inconclusive. The Heirsons undeniably had to be watched. Cal suspected they were planning something treacherous. The duke had always been hungry for power and eyed the throne with lustful longing. However, Cal knew the man was also too satisfied with his lofty position as duke to try anything that might result in him losing his title. Gathering information about Duke Heirson was always similar to walking a tightrope. Cal had to be careful with every step he took. The duke's words could be nothing more than talk. Many of the nobles felt they could rule the kingdom better than King Rupert. Cal suspected it was that way with any monarch. No matter how beloved the king was, there would always be others who were dissatisfied and felt they could do better. After King Rupert's elder brother, Theon, had forfeited his title, many nobility had lost their trust in the Castille family. They saw Theon's abdication as a betrayal to the kingdom. Rupert, having never been expected to inherit the throne, was somewhat unprepared to step into the role of king. Cal knew the man was a wise and kind ruler but it had been a long road for Rupert to gain the trust and admiration of his subjects. Duke Heirson was hardly the only dissenter. So, all Cal could do was keep an eye on the duke and his son and try to not be completely disgusted with them. Someday, maybe, the duke would make a public scene and dig his own grave. In the meantime, they could only be watched very carefully. Cal waited a moment longer before pushing off from the wall and staggering down the hallway. He had places to be and he was eager to leave the duke and his son behind.

CHAPTER 8

Cal picked up his pace as he headed deeper and deeper into the castle. The hallways grew dimmer with dwindling windows and torches. Fewer doors led off to bedrooms, offices, and other gathering places. The walls were blank with no tapestries or paintings covering their surfaces. It was eerily quiet. It was the sound that could only come from a truly abandoned space. There were no knights standing guard or nobles wandering back to their rooms. This area of the castle was as good as forgotten to everyone except a select few.

An uneven set of stone stairs led to a lower level, just below ground. For many, the slightly pitched angle of the steps would be off-putting but Cal didn't even have to raise a hand to the wall to steady himself. He took the steps two at a time, knowing he was already late for the meeting. At the base of the stairs was a narrow corridor. The walls pressed in until there was hardly room for the span of a man's shoulders. A few doors were spaced along the wall. All of them housed the same type of supplies. Cal opened a door at the end of the hallway on the left-hand side.

The supply pantry was filled with worn, moth-eaten blankets, unused candles, and sacks of grain probably unfit for consumption. They were old relics of the War of Three Kingdoms, the Great War. Cal hadn't been alive during that time but he knew the stories. It was a long and arduous conflict and uncertainty had been rampant. The stockpiles in all of the basement closets were kept in preparation of a siege on the castle. They were meager rations in case the residents were trapped inside the fortress. The food wouldn't last long and the candles would burn out even quicker. But it seemed to have offered some peace for the king and nobles. Now, the supplies were little more than trinkets of a war that was won long ago and a reminder of how differently things could have been for Ashnah.

Sir Hayes had suggested to the king that the supplies be replenished, but as of yet, the king hadn't begun stockpiling goods. Cal suspected that King Rupert would send any nobles and servants further inland in the event of a battle instead of encouraging them to take shelter in Castille Castle. The castle was a fortress but it was also a trap, with no easy way to flee should the walls be breached.

Cal sidestepped a stack of blankets to reach the only cleared spot on the floor. A half-hidden latch in the corner of the wall revealed itself. When Cal pulled the latch, a section of stone slid back, exposing a small square door. Cal crouched through the small opening. It had always been a tight squeeze even when he had first ducked through the hole at fifteen. As he often did, he wished the builders had taken into account that some people were not as small as Lark. Cal had long since lost count of how many times he'd hit his head on the edge of the opening. He reached for the ladder on the other side, swung onto it, and closing the trapdoor behind him, started to descend into darkness.

The wood rungs scraped against Cal's calloused hands. He counted them as he went deeper and deeper into the dark depths. Five…Ten…Fifteen. At seventeen, he released his grip and jumped the last few rungs. It was an old habit, long ingrained, and one that despite the years, despite the fact that he was now an adult instead of a teenager, he couldn't break. He landed on the roughly-hewn, planked floor with a satisfying thud that he knew announced his presence to the others. He took a deep breath in an attempt to make himself more alert despite the late hour. The meeting ahead was sure to be a long one and he was already drowsy from an exciting and busy day.

He allowed himself a brief moment before squashing the exhaustion weighing on him and stepping into The Cavern. That was what the spies of Ashnah called their meeting place. The Cavern was deep beneath Castille Castle, hidden and unknown by the court that walked the halls above. The name of the secret place was fitting. Cal wasn't sure who had come up with the title, the old spymaster, Barton, probably. Cal's mentor had possessed a strange sense of humor. In his youth, he'd teased that it was more of a hole than anything. The walls were a combination of dirt and stone, dug into the ground and supported with wooden beams. At some point, someone had attempted to add wooden flooring to the space but the dust that lay below the planks always worked its way to the surface. The wooden boards squeaked and groaned with each step and bent with any weight placed on them. The place was relatively small, with cots in the corners, a table and chairs, and shelves full of maps, parchments, and books. The contents of the collection covered topics ranging from details about the noble houses, information about the knights and archers currently within the king's service, intelligence gathered about Freiwade and Skellas, maps of all three kingdoms, and extensive blueprints of Castille Castle. There were also a large variety of boring volumes of history and past conflicts. Supplies of various types filled every other space. There were blankets, rations, disguises, candles, cloaks, and weapons of all kinds. Then there were the few homey touches spread throughout that made the space less a meeting ground and more a refuge. The undeniable signs of habitation were all around from the clothes strewn on a cot to the eating utensils still laying out from the last meal. And of course, the most undeniable sign of life was the young man sitting at the table.

Dusk nodded in greeting, silent as usual.

"Lark?" Cal asked.

The girl in question thudded down the ladder as if on cue. Her foul mood was clear from the start as she stalked towards the table, yanked out the chair beside Dusk's, and plopped onto it. Cal had to look away from her to keep a straight face. Her petite frame was nearly consumed by her raised shoulders and crossed arms. She blew a curl of her long dark hair out of her eyes with a huff, only for it to fall stubbornly back into place. Her glowering expression might have been intimidating on any other person but to Cal, the effect only filled him with an odd sort of amusement. He knew he shouldn't feel that way. The expression could only mean that her mission hadn't been as successful as hoped. However, it was so rare for Lark's feathers to get ruffled that it was a bit of a treat to see her so annoyed.

Dusk, likewise couldn't quite look at her but Cal was sure the other man's expression was more stoic than his. Lark fixed him with a pointed look, daring for him to comment. Cal cleared his throat.

"Right, now that we're all here..." He pulled a seat from the corner and sat on it backwards, facing his companions.

Cal turned his full attention to Dusk who had moved past any amusement over Lark's behavior and was fixing him with an intense gaze.

"Okay, what do you want to know first?" Cal asked with a slight smile.

Dusk's annoyance at having to stay belowground during such a time of excitement was obvious. The dark, brooding exterior hid an inquisitive and never-resting mind. Cal could only imagine the turmoil his friend must have faced having to wait for information from him and Lark instead of searching for answers himself.

The question was only an invitation. Cal already knew what Dusk would want to hear about most. However, there were more important matters to discuss before they reached that particular conversation. Dusk knew it as well and chose to stay silent instead of answering Cal's question.

Cal shifted in his seat, turning the meeting to the newest issue. "What did you think of the mage?"

"I thought he'd be taller," Lark said sarcastically. Her gravelly tone, as usual, came out quiet. Most would interpret the tenor as shy or uncertain but it was the norm for Lark.

Cal released a huff of laughter, grateful that she at least wasn't upset enough to lose her sense of humor. Dusk shook his head in exasperation. He never quite got used to Cal and Lark's shenanigans.

"Need I remind you two, that boy you're referring so casually about is a mage. That makes him dangerous. We have to be certain he's on our side. This is no time to be making jokes."

"We're well aware of the severity of the situation, Dusk," Cal reassured.

Lark shrugged. "He's just cranky because he had to stay behind and watch the worms fighting over crumbs instead of seeing the mage for himself."

"I'm cranky?" Dusk asked pointedly.

Lark's expression soured.

"Enough," Cal warned. "The truth is the mage was less than impressive."

"Facts and only facts," Dusk said. "I'll form my own impressions."

It was a standard practice in their reports. Dusk's ingenious mind could make better sense of a situation without unnecessary input. Dusk's analysis could also be counted upon to be impartial, more impartial than even Cal's impressions. Even if Dusk hadn't witnessed an event in person, given accurate information, he could typically solve a problem in minutes that had stumped Cal or Lark for hours or days.

"His name is Corin Faye. He's average height, a

little on the thin side, seventeen or eighteen years old. He came from a battle school in Nevara…"

"Nevara!" Lark snorted.

"He didn't meet anyone's eyes," Cal went on, ignoring Lark's interruption. "I found that a little suspicious. He asked for privacy from even Clifton once we'd entered the castle. I thought he might be hiding something so I kept an eye on him. He stayed in the antechamber for a long time but, after he stepped outside, he went right to the great hall. He looked a little sick and even more so when he stepped into the great hall. I watched from a distance for a while but he didn't do much. He hesitated to answer questions but was very polite. Altogether he seemed overly cautious. The question is why?"

Dusk turned to Lark, an eyebrow raised, waiting for her part of the story.

"He went right to his room after the feast. He'd hardly laid down before he was asleep."

Cal looked at her sidelong. "The king gave us strict orders to only watch from a distance. We weren't supposed to invade the mage's privacy in any way."

Lark leaned back in her chair, unconcerned. "What the king doesn't know won't hurt him."

Cal gave her a warning look.

"He's a potential threat," Lark argued, "and I watched from the vent system. He never knew I was there. I left as soon as I knew he was asleep."

Cal didn't say anything further. As the leader, it was his responsibility to berate her for what she'd done. The vent system, built to convey heat from fireplaces throughout the cold, drafty castle was useful for spying but shouldn't have been used to spy on a supposed ally. That didn't mean Cal fully disagreed with her decision. He couldn't blame her for what she'd done. Corin, despite his nonthreatening exterior, still posed a great risk for the kingdom of Ashnah and everyone in it. It was a threat that Cal, Lark, and Dusk were personally responsible for discreetly managing.

Cal rested his forearms against the back of the chair. "Well, what do you make of it?" he asked Dusk.

The room lapsed into silence as Dusk fell into a contemplative state. Cal and Lark exchanged a glance but stayed quiet, giving their companion time to think. Cal wasn't entirely sure what to make of Corin Faye. He had a feeling Dusk would be able to sort through the situation without letting any skewed perceptions get in the way.

"He won't pose a threat." Dusk finally said. "At least, not at the moment."

"How do you know?" Cal asked. He trusted Dusk but he still couldn't help doubting just a little.

Dusk traced a finger along a grain of the table and studied Cal with an expression that said the answer should be obvious. "You think that it was suspicious the mage wouldn't meet anyone's eyes. He wasn't hiding something. He almost certainly has some kind of inferiority complex. You said he was average height and thin. He was in a battle school trained by one of the greatest knights in the kingdom."

"He was used to being the smallest person in the room," Lark put in.

Dusk nodded. "The weakest too. Not to

mention, he's from Nevara. That backwater town is hardly an epicenter for nobility. The baron of Nevara has been trying to shift rulership of that place onto someone else for years now. The boy was forced to go face to face with the only known mage, the legendary Sir Hayes, and the king himself in the space of twenty-four hours. He was probably in shock. That's why he spent so long in the antechamber."

"Probably making friends with the chamber pot during that time," Lark snickered.

Dusk and Cal both ignored her.

"Furthermore, his hesitation in answering questions during the feast was probably because of nerves. He may not have known how to answer or even how to address people properly. He wasn't raised in a court setting and the intricacies of etiquette are headache-inducing even to someone who's spent their whole life learning about it."

Dusk rubbed his forehead as if one of those etiquette-induced headaches was coming on at that very moment. "People, especially nobility, are full of contradictions. Corin was wise to be careful with his words. It's never a good idea to trust too fully."

"I suppose we can't fault him for being cautious," Cal admitted.

"Still, we should keep an eye on him, though I'd be more worried he would make a run for it than cause any trouble."

Lark snickered. "With the way he was looking at Ruena, I doubt he's going anywhere."

Cal stiffened. The last thing he wanted was for Ruena to get involved. It was inevitable that she would be. Still, he'd prefer she stayed away from the mage, threat or not.

Lark nudged him in the side. "Relax, brother bear. Ruena can take care of herself."

Cal rolled his eyes. "It's our job as spies to be cautious. Like Dusk said, Corin doesn't pose a threat, *for now.*"

"Ruena faces enough trouble from the court. Those are the vultures you should be worried about," Dusk pointed out.

Cal waved a hand through the air. Enough about Ruena. Yes, maybe Cal was a little overprotective. But Ruena was like a younger sister to him. They'd grown up around the castle together. They'd been friends for longer than either of them could remember. Cal didn't want anything to happen to her. Fortunately, Lark was right. Ruena was smart and she could take care of herself.

"What about the rest?" Dusk asked, bringing them back to the meeting.

The question was vague but Cal knew exactly what Dusk was asking.

Cal rested his head on his forearms and with a deep breath explained everything he'd heard while listening at the duke's door. He watched Dusk as he spoke, and saw the spy's jaw clench. Otherwise, Dusk's face gave nothing away. It remained stoic and expressionless. When Cal reached the part where the duke had claimed he was willing to do anything to preserve his title and lands, Dusk rose from his chair and began to pace the room. He walked to one of the shelves and then placed a hand against the stacked books as if looking for something. His fingers brushed the covers but otherwise Dusk stayed still, facing the volumes. Cal could practically hear his mind racing.

Cal and Lark almost unconsciously turned their eyes to study the table. Cal finished the story quickly. There wasn't much left of it anyway. He was preparing to move on to the next issue when Dusk spoke, still facing the books.

"When are they leaving the castle?"

Cal cleared his throat, once, twice. "It will be at least a week or so, depending on how things unfold of course. It'll be some time before the excitement of the mage's arrival fades but I suspect the duke will want to return to his land before long."

Dusk sighed heavily and rested his forehead against the wooden shelf.

Lark elbowed Cal in the side.

"We could... um... use someone on the border keeping an eye on things, making sure Freiwade doesn't make any sudden movements."

Dusk shook his head immediately and after taking a deep breath turned to face Cal and Lark again, composed once more.

"I should be here, extracting information and opinions from the visiting nobles. The appearance of a new mage makes for a tense situation. We need to ensure no one will attempt anything against Corin or the crown."

Cal couldn't object to that. Dusk was the best suited for interrogating nobles. He knew how they worked, how they thought, in a way that he and Lark could never understand. Cal was grateful his friend would be there to help during the trying situation at hand. Stakes were high and the discovery of a new mage only increased the risk involved. Dusk would be a valuable asset to have. Cal didn't say anything more. He didn't need to. He only nodded to Dusk with a mixture of gratitude and understanding.

"Then I'd like you to attend the feast tomorrow night. Listen to the rumors and gather as much information as you can from the visiting nobles. Lark can handle listening to the servants' gossip. Just... be careful."

Cal knew he didn't have to issue the warning. If anyone was aware of the risk involved, it was Dusk. Cal turned to Lark next. He was hesitant to even ask what she'd found given her annoyed behavior when she'd arrived. It was obvious her mission hadn't turned out the way she'd hoped.

"What did you find?" he asked her.

Lark sighed with exasperation, a tad dramatically. "Nothing, nothing, and more nothing."

She rested her head on the table. Her forehead thudded against the surface to punctuate her point.

Cal had suspected as much.

"We'll find them," Cal reassured her. "It'll take time."

Lark turned so her head was facing him, her cheek still resting against the wood. "We don't have time and you know it. Every minute we let those spies walk loose around this castle, we might as well be shouting all our secrets to Freiwade."

She spat out the name of the foreign kingdom. The venom in her tone made Cal lean back involuntarily.

"We should keep an ear out for servants or nobles who are dissatisfied with the presence of another mage. Freiwade demonizes magic and while some Ashnans share that view, blatant remarks are suspicious. At the very least, those people might be in league with the spies. It would help us narrow things down if nothing else," Dusk suggested.

The words only reminded Cal of how precarious their situation was and how their enemies seemed to be encroaching on all sides. The greatest threat may very well lie within their own walls. The question was if that threat was the spies or the mage.

CHAPTER 9

Corin awoke to light streaming through the window and the sound of knocking at the door. At first, the sensations blended into his dreams. He could almost hear the sound of the squires moving about, readying themselves for another day of training. He could imagine Burke's voice at the door, urging them to hurry up before they had wasted away the day. But as the knocking continued and the light filtered through his eyelids, Corin slowly realized there were no voices, no squires scurrying around him. He blinked into consciousness and saw a stone ceiling above him, felt an unusually soft bed beneath him. He turned his head and took in the ornate furniture of the castle, Castille Castle.

So, it hadn't been a dream after all. His coming to the castle and being a mage had been real. Corin couldn't help releasing a soft groan. He wanted to bury his face in his pillow and pretend that he was back at the battle school. The sunlight streaming through the window was proof enough that he was far from that place. Burke never would have condoned him sleeping in so late. He would have been forced to skip breakfast to make up for missing the early morning jog around the grounds. Would he be able to take those morning runs here? That short hour had been his favorite part of training as a knight. Despite the cold, blustery conditions of Nevara, running had been the only aspect of training that Corin had excelled at. He was fast and he could keep up a steady pace longer than any of the other squires. They'd teased him that he was great at running away from problems. Corin hoped he could keep himself conditioned even during his training as a mage. Part of him knew that his time at the castle wouldn't last long. Maybe the battle school would take him back if he was able to prove himself worthy. If not, he could look for work as a freelance knight.

Corin was snapped out of his thoughts by the persistent knocking at the door. The noise pounded away at his skull, informing him of a dull headache that he hadn't noticed until then. He desperately wanted to ignore the knocking and the responsibilities he now had but he couldn't. So, yawning and stretching his arms above his head, Corin rolled out of bed. He hated to leave the soft mattress, softer than any he'd slept on before. Walking barefoot across the cold, stone floor served the purpose of waking him up fully by the time he reached the door. He opened it right as the person standing outside raised their hand to knock again.

It was the young boy from the night before. Corin searched his head for the boy's name and after a moment remembered it.

"Morning, Will," Corin muttered tiredly.

The boy took a half-step back, seemingly surprised by Corin remembering his name. A flush crept up his cheeks as he seemed to realize just how incessant his knocking had been. Now that Corin was more awake and aware, he noticed that the boy was shifting his weight uneasily back and forth. Corin wasn't used to the sensation of people being uncomfortable around him. He wanted to say something but the boy spoke before he could find any words.

"Sorry to bother you, Mage Corin," Will said nervously. "Mage Clifton sent me to wake you. He says you are to meet him in his office."

Corin supposed he should have assumed he wouldn't be allowed to hide in his room forever. He was a mage now and it was to be expected that he would be required to act like one eventually.

"Would you wait for me outside?" Corin asked, feeling slightly embarrassed that he didn't know his way around the castle. "I don't think I'd be able to find his office. I might get lost," he added in a whisper.

"But..." the boy looked at him with wide eyes, as if surprised that a mage could possibly get lost.

Corin waited for him to say more but Will only closed the door, waiting as requested. Corin stalked to the desk and rifled through his satchel, removing the only other clothes he had. As a knight-in-training, he'd worn a uniform and never had to worry about not having enough changes of clothing. The clothes he wore now were of better quality than the threadbare garments in his hands but they were also wrinkled and stunk of travel. He looked at the wardrobe in the corner, no doubt full of clothes fitting for a mage. No fancy garments would make Corin feel like he fit the part. He glanced at the simple tunic he held. At one time, it seemed a luxury that he didn't deserve to own a pair of clothes with no holes or tears. He'd felt an immeasurable sense of pride to wear his battle school garments. Now, he knew the simple clothes would hardly be considered presentable, especially in the presence of the king and a mage. He should try one of the garments provided for him by the castle but those robes were meant for a real mage, not Corin.

He changed into his old, worn-out tunic, draping his dirty travel clothes over the back of a chair. He stared at the mirror before him. Corin wanted very badly at that moment to crawl back into bed and never awaken. But Clifton was waiting for him and he had already made the bed. He didn't want to wrinkle the sheets. Corin glanced longingly at his sword, tempted to take it with him. He was a mage now and mages didn't carry swords. Still, the weight of the sword at his hip would bring about a sense of comfort in this odd place. Corin braced a hand on the wall beside the mirror and leaned forward until his forehead was pressed against the reflective glass. How was this happening to him? He didn't feel like any of it was real. He didn't know what to do. What would Sir Burke do? The answer came to him immediately. Sir Burke would pray for guidance. Corin swallowed hard. Never had he needed guidance more but prayer still felt awkward and uncertain. Burke had always been the one to lead prayers with the squires. He'd made it seem so effortless. Corin still couldn't imagine God wanting to listen to anything he might have to ask. He tried anyway.

God, he began and then hesitated, *I...* Corin couldn't find the words, any words. He shook his head to clear it and pushed away from the mirror. He glanced behind him at the sword once more then left it behind.

Will was obediently waiting for him just outside, shifting from foot to foot anxiously. He perked up when Corin appeared and started towards Clifton's office. Corin followed. Silence filled the space between them as they walked. It was an uncomfortable silence and it only made it increasingly obvious how uncomfortable Will was around him. The boy's shoulders were rigid and he hid his hands in the folds of his tunic. They reached a set of stairs that led further up into the tower. The previous night when he'd been tired and weary, Corin had thought he'd climbed to the top of the tower just to reach his room. It turned out he'd only scaled three flights of stairs, though it had felt like an eternity to reach the soft bed that awaited him. With each step, the silence seemed to grow louder until Corin couldn't take it anymore.

"How long have you worked for the king, Will?" Corin asked. It had bothered him slightly the night before, now it was the only question he could think to voice. How had someone so young found a position serving the king's head scribe?

"Two years," Will told him.

Corin halted a moment. That would have made the boy eight, at the most ten, when he started his position.

"I'm twelve," Will went on as if anticipating the question. "I'm just small for my age. But I'm growing fast."

The remark made Corin grin. He'd been small

at that age too. Then again, he was still small for his current age. He was grateful to know that Will's stature was likely due to genetics, not for want of nourishment like Corin had faced on the streets of Nevara.

"You have a lot of responsibility for someone so young. You must be a hard worker and trustworthy too," Corin voiced.

Will tripped on a step but quickly steadied himself. His ears looked just a little red from Corin's view.

"My uncle is a knight," Will explained. "He put in a good word for me. I... I don't want to train as a page like my parents wanted. He thought an apprenticeship with the scribe would be a good alternative. It's only recently that I've started helping Mage Clifton as a secretary. I'm very grateful to the king for allowing me such a position and to my uncle for getting it for me."

And that was how things worked, Corin thought. The easiest way to get somewhere in life was to have connections. He studied the back of Will's head. When he'd been Will's age, his only desire was to survive. He'd had no real hopes or dreams. When Burke appeared, a knight in shining armor, Corin had seen that as the only path for him. If he'd grown up in a real home with his every need provided for, would he have wanted something different than knighthood as Will did? Corin supposed he would never know. He would never know if he could have achieved status as a knight anyway.

Anxiety crept into Corin's chest as they continued up the stairs. His path led in a different direction now. What would be required of him as a mage? How would he adapt to this new life that he'd had no choice but to undertake?

Corin was lost in his thoughts by the time they reached Clifton's office at the very top of the tower. The single tower of the castle was larger than almost any building in Nevara except for perhaps the battle school. Will pointed to a relatively simple door.

"That's the office," the boy explained. He said nothing else before hurriedly turning to descend the stairs.

"Where are you going?" Corin asked.

Will paused a moment. "I have to get to my own lessons. Just because I'm helping Mage Clifton doesn't mean I can shirk my training as a scribe. Besides, Mage Clifton requested privacy for your first lesson."

Will took the steps two at a time, leaving Corin alone in the tower. Corin stared at the door. In a way, it was even more imposing than the entrance to Burke's office. Corin had no idea what lay on the other side. He had no idea what he should expect to find. Half of him feared there would be a dark, dire room waiting for him. Maybe there would be ancient, dangerous relics of magic and books filled with secrets that could drive a person mad. Corin swallowed hard. His hand shook just a little as he reached to knock. The sound of his fist connecting with wood was quiet. Maybe no one would hear him and he could leave, claiming he had at least tried. No such luck. A voice from inside called for him to enter and Corin was forced to oblige.

It was not what Corin had been expecting. The room was bright and airy, the only discomfort coming from the stale quality of the air. There were bookshelves lining almost all of the walls and a desk situated in one corner. Two chairs sat in the middle of the room facing each other. There was a chalkboard that had lots of strange symbols scrawled across it. Writing, maybe? If that was Clifton's handwriting, it was no wonder he needed a secretary. A staircase in one corner led to a loft space above that looked to house even more books and scrolls. Clifton was reaching high above his head for a book from one of the shelves when Corin entered.

"Please, have a seat, Corin," Clifton told him, finally reaching the book.

Corin did as he was told and took one of the two seats. He looked at his hands resting in his lap then glanced around the room before his gaze returned once again to his hands.

"You slept through breakfast so I'll try to make your first lesson short so you can get something to eat. In the future though you'll be expected to have breakfast with the rest of the castle. Your lessons will be immediately after that."

Corin nodded. Half of him had been expecting a greater rebuke at his tardiness, the other half of him couldn't bring himself to care.

"Good. I'll start with a little history lesson. Don't groan just yet. I'm sure you've had your fair share of history lectures from Sir Burke but I'm going to focus on what we know historically about magic."

Corin sat in his chair a little straighter. He had immediately dreaded the next hour or so of his lesson when he heard the word history. It wasn't that he disliked studying history so much. He enjoyed learning about past battles and Ashnah's growth as a kingdom. However, he'd sat through so many lectures at the battle school that he wasn't eager to hear things he already knew once again. Magic was one topic that he knew very little about and he suspected what he did know was tainted by prejudice and superstition. Maybe he might learn something that would help explain his predicament a little further.

"Like most aspects of our history, very little is known about magic before The War of Three Kingdoms. All historical records that mention magic save for a single scroll were lost sometime before the Great War. The story goes that long ago there was a great library full of knowledge and learning that connected the three kingdoms. We don't know as much as I would like about the library or what was stored there but it would have been the primary source of knowledge throughout the kingdoms. Scribes and historians believe that it was destroyed by a great fire. A young scribe stole away a Bible from the burning library, the only copy predating the Great War, and brought it to Ashnah for safekeeping. The only other document salvaged was a single scroll about the gifts we call magic. That scroll offered Ashnah a perspective that neither Freiwade nor Skellas possessed. Magic was not a curse as many believed but a great gift bestowed on a few select individuals by God Himself. We call the abilities magic but in the past, they were known as healing, prophecy, and other similar gifts. The important thing to remember, Corin, is that real, pure ability can only come from God. There have been some over time who have sought to find power for themselves and create their own magic. However, any manmade magic is corrupt and does not come from God. Someday, I'll share more about that sort of corruption, but for now, I want to talk about the magic that you and I were gifted, the true magic."

Corin cleared his throat, hesitant to interrupt but needing to voice his concern.

"The corrupt power, how does someone come by it? How can people tell the difference between it and God-given abilities?"

Clifton rested a hand on the back of the empty chair facing Corin's.

"Gifts given by God are made to glorify Him. Although the circumstances of magic have changed over the years as kingdoms have risen and fallen, the essence remains the same."

"What do you mean changed?"

"In times of peace, magic has been used to heal, to mend, to aid in harvest and growth. In times of war, it has been used to protect, defend, and even in some cases attack. At some times war is necessary. For example, Freiwade detests God and the ruler of Freiwade lives in blasphemy of Christian ideals. The vast majority of the kingdom and especially the ruling family believes that there is no God and that men hold power beyond anything else. Ashnah cannot under any circumstances compromise to that view. So, if Freiwade strives for control over all of the kingdoms, Ashnah must do what is necessary to defend its ideals and beliefs. In that case, war is necessary. You and I as mages have been given the power to defend Ashnah. It is not only our ability but also our duty having been given such gifts. In the end, even battle in this case is used to glorify God by defending the faith we have in Him. Unnatural magic is used for destruction and self-gain."

"But if it doesn't come from God, then where does it come from?" Corin asked.

"There are sources of evil in this world, planted by the enemy," Clifton explained. "Mankind is sometimes led into temptation and falsehood. In the Bible, there are stories about sorcerers and enchanters who sought after false gods. Their power was not from God and was used to trick people and to gain power for earthly desires. They did not serve kingdoms but manipulated rulers. They did not attribute power to God and created pagan rituals that were abominable to Him. They stumbled into their unnatural abilities through their sin. Ultimately that power doesn't come from God but from their seeking after the devil. There is a crucial difference between that kind of sorcery and the magic we possess. That is why we study the true magic gifted by God and why we must be certain to credit Him for everything. He gives gifts and He can take them away."

Corin felt a chill creep over him. He'd been led to believe by superstitions and rumors that all magic was the same. Perhaps that was why so many distrusted it in all forms. However, if Clifton was right, and he certainly knew more about the issue than Corin did, then Corin's view of magic wasn't accurate. Seeing it, not as an all-powerful force used for whatever the mage desired, but as a gift used to glorify God changed everything.

"But we're getting off track, there will be time to discuss this further in future lessons. The point of the matter is that magic is still not fully understood. It likely never will be as it is not by human design. Much knowledge of magic has been lost along with the great library and much has been distorted by biased historians and rulers. The presence of magic had been forgotten for some time before The War of Three Kingdoms. However, during that Great War, a young man joined the side of King Henry Castille, a man by the name of Neos Loch. He wasn't much older than you, Corin, when he turned the tides of war. Of course, you know what he did."

"He was the first mage, sir," Corin replied.

"Yes, at least the first mage within remembered history. He joined the side of Ashnah and before long, thanks to his ability, the war that had lasted so many years was finally won. You know the rest, I assume. Freiwade took control of Skellas and its resources, merging into one kingdom under Claudius Corpin's rule, and a treaty was forged between Freiwade and Ashnah to provide resources and trade between the kingdoms. Then there was the hundred years of peace that followed."

Corin nodded, having heard all of what Clifton said and much more during his studies with Sir Burke. Of course, The Hundred Year Peace was a relative term. There had still been skirmishes between the kingdoms. Men like Burke and Hayes would attest to that. However, those battles had been small affairs and not recognized as conflicts by either kingdom. The knights who'd died during those "skirmishes" and their grieving families might think otherwise.

Clifton sighed, finally taking a seat in the chair opposite Corin's.

"The truth is, Corin, I'm telling you all of this

because we are in a delicate stage of history right now. No doubt you know a bit about what is going on, seeing as you were trained by Sir Burke. Freiwade has never been satisfied with the state of things after the Great War. King Histen Corpin is a proud and brutal ruler and the treaty between the kingdoms benefits Ashnah greatly. Ashnah won the war, after all. Our kingdom has fertile land that supplies us with all of our needs: bountiful harvests, plenty of forestry to use for lumber, wildlife to hunt, a relatively good climate, and conditions that allow for livestock and farming. Freiwade is incredibly dependent on our kingdom for food and materials. While we receive the metals needed for weapons and other tools from their mines, they must rely on us and Skellas's meager provisions for everything needed to survive. With such a proud man as king, Freiwade hates to sacrifice any measure of pride and the treaty deprives them of that most of all. You know about the skirmishes that have continued despite the treaty and the years of peace. Sir Hayes will tell you that those small battles are nasty enough as it is. Freiwade has been testing the waters for years now, determining if they are strong enough to win against Ashnah, trying to find any weaknesses in our ranks. Those skirmishes are only the beginning of what is to come. Freiwade is dissatisfied with the land that has been allotted to them. They rebel against the belief in God that Ashnah maintains. Freiwade has been advancing on our borders, slowly but definitely. And soon, very soon, it is expected that outright war will be declared."

  That word, that awful word had floated unsaid in the air of the battle school classrooms each time

Burke discussed a battle or skirmish. Even when mysterious casualties on the border of Ashnah were reported, even when evidence of battle was all around, it had never been outright spoken. War, there would be war. Corin knew enough to recognize that if Freiwade was going to go so far as to declare war, they were serious about it. They were confident that they could win. The conflict that would come was likely to be just as brutal as The War of Three Kingdoms. And this time Freiwade would not only have a goal but a personal vendetta against Ashnah. Corin's chest throbbed with the realization of how dire their situation truly was.

"Why," Corin swallowed hard, "why is this not public knowledge? Shouldn't the people know the threat that Freiwade poses? Shouldn't the towns start to prepare for battle?"

"King Rupert has tried to keep all of this silent in hopes that it wouldn't lead to mass panic. He, Sir Hayes, and other battle masters around the kingdom have been quietly preparing for the worst. It's only a matter of time before there is no choice but to declare war. Even the nobility are not truly aware of the state of things. You are in a position of great importance now, Corin. It's only fair for you to know that the king himself is in a delicate position. Rupert was never meant to be king. When his brother renounced his position, many in Ashnah were outraged. The fact that King Rupert never produced an heir, makes the situation even more tumultuous. His niece is the only viable successor. As such, many of the nobles have personal designs on the throne and can only be trusted to look after their own desires. The king's authority will be further questioned should there be war. Until things are certain and until the king can create a foolproof plan to defeat Freiwade, a certain level of secrecy is required. That is where you come in, Corin. When King Rupert and I received word from Sir Burke, we were filled with relief. I... I am growing older. You've probably wondered why I require a secretary."

Clifton held out his hand and Corin could see a slight tremor.

"I may be a mage but I'm still human. Years of writing and experimenting with my abilities have taken a toll on my body. My abilities were never as powerful as my mentor's. The Lord has gifted me knowledge most of all. Much of my training, done in times of peace, has been to further understand magic. I'm not equipped for a long and drawn-out battle. But you, you are young, and from the account Burke shared of your fight with young Phineas York, you have a power unlike any I have demonstrated. You could be like Neos Loch. You, Corin, could turn the tides of war."

CHAPTER 10

You, Corin, could turn the tides of war.
The words reverberated around Corin's skull like clashing swords. *He* was expected to turn the tides of battle? Him? Clifton, the king, and everyone else who had come to that conclusion must be a few eggs short of a dozen. How could scrawny, weak Corin Faye from the backwaters of Nevara possibly be expected to win a war? He needed time to think. Brooding was what Sir Burke would have called it. Most importantly, Corin wanted as much distance between him and Clifton's office as possible. In fact, he wanted to avoid everyone in the castle. He didn't think he could bear the amazed and fearful looks and the whisperings of, "Mage." Instead of returning to his room, Corin decided it was past time to explore the castle. He was already tired of feeling lost in the twisting hallways and he didn't want to be so dependent on Will to lead him around.

Castille Castle was magnificent. The further Corin found himself in its depths, the more it stood out as an architectural wonder. Even the stone walls were all flawless corners and elegant lines. Corin went past one section of wall that had a scene of trees, rocks, and a river carved right into the stone. Corin brushed his hands along the careful grooves and ridges. The entire castle was a thing of beauty. It was obvious that had been considered from the start of its construction. Corin had heard that much of the castle had to be rebuilt after the Great War. Enemy sieges were a frequent occurrence then and, on a few occasions, Freiwade soldiers had made it past the exterior defenses and destroyed a good portion of the interior of the castle. It was amazing, Corin thought, what incredible feats men were capable of in times of peace and war. In times of peace, beautiful and extravagant art was created to reflect hopes, dreams, and prosperity. The stone carving was serene. It was obviously the work of a very talented artist. But in times of war, there was another form of art displayed, the art of war. Some might call men like Burke and Hayes "artists" in their own fashion.

Corin moved past the carving. As he continued down the hall, he caught a glimpse of a small, dark-haired woman out of the corner of his eye. At first, he thought she was a child, so small was her stature. Her hair was a mess of untamable black curls and her eyes were fixed right on Corin. Was she a noblewoman? Not likely. She didn't carry herself as a noblewoman. Her dress was basic but she clearly wasn't a servant either. There was a sense of certainty in every line of her body. He hadn't even heard her, only caught sight of her out of the corner of his eye. He was sure she hadn't been there before. He opened his mouth to ask her who she was and why she was staring so intently at him, not with fear or amazement, but with scrutiny. However, before Corin could form a single word, she was gone. It was in the space of a blink. Corin hadn't heard the slightest sound from her small, booted feet as she deserted.

A chill ran down Corin's spine. Eerie. He turned his mind back to his explorations in an attempt to forget about the strange young woman. His mind kept turning back to thoughts of war. War!

Although Corin hadn't lived through the War of Three Kingdoms, he remembered the many lectures Sir Burke had given him and the other squires. "It was a long and difficult war full of despair and bloodshed. Countless lives were lost on both sides. Where before the three kingdoms of Ashnah, Skellas, and Freiwade had lived in good relation, now the moral boundaries between them are as clear as the physical ones. I thank the Lord every day that I wasn't alive during that great and terrible war. I pray that none of you will ever have to live through a war like that."

Burke's words had seemed like just another lecture then. Ashnah and Freiwade had been at a tentative peace for over a hundred years. Another war seemed more like a nightmare than reality. Now Corin was living that reality. And he was expected to play the part of Neos Loch, bringing an end to the conflict. He thought he might be sick.

Corin tried to force the thoughts away. He wished he could pull them out of his head and lock them in a chest somewhere never to see the light of day again. He tried to recapture his amazement in the beauty of the castle. He looked up at the high ceilings, mesmerized. But his gaze quickly fell to the endless expanse of walls. There were doors everywhere. Despite his curiosity, Corin didn't dare open any of them. He noticed the tapestries he'd seen when he entered the castle the previous night. The intricate images were lit now by the many windows spread throughout the hallway. Corin paused to study their detailed renderings. They depicted various scenes of history. Many showed battles, dark and gore-filled to some but full of interest to an aspiring knight. Corin was amazed at the fine detail and a little horrified at its accuracy. What had the weaver seen to be able to so perfectly encapsulate the thrill and devastation of war? Not to mention, the glory of battle. Knights rode on their brazen steeds, battling the seemingly endless foe. Corin tried to picture how he would feel in that moment, the rush of battle that would envelop him.

Next to the first tapestry was another depicting what seemed to be the same battle. Instead of instilling in Corin a sense of awe and reverence, it only made him uneasy. Instead of a knight in the forefront, there was a man, unarmored, carrying no weapon, but emanating power nonetheless. The man stood on a hilltop. His arms were outstretched and an aura of bright energy surrounded him.

"Neos Loch," Corin murmured.

He reached out to touch the figure of the first mage but his fingers hesitated a hairbreadth away. He stared at the outstretched arms and flowing robes depicted so beautifully in the tapestry. Corin tried to picture himself standing so full of power and bravery. He looked away quickly, knowing it was not his place.

There were other tapestries too. They depicted scenes of quiet and tranquility. The Time Before. The words came to him from some recess of his mind that he hadn't even realized still existed. There had been stories of The Time Before while he was in the orphanage.

"Before the Great War, before the heartache and bloodshed, there was great peace in Ademar," Sister Guinevere had said. "The Time Before was full of learning and love. Great poets wrote breathtaking ballads, artists painted masterpieces, and craftsmen and architects built structures that couldn't be rivaled. There was peace and prosperity for the people."

"But what happened to all of it?" a little girl had asked. "What happened to the paintings and poems and buildings?"

Sister Guinevere had shaken her head with dismay. "They were all destroyed in the war. King Corpin, not King Histen Corpin but his grandfather Claude Corpin, brutally attacked Ashnah. The buildings were burned to the ground, the paintings ripped from their frames, and the poems and ballads were used as kindling during the coldest nights. But during the time of peace, Ademar was blessed. Remember that children, there may be times of war, but there are times of peace as well."

Corin thought of the words now. He'd never been particularly fond of Sister Guinevere. Guinevere the severe, is what the children had nicknamed her. But no one else had told the children of Nevara's orphanage that there was hope for peace in the world, true peace and prosperity.

The tapestry that most caught Corin's eye was a small one. It was slightly newer than the rest and not as intricate. It was made as if a novice had created it instead of a master. It still must have been older than Corin was. It showed a scene of a coastal region. Corin recognized it from his cartography classes as Skellas. It seemed to be a beautiful place, surrounded by ocean waves as tall as a castle. There was a brutality underlying that beauty. Skellas, Corin thought, would be a little like Nevara. Only the strong would survive there. The tapestry showed those monstrous waves along with rocky shelfs pockmarked with caves. Corin stared at the tapestry for a long time, wondering why it sent a tingle of unease down his spine. He moved on.

Corin tried to make some sense of the direction as he moved through the castle but after passing door after door, he soon felt himself becoming lost. In the battle school, there had been one simple hall leading to various classrooms and barracks. Castille Castle, on the other hand, had halls that joined together and led off to dead ends and locked doors. Corin found that the best he could manage was to keep moving forward with the hope that he would find his way eventually.

Just when Corin was getting dizzy from all the twists and turns, he found an open doorway. He stepped inside. He would take a moment to catch his breath and try to reorient himself. Corin took in the large windows overlooking the castle garden and the scarcity of furniture. There were no chairs or tables. The only light in the room came from the windows. Corin stepped further inside, enjoying the calming atmosphere and, for the first time since coming to the castle, not feeling the pressure pushing down on him. There were no judging stares or hushed whispers in this room. There was no expectation of finding a destination or missing a lesson. It was quiet, airy, and peaceful. He walked over to one of the windows to look outside. That's when he noticed he wasn't alone.

Sitting with her knees pulled up to her chest on the windowsill, nearly out of sight, was the young lady with honey-colored hair and deep blue eyes. Corin backed up hurriedly, unsure if he was intruding. The girl noticed him before he could make his escape. She looked away from the window and smiled at him.

"Hello, mage. Please, come join me," Ruena said.

Corin felt instantly at ease with her friendly tone and easy manners. He slowly approached her, keeping his eyes focused on the window, the floor, the windowsill, whatever he could to avoid looking her directly in the face. He perched lightly on the very edge of the large windowsill across from her. Her feet, resting on the sill, were only a few inches away from him. It felt too close. Maybe he should leave after all. He was sure he was intruding.

Corin felt like a fool. He couldn't even remember her title. She was a lady; he knew that much. But what was her position in the court? Everything had happened in such a blur after his arrival in the castle. He was certain she had been introduced but try as he might he could only remember her name. He was afraid to speak without knowing her title. It was probably inevitable at this point that he was going to embarrass himself so badly that she would never want to see him again.

"It's beautiful in here, isn't it?" Ruena remarked, turning back to study the castle gardens again.

"Yes." Corin let out a breath of relief and hoped the noise wasn't too audible. At least he'd managed some response. It was better than sitting in silence.

Corin had to keep reminding himself not to stare at her. He lifted his head and accidentally met her gorgeous eyes. They were like a night sky. Corin worried he would get lost in their dark depths. It was a mistake to even look at her hair. The sunlight lit up her light brown tresses, turning them golden. He hadn't known many girls during his time in Nevara. There had been several at the orphanage but he'd thought of them more as family. The battle school was full to bursting with rambunctious and rowdy young men without a single girl in sight. Corin realized with mounting horror that he had no idea how to act around girls.

"They like strong guys," one of the squires had said, "just act tough, it'll impress them."

Corin didn't think that was good advice and he knew he couldn't have pulled it off if he tried. He'd heard plenty of conflicting advice and no-doubt-embellished stories of love from the squires at the battle school. They all had much more experience than Corin and a few had sweethearts waiting for them back in their hometowns. Still, some of their stories of failure made Corin hesitant to emulate them. Ruena studied him, clearly waiting for him to contribute to the conversation. He decided he would treat her as he did everyone else. What other choice was there?

"I'm Corin," he said after a moment. He immediately felt like a fool. She knew that already. Everyone in the blasted castle knew who he was. Corin hated it.

However, instead of teasing him, Ruena smiled

again reassuringly.

"Nice to meet you, Corin, officially."

She offered her hand to him and Corin could only stare at it. What was he supposed to do? She was a lady. Did that mean he should kiss her hand? In battle school, he would shake hands with the squires and Sir Burke. Was that appropriate in this situation? He was seriously starting to wish Burke had spent a little less time on sword drills and history lessons and a little more time teaching them etiquette.

"You can shake it," Ruena whispered conspiratorially. "Most ladies prefer a kiss but I rather like not getting slobber on my hand."

Corin snorted and then stiffened, embarrassed at his outburst. Ruena gave a small laugh of her own. Corin hoped she wasn't laughing at him. He took her hand and gave a perfunctory shake.

"How was your first day as a mage?" Ruena asked.

Corin let out a tremendous sigh as his newfound good mood soured. Ruena laughed. Corin found himself letting out a soft laugh too.

"Was it really that bad?"

"It was just... overwhelming," Corin admitted. "All my life I've been a bit of a nobody. Now all of a sudden I'm important. I'm supposed to turn the tide if..." Corin halted.

How much was he allowed to share? Clifton had said that the war wasn't common knowledge. Corin winced at his slip.

"If there's a war," Ruena finished for him.

"How?"

"I know more than you think I do," Ruena

told him. "Most nobles in the castle know, or at least suspect. Though, I'd still not go around telling everyone if I were you."

Well, if she knew, then Corin supposed he could tell her the rest.

"I didn't even know Ashnah was on the verge of war. It's... it's like coming to the castle is just one huge nightmare." Corin stopped and blushed, realizing he'd been ranting to someone he hardly knew.

"Why is it a nightmare?"

"What?"

"Why is it a nightmare," she repeated. "You say it's different, but are you sure it's different in a bad way?"

Corin thought about that for a moment. Things had changed a lot but they hadn't been that great before. He'd lived on the streets and then he'd barely passed as a squire. Now he was being treated like royalty. Overnight he'd become the hero he'd always wanted to be. Still, the pang in his chest at the thought of all he'd left behind told him that this wasn't what he wanted.

"I suppose I've always just wanted to fit in. Now I'm even stranger than I was before. Where I come from, mages are seen as cursed."

"That's not true though," Ruena protested. "Mages are blessed by God. Even if not everyone admits it, that's the truth. You should be pleased to have such an amazing gift, Corin. Don't you feel seen by God? He's chosen you."

"I don't feel seen or chosen," Corin huffed. "I just want to go back to the way things were. Even if they weren't that great, I knew what I wanted and where I belonged. I can't imagine any of this will last long."

"You belong here," Ruena pressed. "God cares for you and He made you for a time and place such as this."

"How can you sound so sure?"

"Because I've been where you are now."

Corin studied her. The confusion must have been obvious on his face because she hurried to explain.

"I haven't always been at this castle," Ruena explained. She smiled softly. Her smile was like honey, sweet and calming. "I'm the king's niece," she continued. "My parents died when I was very young and my uncle took me in. He's raised me as if I were his daughter, but I'm not. That makes me different. It's hard sometimes to know where I stand. When I first came to the castle, I felt completely out of place and I had no idea what I wanted anymore. Sometimes I still feel that way. But I know that God put me here for a reason. Everything that's happened to me is for a reason. You're here for a reason too, Corin."

She spoke with a powerful certainty but Corin found himself hung up over a single phrase.

"You're the king's niece?" Corin asked. How could he have forgotten something so important? He was suddenly very afraid that he had overstepped his boundaries. He'd been ranting and complaining to the king's niece! He slid off of the window sill. He shouldn't have even been talking with her in the first place. He was a commoner. He wasn't nobility. He knew nothing about etiquette. Oh! He'd shaken her hand! He was a fool, an absolute fool. He had to get out of there.

"I'm sorry for disturbing you," Corin said, bowing slightly, unsure how to act around a king's niece. Did that make her a princess? "I should... get going."

Ruena opened her mouth as if she were planning on saying something more, then hesitated, seemingly having changed her mind.

"Goodbye, it was nice to meet you," she finally said.

Corin looked at her once more and noted the hurt expression on her face and the fake smile she tried to plaster over it. Had he offended her by leaving so soon? It wasn't his place to have a conversation with the king's niece. If he could think of himself as a mage, he might be able to calm his insecurities. But to him, he was still Corin Faye, the pathetic squire. He still wasn't fully convinced that all of this wasn't some huge misunderstanding. As he fled from the room, he could only think of how much he didn't belong. He could never belong in Castille Castle and it was only a matter of time before everyone else discovered that too.

CHAPTER 11

Finch Caraway raced up the northwest tower stairs, hurrying to reach the battlements. He was late. He was so, so late. Sometimes he wondered why he did it to himself. It always happened like that. He would make up his mind to skip training entirely, then, at the last moment, he would grow cowardly and sprint to his post, hoping he wouldn't face the repercussions for his negligence. He rarely got away unscathed but he kept doing it anyway. He thought that spoke more to his foolishness than any sense of righteous indignation that caused him to act in such a way.

Why, oh why did there have to be so many stairs? They always felt endless when he was in a hurry. His shirt was untucked and wrinkled like it'd been wadded into a ball. He fastened his belt as he ran, his fingers fumbling at the buckle. His uniform-issue vest and the short cape that hung over one shoulder were missing entirely. He hadn't bothered to grab them before starting his mad dash across the castle and up the stairs. The only sign of his station as one of the king's archers was the patch sewn onto his pathetically wrinkled shirt and the bow held in his hand. He'd never been one for uniforms. Maybe being sloppily dressed was one of his trademarks. Some of his fellow archers spent nearly an hour every day ensuring every piece of their uniform was neat and in order. They hung their garments every night, fastened the cape at the shoulder, donned the vest and hat, and even went so far as to polish their boots until they shined. Finch only cared about oiling his bowstring to make sure it was in pristine condition. His bow and arrows were what would save him in a battle, not a prissy uniform.

He mumbled and groaned under his breath as he ran. Why did he have to attend training at all? They never learned anything, at least not anything Finch didn't already know. He'd exceeded his commander's talents long ago. Finch's abilities would help him in battle but until he faced conflict, they only painted a target on his back. He had fully intended on skipping training. It wasn't because he didn't understand the importance of practicing drills in case of an attack. He just avoided interacting with the other archers as much as possible.

He'd been determined to avoid the battlements at all costs until he heard that the archers who would be sent to the front lines would be chosen that day. He couldn't miss that announcement. It was inevitable that he would be chosen. His skills and his position among the archers ensured it. He expected his name to be called among the others and he knew that it meant certain death if he was.

There had always been a few archers stationed on the border between Ashnah and Freiwade. It had been seen as a thankless job, the type of post that was assigned to those who were mediocre or troublesome.

However, with the skirmishes increasing in frequency and severity, additional archers had been sent to assist in any battles and to discourage further attacks. Those archers rarely returned and, if they did, they were worse for wear. The position that had been seen as a punishment had become a place where only the most skilled and battle-hardened were sent. Outpost Gray was where good soldiers were sent to die. Finch knew it was only a matter of time before he joined their ranks, especially given his less-than-friendly relationship with his commander. He wanted desperately to ignore the summons. He didn't want to hear his name called. He'd been waiting in dread for more than a month, expecting it. However, he knew he couldn't just ignore it and hope the problem went away.

He mounted the top step of the stairs and strode onto the battlement. His breath came in rasping pants. He bent forward, resting his hands on his knees, and attempted to catch his breath. A scowl crossed his face when he caught sight of his commander. Commander Terin glared at Finch, a vicious look that would often be directed at an invading enemy. Finch had a brief, scant hope that his commander would simply ignore him. No such luck.

"You're late," Terin growled, approaching Finch with a heavy step, "very late."

Finch considered his options. A retort was quick on his tongue. However, he decided silence was his best bet. He ignored his commander entirely. Finch quickly composed himself. Slinging his shoulders back and holding his head high, he went to stand in line with the other archers. They all shot him dirty looks.

"The prancing peacock thinks he's better than us," one of the men, Rory mumbled.

"Maybe because I am," Finch responded.

He could sense the other archers stiffen defensively. All of the castle archers were the best of the best. They were competitive by nature and eager to prove themselves. They knew Finch's impressive skillset. They envied it. Finch was less enthusiastic. He was too good. He wished he hadn't trained so hard to reach that point. At the time, he'd believed it was the only option. Now, he knew it would have been better for him to sink into obscurity instead.

Finch thought that the archers would turn on him, throw the consequences to the wind, and turn the fight from a verbal to a physical one. By some miracle, it was Terin who saved him.

Terin cleared his throat, drawing everyone's attention to him. He was a grizzled man, just past middle age, stout, below average height but with shoulders broad enough to make up for any shortcomings in stature. He was not someone to be trifled with. That was why everyone looked at Finch like he was a madman whenever he did just that.

"War is inevitable," Terin started. "The time for peace is long past. It is our duty as the king's archers and as citizens of Ashnah to protect the front lines. We must stand firm against Freiwade and refuse to retreat even an inch. The king may hesitate to declare war but war is already here. The most talented archers are required to defend our outposts against the enemy."

His eyes met Finch's at the word "talented."

Finch felt his heart sink. He mustered his willpower and kept his head high with a defiant look on his face. It was decided then. He wished more than ever before that he had never been forced into the position of a king's archer. It was an honor, at least that's what everyone told him. But he'd wanted to be a ranger. A ranger wouldn't have to deal with the daily torture Finch was put through. A ranger only protected the forest. It was an obscure position, yes, but it also allowed for isolation deep in the wilderness. No one would know his name. No one would care about him. He would be a nobody and he would be far, far away from the capital. Maybe it would have been squandering his potential but it was all he'd wanted and it had been ripped away from him so he could "best serve his kingdom." He didn't care about serving his kingdom. He only wanted to get away.

His greatest regret was the pride, arrogance, and defiance that had caused him to pick up a bow to begin with. If only he had been a coward and run away when he had the chance instead.

Now, he would be chosen for the front lines. It only came as a shock that it hadn't happened sooner. He knew his 'commander' would be more than happy to see him go. The man could hardly keep the smile off of his face even as he gave his superficial speech. Finch's acts of defiance should have sent him over the edge long ago. He'd been tempting fate on purpose. He'd been starting to wonder if his plan had backfired and protected him instead. If he couldn't be trusted to follow orders at the castle, how could he be expected to do so on the front lines? He knew his actions made his comrades view him as an arrogant coward but he didn't need their respect. He didn't want anything to do with them. They were blind to the truth around them.

Finished with his speech, Commander Terin pulled out the list of men who were to be sent to the front lines. He read the list slowly. After each name, he paused a moment. Maybe it was to give the poor archer selected a minute to let the information sink in. Finch didn't believe the commander capable of such sympathy though. More likely, the pauses were to build anticipation for who would be chosen next. Terin slowed even further as he made his way through the "c's". The commander paused, staring at the sheet for a long moment after reading "Caldwell." He squinted at the list, a sour look contorting his face. His expression was terrifying before he composed himself and kept reading. When he reached "Dracon", Finch wondered if the old man was saving his name for the last to torture him further.

Finch's fingernails cut into his palms. Anger surged in his chest, only overpowered by the anxiety that threatened to burst from him. The waiting was the worst part. The torture of waiting had nearly driven him mad during the last month. He kept on waiting until the commander reached "Yohan" and set the list aside.

"You're dismissed," Terin announced. "Resume your training and posts."

What had just happened? Finch stood frozen for a moment. Why hadn't his name been called? He'd been sure that it would. He'd been positive. Why? Whatever reason, Finch didn't want to stick around in case the commander changed his mind. He turned on his heel and headed directly for the stairs.

"Caraway, you're expected to train," Commander Terin yelled after him.

Finch ignored the command. He stormed down the stairs. How had he not been chosen? Impossible! Was this in itself a special kind of torture crafted just for him? Was he expected to wait with crushing anticipation time and time again? He knew things were heating up on the front lines. Casualty rates were rising, bodies returned to the capital every week. Freiwade had been testing the waters for a while now. They would invade soon enough. The outposts needed any additional help they could get. How was it possible that Finch hadn't been chosen? Even if Commander Terin had the power to stop Finch from being sent away, the man had no reason to do so. It wasn't as if he cared whether Finch lived or died. Surely, he hadn't given the order to ensure Finch wasn't chosen. That was more impossible than anything else.

Finch reached the bottom of the stairs and stomped through the castle halls with his bow clutched in his hand. White hot fury pulsed through his veins. He hated the doubts rushing through his head. What if Commander Terin had removed his name from the list? What did that mean? Finch was so lost in those thoughts that he ran into someone.

"Sorry," Finch grumbled, pushing away from the man, obviously a knight judging by the chain mail that had imprinted on Finch's face.

"Finch?"

Finch recognized the voice. He looked up at the tall knight and saw a familiar face peering down at him. Dorian.

"Oh, Dorian. It's good to see you," Finch greeted, distractedly. It was truly good to see his friend but he couldn't pull himself from the thoughts rushing through his head and the adrenalin still present from expecting to be chosen for the front lines.

Dorian seemed to pick up on the distant, distressed state of Finch's mind. Finch realized he must have worn a pitiful expression on his face because Dorian automatically suspected the worst.

"What's wrong? Were you chosen?"

Finch shook his head. "I wasn't."

"Then... why do you look so upset?"

Finch leaned against a nearby wall. His legs felt weak and shaky. "I just... it doesn't make any sense. I should have been chosen. It's impossible."

Dorian looked at Finch with sympathy. "I just finished training for the day. Since I'm done, care to go for a walk outside? The fresh air might do you some good."

Finch thought about it for a moment then agreed. The fresh air would do him some good. He was sure of it. He wanted to get out of the confining castle and away from his commander.

"I wish I could just run away entirely," Finch confided to his friend.

Dorian paled. "Don't say that. You'd be a deserter."

"So?"

Dorian paused. "There are duties we owe to our kingdom, Finch. We can't forsake those duties, no matter how we feel about the matter. Besides, this place would be pretty dull without you."

Finch snorted. "Please, you'd make a dozen new friends in no time. Every time I see you, you've found another companion. We both know I'm the one dependent on this friendship."

It was true. Dorian was his only friend, the only one Finch trusted. He might threaten to run but in actuality, he could never abandon his friend.

"You'd make more friends if you were more friendly," Dorian teased.

Finch grimaced. "It might in fact kill me to do that. Besides, I don't need any other friends. And being friends with a knight only increases the annoyance the other archers feel about me."

Dorian shook his head ruefully. "I've never understood that rivalry. We're all serving the same kingdom after all. The only difference between us is that some serve with swords and others with bows."

"Well, you are still relatively new to the castle, you'll understand the grudge before long."

"It seems like Sir Hayes and Commander Terin might be the ones perpetuating it," Dorian said with a laugh.

Finch grimaced at the mention of Commander Terin.

Dorian caught the action and gracefully shifted the conversation to safer ground. "Have you seen the new mage? What do you think of him?"

Finch crossed his arms over his chest and gave a noncommittal response. He couldn't care less about the new mage. He only hoped the newcomer wouldn't interfere with his life in any way. He had enough troubles without a mage getting involved.

"Maybe he'll help in the war. Who can say?" Finch responded. He was already sick of all the talk about the mage.

He was too busy stewing in all that had happened that day to say anything further. Dorian kept up the conversation, allowing Finch to maintain his moody silence. Finch wouldn't say it but he was grateful for Dorian's distraction and for having Dorian as a friend. The young knight had entered the castle about a year ago and quickly filled the void of companionship in Finch's life. They made a strange pair, a knight and an archer, but Finch wouldn't trade their friendship for the world. No, he wouldn't desert, despite how miserable Terin made his life, despite the threat of war, and the looming despair of being sent to the outposts. He couldn't leave Castille, at least, not yet.

CHAPTER 12

Corin spent the rest of the afternoon hiding in his room. The events of the day had been frustrating and frankly embarrassing. He wasn't the talented mage that Clifton and the king believed him to be and he'd made a fool of himself in front of the king's niece. Corin felt that there was no other choice but to hide away after what had happened. His room was unfamiliar and much too luxurious for someone like him. It had only been recently that he'd overcome his amazement at even having a roof over his head. Now, he was living in a castle in a room fit for royalty. It was the only sanctuary he had. He'd tried exploring the castle and only run into trouble. It was safest to stay in his room, unseen, unheard, and hopefully forgotten.

Unfortunately, there wasn't much to do while he hid. There were no books in the room except for the ones that Clifton had given him about magic. Corin dreaded to touch those much less read them. He might have written a letter to Burke pleading to be brought back to Nevara but there were no writing materials either. The only thing Corin could busy himself with was the sword. He picked up the blade which Burke had given him and unsheathed the weapon. The light that streamed in through the window reflected off the metal. Maintaining the integrity of a blade was something that had been ingrained in Corin early on in his training. He set about sharpening the weapon with a whetstone. As he worked at the surface, Corin caught sight of his reflection in the blade. He looked tired and much older than he had only a week ago. His hair was getting long too, longer than would have been considered regulation length at the battle school. He had been about due for a haircut when he'd left. He'd have to get it cut soon. Seeing his hazel eyes staring back at him, Corin thought of another set of eyes, dark blue and depthless.

Remembering his encounter with Ruena, Corin groaned. He leaned back into his bed, the sword dangling from his hand at his side. He mourned his non-existent social skills. What had he been thinking? She was the king's niece and he'd made a fool of himself in front of her, stammering and ranting and complaining about his day. Would she tell her uncle the king how much of a disgrace Corin truly was? Would he be thrown out of the castle as a result? That seemed more likely than him "turning the tide of war."

Corin cast his blade aside. What good would a sword do against an invading army, especially when that sword was in the hands of someone like Corin? He couldn't win a practice duel against a squire. How could he expect to win a fight against a battle-hardened knight with the intent to kill?

What am I doing here? Corin called out to God. He wasn't even sure if God would listen to someone like him but who else was he supposed to talk to?

What are Your plans for me? He didn't get an answer, not that he expected one.

He'd always prayed like Burke told him to and he believed in God but he didn't understand the personal relationship that Burke had with God. Corin doubted he'd ever be able to have a similar relationship. Why would God want him anyway? Corin knew and had learned time and time again that he was nothing special. He was ordinary in every meaning of the word. He wasn't strong or powerful or even particularly smart. He didn't have a noble family or talent with the sword. He wasn't especially interesting either. He'd been called dull on more than one occasion. He could hardly imagine God saving him from sin, much less caring enough to talk to him.

Corin pushed the thoughts away and picked up his sword. If he was going to hide in his room, he might as well get something accomplished while he was doing so. He held his sword and slipped into a ready stance. If he were expected to "turn the tide of war" then he would prepare himself the only way he knew how. Not that it would do any good. He started with some basic combinations, deflecting an imagined enemy sword, and striking with brute force at the unseen threat before him. He wished he could practice outside where there was more room and where a cool breeze might cool the sweat from his face but he feared someone might see him. A mage was expected to practice magic, not sword drills. Although he hadn't been told that he couldn't practice, he didn't want to risk having his sword confiscated. It was the only part of his old life he still had, the only reminder of Nevara and Sir Burke. So, he hid in his room, cramped but feeling freedom as he hadn't before. Perhaps later he would go for a run around the castle grounds to feel the breeze against his skin and the breath surging in his lungs. Maybe Sir Hayes would let him join the castle garrison for their morning exercises. No, that wasn't his place anymore. Besides, why would the king's garrison, the best knights in all of Ashnah, want to train with him?

Corin's strikes grew more frenzied as he grew more frustrated. The fluid, calculated movements became sloppy and disorganized. Why did this have to happen to him? If God chose mages and bestowed their abilities on them, then why had He chosen Corin? How could Corin possibly live up to the expectations placed on him? He wasn't special! He was pathetic. He was a weak orphan who hadn't even managed as a squire. Why couldn't he have just stayed in Nevara training under Sir Burke? He'd dreamed of being recognized for some great deed. He'd dreamed of being a hero in battle. Now he only wished to go back to the way things had been before. He craved the anonymity of being a nobody! He felt so lost. He was out of place in this castle among nobility and knights. He was nothing more than a street rat who had been kicked out of battle school.

He had to be on guard with every movement for fear of messing up. He didn't know etiquette or manners. He didn't know how a mage was supposed to act. He couldn't relax even for a moment. Well... that wasn't necessarily true. He had relaxed when he'd been with Ruena. Just for a moment, he'd forgotten his position and hers. He'd seen her as a friend, someone relatable in a castle full of unknowns. Now, he could never talk with her again. He'd lost himself and forgotten his position. He'd overstepped.

She'd said he was blessed but she was wrong. The only thing that had been a blessing in Corin's life was Burke accepting him into the battle school. Now, even that had been ripped away from him. Corin was doomed to a life of failure and hardship. He knew that. Being a mage wasn't a blessing at all.

He wished he had a practice dummy to take his anger out on. He wished for the thrill that came when his sword struck a target, the resistance as he pulled back the blade, and the numbing of his arms as the force of contact surged through him. Instead, he was forced to pull back his strikes before they made contact. Still, Corin could feel the rush of adrenalin, the pounding of the blood in his veins. Sweat dripped down his neck. He fell into a pattern. He repeated strikes and parries. He worked through combinations of attacks that he had never mastered but still knew by heart.

He was so lost in the feeling of familiarity that he didn't hear the knock at his door. Without his noticing, the door creaked open. Corin did, however, hear the clearing of a throat from behind him. Corin spun around, frantic with fear and surprise. He only just stopped his sword before it slashed into Clifton's tall form. Clifton's eyes went wide as saucers and he took a cautious step back. He raised a finger to carefully direct the point of Corin's blade to the side.

"I suppose I should have better announced my presence," Clifton said.

Corin lowered the sword, feeling sheepish.

"Sorry," he murmured, mortified that he had

almost killed Ashnah's mage. He remembered Burke's warning to be careful since the sword was real. He winced, imagining the lecture he would have received if Burke had witnessed the near accident. "Um, why *are* you here?" Corin asked, trying to push the thought away of what had nearly happened. It was a struggle to calm his ragged breathing.

"I came to tell you that dinner is being served."

"Oh," Corin said, and then mentally berated himself for not thanking the mage. "I'll be down shortly."

Food was the last thing on Corin's mind after everything that had happened that day, especially after what had nearly happened just then.

"Well, I'll leave you to it," Clifton said before turning to leave.

Corin delicately, cautiously placed his sword back in its sheath. He stood for a long time trying to determine why Clifton hadn't just sent Will to tell him. He noticed that Clifton still stood in the doorway. Corin voiced the question.

"Why did you come to tell me? Why not send Will or a servant?"

"I wanted to see how you were settling in. I worried my words this morning may have startled you."

"That's an understatement," Corin said under his breath. Fortunately, Clifton didn't seem to hear him.

"I wanted to tell you that things do get easier. Adjusting to the position of a mage takes time. You're very talented Corin and I'm sure you'll find your place here quickly. You may even surpass me before long."

No pressure there, Corin thought. He didn't even know how he had managed in his disastrous fight against Phineas York. Now, he was suspected to someday surpass Clifton?

"I'm fine," Corin said. He wasn't sure if it was convincing or not. "There's no reason for you to check up on me."

"Of course. Then I'll see you at dinner."

Corin turned, already wondering what he should do to make himself more presentable. He was covered in sweat from his training. It may have passed in battle school but he couldn't attend a meal with the king like that. He noticed that Clifton still hadn't left. He turned to study his new mentor.

"Forgive me," Clifton said upon receiving Corin's questioning look, "but I'm curious. Why do you continue to practice with that sword? You're a mage now. Before long you'll learn to control remarkable, unthinkable powers. Why waste your time with a manmade weapon?"

Corin stiffened. "It's not a waste of time to me."

He felt slightly defensive. Training as a knight had been his whole life for a long time now. He couldn't cast it aside so easily. Besides, what would be left for him when he was inevitably kicked out of the castle? He had to keep training. Swordsmanship was all he knew. He hoped his words weren't too informal because of his irritation.

"I've wanted to serve the king as a knight for a very long time. I've worked hard and sacrificed much to do the best I can. It's been an ordeal of blood, sweat, and tears throughout my endeavors to be a knight. I may not be very skilled at swordsmanship now and I know I don't possess the raw talent of some but with practice maybe someday I'll be able to fight. If there's a war coming, then now's the best time to practice."

Corin didn't say the rest of what he was thinking. He couldn't rely on magic. So far it had only caused trouble for him. What if there was another accident like what had happened with Phineas York? What if Corin was thrown out of the castle and commanded to never use magic again? He had to be prepared for that and the only way he could prepare was with his training.

Clifton looked at him for a long while, appraising Corin's thin, sweating form, before he nodded his head.

"Very well, Mage Corin. I'll see you at dinner."

Once the door had closed behind Clifton, Corin flung his sheathed sword aside. His chest still rose and fell quickly with the exertion from his training and his anger at Clifton's remarks. How pathetic he must appear, training with his sword! He knew he wasn't any good. He'd been told so on more than one occasion. There was no future for him as a knight, now more than ever before. Still, he couldn't let go of the only thing he knew. He couldn't! He ran his hands through his sweat-soaked hair, pulling the ends with aggravation. He stared at the sword lying sheathed on his bed. He thought of his initials which Burke had engraved into the blade. Burke had believed in him from the start. How disappointed would Burke be in him now? Without meaning to, Corin let out a dry sob. He quickly muffled it with his hand and took a deep breath to compose himself. He wouldn't allow himself to lose control of his emotions. Instead, he busied himself preparing for dinner. Maybe it was a waste of time. But what else could he do?

CHAPTER 13

Dusk hid in the great hall during the evening meal. He slipped from corner to corner, surveying the crowd of nobles and knights gathered for the feast. The nobles were dressed in their shining finery. The men wore elegant tunics embroidered with gold and silver thread, and the ladies were clothed in extravagant dresses that flowed like rushing water, jewels lying in circlets on their brows, hanging from their ears, and resting at their collars. It was pure opulence. Dusk was used to it but it still made him uncomfortable. How many of those jewels had come from the mines of Freiwade, the very kingdom encroaching on their doorstep? Dusk's midnight blue tunic with black embroidery was simpler than the others. In that way, it stood out. However, it had been carefully chosen. There was a trend going through Ashnah to dress in dark, rich colors such as navy, maroon, and emerald. From the back, Dusk would look like any other. From the front, he would appear a lord or maybe a lord's aid. He would seem to be a nobody who was attempting to fit in with the throng and make himself appear more important than he actually was. It was all part of Dusk's disguise and a good way to be ignored. The petty nobles were terrified of interacting with someone below their rank.

It wasn't likely anyone would take notice of Dusk anyway. All eyes were on the head table. But they weren't looking at the king. The excitement over the new mage was still at its peak. That was the reason the great hall was so unbearably crowded. Anyone who was anyone had found a way to stay at the castle in order to not miss out on the action. Dusk caught sight of Baron Geoffrey and his stunning wife Abigail. Then there was Count Horace, his wife, and their gaggle of preening daughters, Rosemary, Eustace, and Christine. There were a few earls that Dusk recognized, numerous viscounts, and barons. It was his job to know all of these self-important people. It was why he had been chosen to be stationed in the great hall. He'd been given the unpleasant task of trying to pick up snippets of conversation among the nobility.

If there was one benefit to the larger crowd, it was that it made Dusk less noticeable. Normally that would be a difficult task. Dusk's tall frame and dark hair usually stuck out among the lighter shades of the Ashnan nobility. The dark hair and pale complexion were trademarks of the border provinces of Ashnah where intermarrying with Freiwade immigrants was more common. There weren't many nobles who possessed such stark features. However, in such a large crowd, Dusk's hair wasn't a concern. He blended in easily enough. He was grateful for that because the gathering contained two people whom he very much wanted to avoid.

He would have avoided the place entirely if he could but he had a job to do. He'd been given a second chance at the castle and he wouldn't be scared off. He refused to be. The odds of his being found out were slim to begin with. No one would be looking for him. If they did find him, what could they do? Would they even recognize him? He'd changed a lot in more ways than one. Even if he was confronted, he wasn't the one in the wrong. He was the one who hadn't wanted trouble when he had every right to seek it. However, especially now, especially in his new position, it was imperative that he continued to avoid detection and the trouble that would follow.

Dusk was good at gathering information from the nobility. He knew how to get them to talk. So, he bypassed the Baron and his wife, the Count and his, and made a direct path toward the Count's daughter Rosemary. He knew from prior experience that she was the most talkative of the sisters and Dusk had an advantage. Any young man approaching a single noblewoman would be seen as a suitor. The count's daughters, nearing the end of their prime eligibility would be eager to attract a suitor's attention, especially Rosemary, the eldest.

"Good evening, milady," Dusk greeted. He tried to assume his most distinguished gracefulness in his address.

It was another of his talents that he could change from the unimportant aid of a lord to a nobleman of influence and power just by altering his exterior demeanor.

"Hello," Rosemary responded. Her interest in him was evident from the demure tilt of her head and the intensity in her gaze.

"I apologize for approaching you so directly but I couldn't restrain myself. Your beauty captivated me even from across the room. You must be the Lady Rosemary whom I've heard so much about."

Perhaps he was laying it on a bit thick but he knew she would fall for the flattery. Indeed, a blush crept up her already heavily rouged cheeks.

"Yes, I am Lady Rosemary but the pleasure is all mine, milord."

Hook, line, and sink her.

"I pray you are enjoying yourself this evening milady. It is a great turnout, is it not?"

Rosemary nodded, fanning her face in a flirtatious manner. "Yes, the excitement taints the air. I hardly had time to pack my things before Papa brought us here. The news of the new mage's arrival came suddenly and we couldn't bear to miss the celebration."

"Yes, what a surprise this has all been. What do you think of the young mage, milady?"

Rosemary giggled, "I don't quite know what to think. He's so awfully young. It's exciting to be sure. I wasn't alive when Mage Clifton arrived at the castle, though my papa says it was just as incredible an occasion. I hear rumors that this mage is even more talented than Mage Clifton. I… well… it's nothing."

"No, please," Dusk pressed.

Rosemary sighed. "It's only, I can't help being a little frightened. I've heard such dreadful things about magic. I hail from Iverny. It's a relatively small province and our community is closely knit. There's so few nobility in that area that I've resorted to making companions out of some of the village girls. It's embarrassing I know but I must have someone to talk to besides my sisters."

Dusk had to refrain from rolling his eyes. He waved for her to continue.

"I've heard that magic is a curse, like an incurable disease that eats the soul. Maybe it's silly. I've seen Mage Clifton and he hardly seems dangerous. But this new mage, there's something different about him, something unsettling. He doesn't look at anyone. Maybe he's hiding something. I've heard that power corrupts, especially the young and inexperienced. What if this new mage, I don't know his name…"

"Corin," Dusk supplied.

"Yes, this new mage, Corin, what if he's dangerous?"

Dusk forced a smile to his face. "Please don't fret milady. I'm sure he's just as harmless as Mage Clifton and even if he were dangerous I would protect you."

Her face turned the color of roses. "My lord…."

"But tell me, is this fear your own? Does your father feel this way?"

"Oh, Papa isn't afraid of anything. However, he did warn me and my sisters to keep our distance from the new mage. 'It's better to be cautious and see how things play out before we place our loyalties' he told us. Anyway, I'm not afraid now, not with you to protect me," she fluttered her eyelashes at him.

Dusk decided it was time to make his escape. He'd gotten all the information he could from her.

"I am at your service, milady. Unfortunately, I must excuse myself for the moment but I hope to see you again soon."

He bowed deeply as if she were royalty. She held out her hand for him to kiss but he pretended that he hadn't seen it. He turned to leave.

"Wait, I never learned your name!" Rosemary called out after him.

Dusk acted as if he hadn't heard her. The moment he'd disappeared into the crowd, he let the mask of friendliness drop from his face. He felt none of it. He detested the extravagant foolery of the nobles, the reckless emotions that controlled them, and their tendency to follow after their every whim. Dusk had never fit in that regard. He followed his intellect and knowledge, not his heart. The heart was deceptive and cunning. Trust was hard-earned and too easily broken. Rosemary, like the other nobles, was blind to the harsh realities of the world. He felt sorry for them but also a little jealous. He'd been that innocent once. He felt only a touch of guilt at using her in such a way. He hoped she would find someone one day, someone who would care for her and not just her position. Deceit was one aspect of his role as a spy that he was not fond of. He didn't lie to people if he could help it, but he didn't reveal to them who he was either. He allowed them to believe in an illusion. He had over the years gained the gift of gathering information from others without expelling any knowledge of himself. He was a ghost, as subtle and fleeting as the dusk.

He engaged several other nobles in conversation. He flattered aging women with their enduring beauty, acted as a suitor to young, unmarried women, and asked noblemen for their opinions on matters as if he deeply cared what they had to say. Excitement over the new mage overpowered all of the conversations. Although many were excited and thrilled at the prospect of a new mage, others were distrusting and nervous, even fearful.

"I wonder at the safety of having an untrained mage among us," Baron Cleft said.

"I don't like the idea of a mage in the castle," Viscount Harris mentioned, seeming to forget that Clifton was a mage who had been among them for decades.

Some of the nobles ventured to talk to Corin. They approached him at the head table with self-important but cautious airs. Poor Corin looked like he would be sick at each new approach. He mostly stayed quiet and let the nobles do the talking as the king introduced them in turn. Other nobility swept past Corin with furtive glances and crossed themselves muttering prayers as they looked at him. Those were the ones Dusk made a special effort to seek out. He talked with them as if he too were suspicious and uneasy. His purpose, his mission, that night, was to determine if such nobles were dangerous. Would they rebel against this new mage? Would they side against the king in a conflict? Would they find a way to eliminate what they saw as a threat? It turned out that they were mostly harmless, just fearful. Several, however, Dusk made a mental note to keep an eye on.

Fortunately, the man Dusk was most concerned with, Duke Heirson, didn't seem to pay Corin much attention during the feast. Dusk kept an eye on the duke, careful that his attention went unnoticed. Duke Heirson and his son spent the majority of the evening talking with Ruena, a fact that Dusk was sure would make Cal unhappy. It eased Dusk's mind to know that Corin was safe from the duke's attention for the moment.

The knights stationed around the room also talked. They were the most worrisome. Several of them looked at Corin with disgust, some with envy, and many with anger. To the knights, Corin was seen as more than a possible threat; he drew the attention and esteem usually directed towards the knights without doing a thing to earn it. Usually, certain knights were honored for their bravery and talent during the feasts. They talked with the nobility and gained allies among them. They made matches with the noblemen's daughters, gaining property and power as a result.

One knight in particular stared at Corin with an odd look. Dusk didn't like the intensity of that stare. It was a studious look, examining Corin not as a rival but as an enigma to be solved. Dusk made note of it and resolved to find out more about that particular knight.

He was tempted to go engage the knight in conversation but just then Lark sidled up next to him. He hadn't heard her approach and was startled a little when she cleared her throat.

"Jumpy tonight?" she asked.

She had no idea.

He glanced at her. "Is something wrong?"

She shook her head in the negative.

She was much shorter than him and it felt awkward to look down at her. She leaned against the wall at his elbow, casual and sticking out among the proud, straight-backed noblewomen. She didn't mix in with the servants either. She never lowered her head in submission to anyone. She turned her head just a little to address him without looking like she was doing so. They were just two people who happened to be standing next to each other.

"What have you found?" she questioned.

"Not much. There are a few people I'll be keeping an eye on. They're more fearful than dangerous."

"Fear is a special kind of danger," she muttered. "It can drive people to do terrible things."

Dusk grunted in agreement.

"I've had similar results," she told him. She'd been hiding in the shadowy hallways, picking up any gossip that was too scandalous to repeat in a crowded room where it might be overheard and listening for what the servants might be whispering.

She nodded towards the head table and the cowering mage hunched over his barely-touched meal. "Poor bloke," she said.

Dusk glanced at her quizzically. She had a way of expressing things that stood out as obscure. It was common for her but it still always caught him off guard. He fixed his expression and looked at Corin as well.

"I don't envy having that much attention from the boot-kissing nobles."

Lark snorted. "That's not what I meant. Do you really not notice?"

Dusk studied the head table, hoping to see what she did. Corin poked at his plate, organizing the food into categories. Dusk knew it was an extravagant fare. The king had spared no expense this week in spoiling the new mage. Delicacies that were difficult to come by and prepared by the best chefs in the kingdom were set at the head table. It was a shame to let such good food go to waste but Dusk didn't blame the young mage for having no appetite. He knew what it was like to draw attention and he hated it. He couldn't imagine enduring the fanfare that Corin was steadfastly persevering. But he didn't see anything other than the nobles trying to win the new mage's attention. Dusk gave in.

"What do you mean?" he asked Lark.

"You know Dusk, you have a talent for getting nobles to talk but you could use some work on reading emotions."

He had no objection to that. He knew she was right. That had never been his strong suit.

"Take a look at our young mage, a careful look."

Dusk did as he was told. He saw that Corin hardly paid any attention to the nobility. He kept his focus on his food and occasionally lifted his gaze for a moment to look straight ahead. Dusk shrugged; he was still uncertain what Lark was getting at.

"Young Corin Faye may be a mage but he's still a boy. He's been stealing glances at Ruena all night like a lovestruck fool."

It was true, Dusk realized. Corin could hardly help himself, it seemed like it was happening without him even realizing it. But that wasn't all.

"She's doing it too," he remarked.

"Huh, I suppose she is." Lark smiled softly. "Ah to be young and in love." She snickered.

Dusk didn't think it was so funny. He couldn't help but feel a little sorry for Corin. It was only natural for Corin to seek comfort and companionship when he'd been thrown into such an unfamiliar and uncomfortable situation. Dusk had been in those types of situations all his life. It helped to have a friendly face to look at. Although Corin was far less subtle than he thought he was being, Dusk probably never would have noticed his glances at Ruena without Lark saying something. He might be good at gathering information from nobles but that was only from practice. He'd gained the talent of putting on an act and pretending to be sociable but he'd never really succeeded at understanding people. He could only analyze them. As Lark had pointed out, emotions weren't his specialty. He could see that Corin was a little similar in that regard.

Dusk may not be good at reading emotions but he suspected there was something other than Ruena troubling the young mage. He wondered what it could be.

Dusk caught a glimpse out of the corner of his eye that jerked him away from all thoughts about Corin. A head of black hair drifted through the crowd, visible above the others. The person was heading in Dusk's direction. Dusk felt his heart palpitating. His mouth went dry. He clenched his hands into fists and then unclenched them. What should he do? What *could* he do? His eyes fixated on the figure pushing through the crowd. It was too late to avoid detection. It was too late to run. Fear, actual fear, surged through Dusk.

"Dusk?" Lark asked, noticing his changed

demeanor. She followed his gaze and stiffened. "That's not good," she mumbled under her breath. "Is that…"

"Dresden Heirson, the duke's son," Dusk finished for her.

The figure came closer and closer. Lark latched hold of Dusk's hand. It was the only thing she could do to get his attention. He hesitantly took his eyes off the crowd and looked down at her. He was sure his fear was evident on his face.

"Dusk?" she asked quietly. "Will you trust me and follow along?"

Before he had a chance to answer or even comprehend what she was planning, she pushed away from the wall. "I'll distract him. Get out of here."

Dusk blinked at her, realizing what she was planning. "Don't…"

"It's fine but you owe me." She strode towards Dresden. Dusk didn't have time to understand what she was doing before she stood on her tiptoes, leaning too close to Dresden, and whispered something in his ear. Dresden's eyes widened and he bent towards her, his hand grasping hers in an intimate gesture that made Dusk's stomach churn. He knew what Lark was doing but he hated seeing her use those tactics on someone like Dresden. Dresden started to look around the room to make sure he and Lark weren't being watched. Before his head could turn towards Dusk's position, Lark reached up and wrapped her hand around his neck, lowering his head until it was close to her own.

Dusk inwardly struggled for a moment. He needed to get away but he didn't want to leave Lark. He felt a swell of panic. If Cal knew what was happening, he'd probably kill them both. Lark tried to pull Dresden away, towards the other side of the room but he wasn't budging. She managed to turn him around so he wasn't facing Dusk. She looked past Dresden and shot Dusk a look that clearly said 'get out of here'. The flirting was just an act. Lark was all business. Dusk reminded himself that she could handle herself as he hesitantly turned to leave.

Dusk knew that her decision to flirt with Dresden was probably the quickest method to distract him. But he thought of Lark as a sister and a friend. He hadn't been prepared to leave her alone with Dresden. He hated himself for doing so but knew it was necessary. Her quick thinking had saved him. He felt like a coward. As he was leaving the great hall, Dusk glanced at Corin again and felt pity for the young mage. What people like he and Corin really needed were good friends, friends like Lark.

CHAPTER 14

The next morning, Corin rose with the sun.

He was accustomed to early mornings but, in Nevara, they were usually accompanied by only the barest streak of light and a cold, unwelcome breeze. He lay in bed for a moment as the blessed sun drifted through his window. He relished in the warmth it cast on his skin.

He was tired from the previous day's excitement of training, his ruinous conversation with Ruena, and the feast. He was grateful for a new day but worried that he'd mess up this one too. He forced himself out of bed, determined to not cave into the temptation to crawl back under his covers. He dressed quickly and snuck out of his room, grateful to find that he'd woken before Will came to get him. After some confusion, Corin found his way out of the castle and into the morning sunshine. Fortunately, in his rough squire's attire, he was able to get past the guards stationed at the archway. They must have assumed he was a servant being sent on an early errand. They would have no reason to suspect that he was the young mage who had quickly become the talk of the castle.

The castle courtyard was empty at such an early hour and, for the first time, Corin fully took in his surroundings. The castle rested at the top of a slope; a path led from the castle steps to the arched stone entrance. Corin could just make out the stone road that Clifton had stopped the carriage at when Corin arrived. To the right was a grassy field, the castle gardens, and in the distance Corin could see a large building that he suspected was the knights' barracks and training grounds. To the left were the stables close to the castle and beyond that only empty grassy estate.

Corin descended the front stairs of the castle and started running. He ran out all of his frustrations and insecurities. He ran until he was drenched in sweat and he could almost imagine that he was back at the battle school and Sir Burke was yelling at him to run faster. So Corin did. He picked up his pace and lifted his legs higher with every stride. He savored the pounding of his heart and the burning of the air in his lungs as he drew in deep breaths.

He'd always been good at running. His thin frame and determination made it easy for him. Most of all, he liked the feeling of freedom that came with it. He liked the feeling that whatever he might face later, for a moment he was free from it. He felt like a hawk soaring through the sky. He felt like a fierce predator on the hunt. He felt strong. Corin ran and ran until the sun was fully in the sky and the heat dried the sweat from his body as quickly as it appeared. He might have kept running even then, perhaps he would have tried to run back to Nevara, but he ran right into the midst of the knights of the castle making their own jog around the grounds.

Corin paused on the outskirts of their grouping. It was tempting to run alongside them in the middle of their ranks. He stood no chance of passing as one of them though. He didn't have time to take that leap of boldness before they were past him. However, at their tail end, running alongside them, came Sir Hayes, yelling at them to pick up their pace.

"Terrence, if you don't speed up you'll run twice as much tomorrow! I've seen you run faster in your dreams! Dorian, pace yourself, you'll wear out too quickly!" Hayes shouted. He barely seemed to be short of breath.

The king's battle master halted when he saw Corin standing uncertainly on the edges.

"Keep running!" Hayes commanded his knights before he stopped to study Corin.

Corin wanted to race back inside the castle to avoid that questioning stare. He was covered in sweat and dust and panting heavily. He probably looked pathetic in Hayes's eyes. Maybe the knight wouldn't recognize him.

"Mage Corin," Hayes greeted.

Corin felt his hopes combust into a fiery inferno.

"Sir Hayes," he replied timidly.

"What are you doing out here? It's early and your lessons with Clifton will be starting soon."

Corin shrugged, attempting nonchalance. "Old habit. Sir Burke always had us take morning runs. I needed to wear off some energy before the day started."

He felt ridiculous after he'd said the words.

Wear energy off? He sounded like a rambunctious child.

Much to Corin's surprise, Hayes laughed. "I understand. Technically I don't have to run with the men since I'm in charge but I like the exercise. It's good for the mind and body. I try to keep conditioned for battle and I don't like the idea of sitting back and watching others do all the work. Burke has trained you well if you're willing to keep up the routine."

Corin was pleased with the praise for his instructor. Burke deserved all that praise and more. He'd been tough on all of them but Corin was grateful for him nonetheless.

"It's good to train, Corin, but you're a mage now. You should focus on those studies."

Corin looked away. Was this a rebuke? He wasn't quite sure. Hayes's words weren't harsh by any means but they did sound a bit like a warning.

"Of course, sir. But..." he hesitated, not wanting to sound proud or petulant.

"But?" Hayes prompted.

"But I'm good at running. I want to keep it up."

Hayes grinned, the scar on his face stretched with the expression. "There's nothing wrong with that. I hope your lessons go well, mage. Remember that all talent comes from practice. That applies to being a mage as much as it does to being a knight."

With that, Hayes ran off to catch up with his men. Corin wasn't sure how to feel after the encounter. Hayes's words were encouraging but he wasn't sure if he wanted to improve as a mage. He didn't want to train with magic. He wanted to be running alongside the knights of the capital, keeping pace as Hayes yelled at him to exceed his limits.

He knew Hayes was right that his lessons with Clifton would be starting soon. So, Corin snuck back inside. It was difficult getting to his room now that servants were everywhere, already busy for the day. They gave him odd looks as he walked by. He wondered if it was because of his unkempt state or something else. Some of them likely recognized him as the new mage. Corin felt the most intense stares come from these observers.

When he reached the safety of his room, he quickly changed clothes. Both of his outfits from the battle school were in miserable shape. Corin was reluctantly forced to inspect the wardrobe full of fancy, heavily embroidered, and no doubt very expensive garments. He selected the most basic tunic. It was a simple thing in a rust color with brown cuffs and a fine leather belt. He caught sight of numerous robes and overcoats like the ones that Clifton wore. They were scholarly-looking and seemed heavy. Embroidered patterns in gold, silver, and bronze colors were at the hems, wrists, and collars. The long sleeves were slit in the middle to allow easy movement of the arms and hands. Corin noticed that it would be difficult to equip knives or swords in such a robe. It was another reminder that a mage didn't need to carry a weapon. Corin didn't study the garments for long. It made him upset to look at the luxury. He didn't feel right wearing any of the clothes.

He moved to the washbasin and mirror and rinsed off all the sweat covering him from his run. He stopped for a moment to stare once again at his lengthening hair with distaste. He looked at his sword in the reflection of the mirror. It laid on his desk. He fingered a strand of his hair then shook his head. No, that was a terrible idea. Besides, he didn't have time.

He raced off to breakfast before he could change his mind. The run had awakened a sense of hunger in Corin that he hadn't felt since he'd left the battle school. He wasn't willing to miss breakfast even though he didn't have much time left to eat before his mage lessons began. He dodged servants and nobles, aware that he probably looked like a madman running about as he was. His appetite and lack of time propelled him forward faster and faster. He came to a halting stop in front of the great hall's impressive door as he realized there would no doubt be people inside. Corin cringed at the idea of socializing again and enduring the stares and questions he would certainly face. His stomach growled like a wild animal, urging him forward. Sighing in resignation, Corin pushed open the door.

There weren't as many people in the great hall as he'd feared. Many of the tables were empty. Sir Hayes and the garrison were likely still running drills. There were a few archers at one of the tables. Most of them were grouped together and joking as they ate their morning meal. One archer sat at the end of the table and he stared moodily at Corin as he entered, as if his being there had ruined the archer's day. There were a few nobles scattered around the room but they only looked at Corin with the same curious glances and hushed whispers which had been his greeting when he first arrived. Clifton was also absent, most likely preparing for Corin's lesson, or perhaps already waiting for him. Corin looked around hurriedly for a place to sit so he could eat and hurry off to his training. He had already kept Clifton waiting the previous morning. He feared the consequences should the powerful mage be disappointed in him again.

"Corin," King Rupert called from the head table. The king gestured for Corin to come sit with him.

Reluctantly, Corin approached. He kept his eyes downcast as he sat at the king's side. As a result, he nearly didn't notice Ruena sitting across from him.

"Good morning, mage," Ruena said politely.

"Good morning," Corin responded. He couldn't meet her eyes. Instead, he started to pick at the food that was immediately placed in front of him. He knew he should eat quickly and be off but his appetite had suddenly vanished as nerves took its place.

"I heard from Ruena that you went exploring yesterday," King Rupert said. "Did you find anything interesting?"

"I didn't explore for long, Your Majesty," Corin responded.

Had he done something wrong? Why was there always such a lack of formality with the king? He seemed determined to force Corin to engage in casual conversation. It was disconcerting. Corin didn't know how casual he was supposed to be. What would be considered overstepping boundaries? Ruena seemed to sense this discomfort because she expertly distracted her uncle by asking him a question about the state of a neighboring town. Corin gratefully took the opportunity to dig into his food. He ate as fast as he could but he still hadn't finished when King Rupert turned his attention back to Corin.

"Tell me young mage," King Rupert began and

Corin hesitantly brought his gaze up from his food to direct his sight at the king's forehead. He couldn't muster the courage to look the monarch in the eyes, "how are your lessons with Clifton? I hope you're finding them satisfactory."

Corin jerked his gaze toward Ruena for a brief instant before he brought his eyes back to the spot on King Rupert's forehead. The man had a cluster of freckles above his left eyebrow that looked like a constellation of stars. Had Ruena told her uncle about Corin's distaste for his new position as a mage? Corin knew he had to answer the king's question, but a sense of great fear had risen inside him. As much as his new position as a mage felt like a nightmare come to fruition, Corin couldn't bear the thought of being thrown out of the castle. He may not think of it as home, but it was infinitely better than being back on the streets. He doubted Burke would accept him back at the battle school if he offended the king.

Ruena saved him from answering, "Uncle, Corin has only had one lesson so far. He most likely won't have an answer right away."

"Oh, of course," the king agreed.

Corin felt his shoulders sag with relief. Ruena must have not told her uncle about his complaints. Perhaps he wouldn't be thrown out. It filled Corin with a surprising amount of relief to know that his position was safe for the moment. He was starting to realize that, whether he liked the castle or not, he had nowhere else to go.

"Baron Geoffrey and his wife were telling me just last evening that they were planning to renovate their estate's garden," Ruena told her uncle, steering the conversation away from Corin and saving him from further discussion.

Ruena and the king talked about all sorts of subjects and King Rupert attempted to include Corin by commenting on various places in the castle which might interest him. Corin listened and nodded in agreement when appropriate. Mostly, he set himself to the task of devouring his meal. He stole occasional glances at Ruena whenever he lifted his eyes. She seemed nervous, as if speaking up earlier had cost her something. The smile on her face appeared strained. Corin wondered how it was that he could so easily tell the smile was fake yet no one else seemed to notice.

"I was reading an interesting book about the history of Freiwade's trade agreement with Skellas," Ruena told her uncle while Corin continued shoving food in his mouth.

"Really?" King Rupert asked. "That sounds like a heavy topic. You're much more involved in matters than I was at your age. Then again, I didn't expect to be king until later." He grinned, "You'll have to tell me more about it this evening during tea. It might be important in our negotiations with Freiwade."

Ruena beamed at the praise. "Apparently Freiwade..."

She didn't get to finish. A noblewoman attired in an audacious dress of violet purple, a bold color by anyone's reckoning, approached the king.

"Your Majesty, I must say that the meal last night was incredible. It's been such an honor to be here and that roasted venison was to die for."

The king smiled graciously and Ruena sunk into her chair. Corin glanced at her and thought he saw her eyes blaze but she quickly smothered the look and put on that same fake smile. Corin wondered at the woman's rudeness. Why had she so blatantly interrupted? It had been obvious that Ruena and her uncle were deep in conversation. Ruena continued eating without comment as if this were a normal occurrence.

Corin took the woman's interruption as a good opportunity to excuse himself. He muttered a quick farewell and slipped out of the room. He took the stairs to Clifton's tower two at a time, knowing he was going to be late if he didn't hurry. He tried to focus his mind on the upcoming lesson and the trials he would soon face, but with each footfall a different thought assaulted him.

He thought of his first real battle, a fight he'd had with another boy in battle school. It had taken place a few weeks after Corin's arrival at the school. The boy, Earnest Berdict, had insulted Corin. He'd claimed that an unwanted orphan had no place training as a squire. He'd claimed that Corin could never be a knight. When Sir Burke had found the two boys, they'd both been bloodied and bruised, clawing at each other like feral cats. Corin could still remember the animalistic anger that had overpowered him then. Sir Burke had dragged Corin to his office and proceeded to give Corin his first true encounter with fear. Corin had thought he'd known fear before that day. He'd lived on the streets. He'd known the gnawing ache of an empty stomach and the bone-weary exhaustion of sleeping in the cold as shivers wracked his body. He'd never had an easy life and he'd never expected one. Then, Burke accepted him as a squire and gave Corin hope. So, when Burke threatened to expel him if he sought out any more fights, Corin was petrified. He'd worked harder than ever after that to stay out of trouble. Yet, trouble always seemed to find him. Burke had been so, so patient. Corin wondered how far King Rupert and Clifton's patience reached.

He arrived at Clifton's office and, after knocking at the door, waited for Clifton's invitation before he entered. As Corin had suspected, Clifton was waiting for him. So was Will. The boy was sitting at Clifton's desk, writing something. He looked up when Corin entered and smiled in greeting.

Clifton began the lesson as soon as Corin took his seat, refraining from any comments he might have regarding Corin's tardiness.

"You don't have to knock," was all Clifton said. "This office is for the mage of Castille Castle. It's as much yours as it is mine."

Corin nodded but he knew he would knock anyway.

Despite Clifton's silence about his being late, Corin felt that a repercussion was coming. Dread settled in his chest as he thought about the trouble that no doubt waited in store for him.

"Soon you'll learn how to use magic," Clifton told him as Corin settled into his chair. "It's a great gift and it takes time and practice to learn how to best use it. Just as some people are gifted with harmonic singing voices and have to practice their melodies to find the full potential of their talent, so it is with magic. Neos Loch spent years trying to find ways to better understand magic and use it, then he worked hard to teach me everything he knew. Now, it's my turn to teach you, Corin. Just remember, always remember, that your gift comes from God, it's by His will that you're able to use it."

Corin nodded soberly.

Clifton rubbed his hands together as if in excitement. "Great. But before you use magic, you must first understand it. As I mentioned in your last lesson, a scroll containing foundational information about magic was brought to the castle. The rest of what we know was discovered by years of study from Neos Loch. After the war, he journeyed throughout the three kingdoms of Ademar, not only Ashnah but also Freiwade and Skellas. Loch suspected that there had once been teachers of magic who retained the knowledge for future generations. There had been myths of a time when the three kingdoms of Ademar were filled with knowledge and a great library connected Ashnah, Freiwade, and Skellas. The scroll brought to Castille Castle was the first real evidence of such. Loch worked tirelessly to rebuild the knowledge surrounding magic and strived to encourage people to respect mages as they had in ancient times instead of fearing them. He hoped one day more mages would emerge whom he could train. Eventually, I did."

Clifton smiled faintly as he spoke, as if he were remembering fond memories.

"Neos Loch spent all of his life building knowledge of magic and drawing the attention of the gift back to its source, God. His recognition of God's hand in all life and especially in the gift of magic may not have gained him many admirers among people in Freiwade and even some in Ashnah, but I believe it was the reason behind the great power he was blessed with. He passed that responsibility on to me and someday you'll take on that duty, Corin."

For the first time, it truly sunk in for Corin that being a mage was not only about him. It wasn't only a great upheaval in his life but a lifelong commitment that would affect others as well. Would he someday be expected to train other mages as Neos Loch had done and Clifton was doing for him? He couldn't survive the war and just go back to the way things had been. His destiny had been chosen for him and there was no escaping it.

Clifton continued. "Neos Loch discovered that the gift of magic is innate in a person when God has chosen to use them. However, it becomes more prevalent in times of need. For example, if there is a battle, the magic will rise to the surface along with the adrenalin and it can be used as a defense. A mage needs to learn to control their emotions so they do not cause a dangerous accident as you did in your battle with Phineas York when you lost control of your anger. There is a section of the Bible called the Beatitudes. In it, different qualities are highlighted as being blessed. Those who are meek, who hunger and thirst for righteousness, who are merciful, pure in heart, and peacemakers are all called blessed. These qualities are what a mage should seek to obtain. And above all, a mage should trust in God and not in their own abilities. If you can control your emotions, Corin, you will be able to control your magic. If you lose control of one you may lose control of the other. Remember that. Keep in mind that you may have stronger talent with certain skills than others. It depends on what God has blessed you with."

Clifton started to pace the room, lost in his lecturing. Corin watched him as he walked back and forth, back and forth. Corin's mind was distracted by Clifton's warnings. He'd lost control of his abilities during his fight with York and, as a result, had nearly killed the other boy. Magic may be a gift but it was a dangerous one, or at least it had the potential to be if it was used incorrectly. It made Corin hesitate to use it at all. What if he messed up again? What if things didn't end so well the next time?

"Neos Loch also tested the limits of magic," Clifton explained. "He discovered several firm boundaries which cannot be breached."

This piqued Corin's interest and drew him back to the present. He listened intently as Clifton continued speaking.

"As I mentioned before, we call these abilities magic but others have called them prophecy, healing, and other names. Our gifts come from God and are made possible because of Him. Jesus is the Son of God and He is God. The miracles Jesus demonstrated were perfect. No one can ever replicate them. However, when Jesus died, rose, and ascended to Heaven, followers of Him were gifted with similar abilities to continue good work on the earth. His disciples were especially gifted and capable of acts of healing, invulnerability against attacks on their lives, and even on occasion raising the dead. The important thing to note is that they glorified God in all they did and attributed everything to His power and might. Magic has changed since then. Its uses have changed. Raising people from the dead is unheard of now. Neos Loch never accomplished it and I certainly wouldn't be able to. God is in control of life and death; it is dangerous for men to meddle in such things. Likewise, magic can never rewind time or rewrite past events because God is the Creator of the universe and the Judge of all things. Magic cannot fundamentally alter a person or environment because that would be interfering with God's creation. A mage may calm the sea for a moment during a storm, or redirect strength to their bones to make themselves stronger but it is a temporary and surface-level change. And this is not the case in dealing with another person. A mage cannot alter a person's heart or mind or control their actions in any way."

"What about healing?" Corin asked. "You said that the disciples healed people. Can we do that?"

It felt strange using the word 'we' but Corin was growing excited and didn't notice the slip at first.

Clifton shook his head. "Neos Loch and myself never accomplished such a feat. Perhaps it is possible. We know from the Bible that the disciples were able to do so. However, we could never discover how to accomplish it. I suspect that a mage could learn to heal others but not themselves. The Bible never states an occurrence where one of the disciples healed themselves. Several of them had various infirmities that they dealt with their entire lives. Magic requires reliance on God who bestowed the gifts in the first place. Personal pain and injury require seeking the Creator Himself and accepting His decision. I realize that I'm making it sound like there are more limitations to magic than uses but the full range of power has not been discovered. Just remember that magic's primary purpose is life, not death. It acts as a defense. It creates. That is what makes it such a gift."

"Can it be used as a weapon?" Corin asked. "Against another person?"

Clifton paused in his pacing and placed a hand on his desk to steady himself. Will watched the discussion with wide eyes, his pen poised to document the lesson.

"That would be going against magic's very nature, Corin. However, I will warn you again that controlling your emotions and striving for the things that Jesus called blessed are essential. If you lose control of your magic, its power may cause unforeseen consequences. Loch suggested that because of its nature for creation, magic could in some ways be used to destroy. For example, if a person wanted to build a great structure they would have to quarry the stone and fell the lumber first. The destruction of the environment could result in unforeseen injuries to those nearby. It is important to consider that once the stone is cut or the tree is chopped down, it cannot be mended. That is why it is so important to treat your gift with care and work to better your inner self, your heart, mind, and soul, to be able to use the talent God has given you."

Corin didn't know what to make of Clifton's words. He sensed the warning behind what Clifton said. Corin swallowed hard and focused on Will, needing a moment to compose himself as a nervous sort of fear filled his chest. This 'gift' was not something to be trifled with. What if he messed things up and someone got seriously hurt or worse? What if there was another accident like what happened with Phineas York? Corin wished he could stick to practicing with his sword. At least the only one he stood a chance of hurting in that scenario was himself.

Clifton seemed to sense the anxiety coursing through his student. "That's enough for today. I'll assign some reading for you, Corin. Neos Loch and I have written many volumes about magic and its uses, I'd like you to study them. Will can help you; he knows where everything is kept and he can help you decipher my pitiful handwriting."

Corin slowly raised himself to stand. His legs felt weak. He wondered if Clifton was determined to end each lesson in a dramatic tone that would leave him drowning in expectations and uncertainty.

"I saw you out running today," Clifton said, stopping Corin before he reached the door. "You're quite fast. I can't help but wonder if you've discovered how to channel."

"Channel?" Corin asked.

"Yes, it's a technique used by mages to enhance their physical abilities using magic. It's fairly complicated and requires a certain mindset to perform. I can already tell that you are very talented, Corin. I know you still feel some unease about your place in all of this, but I can assure you, you'll make a great mage."

Corin bowed his head and made a quick exit before Clifton could say anything else. He wished people would stop referring to him as a mage. He wished there wasn't so much expected of him. It was unsettling to know that he had been using magic without even realizing it. How many times had he slipped and used it before without knowing he was doing so? How many of his talents were a lie? Had he been using magic to help him succeed all along? He wished he could escape the 'gift' that he'd been given. He wasn't sure how he would manage the expectations and power suddenly thrust upon him.

CHAPTER 15

"Today, you'll be learning how to use your abilities," Clifton announced when Corin took his seat in the mage's office.

Corin hadn't been expecting the announcement. He'd started to suspect he would always be subjected to lectures and history lessons instead of practical uses of his abilities. And worst of all the books. Clifton had already assigned more books than Corin could ever hope to read, especially considering the horrific state of Clifton's handwriting. Will helped the best he could in deciphering the cryptic messages, but it still gave Corin a persistent headache. He wasn't confident that he had learned much from his studies. However, he had learned more about Will. They tended to talk as they worked together to understand the books. Corin knew Will was working hard with his own training as a scribe, he was mature for his age and carried more responsibilities than any twelve-year-old Corin had met before, and he had a timid sense of humor.

"Most of what I do for Clifton is transcribing his books," Will had admitted. "King Rupert wants what Clifton has written about magic to be legible so future generations can easily understand it. I'm also supposed to record any discoveries he makes. Unfortunately, that decision was made after Clifton had already written dozens of volumes on the subject. I have a lot of catching up to do."

Corin looked at the younger boy with a grin when he entered Clifton's office. Will, as usual, was sitting at Clifton's desk, ready to record the events of the lesson.

It wasn't that the constant studying and lack of actual demonstration was a bad thing. Corin certainly didn't feel ready to use magic. He still woke with nightmares about the incident with Phineas York. Sometimes Corin would wake in the middle of the night and by the light of the moon shining through his window, sit at his desk and think about writing a letter to Burke, questioning the man about York's wellbeing. Corin felt a constant dread over what he had done. The idea of trying to use his magic again was terrifying.

As Clifton made his announcement, he seemed more nervous than excited. He paced as he talked, wringing his hands frantically. Corin hoped it wasn't because he was about to teach Corin how to control his magic. Corin was worried enough for the both of them. Would he throw Clifton into a wall on accident like he had with Phineas York? Would he set something on fire or destroy the castle with a single word? Corin shuddered at the thought. But as Clifton paced, he didn't so much as look at Corin. It was as if his mind was entirely elsewhere. Clifton wasn't the only one who seemed out of character. During breakfast, several of the people at the head table, including the king and Sir Hayes seemed to share the unease. They'd glanced at Corin as if he might suddenly burst into flames. Corin knew something was going on but he wasn't sure what.

Whatever it was, Corin had bigger concerns.

"Isn't it a little soon?" Corin stated. "I thought any practical applications wouldn't come for a few weeks. That way I would have time to study the books you assigned me."

Being called a mage was one thing, practicing magic was another entirely. If he made a mistake, he'd be thrown out immediately, Corin was sure of it. He didn't belong at the castle. The doubts kept him up at night. He wondered what the streets of the capital were like. Surely it wouldn't be as cold in Castille as it had been in Nevara. How long would Corin last when they kicked him out? He wasn't a knight-in-training anymore and he didn't possess the skills necessary for a trade. What would he do when the castle finally decided to get rid of him?

Clifton's words made everything seem a lot more real. If he was going to be shown how to use his magic, his position must at least be safe for the moment. Maybe it was foolish to think they'd get rid of one of the only two mages in existence but Corin had ruined everything so far; he was sure he'd ruin this too.

Corin wasn't sure if he should be excited or nervous to see what he was capable of. It would be good to have control over his abilities at least. He hoped he could manage that much so he could avoid another incident like what had happened at the battle school.

"Don't look so nervous, Corin," Clifton said, seemingly reading his mind.

It wasn't altogether reassuring when Clifton looked so nervous himself.

"Remember, you've already used magic before," Clifton reminded him.

Corin shuddered, remembering his fight with York. Yes, he had used magic before and it had nearly gotten his fellow squire killed, not to mention the giant crack through the courtyard cobblestones that he'd left behind.

"I'm not just referring to your fight with Phineas York," Clifton said. "You've also learned how to channel. That's a difficult skill. And you seem to have mastered it. What I'm about to show you will probably come easy."

Corin had no idea how he had done any of the magic in the past so Clifton's pep-talk didn't do its job. Corin could only hope that his abilities would come as easily as Clifton claimed they would. He didn't want to mess up. He knew firsthand that the consequences would be disastrous if he did.

"Today, I'll be showing you how to create a small light in the palm of your hand."

At least that sounded innocent enough. Surely, that couldn't cause too much damage.

Clifton continued, "You'll place the palms of your hands together, then, as you slowly separate them, imagine a light forming. Watch me demonstrate."

Clifton held his tremoring hands together and then separated them slowly. Corin watched in fascination as a bright light appeared in the palm of

Clifton's hand.

"Now, you try," Clifton instructed, clapping his hands together and extinguishing the light.

Corin did as he was told and pressed his palms together. Although he was far from confident that anything would happen, the light sprang to life immediately. It was bright, brighter even than Clifton's light had been. Corin was so shocked that he quickly clapped his hands together, making the light disappear.

"Well done, Corin!" Clifton exclaimed. He seemed just as surprised as Corin. "When I first learned that, it took me three times of trying before I got any light at all."

Corin studied his hands. How had it come so easily to him? It wasn't just easy, it was natural. He hadn't even been fully trying and the light had flared to life out of nowhere. He had doubted that he even possessed the abilities that Clifton claimed he did. The concern that had been on Clifton's face the entire morning faded a little.

"Hmm," Clifton murmured as he walked behind his desk. He rummaged through some papers and then moved over to one of the bookshelves lining the walls. He pulled several books from the shelves, perused them, then returned them to their places. Finally, he seemed to find the one he was looking for. It was an old book, several decades old. The binding was worn and the pages were uneven, some of them had been folded to bookmark certain sections. Clifton pulled open the book to one of the marked sections and his eyes scanned the page.

"Maybe this will be a little more challenging for

you," he said. He closed the book and moved to stand in front of Corin. He made a cross with his arms in front of his body and closed his eyes. He took a deep breath and exhaled.

At the released breath, a large, bronze-colored shield appeared on his forearm. It was slightly translucent but Corin knew it would be just as strong as any shield a knight might use. Clifton allowed Corin to study the shield before he dropped his arm, letting the magic dissipate.

"That is a simple skill for shielding yourself from attack. You only have to cross your arms in front of yourself like a shield, imagining protection from your enemy. When the shield is created, it will attach to the arm placed in front. You should be able to drop the other arm and use it for other purposes. Now, you try."

Corin held out his arms like Clifton had. He kept his right dominant arm behind his left so the shield would attach to his left forearm. He took a deep breath and pictured a shield, the sort he had never been able to lift at battle school. He hadn't expected much but a bronze shield appeared on his forearm just as easily as the light had appeared in his palm. He could only stare at the semi-translucent shield as Clifton approached to inspect it.

"Incredible," Clifton murmured. Without warning, he hammered his fist against the shield, testing its strength. Clifton winced as his hand made contact. "It might even be stronger than mine."

"Cool," Will said excitedly, leaning forward to get a closer look.

There was a look of awe in Clifton's eyes that

made Corin immensely uncomfortable. The shield wasn't any more difficult than the light. It had all come easily. What did that mean? Was it wrong for Corin not to struggle as Clifton expected him to?

"I don't know how I did it," Corin hurriedly explained. "I'm sure it was just a fluke."

"Oh, no," Clifton shook his head. "You undoubtedly have an innate talent for this, Corin. You're a quick learner."

That was something Corin had never heard before. He'd always struggled at battle school. Nothing had come easy there.

"I just can't believe it," Clifton said, plopping down into a nearby chair. "It took me weeks to master that skill. You've managed to do it on your first try."

Corin quickly let the magic shield drop. He rubbed his forearm where the shield had been. It hadn't felt heavy like a normal shield. Clifton glanced out the window before looking back at Corin.

"Well, I'd assumed I would only be teaching you one method today. I have nothing else prepared. You're free to take the rest of the day off while I attempt to find something more challenging to teach you tomorrow. Just remember to keep studying those books in the meantime."

Corin bowed his head and wasted no time in accepting the dismissal. He felt even more nervous and uncomfortable than he had before the lesson. At least nothing had blown up on him. He hadn't expected to succeed at all, much less surpass Clifton's expectations. He wasn't even sure what had happened. He did know one thing; it had felt good to practice magic. It felt like accepting a part of himself that he hadn't known he was hiding. Corin thought about returning to his room to practice sword drills but instead, he found himself heading towards the empty room where he'd talked with Ruena.

Corin hesitated at the doorway. Would she be inside? Did he want her to be? He wasn't sure what he'd do if she was. Would she want to talk to him? Corin knew it wasn't right for him to seek out her company but he craved someone to talk to. Corin peeked his head around the corner of the doorway and found the room empty. He felt a twinge of disappointment. It was probably for the best. Corin entered the room anyway. He approached the window and sat on its sill in the same position he'd faced Ruena before. He pulled his legs up to his chest and leaned his head on his knees. He stared out the window. The garden was beautiful in the afternoon sunlight, more beautiful than anything at the battle school had ever been. Just in the distance, Corin could see the barracks where the king's knights trained. He stared longingly at it.

What a strange turn his life had taken. All he'd ever wanted was to be a knight and he'd been terrible at it. Now, he had finally found something he was really, truly good at, and he hated every minute of it.

CHAPTER 16

It was a sorry bunch of men who made up Freiwade's ranks. The knights of Freiwade's army were far from what Nox had been expecting. He surveyed them with distaste. The vast majority of the men were peasants from Freiwade or Skellas. They'd been drafted into the fighting without a say in the matter. They had been unwillingly dragged kicking and hollering from their homes to join the fight. Only a few of the officers were nobles. Those were flippant about their positions which had been handed to them. They didn't care for the difficult, inglorious aspects of war. They refused to dirty their hands and instead held their superiority over the common soldiers. Nox suspected that the nobles would be the first to fall in a real fight. However, in this war, they'd hang back and let the peasants lay down their lives for Freiwade's honor. It was pathetic, Nox thought, to make men slighted by their kingdom or even those who did not call Freiwade home fight for the benefit of the king. As a result, none of the members of the army were fully dedicated to the cause.

It was a faulty cause to begin with. The entire war was being fought for the sake of King Corpin's pride. Nox would not allow it to be a losing battle. Too much had been lost already. The pathetic lot before him would win the war. Nox would make sure of it. Then, he would deal with the king. King Corpin had blatantly lied to him. He'd told Nox that the army was powerful and would quickly overtake Ashnah. Instead, the men were weak, hungry, and tired. They had not wanted to fight to begin with. They were weary and dejected before the war truly began. Freiwade had been staging skirmishes for years, forcing men like these to fight to test Ashnah's might. Each practice battle had only served to demoralize and weary the soldiers. Now Nox had the task of mustering them into a force that could defeat Ashnah.

The state of the army wasn't the king's only lie. He'd told Nox that he would be in command. However, he had neglected to state that he would be placing his general as a watchdog over Nox's every action. Nox did not doubt that the general and his spies would report the slightest misstep in an instant. Though, what they planned to do about it, Nox had no idea. They couldn't face him. They were afraid to. He'd seen the looks of terror on their faces when he stepped into the throne room. He'd relished the pallor of the king's face and the helplessness that had been instilled in him. In that regard, Nox had already won. He'd still keep a close eye on General Havoc though. The man would prove to be trouble sooner or later.

Everything amounted to a massive disappointment. Nox certainly had his work cut out for him. However, he had bigger problems than the army and General Havoc. His head pounded incessantly. His thoughts felt scattered as if they were ash in the wind. It felt as if something was trying to force its way out of his skull. And his chest felt achingly cold. He'd lived in Skellas all his life. He knew cold. He knew the bitter, biting wind of winter on the ocean's coast. This was wholly different. It was beyond the numbness of frostbite. It was beyond the piercing needles of ice water. It was an empty sort of cold and it felt all-consuming. It emanated from his chest and spread through his limbs. Even more troublesome were the sections of lost time. He found himself losing track of time and space. He would forget where he was and what he was doing. His mind would go blank for long periods. He was overcome on occasion with violent impulses and thoughts. He longed to reach out and strangle a soldier who looked at him for longer than a moment. He wanted to send his dark magic into the general and watch as he burst from the inside out. Nox snapped at people whenever they spoke to him and even when they didn't. He looked down on all of them without any sort of remorse. He knew he was more powerful than any. He knew what was happening and it terrified him. His power was growing and soon it would be beyond his control.

The first night at the camp he'd woken in a cold sweat to find his tent filled with a suffocating darkness that was cold as ice. That was only the first of many similarly frightening situations. Sometimes he felt in control but the other times... It was the most exhilarating and terrifying experience Nox had ever had.

He was tired, so dreadfully tired, and filled with unexplainable anger and disdain for all of those around him. They were just behind the front lines and Nox knew he had to get the men under control. If he didn't, they would lose the war. Ashnah was powerful. Years of prosperity had strengthened them while Freiwade and Skellas languished in hunger and despair. The army of Freiwade needed to be confident in their fight if they were to stand a chance.

"Do you care for this fight?" Nox found himself asking one of the groups of soldiers.

They were silent, terrified of him, and afraid to answer in any way.

"Tell the truth. I'll know if you are lying."

One of the men, perhaps the bravest, perhaps the most foolish, spoke. "Why should we? We're from Skellas, this isn't our fight."

"Yet, you are on the battlefield. If you don't fight well, you will die."

"They'd like that I bet," one of the others responded bitterly. "They don't care about us. They never have. All Freiwade has ever done is starve us and work us to death. Now the king is throwing us into his war to be slaughtered in place of Freiwade soldiers."

"Bold words in the midst of a Freiwade camp," Nox warned the man.

The man straightened. "Kill me if you like then. I'll die before long anyway."

"He doesn't mean that," a third man put in. "We're all just weary."

The first man spoke again, "It doesn't help that General Havoc is a brutally unforgiving slave master."

Nox had noticed as much. Havoc had just enough fear of Nox to leave him alone. The other men were less fortunate. The soldiers murmured that General Ray Havoc possessed all of the worst qualities of a man. He stalked about the camp, waiting for the smallest excuse to turn his anger on an unsuspecting soldier. The men cowered before him and were repulsed by him. They lowered their gazes as he passed by, their conversations halted and their shoulders stiffened in self-defense. Every night Nox had spent with the army, Havoc had spent drinking himself into oblivion. Where he obtained the scarce alcohol, Nox had no idea. The following mornings he would be in a foul mood that no one could rival. If anyone so much as looked at him awry, they'd be hit with the small whip Havoc always carried at his side.

Nox knew he'd have to put the man in his place eventually. Havoc was certain to become an obstacle for Nox and the army. But first, Nox had to gain the men's allegiance. Fear was not enough. Havoc had already proven that the men would not rally under fear. They had to be willing. They had to believe they could win. They needed something or someone to rally behind.

As they reached the border of Ashnah and approached their first target, the strike that would announce the intent for war once and for all, Nox knew he was running out of time. The men were tired and weary, unfit for the battle that would take place that afternoon against Ashnah's determined knights. The outpost was only a few miles ahead. It was a fortress, Ashnah's first defense against invaders. Nox had called for the army to camp out of sight of the outpost, knowing they were in no condition to fight after a hard day of marching. However, the short pause had only caused uncertainty at the thought of the battle to poison the hearts of Freiwade's forces.

It was estimated that there would only be 70 knights and 30 archers stationed at the outpost. Nox knew the army could easily defeat them, even with sections of the main force split apart under the command of other generals to seek entry into Ashnah undetected. Nox's soldiers, the force that would fight at the front lines of battle, could still overwhelm the outpost. However, he feared that the dejected state of Freiwade's soldiers would lead to more deaths among them than necessary. The army couldn't afford to lose any men at the onset of the war. An idea started to form in Nox's mind. He was not sure if it was his own or from the insidious *thing* inside him.

He waited until dawn. Even from childhood, he'd had an uncanny gift for waking himself at a preset time. Now, he rose before any of the soldiers. He could still hear Havoc's drunken exclamations from the tent across from his own. The man hadn't even gone to bed yet. Nox stepped out of his tent. It was a gray day. The cold morning air reminded Nox of Skellas. He closed his eyes for a moment and tried to picture the roaring waves and rugged coastline. All he could see was the darkness of his closed eyelids. He left the camp behind him and headed for Ashnah's outpost alone. As he walked, he gathered his power around himself until it wrapped him like a cloak. It offered no warmth, only concealment. He saw the outpost from a distance. It was along a great expanse of empty field. He was certain his presence was spotted long before the alarm was raised. No one would expect a single man to pose much of a threat. They probably assumed he was a messenger. He faced no opposition until he was standing close to the outpost.

"State your business!" one of the knights called down to him.

"To end you," Nox responded.

Only then, did they start firing arrows. When Nox used his magic to deflect each of the arrows, the reinforced wooden doors of the outpost pushed outwards and knights poured through the opening.

"Demon!" an archer yelled from the parapet.

"Unnatural!" another put in.

The knights assembled a yard away from Nox. They stood uncertainly, hesitating to attack when it was becoming increasingly obvious that Nox was no ordinary man. He was to be feared. The knights formed a defensive line, swords pointed ahead and shields raised at the ready. It was pathetic, so pathetic.

They didn't stand a chance.

Nox took out the archers with one lethal stroke of power. The dark power solidified into a massive scythe that cut through the ranks assembled on the parapet. The arrows pelting the ground around Nox halted. Silence swept through Ashnah's numbers. Nox felt his power fill him to overflowing. It rose in a wave that swept over him, consuming him entirely. It was suffocating. He relished the feeling of absolute power.

The knights overcame their horrified confusion and charged forward. Nox took his time with them. He engaged them one at a time. Each sword that was thrust his way shattered. Each man who came too close was impaled by the dark magic. Eventually, the knights swarmed him, thinking they could overtake him if they fought together.

For a moment, Nox felt overwhelmed by

them. They were surrounding him. They were bigger and stronger than him and armed with powerful weapons. One of the knights surged forward. Caught off guard, Nox could not defend himself against the sword thrust at him. It sliced deep into his arm. The pain was vivid. Nox took a step back and then another. He felt a prying in his mind as if something were trying to break loose. The pounding headache grew agonizing. The prying moved to his chest, even more powerful than before. Something was trying to take over. Despite the great force of it, Nox knew he could fend it off if he chose. He could reject the thing and deal with the consequences. But why should he? He'd wanted this ability. He wanted all of it. He didn't care what happened. He only wanted complete and utter power. Nox allowed the evil to overtake him. He gave in to it willingly, lovingly.

Everything went black.

Nox woke. He wasn't sure how much time had passed. He was standing in a field of blood. The bodies of the knights were strewn all around him. All of them dead. He was covered in blood from his hair to the ends of his fingers. Was he injured? No. None of the blood was his own. The outpost, once towering and impenetrable was now ruins and the Ashnan forces were reduced to corpses. As for Nox, there was not a single scratch on him. Even the wound on his arm was gone. It had vanished. It should be impossible but the skin where the sword had cut was smooth and flawless. There wasn't even a scar left behind.

What had happened? He couldn't remember anything after he allowed himself to be lost to the magic. He felt... empty. It was a strange feeling. There was a complete absence of all physical sensation and emotion. There was only cold, that same cold that persisted in his chest. He felt powerful, more powerful than ever before.

He stood there in that bloody field for a long time, basking in the sensation of unstoppable power and the awful destruction *he* had caused. Then, he returned to the camp. There was still work to be done.

There were exclamations of surprise and horror when he entered the camp, still covered in blood and gore.

"What happened?" one of the three Skellans he'd talked to before asked.

Nox faced the soldiers. All of their eyes were on him. "The Ashnan outpost is destroyed," Nox told them. "Every last knight and archer is dead. I have massacred them. There will be no battle today. You will rest. Tomorrow, we will proceed towards the capital."

They could only stare at Nox in awe.

"You killed all of them?" a hesitant voice rose above the crowd.

"He doesn't even have a scratch on him," another soldier put in. "That's all their blood."

A murmur of praise and excitement swept through the ranks, tinged with a hint of fear. Yes, fear was still necessary. They must not be willing to turn against him. Nox did not have to worry about that. The soldiers of Freiwade and Skellas bowed, one, then another, then every last one of them. They all bowed before Nox. Their loyalty was ensured. In one battle Nox had gained not only their fear but their respect as well.

General Havoc was the only man to stay standing. He looked at Nox with raw and unrestrained terror. Mixed with the expression of utter fear was one of utter hatred. Havoc had much to fear from Nox, not only his power but the threat to the general's authority that he posed. Nox would take away Havoc's men from right underneath him.

Nox nodded to the man. He'd won this battle. He'd won this war. The general had lost his control. His brutality could not save him. The soldiers would obey Nox and no one else. And under Nox's command, they might stand a chance of winning the war, of defeating Ashnah.

Yet, Nox's victory was not without a cost. He felt ill. Weakness and exhaustion permeated every part of him. He'd managed to tell the soldiers what he'd done and he'd stood proud to accept their praises and reverence but he knew he couldn't hold out much longer. He returned to his tent without delay. His body was wracked with cold, bitter agony. His limbs shook with tremors that he could not control and his head pulsated with a migraine unlike anything he had ever experienced before. Suddenly he could not even stand. He sunk to his cot and in a moment fell into a feverish sleep, numb to the world around him.

CHAPTER 17

Finch didn't know what to expect from the invitation. The simple slip of paper led him to the castle's war room where he was met with the sight of an assembly gathered. His commander Terin, several experienced archers, several knights, Sir Hayes, King Rupert, Clifton the mage, and a younger man whom Finch had met though he didn't really know what he did, were all gathered in the room. Stranger still was the fact that the invitation hadn't come from a servant or even Commander Terin but Sir Hayes himself.

The man had directly delivered the paper with a simple statement. "You're to report to the war room. The reason will be discussed there."

It wasn't Finch's first encounter with Hayes, not by a longshot. The man wasn't his commander and didn't hold much authority over the archers, though he was the castle's battle master. Terin and Hayes's roles were of close to equal standing in the castle. It was odd for Hayes to take any interest in one of the archers but that was exactly what he had done with Finch. Hayes had looked out for Finch, there was no better way to describe it. He was likely looking out for Finch again by ensuring the letter reached him. If Commander Terin had been tasked with its delivery, the paper never would have arrived.

Whatever the case, Finch suspected the meeting was serious and for once he didn't attempt nonchalance. He darted through the castle halls on his way to the war room, looking more put together than usual. He'd dressed in his full uniform, marking him undeniably as a castle archer. He was only disappointed that there was little he could do about the wrinkles on such short notice. The short cape draped over one shoulder felt ridiculous to him. He kept shoving it aside as it slipped around. He hadn't worn it often and he'd struggled to get the clasp right when he put it on. The hat with a single feather like that of an arrow's fletching felt even more out of place on him. It was all a show. The only practical aspect of the uniform was the leather cuffs at the wrists of the shirt that protected against impact from the bowstring when an arrow was loosed. Despite how uncomfortable the uniform made him, Finch wanted to present himself at his best in the meeting. Judging by Hayes's face when he'd delivered the letter, Finch knew this gathering must be serious. Finch was rarely trusted or taken seriously. Why had he been invited at all?

He made it to the war room and hesitated to push the door open. It was rare for him or any of the other archers to gain clearance into the important chamber. Normally, he'd face serious repercussions if he was even caught lingering by the entrance. It felt wrong to push the door open but the invitation in his hand was proof enough that he belonged there.

He was met with a cluster of solemn faces gathered around the great oval table in the middle of the room. Despite his intent to be early, Finch seemed to be the last to arrive. He ducked his head, a little embarrassed, then took his place with the other archers. He kept as far away from Commander Terin as possible. He did, however, catch sight of his commander's face as he walked past. Terin looked outraged and disgusted to see Finch enter the room. It was obvious that he hadn't been expecting him. It made Finch's day.

"Any idea what's going on here?" Jem, one of the archers, asked.

"None," was Finch's only response.

Whatever it was, it was important enough to warrant the king's attendance. King Rupert didn't usually attend battle meetings according to Dorian who had taken part in a good number of them before a skirmish or as practice for one. Even living in the castle, Finch rarely saw the king. He caught sight of the man sitting at the head table during meal times but had never really interacted with him. He might serve the king, but Finch wasn't sure how to act around him. This meeting was unnerving. What was so important that it required so many men of importance to be gathered? What had caused Mage Clifton's presence to be required? Clifton never attended these types of meetings. Why should he? He was a scholar, not a tactician. As a mage, he wouldn't be sent into any ordinary battle. And who was the young man hovering just behind Hayes? Whoever he was, he wasn't dressed in armor or any sort of uniform. He wore a simple tunic of a muted green color. There wasn't even a weapon in his belt, at least not a visible one. Maybe he was an advisor but, if he was, he seemed very young for the role. He couldn't have been much older than Finch.

Sir Hayes cleared his throat. "Now that we're all here, I'm sure you've all been wondering what the purpose of this meeting is."

There were nods of agreement around the room.

Terin placed a hand on the table and stared hard at Hayes. "What I'm wondering is why so many unimportant members are present at this meeting? I was under the impression that we were gathered to discuss a serious matter. I don't see why my presence is needed at a meeting filled with so many untrustworthy amateurs."

Ouch. Right from the start.

Finch had expected the commander's objections to be held until the end of the meeting. Finch turned, ready to excuse himself from the room. He was sure it was a mistake that he was there anyway. Hayes's voice stopped him.

"Everyone here has been selected for a reason. However, if you feel your presence is not necessary then you're free to leave anytime, commander."

Terin stiffened and grimaced. Finch had to duck his head to hide his grin.

"Now, if you don't mind. As I was saying," Hayes continued, "you're gathered here because of an event that took place yesterday. A border outpost," Hayes consulted the notes in front of him, "Outpost Gray, it's called, was destroyed."

"Destroyed?" one of the knights voiced. "Do you mean attacked, Sir?"

"No," Hayes said slowly, "I mean destroyed. It was completely leveled to the ground in a single day. Only one survivor managed to escape. It was one of our knights who happened to be scouting around the outpost at the time. He reported seeing the end of the fight and he raced back to the castle to bring the news. The battle brutalized the outpost, there's nothing left."

"Where's the knight?" one of the archers, Remus, asked. "Shouldn't he be in this meeting?"

"He was sent to the infirmary. He was uninjured but he arrived at the castle in a state of catatonic shock and fear. He barely managed to give his report before he fell into a fit of hysterics."

Silence fell over the gathering. What had happened at that outpost? What had caused the knight who'd witnessed it to fall into a state of madness? One thought rang above all others in Finch's mind. Somehow, he'd escaped a similar fate. He'd been so miserably close to being sent to that very outpost. He would have died along with the other archers and knights. Or worse, he could have been driven to insanity like the sole survivor of the ambush.

"Are you okay?" Jem asked him. "You look like you've seen a ghost."

"Fine," Finch muttered. It was the only word he could force out.

Before anyone could say anything about Hayes's statement, Hayes spoke again. "There's more."

Finch felt like he might be sick. More? How could there possibly be more?

"The scout, once we were able to get more information out of him, explained what happened at the outpost. He claimed that all of the damage and death was caused by a single man."

That time, when Hayes was finished, there was an uproar instead of silence.

"That's impossible!" Terin objected.

"I know the knights who were stationed there," one of the knights, Kent, stated. "They couldn't have been defeated by a single man."

"The knight who reported must be lying!" Rory, an archer, claimed.

"Silence!" King Rupert demanded.

Blessedly, the room sank into a state of relative calm.

Kent ventured to speak again. "How many men were stationed at the outpost at the time?"

Hayes sighed heavily. "There were 30 archers and 70 knights."

The uproar rose again, louder and more vehement than before.

"It's a lie!"

"He must have been lying!"

"Enough!" Hayes quieted them this time. "Villagers in a nearby town several miles away witnessed the attack."

"How could they witness the attack from miles away?" Jem questioned. "Correct me if I'm wrong, Sir, but isn't there a forest between Outpost Gray and the town nearby?"

Hayes nodded. "There is. The villagers claimed to see darkness clouding the sky but it wasn't anything like smoke which was what they originally suspected. They heard a great noise and screams as well."

Finch wondered why he was in this meeting. What could he possibly do about that? The news was horrifying. He was just an archer. What could he do against someone so powerful? How was it possible for one man to do so much damage?

It seemed that Remus shared that thought. "No *man* could do that."

Finch glanced across the room at Clifton who never attended meetings like this. Suddenly, a thought occurred to Finch.

"He was a mage," Finch stated, drawing all the attention in the room to himself.

Hayes gave him a proud look, seemingly pleased that Finch had found the answer before the others. Clifton nodded gravely and stepped forward.

"Yes, the man must have been a mage. The problem is, that no mage should be capable of such destruction. Magic is a gift used to create not to destroy. Although the limitations of magic are still being discovered, no magic I have experienced could even come close to what this mage has displayed."

"What do *you* suppose this man is, then?" Terin interjected.

Finch glared at his commander. Terin had never been afraid to talk poorly of Clifton in front of his archers or anyone else for that matter. He'd always dismissed Clifton as an inexperienced fool, even a madman. Then again, he'd done the same for many of the leaders of the kingdom. Fortunately, he'd never gone so far as to say something against Sir Hayes. That would have been as good as a death sentence for him. Everyone in the castle respected and admired Hayes. If Terin had spoken out against the battle master, he would have had the castle staff, advisors, and an entire garrison of knights to contend with. He had no qualms against downplaying Clifton and his role, however.

Clifton shrugged as if the comment didn't bother him in the least. "The man must be a mage but he's unlike any discovered before."

A thought occurred to Finch and it filled him with annoyance. "If the enemy is a mage, then why isn't the new mage, Corin, present in this meeting?"

Clifton looked... abashed. It was surprising to see a mage, someone so powerful, with such a meek expression on his face. "Corin has shown great potential as a mage," Clifton explained, "but he's still settling into his new role. I'll tell him everything when the time comes. For now, Corin needs to focus on his studies."

Finch's annoyance surged. They were coddling their new mage. Corin was young but he was still accountable. With such great power, he couldn't be treated like a child. None of the rest of them received that luxury. No one in the war room, except Clifton, possessed the gift that Corin did. Yet, they were still gathered to discuss an unimaginable foe. What was the purpose of Corin being at the castle if the knowledge of danger was kept from him? There were plenty of objections Finch wanted to make but he didn't say anything further, especially when Hayes fixed him with a stern, warning look.

"So, why are we here?" one of the knights, Adam, questioned. "Some of us don't hold high-ranking positions and I'm sure there are some more qualified to be here. This seems like an awfully important meeting. I'm not sure if I understand why we're being given such sensitive information."

The king himself answered, "All of you gathered here are the kingdom's finest fighters, both archers and knights. Moreover, you've all proven yourselves trustworthy."

Finch wondered how his constant rebellion and indifference to his position could be seen as trustworthy enough to warrant being included in such glowing praise.

The king spoke, "The situation at hand is unlike anything Ashnah has faced before even during the Great War. If a mage is working with Freiwade, and a mage stronger than any we've encountered before, we can assume that Freiwade is more serious about the war they've threatened than we'd realized. They're ready to carry through with it. And now they pose a greater threat than we ever could have anticipated. Ashnah must ready itself for a greater battle than we've ever faced."

"We're in a more precarious position than ever before," Hayes cut in. "The emergence of such a powerful mage working for the enemy is an unforeseen and deadly twist in this war. As of this moment, we have no way to combat such a threat."

"What about the new mage, Corin?" Jem asked.

Yes, what about him, Finch wanted to ask. Why wasn't he here? Why was he being babied when an enemy mage was preparing to attack their kingdom? Why was Finch here instead? This was all ridiculous.

"Corin is very powerful but he's still training," Clifton reminded them. "Neither myself nor Corin possess the same type of twisted magic that this new mage possesses. His abilities do not come from God, they must be of his own seeking. That makes him a truly dangerous, depraved force to be reckoned with. I'm not sure Corin or I could ever hope to face such great evil."

"That's the reason you've all been called here," Hayes reiterated. "More than your abilities, you possess the greatest minds among the castle forces both in intelligence and ingenuity. We request that you all think about this new threat and create plausible means to combat it."

The group went quiet with thinking. A few murmured conversations filtered through the silence. Jem looked like he might try to talk things over with Finch but Finch didn't want to talk with anyone. His thoughts were racing. How could any of them come up with something that would work against such an awful enemy? Finch realized for the first time that the only men present in the room were warriors. There were no advisors or nobles. Why? Was this information being kept from the nobility? It seemed strange to keep something so important private even from the king's trusted advisors. However, Hayes and the king were correct that some of the most brilliant tacticians in the castle were present in the war room. Finch wondered if any of them would be capable of meeting the expectations placed on them. How could they defeat such a powerful enemy? Finch's first thought would have been to use Clifton and Corin to face off against the threat. If they couldn't win against the enemy, then what could?

Terin cleared his throat and Finch looked at him. Surely he hadn't come up with something, not so quickly anyway. Of course, that wasn't what Terin wanted to say.

"I object to all of this," Terin stated. "Not everyone in this room is capable of this task. I don't believe everyone in this room can even be trusted." He looked directly at Finch as he spoke.

Finch looked away, studying the table. He wished he could retaliate but what could he say against his commander? Besides, he might have the nerve to speak against Terin in private but he wouldn't do so in front of Sir Hayes and the king.

"*Everyone* in this room was personally selected to be here by the king and I," Hayes shot back. "The candidates were vetted based on background, skill, and seniority. We don't trust anyone lightly." When Hayes said the last words, his eyes darted to the strange young man who had stayed so quiet throughout the meeting. The movement was quick but Finch caught it. He glanced at the man, wondering again who he was.

"We understand that this new information is a lot to process," the king stated. "You'll all need time to think over things and come up with plans of attack. So, you're all dismissed for now. We'll meet again in a few days. Please be ready with your ideas by then. A messenger will find you with information about the next meeting in due time. The information discussed today is *not* to leave this room. You are instructed to tell no one, not even those you trust the most, about what has taken place."

The warning unsettled Finch. However, he knew it was directed at those who actually had people they trusted and cared about. Finch didn't have to worry so much about that.

"The first step against this unforeseen threat will be to reinforce the outposts near Outpost Gray. We can assume the enemy will be moving towards the capital. Qualified archers and knights will be selected to aid in defending the outposts. That should gain us some time to come up with a more substantial plan," Hayes explained.

"A death sentence," Jem murmured beside Finch. Fortunately, Hayes didn't overhear him. Finch knew that Hayes would never willingly send men to their deaths.

"You're dismissed," Hayes told them, shuffling the papers lying on the table into order.

Finch caught Hayes's eye. He'd have to seek out the battle master at some point and ask him some questions. Why had Finch been included in this meeting in the first place? What made him trustworthy when he'd worked so hard to be taken from his position as castle archer and thrown to the rangers instead?

So many questions bounced around Finch's head that he had trouble seeing straight. He wanted to get out of the war room and find somewhere quiet to think. Fate had other plans for him. Before Finch could escape the room, Terin stepped into his path. Finch was ready to ignore him and leave anyway but Terin moved with him, blocking him from exiting.

"Stop," Terin commanded.

Finch wanted to ignore the direct order but the king and Hayes were still present as well as the stranger who was watching the interaction closely. Finch took a deep breath and faced Terin head-on.

"What?" Finch asked, trying to keep the anger from his voice.

"I'm not sure why you were invited to this meeting, Finch Caraway," Terin growled, "but I know it was a mistake. That mistake will soon be remedied. You don't have to concern yourself with coming up with a plan because you won't be attending the next meeting."

"Hayes made it clear that I was invited on purpose!"

"Hayes doesn't know anything about you or who you really are."

"And you do?"

"I know you should have been sent to that outpost. You would have been best used as cannon fodder for the enemy with the disappointment you've turned out to be."

Something in Finch snapped. He took a step closer to Terin. Finch, like his commander, was below average height. He still leaned so close that only a few inches were between their faces.

"I *know* the reason I was invited to this meeting," Finch hissed. "It's because Hayes knows I'm capable. I wonder why you were invited?"

Terin grabbed hold of Finch's collar. His reaction was so quick that it caught Finch off guard. Finch flinched in surprise. A short burst of terror made him close his eyes for a second, expecting the worst. He quickly pulled himself together and slapped the hands at his collar away. Terin growled at Finch to come back but Finch was already out the door.

Outside the war room, Dorian paced the hallway. He caught sight of Finch and approached him.

"What's going on? Why were you and the others invited to that meeting? What was it about?" Dorian's questions came rapid-fire.

Finch felt his head pounding. He kept walking and Dorian was left to follow after him.

"Why weren't you invited to the meeting?" Finch asked.

"I don't know," Dorian admitted. "It was driving me crazy wondering what was going on though. What happened anyway?"

Finch was about to tell his best friend everything. He glanced back to make sure Terin wasn't following after him and instead caught sight of the strange young man exiting the war room. The man fixed Finch with a stern look. The action reminded Finch of the king's command for absolute secrecy. He shut his mouth.

"I can't talk about it," he told Dorian. "It's nothing you need to worry about."

Dorian frowned, clearly not buying it. He didn't press the issue, though Finch had a feeling he'd ask about it again later. He realized his friend must have been excluded from the meeting because he lacked seniority at the castle. It seemed a foolish reason to Finch, one that suddenly made him angry at Hayes and the king. Why leave someone like Dorian, talented and logical, out of the meeting but include Terin? Why was Terin allowed to maintain his position despite the conflicts he constantly created? Finch knew the reason; it was the same reason he hadn't been allowed to run off to the rangers. Their talent couldn't be squandered, despite who they were and how they acted. The similarity between his own situation and Terin's made Finch feel sick.

"Come on," Finch told his friend, "let's get out of here. I've had enough thinking for one day."

CHAPTER 18

Ruena lingered in a corridor just outside the war room. The hallway was positioned so she could see the door but anyone exiting the room wouldn't notice her. The shadows covered her position well. Besides, who would question her wandering around the castle? She was the king's niece after all. It had been troublesome to get alone. She'd had to send her maid, Vesta, on an "errand" to obtain the precious privacy. Vesta had eyed her suspiciously when instructed to hunt down some rose petals for Ruena's evening bath. Ruena wasn't prone to indulging in luxuries but she'd had to find something to get rid of Vesta. She knew Vesta meant well, she was only doing her job as Ruena's companion and escort. In fact, Vesta had exceeded the requirements of her job and become a friend to Ruena. However, no matter how much Ruena enjoyed the quiet girl's company, she couldn't allow Vesta to overhear the conversation she was about to have.

Once she was alone, it was simple enough for Ruena to sneak into a dimly lit hallway beside the war room so she could wait for Cal to arrive. Ruena watched as knights, archers, and advisors slowly filtered out of the war room, murmuring among themselves. A lone knight stood waiting outside the door to the room. He'd been there a while, pacing back and forth as if waiting for someone. Eventually, an archer joined him and the two proceeded down the hallway. A moment later, Cal's figure appeared silhouetted. Ruena took one look at his face and felt her heart drop to her feet. "It's bad, isn't it?"

Cal only nodded.

Cal had been like a brother to her since he'd come to the castle to serve as a spy. He'd been welcoming to a lonely, scared girl who'd felt lost in the massive, cold castle. He didn't often show his worry so plainly on his face. Whatever had happened, was nothing to take lightly.

He moved to stand hidden in the shadows, positioned across from her in the narrow hall. "Freiwade has a mage," he said. Nothing else needed to be said. That was bad enough.

Ruena had heard rumors. She'd gone to see the hysteric knight in the infirmary herself, though she hadn't questioned the poor man. Ruena knew her uncle was worried. Now, she knew why. Freiwade had a mage. Ruena's heart tightened and twisted with dread. A small part of her wished Cal hadn't told her. Now she couldn't hide from the awful truth. More than that, she felt a responsibility to do something about it and a helplessness to fulfill that duty. One day she would be queen. She had a duty to her people to protect them and lead them even in times of war and terror. But she was only one person and a woman no less, how could she lead them if no one wanted to follow her?

It was why she had to hide in a dark hallway

to receive such crucial and devastating news. It was why the spymaster had to tell her the affairs of the kingdom in secret. The advisors and nobles didn't accept Ruena as the rightful heir. She was not only a woman but also not the king's child. Things would have been better if her uncle had produced a direct heir but Rupert's wife, Trinity died young and barren. The brokenhearted king had never remarried, despite the consequences that had for the kingdom. The nobility didn't outright deny Ruena's right as heir but she knew she had plenty of enemies waiting to strike after her uncle's death. They acted civil and courteous around her but she knew they would turn on her like a pack of blood-thirsty jackals. Duke Heirson was example enough of that. He'd been trying to worm his way into her good graces since he arrived at the castle. She could only pray that God would protect her from such unseen threats.

Cal, unlike the others, knew that if she was to rule, she had to be kept informed of what was happening in the kingdom. He loyally reported everything to her, even the matters in which the advisors and generals refused to involve her. She waited for him to compose his thoughts, knowing he would tell her the rest of what was discussed in the meeting in due time.

"Freiwade has a mage," he repeated as if he, himself, could not accept it. "Mage Clifton claims that the man has more power than any mage before him. It's a wicked sort of power that doesn't come from God but from an evil source. Clifton isn't sure if he and Corin could stand against it. Hayes and the king have gathered together some of the greatest and most trusted strategists of the kingdom to come up with a plan but I don't have high hopes. The man was able to destroy an entire outpost and 100 men by himself. Imagine what he could do with an army backing him up."

Ruena shivered. Worry crept up her spine like a snake. It wasn't just worry for herself but also for the kingdom. Most of all, she worried for Corin. She hardly knew him but she couldn't bear the idea of the self-conscious and kind young man facing off against an evil force such as Freiwade's mage.

"Does Corin know?" she asked Cal.

Cal sighed. Was that annoyance she detected in his tone? "Clifton is keeping the news from him, probably to avoid scaring him off. It's exasperating. He and the king are coddling Corin. He'll never rise to the challenge and the expectations laid on him at this rate."

"I've talked with Corin," Ruena objected. "I know why Clifton has decided to keep this from him. He's not ready. He might very well run if he knows about the enemy mage. He hasn't accepted his position yet or the power that comes with it. He's afraid and confused. Knowing about this would only make things worse at the moment. He needs time. I'm... I'm worried about him."

"Ruena," Cal's tone was full of warning, "Corin is still an unknown. We don't know where his loyalties lie. He's been pulled away from his home and everything he knows. He's dangerous and, at the moment, his emotions are volatile. You can't fully trust him. You might get hurt if you do."

Ruena felt strangely defensive at Cal's words.

She knew he was only being protective as he always was, but she didn't like how he talked about Corin. "I know hurt, Cal. I don't think Corin will hurt me. What really hurts is not being able to convince him that he matters and that he's welcome in the castle. He doesn't believe his power is a gift from God. Until he does, he'll never find his place. He's been hurt in the past too. I can tell."

Cal released a long breath. "Your heart is too soft, Ruena. You've always been one to take in the outcasts."

Ruena smiled fondly. "It's because I am one. I'll never truly fit in anywhere. I'm not a princess. I wasn't born in the castle. I might rule but I'll never be the king that everyone wants. I'm an outcast just like him. Besides, you can't say much. You might pretend to be a distant and practical leader but I've seen you with Lark and Dusk. You care about them deeply. They're just as much outcasts as Corin and I. And I know how you treat me too. You worry about me like an overprotective brother."

Cal leaned his head against the wall and gazed at the ceiling high above him. "You're right. You are like a sister to me, Ruena. You remind me of Elizabet."

Elizabet, the younger sister whom Cal had lost. That loss was the reason Cal had come to the castle and joined the spies. Elizabet would have been younger than Ruena if she were still alive. The girl had died in a border skirmish between Freiwade and Ashnah. She'd been five at the time, an innocent caught in the violence and killed amid the chaos. It was a reminder of the casualties of war and the innocent bystanders who paid the price for it. It had led Cal to seek out a position as a knight. He'd soon proved that his talents were better suited elsewhere. His intelligence was unmatched among the other knights in training. He was skilled with knives and staying hidden during practice skirmishes. He was an expert at hand-to-hand combat. Most impressive was that he had somehow managed to memorize the names of every town and outpost in Ashnah and Freiwade in the space of a year and he could predict where an enemy might stage an attack by just glancing at a map. His skills were unorthodox and the king and his generals had soon taken notice. They'd recruited Cal as a spy. Cal, hurt from the loss of his sister and eager to serve his kingdom, quickly accepted. He'd become the youngest spymaster the kingdom had ever known. He'd managed to gather information in the most honest and harmless way possible, determined not to sacrifice his morality while serving his kingdom. It was all because of his dedication to his sister, Elizabet. It was an honor for Ruena to fill that void in his life.

"You warn me that I'll only get hurt, but you don't think about that when you take in outcasts. You treat others with kindness despite the losses and hurt you've felt," she told him. "I'll keep reaching out to Corin just as you reach out to those around you. I'm not afraid of being hurt."

"I couldn't stop you if I tried," was his only response.

Ruena decided it was time to steer the conversation back to the problem at hand. "What do *you* think about the enemy mage and the threat he poses?"

"I'm worried. I'm not convinced that Corin or Clifton will be able to stand against the threat. No regular human stands a chance. The knight who gave the report said that the outpost was decimated. There was nothing left, Ruena, not even a weed. It was as if everything that was living, every person, every animal, every seed of grass, was dead."

Ruena stared at him. He looked stricken. She reached out and touched his hand, clasped it for a moment in a show of support before releasing it again. This threat was bad. It was worse than anything Ashnah had faced before. Could they stand against it? She wasn't sure. However, she did know one thing.

"We have God on our side, Cal. If He wills it, we will prevail."

Cal swallowed, his throat bobbing with the motion. "I know. We have no hope without Him."

That wasn't a small hope, not at all. God was greater than any threat they might face. Ruena found that she wasn't afraid. She trusted that God would give them strength and protect them. No person, no mage, could stand against God.

"Maybe you're right," Cal told her. "Maybe it is important that Corin starts to step into his role as a mage before he gets involved in this. I think he might be our only chance at victory. He has God's power in him. He's been blessed with a weapon more powerful than swords and cannons, fire and pestilence, and a defense greater than the strongest wall or the deepest moat."

"If only he would accept it and allow God to use him," Ruena murmured.

"I guess the only thing we can do is pray and be patient," Cal agreed. "That's no easy task in a time of war."

Ruena could tell Cal had finished his report and she didn't want to linger and raise suspicion. She turned to leave.

Cal touched her arm to stop her. "Ruena, remember, many of the nobles, especially Duke Heirson, will rebel if they hear this news. They don't think King Rupert is powerful enough to rule during times of war and they don't want you to take the throne."

Ruena was getting tired of the snake-like nobility. "Their problem is that they don't look close enough. They see kindness as a weakness. That's why they look down on my uncle and I. They don't see the strength underneath."

"Not everyone is like that. I'm not. I know that King Rupert is the best ruler we can have during this time and someday you'll be the ruler we all need. But be careful around Heirson."

Ruena nodded. She didn't tell him about the duke and his son Dresden's attentions the last couple of nights. She could and would handle it. It would only cause Cal to unnecessarily worry about her.

"Thank you," she told him. "But first, we have to survive this war. And Corin, Corin is the key."

CHAPTER 19

As Cal headed for the king's room, he wondered vaguely if he was in trouble. It was rare for him to meet the king in such a private space. Cal reported to the king often but usually in a meeting room surrounded by the few advisors and generals who knew about Ashnah's spy force. Cal rarely, if ever, met with the monarch alone. Whatever the reason for this meeting, it was a sensitive one. Cal tried not to overly worry as he wound up the spiraling staircase of the castle's northeast tower towards the king's personal rooms. He passed by Ruena's chamber as he went, and then picked up his pace, not wanting to be late. His heart was pounding from exertion and dread by the time he reached the king's door, knocked, and entered.

The room was as Cal had remembered it from his first and only visit years ago when Barton, the old spymaster, had brought Cal to the king and proposed stepping down from his position and establishing Cal as spymaster. The memory brought a fond and calming feeling to Cal's chest. He wondered how Barton was getting on, somewhere undisclosed in the countryside. Cal imagined his old mentor sitting by the fire of a modest cottage, perhaps a few sheep grazing outside. It was strange to think of the old spymaster in such a fashion. The thought served to calm Cal's racing heart.

Inside the king's room, there was only King Rupert and Sir Hayes. The men sat at a small table as equals. A third chair was pulled out for Cal.

"Cal," King Rupert greeted. The greeting wasn't warm or cold, only business-like.

King Rupert was a friendly man by nature. His severe expression caused a shiver of unease to ripple through Cal's body. His feelings of warmth fled. This meeting was undeniably serious; it was no social gathering.

"Your Majesty," Cal responded.

"Have a seat," Hayes told Cal.

Cal did as he was told, though he had a feeling he'd rather be standing for the present conversation. He waited for his superiors to speak.

"I'm sure you're wondering why you've been called here to report," the king stated.

Cal nodded.

"We've called you here to talk about the spies," Hayes explained.

Cal stiffened. "I can assure you that Lark, Dusk, and I are doing everything in our power to do our duties, Your Majesty. We are working hard to learn more about the enemy."

"Not your spies, Cal," the king waved off Cal's objections. "We're referring to the enemy spies."

"Oh." Cal wasn't sure if he should be relieved or more worried than before. Certainly, it had made him anxious to think the king had objections against his spy force. However, the conversation about the enemy spies was doomed to be even more dire. Cal prepared himself for a berating. He had let the enemy spies hide in their midst for too long. He should have discovered their identities long ago. The fact that they still eluded him was a sore spot that was sure to be poked in this meeting.

"We're concerned about the spies," Hayes said calmly, seeming to sense Cal's growing unease. "We understand that you and your spies are doing the best you can to uncover their identities. I have also been keeping an eye on those under my command. Whoever this spy or spies are, they are talented at remaining unnoticed. The king and I understand that it's no easy task that has been placed on you, Cal."

"This meeting is not to rebuke you. Hayes and I only wish to discuss the matter. We must find a solution to this problem and discover the identity of these spies. I would like to debate some of the likely suspects."

Cal sighed in relief at the king's words. Good. He wasn't sure with all of the stresses pressing down on him from all directions that he could handle a reprimand on top of it. With Corin's arrival at the castle, the duke's visit, the constant threat of the enemy spies, and now an attack on Outpost Gray, Cal and his spies were spread thin.

"I'm more than happy to hear any ideas you might have," Cal replied. "My spies and I have a few suspects but the situation is constantly changing and throwing new individuals into suspicion."

"Do you have a criteria for suspecting someone?" Hayes asked, ever the tactician.

Cal nodded. Dusk had made sure of that. Dusk

had warned Cal early on that they needed a method to determine who was the most likely culprit and what behavior was suspicious enough to consider a person as a suspect.

"A person is considered a suspect when they meet one or more of the following criteria," Cal explained. "They should have a clear motive for working against the kingdom, the capability to deliver news to an outside source, respect or rank within the castle, and they must be in a role where they can gather key information."

"Unfortunately, that doesn't narrow things down much in a place like Castille Castle," Hayes stated.

Cal couldn't help but agree. The criteria was good but not good enough. The majority of the occupants of the castle met one or more of the criteria. And motives were the most difficult to determine. Someone trusted in all other regards could easily be hiding a strong motive to work against Ashnah.

"So, who are the primary suspects?" King Rupert asked.

"The spies and I suspect Duke Heirson of working against the kingdom but he doesn't have the ability to gather much of the information that is finding its way to the enemy."

"He might be working against King Rupert in an attempt to claim the throne for himself but I doubt he would go so far as to work with the enemy," Hayes added. "We should at least for now, set him aside as a suspected spy. He's sure to make trouble for us eventually but I doubt it will be in such a traitorous fashion."

Cal and the king silently agreed.

"He's bitter because he preferred my brother as king," Rupert stated. "Now, he'll do almost anything to ensure I don't remain on the throne. He's always been hungry for power, even when we were children. But I believe he is loyal to Ashnah, if not Ashnah's current ruler."

Cal didn't admit that his reasoning against the duke being a spy was attributed more to the man's lack of capability, than his lack of will.

"Are there any of your own that you suspect, Hayes?" Cal asked the battle master. Hayes knew his men better than anyone, even Cal. If there was the chance a spy could be hiding among the knights, Hayes would stand the best chance of knowing.

Hayes looked conflicted. "It's hard to say. The knights of Ashnah are the most skilled and loyal in the kingdom. They were all carefully selected and they have undergone strict testing and training. I would hesitate to suspect any of them, especially under your criteria. There are a few that would be privy to important information, the kind of information that has found its way to Freiwade. But their frequent training and duties would prevent them from delivering information to a source outside of the castle. If one of the knights was a spy, they would have to be working with another. The real problem of the matter is motive. Without knowing the motive, it's impossible to know whether to suspect someone. To the best of my knowledge, none of my knights have the motive to act against Ashnah."

"I've looked into each knight before they were accepted to the royal guard," Cal added. "None of their backgrounds raise suspicion. Of course, information can be falsified, but if that is the case, then it took a skilled hand to do so."

"What about Commander Terin?" Hayes asked.

The room fell into silence.

"He is the commander of my archers," King Rupert finally said. "I know you dislike the man, Hayes. Frankly, I do too. But his skills speak for themselves. He may be thoroughly unpleasant but I believe he is loyal to Ashnah."

"It isn't unwise to suspect him," Cal said. "He has openly spoken out that he thinks the king is weak. He isn't afraid to make his opinion known. He thinks King Rupert cannot lead during a time of war. I'm not sure if he would go so far as to act out on any of those claims but it's worth keeping an eye on him."

Hayes looked displeased by the answer. Cal could understand the dislike Hayes had for Terin. However, Cal also suspected there was something deeper about the grudge the two commanders had for each other. Cal wasn't ready to discount that Terin could be trouble. However, the chances of him being one of the spies was slim.

"There is one other suspect who must be considered," King Rupert said.

Cal looked at the man, expectantly.

The king hesitated a moment before speaking. "Lark."

"Lark!" Cal objected vehemently.

Why Lark? Lark was one of Cal's own spies. Surely his spies were above suspicion. Cal's heart pounded with the accusation. It felt as if the king was accusing Cal himself of treason.

"Cal," Hayes said calmly, "stop and think for a moment. What do we know about Lark? She appeared at the castle suddenly. She wouldn't reveal where she was from, why she had come to Castille, or even what her real name was. She refused to tell us anything about herself and her background. We accepted her as a spy, perhaps unwisely. Even Barton had his doubts about training her. Have you looked into her past?"

Cal swallowed hard. Yes, he had tried to learn more about her but perhaps he hadn't tried as hard as he should have. He'd felt like it would be intruding into a personal life that she clearly wanted to keep hidden. When he had looked into her past, he hadn't found anything. It was as if Lark had never existed at all. In a way, she hadn't. The Lark that Cal knew down to the simple detail of her name was an illusion. What Lark showed others was an entirely falsified persona. In reality, he knew nothing about who she was. But he knew, he *knew* that she couldn't be an enemy spy.

"No," Cal told the king, trying to keep his voice civil. "Not Lark. I trust her. I would trust her with my life."

"Do you have good reason to?" the king asked.

"King Rupert is right, Cal," Hayes said. "You have no real reason to trust Lark. You know nothing about her. She has willfully hidden every detail about herself from us. She refuses to reveal anything about her past. She fits all of your criteria for determining a suspect. She has the ability to sneak out of the castle, she is in a position of importance within the castle, and she is privy to key information that has been leaking to Freiwade. We don't know her motives but we do know she is hiding them from us."

"She wouldn't," Cal said lamely.

"We don't know that," King Rupert reminded him. "We don't know what she would or wouldn't do."

"Just think about it, Cal," Hayes said. "Can you really trust her?"

Cal wanted to say yes. He wanted to argue against everything they had said. But… some dark corner of his mind urged him to consider their words. The thought of Lark being a traitor was like a weed that once it had taken root, dug deeper, and spread throughout the garden of his mind, suffocating every good thing. Cal couldn't ignore the words. And a sickly distrust wormed its way into his heart. Who could he trust? Could he trust Lark? As the king and Hayes said, he knew nothing about her and who she truly was. She kept secrets from him, there was no denying that. How much did she keep from him? Was she a traitor? Cal's heart reared against the idea but his mind refused to cast it aside so quickly.

He knew that this meeting had changed everything. From that moment forward, like it or not, he knew he would always doubt her just a little. He would never be able to go back to the way things had been before when he had blindly trusted her.

Hayes's words echoed in Cal's mind as he left the room, feeling sick and confused. "Can you really trust her?"

CHAPTER 20

Corin was disobeying orders. At least, that's how he saw it. They weren't orders per se but he was shirking the only responsibility he'd been given. When he woke up, he couldn't bring himself to attend his lesson with Clifton. It was more difficult and nerve-wracking to forgo his lesson than anything Corin had attempted to do in the past. He'd never been so bold in ignoring the rules before. He knew Clifton and everyone else would be disappointed in him and he could get in serious trouble because of it. Still, he couldn't do it, not today. He pulled himself out of bed at dawn after a restless sleep, filled with nightmares of losing control of his abilities and causing all manner of catastrophes. He hurriedly dressed himself in the threadbare outfit he'd come to the castle in.

The previous lesson had snapped something in Corin. The rope had been fraying ever since he'd arrived at the castle. Learning how to use his magic was the last thread to break. It made everything real. He was a mage; he was really a mage. He could create a light in the palm of his hand or form a shield at his arm. It was easy and natural and it felt right. He couldn't accept it. There was no way that the only thing he was talented in was the one thing he didn't care about. He wasn't a natural, he wasn't a prodigy, and he wouldn't surpass Clifton. He was just Corin and he was notoriously bad at *everything.* Magic was no different, even if it was a gift from God.

He wouldn't go to his lessons. If he were being honest with himself, he was a little afraid he'd enjoy it. It had felt nice to be good at something but he didn't want to be good at magic. He wanted to go back to the way things were. He wanted to be a knight. That was what he knew and pathetic as he might be at sword fighting, at least it didn't have the potential to destroy like his magic did. He wasn't too proud to admit that he was terrified of the abilities that he possessed. He didn't want to be at the castle in the first place. He knew his position was tenuous. It wouldn't last long. It couldn't. Nothing good ever did. He refused to get comfortable or become at ease in such a place.

What about your honor? This is your duty, a tiny voice in the back of his head whispered.

That, Corin knew, was the ultimate dilemma. When he'd trained as a squire under Burke, he'd taken an oath. He was duty-bound to serve God and kingdom in whatever job was set to him, even if that task was something Corin was terrified of doing. He knew he wasn't the right person to hold such power. He wished God had chosen someone else. Corin sat on the edge of his bed. What was he doing? He should be getting ready for his lesson. He was a mage now, whether he liked it or not. He was being selfish and ungrateful. All he'd thought about since Burke and Clifton told him he was a mage was himself. This, none of it, was really about him. His duty now was as a mage.

"God," Corin voiced aloud, feeling silly for doing so, "I could really use some guidance right now. I'm not like Burke. I'm not good at praying or seeking You and I can't comprehend the idea of You listening to *me*. But I don't know what else to do. I don't want this. I don't want to be a mage. I know it's selfish but I don't think I can do this. What if I mess up? What if I hurt someone? I just want to go back to the way things were. If this is a gift from You, I have to admit it doesn't feel like a gift. But if it is, could you please just give it to someone else, someone more capable?"

Great, first he'd ranted to Ruena, now he was ranting to God. Corin felt wretched. As he expected, there was no answer. Would God ever answer him? Burke had talked about answered prayers on more than one occasion, some of the other squires had too. Maybe Corin was just the type of person God didn't bother with. He sighed heavily and shoved himself up from the bed. He missed the battle school. He missed cold, miserable Nevara, and Sir Burke even when he was yelling at him. He missed the obnoxious squires, all of them, even Phineas York. Corin moved to his bedroom window and looked outside. He couldn't see the castle garrison from here. He wished he could see the knights training, just to remember old times. And to see what he was missing.

Why couldn't he?

The garrison wasn't far from the castle, it was still on the royal grounds. Corin could easily sneak away and watch the knights train from a distance. No one even needed to know he was there. He could see what he was missing and what he might have become if not for the magic. He attached his sword to his belt and then slipped into the hallway. He took the stairs quickly and bowed his head to avoid anyone seeing his face. Servants bustled about preparing for the day. Fortunately, Corin didn't spot anyone he knew. They seemed to know him though. Although he was in his old clothes instead of the garments of a mage, he was starting to become a familiar fixture in the castle. The servants parted for him as if they feared his touch was poisonous. They were afraid of him. That frightened Corin. He wanted to reassure them that he was harmless. He wasn't about to hurt them with magic or the sword hanging from his belt. He had a feeling it wouldn't do any good. Even he wasn't fully convinced he wouldn't suddenly explode. He was in a hurry anyway and it helped to not have anyone stop him for conversation. He wanted to be out of the castle before Clifton noticed he hadn't shown up for lessons.

The knights guarding the entrance of the castle didn't question him as he stepped past them. Corin tried to act as if he was meant to be there.

"Mage," one of the knights said, "don't venture outside the gates. It might not be safe for you."

Corin nodded. The warning was unsettling but he tried not to think too hard about it. Something bothered Corin about the knight's caution. Had the knights of the castle been instructed to keep Corin inside the castle grounds for his safety or to prevent any attempted escape? Corin was tempted to ask but instead, he headed for the garrison's training grounds. Once he was out of sight of the knights at the entrance, Corin raced across the open grounds. It didn't take him long to reach the garrison field and barracks. He surveyed the area to ensure that no one was watching him. All of the knights seemed to be inside the courtyard that lay in the middle of the barracks. Corin snuck through the open door to the courtyard and ducked behind a pillar to watch the knights train.

Castille Castle's garrison was set up much like the battle school in Nevara. In the center of the field was the courtyard where the knights would train. A covered outdoor hallway supported by pillars surrounded the whole place. Along the hallway were doors that led to barracks, washrooms, classrooms, and a dining hall that the knights would use when they didn't take meals at the castle. It felt like home to Corin, though in reality, it was much more expansive and impressive than Nevara's battle school. The pillar that Corin used as a hiding place offered him a perfect view of the courtyard while preventing him from being seen.

He could see the knights training. It was incredible to watch them. They were the best knights in the kingdom and it was obvious why. They sliced and hacked with such force that they pushed each other back. There were real swords in their hands, sharpened to wicked points. They possessed remarkable control, pausing when a strike was about to make contact and halting the blade before it could connect with flesh. The sparring was incomparable to the bouts in Nevara. These knights were experienced and filled with an innate talent for the craft of swordsmanship.

Sir Hayes stood off to the side, shouting encouragements and instructions.

"Block it! Block it!" he yelled at the knight currently on the defensive. "Don't let him past your defenses!"

Corin leaned forward to get a better look at the men. He pressed himself against the pillar, standing on the tips of his toes. His heart pounded with excitement and his ears rang with the clamor of clashing swords. Unconsciously, he started rooting for one of the knights, the smaller of the two. He winced with every strike the knight barely blocked with his sword. He had to refrain from cheering when the man got in a few good hits of his own. Corin soon realized however that the smaller knight was incredibly outmatched. The taller of the two knights stood out. He was brilliant in his maneuvering, fast, and strong as an ox. The other knights who stood by watching knew he was sure to be the victor. They all cheered for him.

"Dorian! Dorian!" they yelled.

The knight embodied everything Corin had hoped he would one day achieve in his training. His skill was unrivaled. But the most surprising thing about him was his humility and friendliness. When he inevitably won against his opponent, to the raucous cheers of his companions, he extended a hand to help the other knight to his feet.

"It was just a stroke of luck," Dorian told the defeated knight. "I'm sure when we fight again, you'll beat me."

The defeated knight grinned and took the proffered hand gratefully. "Sure, Dorian, sure."

The knights who'd been watching surged towards Dorian, clapping him on the back and congratulating him for his victory. Dorian waved off their praise. They all seemed to adore him. He only nodded humbly and approached Sir Hayes to receive the feedback that he seemingly craved.

"Good overall, Dorian. Keep an eye on your left thrust. You stamp your foot before you strike. It's a dead giveaway. Otherwise, you're improving. Just remember, there's always room to be better."

Dorian took Hayes's comments gratefully and thanked the battle master before wiping a gloved hand across his sweat-soaked forehead.

"Go, cool yourself off," Hayes instructed Dorian and the other knight who had been battling. "But first, I have an important announcement for all of you."

The knights all stood in rapt attention, hanging on to Hayes's every word.

"With the growing trouble at the border, it has been decided that the outposts along the border should be reinforced with capable and skilled knights to bolster the forces already there. Several of you will be selected to fill that role. Trenton, O'Hair, Kellen, and Dorian, you four will be sent to Outpost Verin." Hayes continued to name other knights who would be sent to other outposts.

Two of the knights in the courtyard looked at each other and shifted uncomfortably but said nothing. Corin noticed that those two were among those not selected. Hayes spoke with severity and a sense of dread settled in the air of the courtyard. When he was finished speaking, Hayes dismissed Dorian and the other knight then called for two others to step forward to spar.

Corin watched as Dorian exited the courtyard

down one of the hallways before he drew his attention back to the other knights who were still fighting.

Corin pictured himself fighting among them. He could imagine himself dressed in chain mail as they were, with his sword gleaming as he fended off attacks. It was the same dream that he'd had for as long as he could remember. Something was different about it this time. Now, he imagined himself with a glowing bronze shield on his arm, semi-translucent but stronger than any real metal. Corin grimaced at the thought. A realization was starting to occur to him and he couldn't ignore it. Even if he still wanted to be a knight, he couldn't fully go back to the way things had been before. He'd always be a mage whether he was at the castle or not. Now that he knew the truth, he couldn't ignore it.

He needed to get to his lesson with Clifton. He never should have left the castle in the first place. He shouldn't have avoided his responsibilities no matter how he felt about them. Corin was about to push away from the pillar when he heard a voice behind him.

"What are you doing here?"

Corin slowly turned, feeling incredibly guilty. Now he'd be in trouble, big trouble. He turned to face the speaker and saw that it was the same knight who had just been fighting, Dorian. Corin sputtered, trying to think of an excuse for his actions.

"I... I," Corin couldn't think of any way to explain why he was hiding behind a pillar and watching the knights train.

Dorian's eyebrows drew together in concentration. "Wait a moment. You're the new mage, aren't you?"

Corin hesitantly nodded. He wished he didn't have to reveal to the knight who he was but he felt no other choice.

"What are you doing here?" Dorian repeated, sounding less angry than before and more confused than anything.

"I'm just…" again Corin couldn't find a suitable answer.

"Can I help you with something?" Dorian asked, seemingly eager to be of assistance. He didn't look scared of Corin. Instead, he seemed almost eager to talk with him.

Dorian's gaze dropped to the sword hanging at Corin's side. He pointed to it, "Are you a fighter too? Are you skilled with the sword?" There was a genuine curiosity in Dorian's questions.

"I'm not very good at it," Corin admitted. "I was training as a knight before I came here. Someday I still hope to be one. I guess that's a ridiculous dream now. I'll never be as good as you."

A change swept over Dorian. The suspicion disappeared from his expression and was replaced with a jovial smile. "I'm not that good, not like Sir Hayes," Dorian remarked. "I've only reached the point I'm at because of a lot of practice. If you practice, you'll get better too. I'm a little surprised that you would want to practice at all since you're a mage."

"I don't want to be a mage," Corin admitted bitterly. "I would rather be a knight."

"Being a mage is an important job. Surely, you want to get better at your magic like you would with a sword. Are you very good at using your magic yet?"

Corin didn't want to talk about his magic but he

also didn't want the conversation with Dorian to end. Dorian was one of the few people who was willing to talk with him. "It's a little unsettling how easily it all is coming to me. Unlike my practicing with the sword, the magic feels natural. Even Clifton is surprised at the pace I'm learning."

"What are you learning? What can you do with your magic?"

Corin shrugged. "I've only been shown how to create a light in my hand and a shield on my arm so far. There was an accident at the battle school before I came here so I'm not in any big hurry to learn anything dangerous."

"An accident?"

Corin nodded bleakly. "I accidentally threw another squire into the wall. He... he nearly died."

Dorian's eyes went wide not with fear exactly but with unease. Corin wished he hadn't said anything. He decided it was time to steer the conversation back to Dorian.

"It was amazing to watch you fight. You're very talented."

Dorian brushed off the compliment. "I just do my best. Like I said, it's all a matter of practice. I haven't been here long so I feel like I have to prove myself. But what about you, Corin? What do you think about the castle and your position here?"

Corin rubbed his arm. "I don't know. It's all a little overwhelming. I still don't know where I fit in."

Dorian took a step towards him. "Well, if you ever need someone to show you around the place, I've gotten pretty good at figuring my way around. I could help you train with your sword too if you like. I know that it can be lonely here but it doesn't have to be. You seem like a nice person, Corin. Although things may have taken a different direction, I think you would have made a good knight."

Corin knew that he wasn't a knight though. He had dreamed of being one but now he knew there was another course for his life. Watching the knights train had only proven to him that he didn't fit in among them. The problem was that he didn't feel like he fit in as a mage either.

"No, I know I'm a mage. But thanks anyway. I'd like to train with you sometime. It would be nice to have a friend in this castle."

Dorian grinned. "It would be my honor."

CHAPTER 21

Finch felt strangely uneasy. It was an uneasiness that, try as he might, he could not explain. Dread crept up his throat and settled there, suffocating him. It became unbearable to carry on with his daily tasks and pretend that his insides weren't tearing themselves apart with an unknowable terror. But that was what he had to do. He went about his day as usual, waking, eating, and even performing his duties as a king's archer. He even put up with Terin's insults and glares.

It wasn't until the afternoon, just when he was heading towards the great hall for his midday meal, that a reason appeared for his inner turmoil. Finch was approaching the great hall when he caught sight of Dorian heading in the same direction. He ran a few steps to catch up to his friend.

"Dorian!" he called out.

Dorian looked up and, catching sight of Finch, slowed so Finch could catch up with him. Finch realized immediately that something was off about Dorian. The knight seemed strangely subdued, not quite melancholy but certainly not as cheerful as he usually was. The two friends walked a few steps together before Finch spoke.

"Is something wrong?"

Dorian seemed to shake a weight off his shoulders and straightened with a smile. "No," he said, a little too cheerfully. "Nothing's wrong."

"I don't believe you."

"Really?"

"You're too honest, Dorian, you couldn't keep a secret from me if you tried. Besides," Finch added as an afterthought, "you never let me get away with brooding over something. Spill it."

Dorian laughed softly and halted to the side of the door leading to the great hall. "It's nothing to worry about. I'm just a little surprised. Sir Hayes gave the announcement during our training today that he would be sending several knights to outposts around the border to bolster the forces there. I'm to be sent to Outpost Verin."

The dread that Finch had almost forgotten roared to a vicious new life. "What?"

"It's no big deal, really," Dorian reassured him. "Hayes says it will only be for a few weeks. It's more of a training exercise than anything."

But Finch knew it was no mere training exercise. Hayes was covering the outposts in preparation for another attack from the enemy mage. And Outpost Verin was the closest outpost to Gray which now lay in ruins. Dorian wasn't being sent on a training exercise; he was being sent to die. Finch felt the blood drain from his face and he reached out a hand to steady himself against the wall.

"What's wrong?" Dorian asked him. "You look like you're going to be sick."

Finch didn't answer. He couldn't answer. He'd been sworn to secrecy about the enemy mage and the attack on the outpost. But didn't Dorian deserve to know the truth? Finch opened his mouth to tell his friend everything, then stopped uncertainly. He felt a wave of anger rush over him and he hated Hayes and the king for demanding silence on the subject. Finch normally wasn't one to obey orders without question but in this case, he saw the necessity of it. If news got out that there was an enemy mage, then there would be mass panic. Besides, he couldn't tell Dorian. He couldn't tell Dorian that Hayes was sending him on a suicide mission.

Finch had been uneasy at Hayes's plan to bolster the ranks at the outposts but that had been before Dorian was selected to join the ranks. Now, Finch saw the idea as nothing short of cruel and inhumane. He had never thought that way about Hayes before but now Finch was filled with anger at the man he had so looked up to. How could Hayes do it? How could he send those knights to die? Finch couldn't stay wholly silent. If he didn't warn Dorian, it would be like he was sending his friend to his death.

"Dorian, maybe you shouldn't go, to the outpost I mean."

Dorian looked at him like he'd lost his mind. "What are you talking about? It's not a suggestion, Finch. It's an order. I have to go. Why shouldn't I?"

"Tell Hayes you're sick or request to be stationed at one of the other outposts. Ask to visit your family. Stage an injury during your next sparring match. Something. Anything. Just don't go."

Dorian put a hand on Finch's shoulder. Finch

realized he was shaking.

"Is something going on?" Dorian asked. "Does this have to do with that meeting? You can talk to me, Finch. Tell me what's wrong."

"I... it's just," Finch hesitated. "It's just, you know there's danger on the border. The conflict between Freiwade and Ashnah is getting serious. You'd be right on the precipice of the conflict."

"That's what being a knight is all about. Don't worry so much. I'll come back. It's only for a few weeks. I doubt Freiwade will attack during that time."

Finch wasn't so certain. If Dorian knew what Finch did, then he wouldn't be so nonchalant either. Finch felt that he was betraying his friend by not saying more but Dorian didn't give him the chance to add to his argument.

"Come on, let's go get something to eat. You're like a mother-hen worrying so much."

"You're my friend," Finch said with a lump in his throat, "aren't I supposed to worry about you."

Dorian laughed and Finch tried not to think of the fact that it might be the last time he ever heard that laugh again.

CHAPTER 22

Corin's next lesson began with a lecture of an entirely different sort.

"You must attend your lessons, Corin," Clifton scolded, sounding more fearful than angry. "I understand the difficulty of adapting to your new position and learning that you are a mage, but you must train and learn as much as you can. You must master your abilities. Besides, you can't just disappear with no warning. Anything could have happened to you. You could have been attacked. You must realize that your powers make you a target for enemies of Ashnah. Some in Ashnah itself see you as a threat. You have free reign of the castle grounds but you must not leave the area unattended."

"I never left the grounds," Corin reassured the mage. "I just wanted to see the garrison. I'm sorry."

Corin wasn't surprised at the scolding but he was surprised at the intense worry behind Clifton's words.

"I promise that it won't happen again," Corin said with sincerity, then added, "I'm sorry for any worry I might have caused."

Clifton sighed heavily and waved a hand

through the air in dismissal. "Just, please understand the situation you are in Corin. You're not a squire anymore."

"I know," Corin snapped a little hotly. He immediately regretted the sharp edge to his response and he bowed his head to look away from Clifton.

Clifton cleared his throat and ignored the outburst. "Now, onto the lesson. I have more to show you today."

Corin's throat went dry, wondering what Clifton had in store. He knew he had to start taking his training seriously. His trip to the garrison had shown him that. Like it or not, things could never be the same as before. He couldn't just stop being a mage. If he was doomed to that fate forever, then he'd better learn how to control his power.

While Clifton was moving around the room, looking for a book that he seemed to have lost, Will slid out from behind the desk and crossed over to Corin. Corin didn't look at the boy until he was standing right in front of him.

"What is it?" Corin asked quietly.

Will responded even more quietly. "Did you learn anything at the garrison?"

"The truth," Corin responded. "I can never be a knight, not like them. But I don't think I can do this either."

Will's expression turned serious. "You can and you will. You don't have to be perfect. You just have to try your best. You're still learning after all."

Corin studied Will and saw the sincerity in the boy's words. He smiled a little in gratitude. "I'll try."

Satisfied, Will crept back to the desk and was

back to work transcribing notes by the time Clifton had found his missing book.

Corin attacked the training with an energy and determination that he hadn't possessed before. He knew he couldn't hide from the fact that he was a mage forever. Still, every time he learned a new skill, he flinched away, remembering the accident with Phineas York. He felt like he was playing with fire. He feared that he was a danger to himself and others. It didn't help that everything came easily, too easily. Corin yearned for the past, the days spent training at the battle school, and the future promise of being a knight. Everything made more sense then. He followed Clifton's instructions regardless of how he felt. He knew he needed to prove himself and make up for the trouble he'd caused by missing the previous lesson. Clifton showed him several skills. The first was simple enough, a way to draw an object toward him.

"Just don't become lazy with this one," Clifton teased.

Corin wasn't intending to use it often. On his first attempt, the book he'd been trying to draw close flew across the room without hesitation and, instead of landing in Corin's outstretched hand, knocked him painfully on the forehead. He winced at the impact but even he wasn't prepared for the additional book that followed after the first, making contact at the same spot.

Will couldn't restrain a snicker of amusement. Corin glared at him.

"We'll have to work on restraint," Clifton mused. "It seems that you have no trouble in using the magic. Your gift is strong and the skills I've shown you so far are relatively simple. I want to make sure you can control your power and only use what is needed before we move on to more difficult magic. Sometimes, an excess of power in a simple command can cause unforeseen damage."

Corin didn't like that phrase, *unforeseen damage*. He felt like those two words could have summed up his entire experience as a mage thus far. Corin practiced the summoning skill a few more times until he managed to draw near a single book that landed neatly in his hand. Then, Clifton moved on to other techniques. He showed Corin how to create a small raincloud in the air, a useful skill for agriculture according to Clifton. Corin managed that ability better than the summoning and they quickly moved on.

The next piece of magic that Clifton showed Corin was how to stitch fabric together again.

"This can't be used on living fibers such as skin, as far as Master Loch and I discovered," Clifton warned him.

"Why not?" Corin asked as he mended the torn fabric under Clifton's watchful eye.

"Although magic is used to create or mend, life is an entirely different matter. Life is made by God and tampering with it is something a mage should try to avoid at all costs."

"What about healing someone?" Corin asked. "Wouldn't that be helping with God's creation, not tampering with it?"

"There is a time and season for everything, Corin. God gives and He takes away. If a person is dying, though we may not understand it, that is God's will as well. Some in Biblical times were able to heal those who were sick or injured but that is because they were gifted with abilities to do so. Did they ever once take credit for that power? No. They gave all the glory to God. They used prayer to heal and mend, not personal power. Your magic is the same way. You are given certain abilities much like some are given brilliant singing voices. However, the things that directly interfere with God's creation, only He can alter those things. If a person is ill or dying, He must be the one to heal them. He may do so through you, but your magic will not be responsible for it."

Corin felt puzzled. He shook his head. "I still don't understand."

"Neither do I, really," Clifton laughed. "The extent of God's power is incomprehensible to man. Magic is similar. Magic is a gift from God and I'm afraid Neos Loch and myself could not fully understand it. Despite your talent, Corin, I doubt you'll be any more successful. The important thing is to listen to God's instruction in your life. He will guide you and make use of your abilities. You must trust in Him. That includes the matter of mending. Trust in His will for human life and keep your hands clean of it unless He instructs you otherwise."

Corin nodded but he felt dissatisfied with Clifton's explanation. He'd never felt God specifically leading him or instructing him before. How would he even know if God was trying to tell him something? Corin didn't have long to ponder over the dilemma because Clifton quickly moved on to the next skill, eager to proceed given Corin's rapid progress.

"The next ability is called *grounding*. Quite

simply, it steadies you. If you use it right, you should be able to walk around and no one will be able to take your feet from under you or put you off balance. Be warned though, that it's difficult to move around while using it. You feel heavy. So, it's best not to use it in a fight. Neos Loch believed that its practical purpose was to give men firm purchase on ships while at sea. They wouldn't be knocked back and forth with each wave."

Corin managed the ability easily enough though he hated the feeling of heaviness as if he was filled with lead. Clifton even called for Will to try to push Corin over to no avail. Corin imagined himself on a ship at sea and could see the practicality of such an ability in that scenario. He realized that each skill that Clifton had shown him had a practical purpose and application. The magic was useful for agriculture, tailoring, and seafaring.

Once again, Clifton ran out of material before the allotted time for the lesson had ended.

"You're a natural at all of it," Clifton announced. "You've demonstrated more talent with magic in your first few days as an official mage than I did during my entire first year."

What the older mage didn't realize was that Corin possessed something that Clifton didn't. Corin had spent his entire life trying to succeed at something he was terrible at. Now that he'd found something he excelled at, he had the motivation to continue in his training. If he could only wrap his mind around the idea that magic would be an advantage, not a danger, then nothing would be able to stop him.

"I know!" Clifton announced, raising a single finger in the air. "You haven't seen the town yet. Since you shouldn't go alone, I'll give you a tour."

"What?" Corin couldn't find any other word to express his surprise. He wanted to argue that he didn't particularly care about the town. Clifton's earlier words about danger made him hesitant to venture outside the castle grounds any time soon. He didn't want to be around so many people, all of whom were likely to fix him with that penetrating and judgmental stare that he so hated. He'd chosen to wear one of the tunics the castle provided him with that morning and even one that was a brighter shade of green. Corin deeply regretted that decision now. But he was a little curious and Clifton seemed so excited at his idea that Corin couldn't find it in himself to object.

"Will should come too," Corin suggested, suddenly wanting the boy present so he wouldn't have to make conversation alone with Clifton.

"I have to get to my lessons with Master Murdoch in the library," Will said apologetically. "I'll see you this afternoon to go through Clifton's books again."

Corin wanted to object further but he couldn't think of anything to say, so he had to assent to Clifton's suggestion. Clifton grabbed his cloak, finely cut with embroidered symbols on the edges, and made for the door. Corin had no choice but to follow him.

Corin followed behind Clifton like a confused child as they wound down the tower, passed through several hallways, and headed for the castle's exit. As they drew near the great hall, Corin could hear voices raised in argument. He tried not to look but he couldn't help himself. An archer, dressed haphazardly in random portions of his uniform and another, older archer with a bright red badge on the sleeve of his coat, denoting his rank as commander, faced each other, both looking ready to fight.

"You have no right to deny me this," the younger archer objected.

"What part of me being your commander do you not comprehend Caraway?" the older responded.

"You had no objections to sending me to Outpost Gray. I know you intended to ship me off to die there. Why won't you agree to station me at Outpost Verin?"

"That is *my* decision to make. Not yours. It would do you well to learn to obey orders. Why is it that you'd want to be sent there anyway? You may be incompetent but you know as well as I do that those knights and archers are never going to return from that death sentence."

"As if you care whether I return or not."

"Believe me, I'd be happy to be rid of you but I'm not sending any more of my archers to that forsaken place. Hayes can do as he wishes with his men but I have no intention of wasting valuable soldiers on a mission doomed to fail."

"That's why I have to go. I have to be there. If you have a heart, if you care even a little, you'll send me."

"No," the older archer said with finality.

The younger archer's face turned red with fury. He looked ready to say more but he looked up and saw Clifton and Corin walking by. He glared at Corin and Corin recognized the archer. He'd seen him in the great hall once, fixing a very similar glare on him.

"Move along mages," the older archer said.

"We were just passing by, Commander Terin," Clifton responded calmly.

The commander turned to the young archer. "Get back to your post, Finch. You're not going to Verin. That's final."

The archer fixed his commander with a murderous look before stalking off. Terin seemed like he might say something more to Clifton but, before he had a chance, there was a welcome interruption.

"Corin," Ruena said.

Corin looked away from the threatening commander to Ruena. He swallowed hard. She was dressed in a honey-colored day dress, simple but incredibly flattering to her complexion. A step behind her was another girl, a servant. Corin had seen the girl following Ruena often and recognized her as the servant who had taken his sword to his room the night he'd arrived at the castle.

"Where are you going?" Ruena asked him.

"I was just going to give Corin a tour of Castille town," Clifton explained with a smile. "He's excelling at his lessons and I've already run out of material to show him. I thought an outing would do us both some good."

"That's sounds wonderful," Ruena agreed. "I wish I could join you but I have a meeting with my uncle. I hope you enjoy the town, Corin. I'm sure it's much different from Nevara but it's a sight everyone should see at least once."

Corin didn't know how to respond and was

grateful when Ruena turned to address Terin. "Commander Terin, shouldn't you be supervising your archers?"

"Of course, Ruena," he responded coldly.

No title, no formalities, nothing. The disrespect the commander showed Ruena made Corin shift uncomfortably. Ruena paid it no attention and only fixed the commander with a stern look until he turned and left.

"Have fun in the town, Corin," Ruena said, turning to smile at him before she too departed.

Clifton had already made it outside the castle before Corin could even think to ask him if he could change out of his mage's clothing. It wouldn't have done much good if he had since Clifton's clothing was so obviously that of a mage. Clifton stayed in the lead as they walked, seeming overly pleased with his idea. The castle wasn't far from the town surrounding it and the walk was downhill so it was pleasant as the sun beat down on them. Corin studied Clifton on the way. He was surprised to feel a slight grin creep to his face as Clifton kept up a steady conversation about the history of the capital town. It was boring nonsense about when the streets and sewage systems had been built, and certain important events which had taken place during its history. Corin realized with a shock that he didn't mind Clifton's company. The man was a bit like a strange uncle who would drop in unexpectedly and simultaneously dote on and confuse his nieces and nephews. Clifton was nothing like Sir Burke but the mage had attempted to make Corin feel welcome in the castle and in his new role. Corin suspected this outing was just another attempt to make him comfortable in Castille.

When they arrived in Castille town, Corin was surprised at how different the place was from Nevara. The streets were cleaner and newer. The buildings were taller with fine architecture instead of blocky stone and wood, and there seemed to be some sort of market going on. Booths lined the streets; colored canopies dotted the scene in varying shades and patterns. People filled the tight streets, pushing past each other to look at the produce and other selections. That, more than anything, separated the capital town from Nevara. In Nevara, people avoided being outside at all costs, in Castille, it appeared a common pastime.

"Welcome to Castille," Clifton told him. "As you can see, the weekly market is going on today. That's a stroke of luck for us. It's quite a sight to behold. They sell all sorts of things here: food, clothes, and antiques. Much of it comes from the farms around this area. There are woolen garments and yarn from the sheep, dairy products and eggs from the livestock, and baked goods too."

Corin saw that Clifton was right. Even from the entrance to the market, he could see a wide selection of goods. There were other things besides the farm goods. There were carvings made from different types of wood, some dark, some light, and some with waving patterns. There were imported goods as well, seashells and seashell jewelry from Skellas. Corin had never seen anything like it. Nevara rarely received imported goods, not from as far away as Skellas at least. Corin had seen one of the prized seashell and pearl pieces on the neck of a visiting noblewoman once but such symbols of status were rare so far north.

All of the goods in the market were foreign to Corin. Nevara didn't have markets like this one. In Nevara, most of the food was homegrown, wool homespun, and clothes worn and hand-me-down. Imported goods were always stale or overly expensive.

Clifton caught him staring at the jewelry. "It's exquisite, isn't it? We don't get the imports as often as we used to and they run a high price. The fine jewels that usually come from Freiwade are becoming even more rare. I haven't seen any in weeks now and I'm sure they'd be set at a lofty sum for purchase."

Yes, Corin supposed that, with war looming, Freiwade wouldn't be eager to continue trade with Ashnah. It was a little thing but another reminder of the tumultuous time they were living in and the weight resting upon Corin's shoulders. He studied one of the increasingly rare seashell necklaces interspersed with small shells and pearls. His mind went unbidden to Ruena and he imagined the necklace resting at her collar. The polished blue of one of the shells was nearly the color of her eyes.

"This piece would look lovely on any young lady's neck," the woman behind the booth told him. "Do you have someone particular in mind?"

Corin blushed and stuttered. He heard Clifton snort behind him.

"There's no one!" Corin objected. "I just haven't seen this type of necklace before."

He quickly backed up from the booth, hands raised in defense. The woman seemed disappointed at losing a potential customer though she wouldn't have had much luck with Corin seeing as he didn't have a single coin to his name.

Clifton patted him on the shoulder. "That was a beautiful shade of blue, wasn't it? Like the shining in someone's eyes."

The words hit a little too close to home for Corin. But how would Clifton know who he'd been thinking of when studying the necklace? Corin shook his head and pushed on into the crowd, leaving Clifton to follow quickly behind. It didn't take long for Corin's thoughts to be pulled in an entirely different direction. He realized that silence had stretched through the crowd and everyone was looking at him and Clifton. The market-goers studied the two mages as if they were oddities put on exhibit. Something was inherently different about the looks these people were giving him. There was no mild unease or simple curiosity, no wonder and awe, or subtle distrust, as there was at the castle. The atmosphere in the market as people began to realize that Clifton and Corin were mages, was purely cold and edged with… hate. There was no other word for the intensity in those gazes. Clifton noticed the looks too. He planted a hand on Corin's shoulder.

"Follow me," he instructed, steering Corin down a less populated side street.

There were still booths down the street but they were further apart and possessed less desirable products. Clifton watched him worriedly. Corin realized he was shaking. His hands were sweating and he felt short of breath. Those stares. They were awful. Corin blinked a few times, trying to erase the looks from his mind. He could still feel their eyes watching him. He detested all the attention. For so long, he'd been invisible, but now…

"W... why were they staring at me like that," Corin murmured, taking several deep breaths to calm himself.

"It wasn't just you that they were staring at," Clifton responded. "I shouldn't have brought you here."

"To the town?"

"To the castle."

Corin blinked at him, uncomprehending.

Clifton sighed. "When King Rupert first became king, he set a watch for mages throughout the kingdom. If anyone showed signs of possessing magic, they were brought to the castle to be trained and to serve the kingdom. After Neos Loch died, I was given the task of keeping an eye out for anyone who might be a mage. I was to bring them to Castille if they were found and anyone who knew the whereabouts of a mage was to report to me. It was a different method than was used in my day. Both Neos Loch and I presented ourselves to the kingdom when we discovered our power. We did so by choice. I was frightened by the abilities I started to demonstrate and I recognized them as similar to those of Neos Loch. I went to the castle without hesitation because I didn't know what else to do. I wanted to understand my gift. I don't regret my decision. Neos Loch was the best mentor I could have asked for. He made me feel less alone and strange. But there are times when I wonder what would have happened if I'd kept my abilities secret and lived a normal life." There was a depth to Clifton's expression that made Corin again question how old the man was. He seemed to possess experience beyond his years. Was that the fate of all mages?

"I made my choice, Corin. I was given a choice. I regret that you weren't. When I received the report from Sir Eamon Burke that he believed you to be a mage, I was torn. It was fantastic news that another mage had been found, especially because of the turmoil on the border. I was eager to not be alone. Perhaps that was selfish of me but it is often the position of a mage to be isolated. It was encouraging to know I could train someone as Loch had trained me. But I was also concerned for you, Corin."

"Concerned for me? Why?"

"You forget that I've gone through what you're going through now. Being a mage means constantly being the center of attention, not always in a good way. Many people are superstitious and think that having these abilities is unnatural. They don't understand that it is God's gift. They don't trust us and they never will. And then there's the expectations, they'd crush anyone under their weight. As a believer in God, it's difficult to be treated like you are forsaken instead of blessed. I know that it made me doubt everything I believed in for a time. Without Neos Loch, I may have gone astray, believing the rumors people whispered about me. I was faced with rejections that pierced my very soul, all because I was a mage. My family," Clifton hesitated. "My family disowned me when I revealed what I was and stated my intention to go to the castle. They believed like many others that I was cursed. My friends hated me and the woman I loved was disgusted at the mere sight of me."

Corin thought about that level of rejection and

shuddered. At least he hadn't had many people he'd been close to before coming to the castle. Maybe that was a blessing in disguise. He wasn't sure he could have endured the amount of heartache Clifton had.

"I didn't want you to have to experience the same things and worse," Clifton told him. "I was a mage after the great war. I never experienced what Neos Loch did, though I saw the lasting effects of the battle on my mentor," Clifton hesitated again. It seemed that he wanted to say something further but he stopped himself before he could. "This new war, if it comes, will be like nothing we've ever faced before. If it weren't for the war and my selfish desire to have someone who understood what it's like to be a mage, then I would have ignored and discounted Burke's report and let you live whatever kind of life you wanted. I'm sorry Corin. I'm sorry that this had to happen to you like it did to me."

Corin couldn't believe what he was hearing. Clifton regretted bringing him to the castle? A wave of overwhelming confusion and pain swept over him and he steadied himself by leaning against the rough stone wall of a nearby building. He pressed his fingers to his temples. Even Clifton hadn't wanted him, not really. First his parents, then the orphanage, then Burke, and now even Clifton. None of them had wanted Corin. Was there nowhere he belonged? Clifton regretted bringing him to the castle. He would have rather lied about Corin's powers to prevent his involvement. Was he as bad, as useless, as that? It was like he was a crippled mule or a broken hatchet. No one wanted him and he had no place. Why was he so surprised? That was the way things always happened.

He wished Clifton *had* ignored the report about his power. If no one wanted him, then he should have at least gotten to choose where he ended up. He wished he was back at the battle school.

"So, people... hate us for being mages?" Corin asked. *You hate me,* Corin wanted to add but prevented himself at the last moment.

"Well, not hate exactly," Clifton said. "They distrust us and they're afraid of us because they fear magic. They don't understand it and they don't see it as the gift that it is. Not all people are like that though, King Rupert for one, and some of the nobles who frequent the castle. But yes, many are so afraid of us that their fear is represented through hate or disgust."

Corin felt sick. Would he live the rest of his life feared and hated? Would he never find a place where he belonged? Even Clifton didn't want him at the castle and regretted bringing him there. Corin looked down at the elegant clothes that marked him as a mage, his hands that possessed a power that could be used for great creation or, in the case of his fight with Phineas York, great destruction. Corin was one of two people who could control that God-given power. It was something he couldn't take lightly.

Corin looked at Clifton with his white hair and wrinkled eyes. Clifton had been a mage for years. He had aged before his time due to the strain and expectations placed upon him. Yet, Clifton had been given the choice of whether to live that kind of life or not. Corin had been forced into his role as a mage. He'd been given no choice and no chance of escape. He knew that his path would not be an easy one. His life would be full of difficulties and heartaches because he had been chosen to carry such an amazing power. He'd spend his entire life feared and scorned by others for that "gift." Corin also knew that it was his duty to God and his kingdom to continue that path. He couldn't back down, he couldn't retreat. At least, not yet.

CHAPTER 23

Corin was downcast as he and Clifton continued through the market. He ignored the pointed stares, silently wishing Clifton would just take him back to the castle. His mentor continued with mindless conversation but Corin didn't listen. All he could think of was the fact that Clifton regretted bringing him to the castle. Just when he'd started to grow more at ease, Clifton was having second thoughts about his presence. Would he try to get rid of him? He probably would if not for the war. If any of them survived the coming conflict, would Corin be cast out of the castle, left to fend for himself once again?

Clifton came to a sudden stop up ahead and Corin, not paying attention, bumped into the mage's back. Corin staggered a step back and steadied himself.

"What?" he asked, leaning to look around Clifton.

Standing in the middle of the path was a strange man, dressed in practical, dull gray clothing. A veil of sorts covered the lower half of his face so only his dark eyes could be seen.

"Corin, get behind me," Clifton commanded. His voice was stern like Corin had never heard before.

"What's going on, Clifton?" Corin asked.

The strange man took a step forward and Corin saw something flash at his side. A knife. It wasn't just any knife. It was a long, wicked-looking blade, slightly curved. It was a warrior's weapon. Sir Burke had talked about such knives during training. They were difficult to forge and made from only the strongest metal. There was a special technique used to strengthen the metal that Ashnah had yet to discover. Those precious blades were difficult to come by and created exclusively by Freiwade smiths.

"He's from Freiwade," Corin stated with shock and awe.

"Corin, get behind me!" Clifton yelled.

Shocked, Corin did as he was told. He still peered over his mentor's shoulder to see what was happening.

"Who are you and what do you want!" Clifton called to the strange man.

The stranger brandished his knife and took another step forward. A light flashed to life in the palm of Clifton's hand. The market-goers, noticing the commotion, retreated. Their frantic murmurs and exclamations rang in Corin's ears but he kept his attention focused on the Freiwade man.

"Mages," the man snarled. His voice was muffled from the cloth around his mouth but the hatred in that word was still audible.

Corin felt a shiver of fear run down his spine.

"Don't take another step forward," Clifton demanded. "You know what I am, what I can do. You won't win this fight."

"I haven't come for you, old man," the stranger snarled. "Give me the boy."

Corin's heart leapt to his throat. What did the stranger want with him? He was a nobody, a useless squire from Nevara. But then Corin remembered that he wasn't just an orphan from Nevara anymore. He was a mage.

"Clifton," Corin murmured worriedly.

"Go back to the castle, Corin. Run."

"I can't leave you."

"Go!" Clifton urged him.

But even if Corin had wanted to run, his feet were anchored. He couldn't move. Dread weighed him down until he was cemented to the spot. There was no time to react. As Clifton spoke, the strange man surged forward, knife flashing in the midday sun.

He moved quickly, fluidly. His movements weren't those of a knight but someone taught to kill quietly without drawing undue attention. Clifton stepped back, shoving Corin to the side. He took a deep breath and with a yell waved his hand, sending a rush of wind towards the enemy. The man staggered back, losing his balance and falling to the dirt road. He quickly regained his feet and rushed towards Clifton again.

Corin wished more than anything that he had his sword. He was useless as a knight but the blade would still offer some protection. Clifton waved his hand again and this time the wind buffeted the stranger so hard that he flew into the wall of a nearby building, dropping his knife in the process.

"Unnatural filth!" the man yelled at Clifton.

Corin realized that the man was frightened. His eyes, the only part of his face visible, betrayed him. He bent slowly to retrieve his blade but Clifton sent another blast of wind to carry the weapon away.

"Go back where you've come from," Clifton ordered, "and I'll let you get away. But if you ever return here and threaten me and my pupil again, you won't be so fortunate."

The man hesitated and Corin thought he would attack again. Instead, he did as Clifton said and ran. The stranger disappeared down a narrow alleyway and Corin released a breath of relief. His heart pounded in his chest. Shock over what had happened overwhelmed him. He looked slowly to Clifton. The mage was leaning heavily against the wall of a nearby building, panting.

"What's wrong?" Corin asked with concern.

Clifton looked exhausted and in pain. He winced, holding his hands gingerly in front of him. Sweat beaded on his forehead.

"Are you alright?" Corin asked again.

Clifton nodded slowly, still breathing heavily. "I'm fine, Corin. Just give me a moment." He gasped as he said the words. His hands were shaking worse than Corin had ever seen them before.

"Your hands," Corin said.

"I'll be alright. This happens sometimes. I'm just getting old, that's all," Clifton said with a self-deprecating laugh.

Corin didn't quite buy it. He watched his mentor with concern. "We should get back to the castle," Corin suggested.

"Yes. I believe that would be wise. We've had

enough excitement for the day."

"How..." Corin couldn't finish the sentence. How had the assassin or whoever he'd been known he and Clifton would be in the town?

Clifton seemed to understand what Corin meant to say. "I don't know."

Clifton pushed away from the wall, cradling his hands close to his body. He took a step and staggered. Corin moved quickly to steady him.

"It's nothing," Clifton repeated, seeing Corin's concern.

Clifton took a breath and then began to lead the way back towards the castle. Corin followed close beside him, ready to steady him again if necessary. He wasn't sure why Clifton seemed so weakened after using the magic. But Corin suddenly remembered that Clifton only ever demonstrated techniques once during their lessons. Corin had never seen Clifton use magic in any other circumstance. Did it pain him to do so? Corin eyed his mentor's trembling hands as they headed towards the castle. Was that in store for him someday as well?

They returned to the castle in silence. Corin was grateful for the time to think. He only wished he could find a solution to the thoughts racing through his mind. Someone had tried to kill him. Or had he? The man had said he was going to take Corin. Where? Freiwade? For the first time it was truly beginning to sink in for Corin that being a mage was dangerous, not just because of his power but because he was a target for the enemy.

When they entered the castle, Clifton addressed him. "I have to report what happened to the king and Sir Hayes. Will should come to help you with studying the books of magic this afternoon but given the day's events, I won't be expecting much progress from you. And Corin, for the time being while what happened is sorted out, please keep what happened quiet. There's no need to concern anyone over this."

Corin nodded in assent but he wondered why such an attack should be kept silent. "If there are assassins from Freiwade wandering the streets of Ashnah, shouldn't the people be warned?"

"Perhaps they should and perhaps they shouldn't. That is up to the king and Sir Hayes to decide. But consider for a moment how the people will react when they learn that their mages, the strongest among them, were attacked by Freiwade. They will be afraid that a similar attack could happen to them at any moment. They will question the king's ability to lead them and protect them when he wasn't able to prevent a conflict between his own mages and the enemy."

Corin knew Clifton was right but he still didn't like all of the secrecy. He would stay quiet about what had happened for now but he hoped and prayed that the king would do something about it before someone else got hurt.

CHAPTER 24

Talbrandt was one of the smallest villages in Skellas. It was nothing more than a tiny fishing community right on the coast of the once-independent kingdom. It wasn't much, but to Aster Kadesh, it was home. It was where he laid his head at night, and where he made his work spending long, cold days on a fishing boat along the coastline. Only a cup of mulled cider and a warm fire could chase away the aching cold after a day at sea. It wasn't an easy life by any means but it was the only life Aster knew.

He hauled one of his nets out of the water. The salty sea air left a tang on his lips. He breathed in deeply. The net was caught on something and Aster had to renew his efforts to free it. When he finally managed to drag the heavy ropes into his small boat, he was rewarded for his struggles. The net had caught a bounty of fish. There would be a few left over to keep for himself and the other townspeople once the required quota was sent to Freiwade. Aster set the largest fish aside for Amery. He smiled to himself, thinking of the pleased look that would cross his love's face when she saw the treasure. Maybe it would even bring a grin to the old man's dire expression. It was rare these days to see anything beyond a grimace of pain or a frown of worry on Amery's father's face. Aster couldn't blame the man. The family had been struggling to make ends meet after old Sunder had lost his arm in an accident with his ship's netting while at sea. Aster had done everything he could since then to help the family. It was his duty as Amery's betrothed but also as a member of the community. They all had to look out for each other in Skellas, especially in a little town like Talbrandt.

As Aster reached for his other net to start dragging it in, he glanced back at the shoreline. He was forced to squint against the glare of the sun on the water and the mist hanging in the air. He could see the little huts lining the shore, the remains of bonfires along the sand, and the cobblestones of the town square. He was about to turn his attention back to his work when he saw an unwelcome sight. There were large wagons spread throughout the town square. Aster had keen eyes from his time on the water and he could see the black and gray uniforms pouring out of the wagons and into the town.

Trouble. It could only mean trouble. A small, cowardly part of Aster wanted to stay out at sea. His little boat would likely go unnoticed from the shoreline. He could wait until the Freiwade soldiers left. However, he knew that as one of the prominent members of the small community, he should be there to fend them off.

He turned his boat back towards land. This day had been inevitable. The soldiers had finally come to take him and the other young men away to fight in Freiwade's war. Aster felt a twinge of unease. He'd seen what Freiwade had done to his people. He didn't want to fight for them, not in a war for power. King Histen Corpin had already taken their food, their labor, their freedom, and even their lives. If a Skellan even attempted to stand against Freiwade's tyranny, they would be publicly executed, or worse, dragged away to Freiwade's capital to serve in the castle or for one of the petulant nobles. To the Skellan people, that was a fate worse than death. But there was nothing they could do against Freiwade. The kingdom was too powerful. The most Aster could do was return to the land, face the soldiers, and try to protect his people.

The community of Talbrandt had taken care of Aster when his father was lost at sea, his mother killed by Freiwade, and his sister dragged to the capital. He had no family left, for he was sure his weak, sickly sister was long since dead. The villagers of Talbrandt were the only family Aster had. They had protected him in his youth. Now it was his turn to protect them.

He drove his boat ashore and jumped over the hull. His soft-soled boots softly impacted against the sand. He hurried across the beach and up to the town square. He knew trouble was awaiting him before he even laid eyes on the soldiers moving about.

"Everyone line up!" one soldier who seemed to be in charge yelled. "Every man young and old is to line up to be inspected!"

Inspected. Inspected for battle. Aster stood on the cusp of the beach and town, watching the chaos unfold. Soldiers dragged the unwilling or unable from their homes and threatened them at sword point to assemble. Men in their eighties, unable to walk without assistance were dragged to the town square and made to stand and wait. Boys barely past their infancy were snatched from their mothers' arms and placed along the line. The screams of the children rang in Aster's ears. Women and girls were instructed to gather in a group at the corner. They were not permitted near the men and the soldiers treated them just as roughly as they were shoved to the side.

Aster looked through the crowd. All of the faces were familiar to him. He knew each person by name. He knew what they liked and didn't like, he knew their dreams and fears. They were his family. He searched the crowd for Amery and her family. Old Sunder, his arm still heavily bandaged at the stump where the amputation had ended, was pushed into the line next to his fourteen-year-old son, Hagan. The young man supported his father almost entirely. Aster looked at the scene with distaste. Poor Hagan had matured beyond his years in the last few months. The boy was barely past childhood but he'd been working just as hard as Aster in an attempt to provide for his family. He'd become the sole provider in his father's inability to do so.

One of the soldiers caught sight of Aster and latched onto his arm. "All men are to gather in the town square," the soldier snarled.

Aster yanked his arm free of the brutal grasp. He took a step closer to the man, a good three inches taller than the soldier. He squared his broad shoulders and leaned forward until his stubbled chin was only a hairsbreadth away from the soldier's clean-shaven face.

"What is the meaning of this!" Aster demanded.

Two more soldiers, seeing the trouble Aster was causing, approached. "In line!" one of them shouted. Aster didn't move. The soldiers, all three of them, grabbed hold of Aster and forced him forward into the assembly. Aster fought against them for a moment, not in an attempt to escape, but to make the task more difficult for them.

"Do you not see the insanity of this?" Aster objected. "These 'so-called' men you are forcing to bend to your will are children and elders. This is cruel and unjust!"

They ignored Aster's protests and shoved him into the line. Aster took a step to go after them. He would fight them if he had to. But a calming hand was placed on his shoulder and he stilled.

"Calm yourself, Aster. Now is not the time to rebel," the voice belonged to Arlen, the old village leader.

Aster shrugged off the hand. He looked at Arlen. The man was grizzled with shaggy gray hair, and eyes so squinted it was a miracle he could see anything at all. His hands were wrinkled and calloused, the flesh dotted with discolored spots denoting his increasing age. Arlen was standing in the line beside the young men despite his age and his constant limp, a result of arthritic muscles. Aster silently seethed at the treatment of his people.

"This isn't right," he muttered.

"We are strong," Arlen reminded him. "We have suffered much in this village but we will persevere as we always have."

Aster glanced worryingly at the soldiers. Just what did they have in mind? Aster hoped Arlen was right but he also knew that their village had been battered to the point of no return. Aster wasn't sure if they could handle another defeat.

"Aster," Arlen said warningly, "the people will imitate your actions. Act wisely."

Aster knew Arlen was right. If he tried to fight back against the soldiers, the others would follow and someone would inevitably get hurt.

One of the soldiers, the leader, stepped forward. He cleared his throat and held up a piece of parchment then began to read off a speech. "By the decree of King Histen Corpin of Freiwade: any able-bodied man between the ages of fifteen and sixty must present himself to serve his ruler and to fight in the war against Ashnah. Failure to do so will result in immediate execution as an enemy to the king."

So, this was it. It was bound to happen eventually. Aster supposed the only reason their town had been drawn into the war so late was because they were far away from the capital of Freiwade and they provided most of the food for the land-locked and barren kingdom. The king's desire for power had finally outweighed the necessity of workers to provide food for the kingdom. Besides, there were always the women and children to do the heavy work in the men's absence. Aster was disgusted by the decree. He knew without a doubt that he would be forced into the king's service.

He was one of the strongest of the villagers and, at twenty-two, he was the ideal age to fight, or rather to die in service. Arlen gripped Aster's shoulder. The old man knew Aster's fate as well as he did.

"God be with you, boy."

What God? Aster wanted to ask. What God would forsake Skellas so entirely? The once great kingdom was nothing but a shell now. It had been utterly destroyed by Freiwade and left to a destiny of servitude and disgrace. But if there was a God, then Aster was desperate enough to plead for help. *Please,* Aster silently begged. *If You are out there, save my people. I care nothing for my own life but preserve them. Preserve my beloved Amery.*

Aster couldn't meet the eyes of his betrothed as the soldiers went along the line of men. They declared some unable, too young, too old, too frail. They pulled the men and boys from the ranks and threw them aside.

"This one's just a useless cripple," a soldier said, surveying old Sunder. "Too old anyhow."

Aster let out a breath of relief. At least Freiwade wasn't desperate enough to force Amery's father into battle. The man wouldn't last a moment with only one arm and his undominant one at that. Aster drew his attention back to his own troubles. A soldier was approaching him. Aster stood stock still in line as Arlen was dismissed as too old. The boy to Aster's left, Tinny as he'd been nicknamed, a lad of barely five years old was fortunately pulled from the line and returned to his sobbing mother. Aster was next.

However, before the soldier could inspect him, there was a cry of horror from behind Aster. He recognized the frantic, pleading voice of Amery.

"No!" she screamed. "No, he's too young, please! Take me instead!"

Aster swung around, feeling dazed and petrified. No. No, not that. There were cries of outrage from the villagers. Aster wondered if a mob might form and drive the Freiwade soldiers from their midst. He hoped not. The people of Talbrandt had a higher chance of being massacred by the sword than of succeeding against Freiwade's soldiers.

One of the soldiers had a hand on Hagan's arm, pulling the boy forward out of the line. Another soldier was busy restraining Amery. Poor Sunder couldn't even manage to fight for his son. Aster pushed past the soldiers, desperate to reach Hagan.

"Stop!" he objected. "Stop, he's not fifteen. He's too young to fight. And he's the only male heir in his household. He has to be left to provide for his family."

Aster's statements were ignored. Two soldiers grabbed him from behind, yanking his arms back so intensely that Aster yelled in pain and frustration.

"Aster!" Amery cried out. "Let him go!"

The soldier grasping Hagan's arm turned to survey Aster with distaste. "The boy looks old enough to me. He'll fight."

"Please, you can't do this!" Aster's words turned into pleas. At that moment, he would have done anything to erase the terrified expression on Hagan's young face. The boy's face was still soft and innocent with youth. He'd matured because of his father's injury, but he was still young. He was wholly inexperienced in the ways of battle. Aster couldn't let them take him.

"Please, don't do this. Have mercy!" Amery cried. She managed to break free of the soldier holding her and she latched onto her brother, refusing to let him go. One of the soldiers unsheathed his sword.

Aster struggled harder against the hands

restraining him. "No!" he screamed. Desperation and absolute terror overpowered him. "Not her!" Anyone but Amery. Her face was tear-streaked but resolute. Aster knew she would die protecting her brother. Hagan knew it too.

"Amery, you have to let me go," Hagan pleaded with her.

"Never," she stated.

"Amery," it was Sunder. He mustered the strength to lay his good hand on Amery's back. "Amery, let him go. There's nothing we can do."

Those words broke something inside Aster's chest. There was nothing they could do. They couldn't fight back against Freiwade. They couldn't even save one of their own. He wanted to scream at the injustice of it all. Amery's beautiful, kind face was stricken. But she realized that her father was right. She hesitantly released her brother. When the soldiers grabbed hold of Hagan again, Amery let out a heart-wrenching sob.

How would Amery and her father provide for themselves without Hagan, without Aster? The villagers would try to take care of them but they would be hard-pressed even to meet their own needs with the very old and the women forced to do all the labor and send the majority of their work straight to the nobles of Freiwade. They'd keep little to nothing for themselves.

"You can't do this!" Aster protested, struggling against the soldiers restraining him. "If you send all of the men away, these people will die. They'll starve! Your people will starve. How will Freiwade get its food without us?"

The leader of the soldiers slapped Aster across

the face. Aster's ears rang, his eyes watered, and he felt blood dripping down his cheek.

"That's none of your concern," the soldier told him. The soldier drew his sword and pointed it under Aster's chin. "You seem strong and capable. You'll certainly be sent to the front lines. That's where most of the Skellans go. After all, they're best used as cannon fodder. You'll be a good addition to that group."

Aster felt a soldier tying a rope roughly around his wrists. "Don't go getting any ideas of escape," the man murmured in Aster's ear. "You'll be branded a deserter if you do. There are worse things than death that Freiwade rewards deserters with."

Despite himself, Aster shuddered with fear. What would become of him? What would become of all of them? Aster looked to Amery. Would it be the last time he saw her?

"Amery!" he called out to her. "I love you!"

"Come back to me!" she pleaded.

Aster didn't answer. He couldn't bear lying to her. The last thing he saw was Amery's tear-filled eyes as he and the other men were dragged into the wagons and hauled away to fight in a war they had no stake in, a war that would only cause them suffering and pain.

CHAPTER 25

Corin was starting to become accustomed to the stares from the nobility, servants, and knights around the castle. He still didn't appreciate the attention directed at him, but he chose to ignore the looks. As long as it wasn't like that moment in the village with the pointed stares of hatred, Corin could bear it. Probably, the stares would never stop. He better get used to them. Corin had seen people distance themselves from Clifton even though the elder mage had been in the castle for decades.

Corin concocted a strategy for making it a little easier to bear. He moved around the halls of the castle with his head down and his eyes averted. He refused to meet the gaze of anyone he passed. That way, he only *felt* the stares brushing over him instead of having to meet them head-on. The whispers were bad enough, much worse than the stares. He couldn't decipher most of them. His ears were attuned to yells from Sir Burke and other squires, not whispers. However, he did pick up bits and pieces. The words, "strange," "unnatural," "dangerous," and "can't be trusted," were used the most. Each one burned Corin like a blazing ember.

The king and the others at the head table seemed at ease around Corin but everyone else was on constant alert. When Corin passed a noble in the hallway, they would hurriedly move out of his way. When he tried to converse with a knight, they would subtly rest their hand on their sword hilt. And when a servant came to refill his glass at dinner, their hand would be shaking so much that the water would slosh as it was poured.

One day as he was walking past a hallway full of bedrooms on his way to the great hall, Corin overheard a particularly troubling conversation. It was so absurd that part of Corin wondered if it was staged intentionally so he would overhear it. Duke Heirson and his son, Dresden, stood outside their room in conversation.

"All this fuss about the new mage is only a distraction to cover up the king's incompetency," Duke Heirson stated to his son. "It's not a very good distraction either. That mage is just a boy. He doesn't stand a chance of stopping this coming war. He will only make Ashnah a bigger target. The king should get rid of him while he still has the chance and dispose of him so that he won't fall into the hands of the enemy."

The words were harsh, broaching on treacherous. It shocked Corin and rattled him to the bones. He felt tears burning in his eyes, whether from anger or fear, he wasn't sure. It was no secret to Corin that some of the nobles wanted him gone, but *disposed* of. No, it was definitely anger that Corin was feeling mixed with a hint of disgust. What right had that man, duke or not, to say such things? Corin's mind flashed back to the assassin from Freiwade. He wondered if there was just as much danger inside the castle walls as outside. Would he have to live the rest of his life looking over his shoulder in fear?

Corin stormed past the men, allowing them to see him and wonder to themselves if he'd overheard their conversation. He even dared to lift his eyes for a moment to glare at the duke and his son. When Corin turned his gaze away from the two noblemen, his eyes caught on a shadowed hallway. A tall, dark-haired man leaned against the wall of the corridor; his fists were clenched at his sides. As Corin neared closer, he saw a pained expression on the stranger's face. The look was quickly changed to a mask of nonchalance as Corin passed by. Whoever he was, there was no doubt that he too had overheard the conversation. He seemed even more upset by it than Corin. It brought Corin a small sense of peace to know that there was someone on his side who had felt the same disgust and anger at the duke's insulting speech.

Corin knew the insults and fear arose from the rumors that circulated about mages. He had lived in a small town where stories traveled fast. They were harsh, dangerous rumors. Corin had known next to nothing about mages before arriving at Castille Castle. What he did know was less than accurate. He had feared mages and believed magic was a curse instead of a gift. He knew he had to expect the same behavior from others no matter how much it hurt. The only people who seemed to think of Corin as a person instead of just a mage were Ruena, whom he feared he'd offended and didn't dare speak to again, Clifton, who was a mage himself, and Will. Will had been nervous around Corin at first but he'd quickly warmed up to him. He treated Corin with a sense of awe as if he were someone important to be looked up to. Corin wasn't sure how to handle that reaction but he appreciated the fact that Will didn't seem afraid of him.

The previous evening after the attack in the village, Will had come to Corin's room to study Clifton's books. Noticing that something was troubling Corin, Will had offered a listening ear. It was good to talk to someone about what had happened and Corin had felt like a great weight was lifted off his chest after doing so.

"Safety isn't guaranteed anywhere," Will had said with wisdom beyond his years. "Even training as a scribe in the castle, I know that life is uncertain. Anything could happen even to someone like me. That's why it's so important to live in the moment and treat every instant like it's precious."

Corin knew Will was right and tried not to worry too much about what had happened.

There was one other individual, Corin supposed, who had treated him like a person. Dorian the knight had offered to be his friend and train with him. Corin hadn't had many opportunities to interact with Dorian because of their differing and busy schedules. It had been several days since Corin had seen the friendly knight. But the times when they had passed each other in the hall, Dorian had offered a smile and asked how Corin's training was going.

Corin had plenty to report in that regard. Clifton was running out of magic to teach him. He quickly picked up new skills and mastered them with little difficulty. Corin had started to look forward to learning more about magic and experiencing the thrill he felt when he practiced it. However, with Clifton searching for more complicated lessons to keep Corin busy, and Will occupied with his own lessons, Corin was given plenty of free time which he had no idea what to do with. Corin had never liked having free time. He liked being busy. It kept his mind from wandering to places he didn't want it to be. Corin had always been told what to do and when to do it at battle school. Under Sir Burke's command, there was no such thing as free time.

Unsure how to use his newfound independence, Corin found himself practicing his sword drills while he waited for Clifton. He trained hard but he could only manage an hour or two at a time before he became exhausted and had to set his sword aside. He ran in the mornings while it was still cool before he arrived for his lesson with Clifton. After his annoyingly short lessons, Corin still had hours of spare time he had to make use of before he met with Will to read through Clifton's books. He took to wandering the castles with no destination or purpose in mind other than to pass the time.

He kept away from the nobles and servants and wandered the less-used corridors and halls of the castle. He peeked through open doorways to see what lay beyond, ventured into empty rooms, and twisted deeper and deeper into the castle. If there was one advantage of his mindless wanderings, it was that Corin finally found that he was gaining a better understanding of his surroundings. He knew every hallway and where it led. He even gained an idea of which nobles were housed in which rooms and that helped him steer clear of those he suspected disliked the idea of having a mage in the castle the most.

Every day he found himself walking past the same room. He always peeked through the open door of the empty room that overlooked the garden, the room where he'd talked with Ruena. He never ventured inside but he always looked. Sometimes he would see her sitting on the windowsill and he would watch her for a little while, knowing that she was unaware of him standing there. Usually, he would just walk past. It wasn't his place to talk to her, especially unattended. He might have the courage to say a word or two to her at a meal but he never sought out conversation on his own. Sometimes another girl, the servant who had taken Corin's belongings to his room the day he arrived at the castle, and whom he'd seen with Ruena often, would be in the room with her. The girl would sit on the other side of the windowsill where Corin himself had sat when he talked with Ruena. Sometimes the girl would lean against the wall waiting for her mistress.

Corin knew he shouldn't watch Ruena but he couldn't help himself. He knew he could never talk to her. Seeing her in her element, watching out the window or reading on the windowsill, was the best he could hope for. One day as he was walking past, Corin noticed Ruena's maidservant standing outside the room. The girl didn't pay any attention to him. She was leaning against the wall beside the partially closed door. Corin overheard lowered voices coming from inside the room, two voices. He heard Ruena's feminine tone but also a masculine voice. Corin hesitated, confused and curious. He glanced through the slight opening of the door and saw a man whom he didn't know standing inside talking to Ruena. Corin only glimpsed the back of the man's head and the side of his face as he spoke. He felt like he'd seen the stranger before, briefly and without introduction, but he wasn't sure where.

The maidservant noticed Corin watching and glared at him but the girl didn't say a word. She was very close to the door and Corin wondered if she was listening to the conversation as well. If she was, she probably wasn't getting much from it. Corin couldn't understand a single word murmured from inside. Corin knew she acted as Ruena's escort. She probably disapproved of the idea of Ruena alone in the room with a strange man. Corin wasn't sure how to escape now that the maid had caught sight of him. It was obvious that he'd been looking inside the room. Corin fumbled to try to come up with an excuse for his actions. He didn't get a chance because, at that moment, the man's voice faltered and stopped. Corin could see through the crack that the stranger had turned to look towards the door and saw Corin's face peering through the opening.

Corin's heart leapt to his throat. He turned, ready to make a run for it. What had he interrupted? Why had the man been alone inside the room with Ruena? Whatever was going on, Corin knew he wasn't supposed to be there. The maid leaned quickly away from the door as it swung open. The man stood in the opening, studying Corin. Ruena was visible still sitting on the windowsill and she saw Corin standing at the doorway.

"Corin," Ruena called to him.

The man turned to Ruena for a moment. "Excuse me, Ruena. I'll speak with you more on the matter later." Then the man left, pushing past Corin with an intense look.

The maidservant perked up at the man's appearance. She smiled warmly, the first friendly expression Corin had ever seen on her face.

"It's so good to see you, sir," she greeted the strange man almost flirtatiously.

The man didn't respond. The girl seemed to hesitate, obviously wanting to go after the man but she couldn't leave her mistress. She glared at Corin as if taking out her frustration on him.

Corin watched the strange man disappear down the hall. Corin thought it would be a good opportunity to make his escape but Ruena called to him again.

"Come inside, Corin."

He took a deep breath. He couldn't avoid her so blatantly; it would be insufferably rude. The maid gave him a warning glare.

"Don't try anything, mage," she spat out.

Corin winced and stepped into the room, leaving the door wide open behind him.

"If you're busy, then I won't keep you," Ruena told him. She looked away, seeming to run through the words she'd said and find them unsatisfactory. "It doesn't matter," she added quickly. She looked down at her hands and pulled her knees a little higher up.

Corin shook his head without thinking. "I've been given the rest of the afternoon off."

He was instantly annoyed at his automatic reaction. She'd given him the perfect outing if he wanted to leave. Now that he'd made it clear that he had nothing pressing, there was no excuse he could use to escape the no-doubt awkward conversation that was sure to come.

He was glad he'd been honest because Ruena brightened at his words, a real smile crossing her face. She gestured towards the windowsill. "Have a seat, please."

Corin perched once again on the very edge of the windowsill. Surely it wasn't overstepping boundaries if she had invited him. Ruena grinned at him but shifted in her seat, seemingly just as uncomfortable as he was. She blushed then straightened herself out so she was in a more dignified position. Corin waited for her to speak without fully looking at her. When she stayed silent, he prepared to leave.

"Wait, Corin. How was your trip to the town?"

Corin cleared his throat. She must not know what had happened. He thought about Clifton's request for him to keep quiet about the attack. It wouldn't be wise to worry Ruena. "Good, thank you."

Ruena sighed. "I'm sorry if I'm bothering you. I only thought that I hadn't talked with you much. I wanted to make sure you were doing well and that you were comfortable here in the castle. I've wanted to talk with you for a while actually but I knew you'd need time to settle in. I didn't want to interrupt your busy schedule. Besides, it's not my place to interfere with your business as a mage."

Corin looked at her with surprise. "But you're the king's niece."

Ruena twirled a strand of her hair between her

fingers. "Yes, but I'm not a princess. I'm not royalty either. I'm more of a guest here. I don't fit in anywhere in the social order of things. Technically, you outrank me. I shouldn't be bothering you. I've never cared much for courtly protocol though."

Corin leaned back against the wall so he was directly facing her. He let that information sink in for a moment. He outranked her? But he was just a peasant from a small, insignificant town in the north. He hadn't even been knighted. He was just Corin, not Sir Corin, or Lord Corin. The title "mage" didn't even seem fitting. If Ruena wasn't a princess, then she must be a lady. Somehow that title seemed a lot less intimidating. He felt a little more comfortable talking with her, knowing they were on more equal footing and that she didn't care much for the niceties of court.

Corin scratched the back of his neck and hesitantly met her eyes. "I don't mind sitting here with you," he said. "I've wanted to talk to you too but I was worried I'd offended you by leaving so abruptly during our last conversation. I was too much of a coward to seek you out again."

Ruena smiled, a dazzling smile that made Corin's heart skip a beat. He realized that he was smiling too, the first real smile he'd had in a while.

"You know," Ruena started to say as she stared out the window again, "I was excited to learn that you were coming to the castle."

"Really?" Corin asked with genuine surprise. "Why?"

He could see Ruena smile even though her head was tilted away from him. "I'd heard you were seventeen. I was eager to get to know someone my age. The castle is wonderful but there are mostly just nobles around all the time. There are a few knights and archers my age but they're busy with their duties. The nobles who have children only seek me out in hopes of making an alliance." Ruena winced at the statement.

Corin shifted uncomfortably, hating the change in topic. "What about the young man who was just here? What's your relationship with him?" Corin was almost afraid to hear the answer to that question.

"Oh, that was just Cal. He's an old friend of mine. He kind of adopted me as a little sister when I first came to the castle." Ruena didn't mention who Cal was or what he did but Corin was satisfied at least knowing he wasn't a suitor.

"How long have you been at the castle?" Corin asked. "Why are you staying with your uncle?"

"I've been here as long as I can remember. My father was supposed to be the king but he forfeited his position when he married my mother. It was a love match. She had no title or position in court. They moved to the country to start a family away from the drama and expectations of the court."

Corin listened intently, enjoying the silky sound of Ruena's voice.

"Of course, I never really got to grow up there. My uncle told me that there was a fire. The little country estate burned to the ground with my parents still in it." Ruena said this all with a straight face and a monotone to her voice. It was as if she were reciting a story that was frequently told. "They were sleeping and didn't notice the fire in time. Parts of the ceiling had collapsed and the door was blocked. They threw me out a window to save me. I escaped. They weren't so fortunate."

Corin had to fight to keep the emotion from his face. Horror at what Ruena, kind, friendly Ruena had faced, crept into him and settled in the pit of his stomach. The story was awful.

"Please, don't look so sad," Ruena said, gently touching his arm. "I was too little to know them well. My uncle says they were devout Christians so I know where they went when they died. My uncle was kind enough to take me in and treat me like the child he never had. I'm very blessed to have the life I do. I know this is where God wants me to be and that He has a plan for me. I won't be sad about what might have been."

Ruena smiled at him and Corin was overwhelmed by her positive nature.

He'd been so ungrateful about his situation when hers was infinitely worse. He wished he could trust in God as she did. She didn't dwell on all the could-have-beens. Instead, she focused on where she was and what the future had in store.

"I never knew my parents either," Corin found himself sharing.

Ruena watched him, her midnight blue eyes wide.

Corin picked at the hem of his tunic. She had told him about her family, it was only fair that he share also. "I was in an orphanage for as long as I remember. The orphanage never told me about my parents. Sometimes I wish I knew if I took after them or if they would be proud of me for who I've become. I'll never know. When I was thirteen, I was sent away from the orphanage to fend for myself. I found myself in a bit of trouble before Sir Burke came along and allowed me to train as a squire."

Corin felt embarrassed after he'd finished speaking. Had he overshared? He didn't want her to think he was setting his position up as worse than her own.

"Thank you," Ruena said.

"For what?"

"For telling me. It's nice to talk about things like this with someone who knows how it feels. My uncle tried his best to understand. When I lost my father, he lost his brother. It isn't quite the same though. I never knew them, yet, there's this small ache of loss anyway. The grief I feel isn't so much because I lost someone close to me but because I lost those experiences and happiness that I could have had."

Corin understood the feeling perfectly. How many nights on the streets of Nevara had he wondered what it would be like to be bundled up around a fire in a warm, loving home, his father reading a story and his mother embroidering in the corner? He still wondered about that dream sometimes. He wondered what his life could have been.

Corin cleared his throat. He wanted to change the subject to a more positive note.

"I don't think your maid likes me very much," Corin stated. He could still feel the girl's glare.

Ruena was caught off guard by the sudden change in subject but after a moment she seemed to understand what he was doing. She laughed. "Why do you say that?"

"She glares at me every time I see her."

"Her name is Vesta," Ruena explained. "She can be like that, but she means well. My uncle believed I needed a female companion around the castle and someone to act as a chaperone for me as I reached the age where I would need to interact with suitors. I've always tried to avoid those types of interactions but I knew my uncle meant well by wanting a friend and companion for me. There was a grand search for a suitable maid to fill the position. I liked Vesta the best. She had just come to the castle seeking work and I thought she'd be perfect. She's kind enough but has a no-nonsense attitude. She's quiet and keeps to herself."

"If she's a chaperone why isn't she always with you?" Corin asked.

"She's gone from the castle on occasion because she has an ailing mother she has to take care of. It suits me just fine not having her looking out for me all the time. I wouldn't say Vesta and I have a friendship exactly but we have an agreement. She leaves me alone unless she's needed and she's able to tend to her mother. We're on friendly terms but nothing too personal."

"I must come across as an undesirable acquaintance for you then," Corin thought out loud, "since she's always trying to fend me off."

Ruena rolled her eyes. "I doubt that very highly. I'm sure she's just being protective. She comes from a border town. She's probably overheard plenty of those awful rumors surrounding mages."

Corin felt a twinge of disappointment at Ruena's words. It seemed everyone had heard those rumors and was eager to accept them as fact.

"Vesta, like many others in the castle, will come around eventually. They'll accept you, Corin, once they get to know you a little better."

Corin doubted that. He'd seen how they reacted to Clifton who'd been in the castle for years and years already. Corin didn't particularly care if Vesta or the nobility personally liked him but he didn't like the idea of always being distrusted.

Ruena noticed the look on his face. "People *will* come around. Even if they don't, it doesn't matter because the important people already know who you are, Corin. I know that you're a good, trustworthy person and you've been given an incredible gift from God. I'm honored to know you."

Corin blushed at the words. "Thank you. I should be going."

He had nearly made it to the door when she stopped him. "Wait, will you meet me here tomorrow?"

Corin smiled. A warm feeling filled his chest. "Of course."

He rushed from the room with the memory of Ruena's smile filling him with a sense of companionship that he hadn't experienced in a very long time.

CHAPTER 26

When the Skellans came, Dane didn't join his father in the courtroom. He didn't care to see the downtrodden men herded like lambs to the slaughter. They weren't technically slaves, but they might as well be. Dane had no desire to see the faces of men who would surely die in battle for Freiwade. He knew how his father would treat them. The Skellans would be sent directly to the front lines while the Freiwade soldiers were held back in reserve. The Skellans would take the brunt of the enemy's attack. They would fight and die for a kingdom that had only persecuted and abused them.

It all made Dane sick. He couldn't bear to watch as his father the king inspected the men before they were sent on to join Nox's forces. Or, at least, he couldn't stand on the dais and watch them be paraded in front of the king like auctioned goods. Instead, he found a corner outside the courtroom where he could catch sight of them before they entered.

Dane stood in the corner, hidden by shadow. He heard the heavy, reinforced door to the castle groan open. He heard the commands of the soldiers, urging the Skellans forward. He heard the stamp of hundreds of feet, and the murmur of hundreds of voices. He could feel the despair hanging heavily in the air. What must it be like to know you would die, Dane wondered. What agony would one feel at such knowledge?

Dane hadn't planned to look at their faces but as they shuffled past him into the courtroom, he dared to lift his eyes to seek an answer to his questions. But the face he met as he looked up wasn't filled with dejection or terror but raw, fierce, and unyielding anger. The look on the Skellan's face made Dane's breath catch. The young man was perhaps twenty-five, no older. His shoulders were broad and his skin tanned from long days of work in the sun. His eyes were as fierce as a storming sea and his hands were clenched until his knuckles turned white. There was no fear on his face. No, that was the type of face that the king of Freiwade should fear.

Next to the young man was a boy, younger than Dane. Even that boy walked with his shoulders squared. His lips quivered, betraying his fear, but he still maintained composure. Dane knew it was more than he could have managed in that place. In that instant, Dane felt a respect for the Skellan people that he didn't feel for his own family and kingdom. His father was cruel for taking the Skellans from their homes and their families to fight in his war.

The doors to the courtroom opened and the Skellans were shoved unceremoniously inside. The doors closed and Dane was consumed again by silence. He was preparing to leave, having seen enough, but when he took a step he felt something sharp press against his back.

"It would be so easy," a voice hissed behind him.

Dane froze, terror piercing into him as the knife pressed more firmly into his side. Dane felt the fabric of his tunic tear and the cold blade of the dagger touched his bare skin.

"I wouldn't move if I were you."

It was Horace. Dane could tell not only by the tone of the voice but also by the slight shaking of the hand holding the knife. Horace's hands always shook. The illness that had plagued Horace since childhood had grown much more severe recently.

"Horace," Dane pleaded, "don't."

Horace scoffed. The sound was cut off by a hacking cough. Dane waited, holding his breath as the knife wavered with each cough. Horace finally calmed himself and steadied the knife.

"It would be so easy," he said again. "I could kill you right here and no one would know it was me."

Dane stayed perfectly still. He knew Horace wasn't bluffing. He knew that Horace would kill him in an instant if the fancy struck him. The question was whether his brother would follow through with it.

"No one would miss you, runt," Horace growled. "I'd be doing all of us a favor."

"Father would be angry. They would find out it was you eventually and you would be punished for it."

"Father wouldn't miss you, not for long anyway. You're only a spare, there are seven more sons to take your place. I doubt he'd even notice you were missing."

Dane feared Horace was right.

"You don't belong here," Horace said, his voice shaking as he fought off another cough.

"You're right," Dane agreed.

"Why does he care about you at all? You were never meant to be born. You were never meant to be here," Horace's voice trembled. Was he going to cry?

The knife pressed firmer into Dane's side. Something wet... blood, dripped down his skin. Then just when Dane thought it would all be over, it was. Horace dropped the knife. It clattered against the flagstones. Dane gasped and fell against the wall, his legs refusing to support him. He looked at Horace with horror. Horace stood, panting.

"Next time... next time."

Dane didn't doubt it. He hadn't been nearly as careful around Horace as he should have been. He wouldn't make that mistake again.

Horace retreated down the corridor while Dane stayed pinned to the wall, unable to move. No sooner had his brother's figure disappeared around a corner than the door to the courtroom was thrown open. There was the sound of a commotion from inside and the Skellans were herded out. The rebellious young man from earlier was being dragged from the courtroom, kicking and thrashing as he went. As he crossed the threshold, he turned in his restrainers' grip and spat back towards the courtroom, towards the king. Dane was horrified at the show of disrespect. No one acted in such a way towards the king of Freiwade. The soldiers tightened their hold on the man.

"You're a coward! A coward!" the Skellan yelled in defiance.

A third soldier clubbed the young man over the head with the hilt of his sword and the Skellan sunk into unconsciousness. He was dragged from the castle without further protest.

A moment later King Histen Corpin, Warson, and Claude appeared at the doorway. They didn't see Dane still hidden in the shadows of the corner. He started to leave, hoping to avoid their attention when he heard their conversation and paused.

"Skellans," the king spat out in disgust, "I have half a mind to massacre all of them."

"Just say the word and I will exact your wish, father," Warson said.

"No. They are troublesome and petulant but I hope the war will take care of them for me. Claude, what is the report from your spies?"

"Ashnah is on guard but not fully aware of the threat we pose, the threat Nox poses. They've seen the outpost and there is discussion among their leaders of what to do about Nox. They've sent extra soldiers to reinforce the outposts nearest Outpost Gray. It won't do them any good."

"I still think the spies can't be trusted. Their job is deceit. How can we be certain they are telling us the truth in their reports?" Warson said ill-naturedly.

"Leave that to me, brother," Claude responded. "They won't betray us. There is too much at stake for them. Their families are being closely monitored. If they step out of line, they know their families will pay the price for that insolence."

Dane had to clench his fists to hold back his anger.

"That is the way to true loyalty, Warson,"

Claude continued. "Encourage obedience and threaten the consequences of disobedience. Exploit weaknesses but never reveal your true cruelty until necessary."

"I prefer a more direct approach," Warson responded.

"That is good for a potential king. Just leave the subtle deceit to me and my spies."

The king gave a cruel laugh. "You two talk as if your positions are solidified. I wouldn't be so certain. You must keep proving yourselves and stay on guard. If you're not careful, I may just make Dane king instead."

Dane felt a chill creep down his spine. He knew the king was jesting. He would never make Dane king. He hardly tolerated Dane's presence in the castle and he constantly stated that Dane didn't possess the backbone to rule. Dane wished his father wouldn't say such things even in joking. It only served to fuel his brothers' hatred for him, the same hatred that had nearly gotten him killed only moments before.

Claude and Warson exchanged a look behind their father's back. It was a dark look full of hidden meaning. Dane wished he could decipher it. They were planning something. Dane trembled thinking what it might be.

CHAPTER 27

The news came in the dead of night.

Another attack had taken place. Cal was roused from bed by Sir Hayes himself.

"A scout's just come. Bad news. Get up and dressed. Be at the war room in five minutes."

The severity of Hayes's words was enough to knock any sleepiness from Cal and put him on high alert. Cal expected the worst and he was not disappointed. It turned out that even his imagination could not conjure up the trouble which had taken place.

At such a late hour, the meeting was only composed of the most essential persons. Sir Hayes, the king, Clifton, and Cal were gathered in the war room to hear the scout's report. The man was quaking with terror. He looked like he'd ridden long and hard to reach them. He was covered in dirt and sweat. Dried blood stained his forehead.

"It... it happened so suddenly," the man stammered. His eyes were wide as a spooked horse's, his breath came in erratic gasps.

"Where?" Hayes pressed. "Where was the attack?"

"Orion Outpost."

Cal sorted through a mental map, trying to remember the name Orion. "But that's well beyond the border," Cal said when his memory landed on the place.

"None of the reinforcements were sent there. I never expected the army would move so quickly and to Orion instead of Verin or Fenley," Hayes stated.

The scout nodded shakily. "The last we'd heard, Freiwade's army was at Outpost Gray. That's miles to the west, right on the border of Freiwade."

"How did they cover so much ground in such a short time?" the king wondered aloud. "It's only been a week since the first attack."

"How'd they get past the other outposts on the way?" Hayes commented.

Cal feared the answer to that question. "Were all of the outposts between Outpost Gray and Outpost Orion destroyed?"

The scout shook his head again. "I... I don't know. All I know is that suddenly there was an attack. The lieutenant," the knight hesitated as if in pain at the remembrance.

"Take a deep breath," Hayes placed a hand on the young man's shoulder. "You're safe now. Just try to give your report then get some rest."

"I'll never sleep again," the scout stated. "I'll never forget it."

"Never forget what?" Cal asked.

"That... thing. I can't even call him a man. He was horrible. The lieutenant saw him and somehow knew what was happening. We'd heard about Outpost Gray. I was told to run and warn you."

Cal studied the scout. It was true that the man hadn't even had time to don his armor. He was still in a state of undress. He'd hurriedly shoved a tunic and pants over his nightclothes and his boots were partially unlaced. Cal poured the man a glass of water from the basin on the oval table. He handed the glass to the man but the scout's hands were shaking so badly that he sloshed the drink down his front. He gestured for Cal to set the drink aside.

"Did you see what happened before you rode here?" Hayes questioned.

The scout swallowed hard. "Yes. There was no way I could miss it. I was far past the outpost but I still saw it. There was something like smoke but not smoke. Then there was a blast so powerful that I was thrown from my horse. I hit my head on something, I'm not sure what. When I managed to get up, I saw it. Or, rather, I didn't see it. The outpost was just... gone. And with it several dozen houses from the town."

"Wait a second. Town?" Cal asked. Yes, there was a town near Outpost Orion. It was small and not many people lived there. But several dozen houses? Gone in an instant. How horrible.

"Everyone defending the outpost was slaughtered," the scout spat out the word then dissolved into a sob.

Hayes dismissed the man to try to get some rest and instructed him to see a surgeon about his head as well.

"I don't like the sound of this," Hayes stated.

Neither did Cal. But something bothered him about the whole thing. Something didn't add up. "Why was there such a long delay between attacks?

Surely we would have heard if the other outposts were destroyed. The army must have moved through the area without making contact with our outposts. But if they have the power to destroy us, why didn't they?"

"The mage," Clifton voiced. "That kind of power is not made for human flesh to possess. I wouldn't be surprised if he was incapacitated for a while after attacking Outpost Gray."

"He has an entire army to back him up," Hayes reminded them. "It would make sense for them to keep moving forward even if the mage couldn't fight. They would choose their targets carefully and only engage the outposts that would strain us the most. Orion is… was, one of our strongest outposts. By choosing their attacks carefully, they could cause the most damage to us without risking their men beyond what was necessary. Sending reinforcements to the outposts was useless. Even if the mage had attacked Verin or Fenley, the extra knights would have only been added to the casualties. Until we can find a way to stop this mage, I won't put more men than necessary at risk."

Cal considered the attacked outpost, carefully chosen. It made sense for the mage to only attack the most important outposts, especially if he was limited in how often he could use his powers.

"I'm not satisfied," the king spoke. "I want to know more about what happened. Cal, I want you to go investigate the scene of the attack right away. If you ride hard without rest, you should be able to reach the area by midday and return here by tomorrow. Then, we'll call our counsel together and discuss a plan of attack."

Cal nodded and prepared to go. Sir Hayes halted him at the door. "Be careful. Don't take unnecessary risks and keep an eye out in case the army's moving this way."

Cal agreed to be cautious and rushed to the stables to ready a horse. He had hardly gotten the bridle latched when he realized someone was standing behind him.

"You're not going without me," the girl said, resolute in her decision.

Cal sighed and leaned his head against the horse's neck. "Lark. How is it that you always seem to know what's going on?"

"I was keeping my watch on Duke Heirson. I was just heading to bed when I heard the commotion. I heard what you discussed in the war room."

"That was a secret meeting."

Lark shrugged. "I'm a spy."

Cal couldn't argue with her there. Still, it made him subtly uncomfortable. He thought of his conversation with the king and Sir Hayes. Lark was always listening in on conversations that she shouldn't. He'd always written it off before but now he couldn't help wondering if she was gathering information for the enemy. He finished latching the last buckle of the bridle. "You can't come with. It's too dangerous and I'll have to ride fast to get there."

"Then you better keep up," she stated simply.

Cal knew there was no arguing with her. He might be the leader of the spies but he knew she wouldn't listen, not when danger was involved. He hoped he wasn't making a mistake in trusting her. He couldn't help but do so. He didn't bother to object further and before he knew it he and Lark were racing towards the outpost.

They reached the area at midday, having to switch horses twice at small towns along the journey to keep up their speed. They were both exhausted and utterly worn by the time they reached their destination. They saw the town of Orion first. Its inhabitants were distraught over what had taken place and rightly so. The attack had come unexpectedly and with absolute brutality. The townspeople were frantic with confusion and fear. They mourned the lives that had been lost and studied the decimated remains of the houses that were destroyed.

"Freiwade should pay for this," Lark said angrily as she took in the sobbing women and children, the shocked and angry men.

Cal felt something stirring inside his chest. Would a Freiwade spy say something like that? Maybe if she were trying to throw off suspicion. Cal hated that his mind instantly went to such thoughts when in the past he never would have questioned such a simple statement.

"We'll come back," Cal told Lark. "I want to see the outpost first."

They rode on through the village. Suspicious looks were thrown their way as they went. Cal suspected the townspeople assumed they were travelers. He and Lark didn't wear anything that would denote them as members of Castille Castle. Cal was grateful for that. He didn't want to answer the inevitable questions about what the king would do about this attack. Cal didn't know the answer and he suspected the king didn't either. What could be done against such a wicked enemy?

Cal and Lark kept riding until they passed the ruins of the houses that lay on the outskirts of the town and reached the outpost. They pulled their horses up short, shocked and horrified by the absolute destruction that they found. The outpost was quite simply gone. The tall, seemingly indestructible structure was reduced to rubble and debris. A hush filled the air between them. Lark glared at the remains of the outpost; her eyes filled with tearful wrath. Cal let her keep her silence. This place demanded quiet. A solemnity at the horrible events which had taken place hung in the air all around. Cal didn't dare say a word to break the silence.

The two spies slowly dismounted from their horses. The animals were spooked at the scene around them. Cal had to yank on his horse's bridle as it reared up and snorted. Its eyes were wide and white, its nostrils flaring. Lark didn't even look at her horse as it stamped the ground and shifted back and forth. She gladly passed over the bridle to Cal when he reached for it. He led the horses to the edge of the tree line and found a sturdy branch to tie them to. Then he rejoined Lark, intent to investigate the area and get away as quickly as possible.

The worst part of the scene wasn't the debris but the bodies. Cal wasn't sure if they could even be called human anymore. They were ghastly. The knights and archers stationed at the outpost were gone, not just dead, but gone. They were charred in places like cremated corpses but the act was not done by fire. Something else was responsible.

"Lark, wait with the horses," Cal instructed her. He didn't want her to look at the remains.

She shook her head and shoved past him. "I came with you for a reason," she ground out past barred teeth. "I want to see it all. I want to remember what they've done."

Cal was grateful he hadn't had time to eat before he'd ridden out. He was sure he would have lost any food he had in his stomach. As it was, he gagged and had to look away from the bodies. Their veins stuck out black against deathly pale skin in the few areas not burnt away. The ones who still had faces intact stared at him with open eyes still full of the horror they'd experienced in their last moments. Cal mustered the courage to reach out and close the eyes of the fallen knights and archers. May they have rest in death as they did not in life. Lark went along beside him, pressing their eyes closed and murmuring prayers over them. A few times he caught her saying something but she spoke so quietly he couldn't hear her. Finally, he asked her what it was she was saying.

"Peace," she said. "After this, I hope they've found it."

Cal hated to leave the bodies strewn carelessly about the field but he'd been given orders to investigate the area and return quickly. Someone else would be along soon enough to retrieve the bodies and return them to their families for a proper burial as well as to take note of their identities for record. Some of the bodies would be difficult to identify and Cal's heart ached for the families who would have to take on that task.

Cal felt a lingering darkness settle over the

area. He felt uneasy and on edge. A heavy feeling crawled into his chest. It was as if something was pressing down on him, driving him to the ground. It was evil, unlike anything he'd ever felt before. He wanted to get out of there quickly. Lark hovered close beside him. Her hand clutched at the sleeve of his shirt. At first, Cal jerked away at the touch. He didn't want to believe that she would hurt him but if she were a spy for the enemy... Cal quelled the thought and settled, allowing her to hold onto the very edge of his sleeve for comfort.

"Do you feel that?" she asked breathlessly.

Cal nodded.

"God, protect us," she muttered under her breath.

Cal swallowed hard and with Lark at his side, investigated the scene of the attack. He'd heard about the state of Outpost Gray after the attack but nothing could have prepared him for seeing the wreckage firsthand. The descriptions of the first attack matched and were amplified in what Cal saw. He was confident the attacks were caused by the same man or rather mage.

"Cal, look," Lark pointed to a spot on the ground.

Cal bent to study it. There was a drop of something that looked like oil staining the ground.

"What is it?" Lark asked.

"Oil?" Cal wondered aloud. But the words had no sooner left his mouth than he realized that it wasn't oil at all. It was blood. Black, blood.

"It's blood," Cal told her, "the mage's blood."

He felt a shiver run over him and Lark clutched his arm with a deathly grip.

"Let's get out of here," she said roughly.

Cal readily obliged. They retrieved their horses and returned to the small town.

"We should talk to some eyewitnesses before we leave," Cal said, though all he wanted to do was ride back and get far, far away from the destroyed outpost. Lark looked like she felt the same way. She seemed weighed down by a deep sadness. Her steps dragged and her gaze focused on her feet as she walked. Cal placed a hand on her shoulder in a show of comfort. She ignored the gesture.

They went from house to house asking questions of the survivors. Sometimes the townspeople answered with confusion or anger, some only responded with sobs. Some of them had been sleeping but those who'd been awake all saw the same thing.

"A strange man approached the outpost," the town's butcher told them. "I was just closing up my shop. I looked outside, you know we can see the outpost from here, and I saw the man along with a group of Freiwade soldiers. I knew it was trouble right away so I watched from my window. It was strange, the soldiers stood a ways back from the strange man, almost afraid of him. I saw why before long. A change came over the stranger and the sky filled with a blackness like smoke, it stood out even against the dimming sky. The man started to direct the darkness all around like spears. The knights and archers at the outpost were gone before they fully realized what was happening. Then the darkness kept on spreading until it reached the houses on the edge of town. It destroyed them and killed anyone unfortunate enough to be inside. We all thought we were going to die but then the darkness suddenly stopped. The man fell over as if he were dead and the soldiers dragged him away. I knew then that it was no man at all but a demon, maybe the devil himself. Only a few of us dared approach the outpost but we didn't stick around for long. We knew it was dangerous for us there. Something in the air wasn't right. Those who stuck around the village said that it was an overwhelming sense of fear that kept them away from the ruins."

The butcher's story was unsettling. It only served to cement in Cal what a terrible enemy they were facing. He suddenly dreaded the idea of the ride back to Castille. He was tired, so very tired, and he didn't want to give the awful report to the king and Sir Hayes.

"Come on," he told Lark, "let's get a drink first."

They headed to the town's small tavern and ordered hot ciders to rid the chill from their bones. The cook persuaded them to add a hearty meal of steaming and savory roast beef on bread to their orders. Neither of them had much of an appetite though. Cal glanced across the table at Lark. Her face was twisted with concern.

Cal wished more than anything that he could see inside her head. What was she thinking about? Was she working with the enemy? Would she betray him as he so feared she might?

"Lark," he waited till she met his gaze, "what are you thinking about?"

Lark took a sip of her cider, hesitating before she spoke. "I know I couldn't have done anything about this. It's just, sometimes I'm overwhelmed by how powerful Freiwade has become. They seem unstoppable."

Cal poked his fork at the meal in front of him. His stomach was in knots. He didn't think he could manage even a bite. "You know, in the Bible, there are many times when battles seemed to be favored for the enemy but God saved His people."

"I know but I just wish there was something else I could do to stop them. It makes me so angry to know that they've hurt so many people. The king has hurt so many, even his own people."

Cal studied her closely. He'd suspected for a long time now and only grown more certain with each passing day, that somehow Freiwade had hurt her too. If she was a spy for Freiwade, could she have a good reason for doing so? Cal had joined Ashnah's spies to make a difference after his sister's death. Maybe Lark was doing the same for Freiwade. Cal just wished he knew more about her. The only thing he knew was that she'd come to Castille desperate and frightened. What had happened to her? Had it all been an act? Cal didn't voice his thoughts, he never did. If she wanted to tell him, she would. Part of him didn't want to know the truth. He didn't want to find out that he had been wrong about her after all the years he'd trusted her.

Cal cleared his throat and pushed his doubts aside. "It's true that Freiwade has hurt many people and they'll likely hurt many more but I believe that God will save us from this battle. I believe that the power of Freiwade will be stopped."

They fell into silence after that and they stayed that way the entire ride back to Castille.

CHAPTER 28

Finch was summoned to the war room with such haste that he didn't bother with his appearance. He'd made an effort to present himself well during the first meeting of the war counsel but now, he didn't bother. If Hayes wanted him there, the man wouldn't care about his untidy uniform. Besides, it would serve to annoy Commander Terin.

A servant came bearing the message to come to the war room immediately and Finch wasted no time in obliging. He ran through the corridors of the castle like a madman, hurrying to reach the dreaded meeting. Had there been another attack? Finch could think of no other explanation for such an urgent calling. Was Dorian alright? He rushed into the meeting, instinctively knowing that things must have gone from bad to worse. The look on Sir Hayes's and the king's faces spoke for themselves. The occupants of the room were silent, waiting for the bad news. They all held their breaths in anticipation and dread.

"There's been another attack," Hayes said somberly.

Finch was desperate to interject with questions and concerns. Was it Outpost Verin? Was Dorian dead? But Finch noticed the exhaustion lining Hayes's eyes. He hadn't slept. Finch wouldn't interrupt just yet. But, if the attack had taken place during the night, why hadn't they been called to the meeting sooner?

"The outcome of this attack is even more dire than the previous. Civilians in a town near the outpost were killed and their houses destroyed. The outpost is gone and the destruction left in the wake is horrifying," Hayes continued.

Finch searched his mind, trying to recall whether Outpost Verin was near a town. He couldn't hold back his questions any longer. He was ready to speak when Jem, his fellow archer beat him to it.

"What outpost was it?" Jem asked.

Finch knew why his fellow archer was concerned. They knew people stationed at nearly every outpost in Ashnah. They had friends and even family risking their lives on the front lines. The attack on Outpost Gray had been difficult enough to accept, now there had been another attack. Finch should have tried harder to go with Dorian to Outpost Verin. He should have disobeyed orders to get there if he had to. He never should have abandoned his friend to such an awful fate.

"It was Outpost Orion," the king stated.

There were a few gasps around the room and snippets of murmured conversation. Finch's heart nearly burst out of his chest. He gasped with relief. It wasn't Verin. Dorian was safe. At least, Finch hoped Dorian was safe. Instantly, Finch felt guilty at his relief when he looked around the room and saw the stricken expressions on so many faces. His friend might have escaped the attack but others had been less fortunate.

Finally, one of the knights worked up the courage to speak.

"The men, sir? I have a friend stationed there. Were there any survivors?"

Hayes looked at the table. He closed his eyes as a pained expression crossed his face. "No. There was only the man who carried us the news. I'm sorry."

The knight took a deep breath to compose himself and nodded in acceptance. The mourning would come later for all of them. They were all accustomed to loss. It was no easy thing but they had to stay strong not only for themselves but for their kingdom.

A disturbing thought rose above all others in Finch's mind. He tried to sort through the thought quietly and find an answer but at last, he voiced his concern.

"Outpost Orion is further inland," he stated. "How did the enemy cover so much ground so quickly? Did they attack the other outposts on the way?"

Hayes shook his head in the negative. "I requested reports from the other outposts but as of the moment, there's been no word of attacks."

"I believe that the enemy mage is wearied by his power and must refrain from frequent attacks," Clifton explained, stepping forward.

"We suspect that the mage and Freiwade's army are selecting advantageous attacks to disable us as opposed to striking randomly," Hayes explained.

"How would they be getting that information?" Finch wondered aloud. "How would they know what places to attack to harm Ashnah the most?"

Finch received no answer but he thought he'd figured it out anyway. There was a reason why only the most trusted in the castle were gathered in the war room. There was a reason these attacks and the plan against them were being kept so secret. There was an enemy spy in the castle, there must be.

Hayes gestured the strange young man from the previous meeting forward. "Everyone, this is Cal."

The young man nodded to them in greeting.

"You've probably seen him around the castle but are unaware of who he is. That is by design. As I said before, you've all been selected because you are the most trustworthy tacticians in the castle. It is because of the trust we have in you that we are revealing this to you now. Cal is the kingdom's spymaster."

Well, that explained a lot, Finch thought. He studied the young man in a new light. He was relatively unassuming. That was probably the point. Looking at Cal, no one would expect him to be in such an important or dangerous position. He looked like a simple nobleman or maybe an advisor to a nobleman. His youth especially concealed the truth of his position.

"Impossible!" Commander Terin objected. "He's too young. Besides, why wasn't I aware of his position earlier?"

Hayes sighed heavily and looked at Terin with distaste. "Yes, he is young. However, he's more than proven himself in his short time working for the king. I would venture to say he's more capable than many high-ranking officers in this very room. And perhaps you are not as trustworthy as you believe you are, Terin."

The look Hayes gave Terin made Finch snicker. He immediately covered his mouth when Terin glared at him. He shuddered at the piercing look on his commander's face.

"The reason so few knew about my position," Cal explained, "was for my safety and theirs. Even those who are trusted may make an accidental slip of the tongue on occasion. Such a mistake would put me and the person who spoke in danger as well as endanger the effectiveness of my work. The truth is, that the kingdom of Ashnah has had a force of spies since the War of Three Kingdoms. I was trained by the last spymaster and then took over the role when he retired."

"Force of spies?" Finch questioned.

Cal nodded at Finch's perceptiveness.

Hayes took the lead again. "Cal and his small group of spies have been conducting intelligence gathering on the enemy mage and the aftermath of the attacks."

"We've investigated the scenes of the attacks and interrogated eyewitnesses if there were any. I've personally gone to Outpost Orion to survey the area. It's unlike anything I've seen before. All of the witnesses claim there was something like a black cloud of smoke in the air and that the mage was able to control it. They said he was inhuman. Rubble is the only thing left in the destruction. The bodies," Cal hesitated, looking to the knight who'd spoken earlier before continuing, "the bodies are disfigured. Whatever power attacked those outposts was grotesque and the evidence is all around. I journeyed to Outpost Orion yesterday as soon as we received word of the attack."

That would explain the delay in the meeting. They'd wanted to get more information first. Finch almost wished he could have seen the outpost to know firsthand what they were facing. However, by Cal's description, he was also grateful he'd been spared from the sight. Cal looked like he hadn't slept since news of the attack had arrived.

"During my investigation of Orion," Cal continued, "I found something disturbing that hadn't been noticed at other scenes. There was blood, but not just any blood. My companion and I believed it was the blood of the mage. It was black like oil."

Interesting, Finch thought.

Everyone turned to look at Clifton.

"I assure you that is not normal for a mage," Clifton told them. "Certainly not for me and I'm assuming not for Corin. However, you must remember this mage possesses an unnatural, corrupting magic. His power may have corrupted his very blood."

"That's beside the point," Terin interjected. "The blood proves that this mage can be stopped. He can be injured."

"But who would be powerful enough to inflict that kind of damage on him?" Kent, one of the knights asked.

"That's a good point," Remus, the archer, agreed. "I don't think anyone in the village would have been able to stand against the mage and all the men in the outpost died except for a messenger I'm assuming.

Who was able to draw the mage's blood?"

"No one," Hayes answered simply.

Clifton moved to explain. "Cal has reported that some of the witnesses saw the mage collapsing after he attacked the outpost. I believe the blood was a result of internal stress on the mage."

"A nosebleed?" Jem asked.

"Yes, a nosebleed."

"So, his magic is working against him?" Adam, another knight, questioned.

"Possibly," Clifton spoke, "though we shouldn't count on something like that working in our favor."

"That," King Rupert said, "is why we need to come up with a plan. We cannot allow these attacks to go on. The war may just be starting but this mage must be stopped soon before he can cause any more damage. We cannot allow him to reach Castille or one of our other strongholds. We must not let him be the driving force of this war."

Hayes addressed them all, "I apologize for the short notice but you'll need to bring forward any plans you may have come up with to stop the man. The time for waiting and thinking is over. It's time to act."

Several of the knights and archers began to share their ideas and work through any shortcomings in their plans. They voiced notions such as attacking the enemy directly, using flaming arrows, attempting to poison the enemy, and other even wilder plans. Terin had the especially impractical idea of sending an assassin into the enemy camp to kill the mage.

"No, absolutely not," Sir Hayes, the king, and Cal all shot down the idea immediately.

"It's far too risky," Hayes explained. "What if the mage woke up? Not only would the assassin be as good as dead, but he would know we were attempting to strike back. The assassin could be tortured for information and reveal something detrimental to us."

"Besides, those are not the kind of tactics Ashnah uses," the king added.

Terin snorted. "Desperate times call for desperate measures, king. Would you rather lose the war than resort to 'dirty' tactics? It takes a leader willing to do anything to win a war."

"Careful, Terin," Hayes warned.

"No, maybe he's right," the king stated, "though in the last war this kingdom faced, we were victorious and not because we resorted to assassination attempts. The king of Freiwade was willing to do whatever it took, no matter how terrible, to win the war but my grandfather refused to sacrifice his morals. Still, Ashnah prevailed. It's not ruthlessness that wins wars, Terin, but wisdom. That's something you should focus on."

Terin turned red with humiliation but he couldn't speak against the king. There were a few snickers from the knights which only made the situation worse. The archers knew better and kept silent. They'd all seen Terin angry and none of them wished to relive that experience. Finch sunk back, leaning against the wall and wishing he could disappear into it. He barely breathed, for fear he'd draw Terin's attention to himself.

Other ideas were voiced and Finch's mind eventually turned from concern about Terin to his own plans. His thoughts raced at a breakneck speed. Finch thought about what he'd learned about the attacks. The second attack came sometime, approximately a week, after the first. As far as they knew, no other outposts had been attacked in the meantime. The mage had reportedly collapsed after the attack and his blood had been at the scene of the destruction. A spy was feeding information to Freiwade about what outposts would harm Ashnah the greatest if they were destroyed.

"Can I see a map?" Finch asked.

His question drew everyone's attention to him. He winced at the looks. Hayes laid a map of Ashnah on the oval table and spread it out. Finch leaned forward to study the map. He'd never been great at reading maps; it wasn't something that archers spent a lot of time on. He gestured to Cal.

"Could you show me where the attacks were?"

Cal easily pointed out Outpost Gray and Outpost Orion.

Finch traced a finger from one outpost to the other. If the mage was heading for the castle, which it could be assumed he was, and he was unable to attack often, which seemed likely, then he would have the chance to attack one more outpost before he reached Castille.

Finch voiced his concerns, "It seems that the mage is only able to attack once a week, approximately. Freiwade's army is trying to cover as much distance as possible during that time while remaining unnoticed and they are striking where it will hurt us the most. They're making good time so I think they'll only be able to attack one more outpost before they reach the castle."

"That's unlikely," Terin said. "We still have plenty of time before they reach Castille if they're only at Orion now. They'll have to face four outposts between here and there."

"But they're not attacking every outpost," Finch stated. "They're picking the ones which will do the most damage. They're staying hidden when possible and only attacking when the mage is able to aid them. That means, there's only one outpost left before they reach Castille. Given the direction the army is heading and the amount of destruction it would cause, it's likely they'll choose to attack Outpost Halliday."

"Quiet, boy. You've never excelled at maps. You don't know what you're talking about."

"No," Cal interrupted Terin, "he's right. I'd made the same connection earlier. It's good that someone else has seen the pattern and confirmed it."

Finch was uncomfortable at the praise. Maybe he shouldn't have spoken out. He wished Cal hadn't said anything. Terin wouldn't let any praise of Finch stand. A vein was bulging at the commander's forehead. He'd been humiliated and Finch had been praised. That would only spell trouble for Finch later.

"We have to slow down the pace Freiwade's army is making," Hayes agreed. "Our army and our mages need time to prepare. If they attack another outpost and destroy it, that won't delay them more than two weeks. It will also cost us dearly in terms of men and morale. So, what can we do to prevent another attack and delay the mage and the army?"

Finch's mind came up with a solution almost immediately but Terin's brutal glare that promised punishment should he speak caused Finch to keep silent. It made him angry. Why couldn't he be brave enough to speak out against Terin to help his kingdom? He couldn't find the courage to do so.

Hayes met Finch's eyes, seeming to notice his hesitation.

"Finch, do you have a plan?" Hayes asked.

Finch wanted so badly to say yes. He knew it was a halfway decent plan. It could work. It could force the enemy army and the mage to slow their pace. He glanced at Terin who fixed him with a warning glare. Finch took a step back until he was up against the wall.

He shook his head. "No, sir."

Hayes kept staring at him, obviously not believing him, but the battle master didn't press the issue.

"Will Ashnah's mages be able to fight Freiwade's mage if he reaches the castle?" Kent asked

Finch noticed then that at some point, Clifton had left the room.

"The mages are working as hard as they can to ready themselves," the king assured them all.

Finch certainly hoped so because it was likely Clifton and Corin were their only chance of surviving against such a terrible threat.

Hayes rested a hand on the table and leaned heavily against it. "I'm sorry again for expecting you all to come up with a solution on such short notice. For now, you're all dismissed while the king and I think over your ideas and come up with a plan. You can expect to be called upon again for another meeting once a decision has been reached. Thank you."

The knights and archers began to filter out of the room, discussing what had happened amongst themselves. Finch prepared to join them.

"Cal, Finch, please stay behind a moment," Hayes called out.

Finch froze. Was he in trouble? Had he overstepped by sharing his observation earlier? Terin's look of glee hinted that he suspected Finch was about to face some sort of repercussion. As the others left the room, Finch wondered just how much trouble he was in.

CHAPTER 29

Cal knew why Hayes had requested him and Finch to remain behind. He'd seen the look the battle master directed at the young archer. Finch had a plan, a plan he was refusing to share for some reason. Cal only wished he'd done so earlier. He was so tired he could hardly stand. All he wanted was to crawl into bed and sleep for a week. However, he feared the nightmares he might find waiting for him when he closed his eyes.

Hayes waited until every last person was out of the room, even the king. Cal had to keep blinking to try to stay awake. Once the meeting was over, he could get some sleep, that is, if he could erase the images of what he'd seen at the outpost from his mind.

"Now that everyone's gone, what's your plan?" Hayes demanded of Finch.

"I'm not sure what you mean, sir," Finch feigned misunderstanding. It fooled no one, least of all Hayes.

"I saw it in your eyes that you had a plan for stopping the mage and halting Freiwade's army. I want to hear it. You won't be leaving this room until you share it."

Finch looked away, refusing to meet Hayes's eyes. "It doesn't matter. It probably won't work."

"I don't care. Let's hear it anyway."

Finch glanced at Cal then back at Sir Hayes.

"It's not a complete plan and I don't know how practical it would be," Finch said hesitantly, "but I was thinking about the mage. What exactly happened at Orion?"

Hayes looked to Cal in deference.

Cal sighed heavily, reluctant to repeat his report but knowing it was necessary. "The outpost was in ruins, the houses on the outskirts of the town were completely gone. The bodies were charred and disfigured and everything in close proximity was dead: the grass, the trees, even the dirt looked like it had been made infertile. A heaviness hung in the air all around. It was difficult to get close without feeling sick and weighed down. Our horses wouldn't get near the place. Lark and I found the black blood in the right spot for it to have come from the mage. The eyewitnesses said they saw a cloud of something black like smoke and it encroached on the village destroying a few houses before it finally retreated."

"So, the smoke got to the edge of the village and then suddenly disappeared, destroying a few houses but not all of them?" Finch questioned.

Cal nodded.

This seemed to cement whatever idea had been forming in Finch's head.

"Based on the time between attacks and the eyewitness reports, he might be struggling to control his magic," Finch stated.

"What do you mean?" Cal asked.

Finch shrugged. "It seems like he might have lost control of his abilities during the last attack. It could be that he wanted to attack the town as well as the outpost to demonstrate his power and ruthlessness. But why would he attack more than necessary if it causes him harm? If he was going to attack the village, he could have destroyed the whole thing, not just a few houses. I think when he was weakened from his attack on the outpost, his abilities overwhelmed him. Clifton says that this magic is unnatural. He said that it may be corrupting even the mage's blood. What if the magic is trying to gain control over the man? The mage was reported to undergo a change during the attack and he didn't seem human. The magic kept growing and expanding even after the outpost was destroyed but then it was cut off suddenly during the destruction of the town. I think it may have been unintentional."

"Maybe," Hayes admitted. "That would explain why he is so weakened after an attack and why there was blood left behind."

"The magic is fighting against him and when he tries to control it, it weakens him," Cal thought out loud.

"So, what do you propose we do?" Hayes asked Finch.

"Well, we clearly need to stall for time. Our army and our mages aren't prepared to face such a threat. We also need to weaken the enemy mage. With the power he possesses now, we wouldn't stand a chance of stopping him." Finch pointed to the map still lying on the table. "Like I said earlier, it's incredibly likely he'll attack Outpost Halliday next.

Fortunately, Halliday isn't near a town like Orion was. It's surrounded by a forest too. It seems to me like it would be a great place to stage an ambush."

Cal was impressed with the idea. Although others had suggested an attack as well, Finch seemed to have actually thought out the plan. The forest would provide plenty of cover to hide knights and archers, and without a town nearby, they could avoid civilian casualties. By noticing the pattern of attacks, Finch had also allowed them to prepare in advance to meet the enemy.

Finch continued, "The goal should be not to stop the man, we're probably not capable of that, but to at least incapacitate him for a while to buy us more time. If we force him to exceed the limits of his abilities, it could cause the magic to turn against him, requiring him to refrain from using it for a longer amount of time. If we could injure him somehow, that would also cause an increased delay. The blood proved that one way or another he can be hurt."

"So, you suggest we encourage him to attack using more of his power?" Hayes asked. "What about the destruction that would cause? Halliday is one of our most important outposts. The loss of life there would be tremendous."

"I thought of that already," Finch stated. "What if we fill the outpost with dummies? A little straw and canvas dressed in armor could go a long way. We would make sure the dummies resembled knights and archers and position them around the outpost. It wouldn't hold up on close inspection but, from a distance, they would pass as real soldiers. That would mean no loss of life at all."

"Wouldn't the mage and the army be suspicious that no one went out to meet them in battle?" Cal asked.

"Not necessarily. They would know that reports have reached us by that point and they would suspect that the men stationed in the outpost were afraid and believed that the stone walls would offer them protection. From a distance, the dummies would be believable enough. If we could rig arrows or projectiles to be thrown from the outpost, it would make it seem as if there were people there."

"It could work," Cal admitted, impressed at the young archer's idea.

"Just how do you plan on injuring him?" Hayes asked, slightly more skeptical.

"We would wait until the mage had attacked the outpost and was weakened, then we would have to move quickly. A group of knights and archers from Ashnah would pick off as many of the enemy soldiers as possible while simultaneously attacking the mage. A bombardment of arrows while he is down and recovering might do some damage."

"Clifton believes the mage is capable of healing himself, an attack may not harm him at all," Hayes commented.

"Then at least the enemy soldiers would dwindle in number."

"We also don't know the full limits of the mage's power. The attack may be fruitless," Cal added.

Finch studied the map. Despite his earlier hesitations, he now seemed determined to have his plan accepted. "Yes, it's a risk. But it's one I think we have to take. I doubt we'd be able to kill the mage or even halt him for long but this is the best way to slow him down."

Hayes paced the room, considering. "Once we use this attack, Freiwade won't fall for it again. We would have to ensure that it worked the first time. But… it is a good plan, maybe the best option we have. It's a lot to think about but I'll suggest this plan to the king. Thank you, Finch, for your input. It's been invaluable, as I knew it would be."

Finch's ears reddened with embarrassment at the praise. He looked up at Hayes. "Sir, why exactly did you want me on this committee in the first place?"

"It should be obvious," Hayes stated. "You're smart and resourceful as well as one of the best archers in the kingdom. You think outside of the box and you're not afraid to take calculated risks. More than that, I trust you explicitly. I know that no matter the cost to yourself, you'll do your duty."

Cal could see that the words impacted Finch greatly. The young man's throat bobbed with emotion and he ducked his head. "I should go, sir. I have a watch this afternoon." With that, the young archer exited the war room leaving Sir Hayes and Cal alone.

Cal thought about the young man and wondered why he hadn't shared his plan during the meeting. Certainly, it would have gone over well. Finch would have earned high praise from all those present. Yet, he had kept the plan to himself instead. It had taken Hayes practically dragging it out for him to speak. Cal had done background research on every individual who was part of the committee. He'd personally ensured that they were trustworthy individuals. To do so, he'd had to look into their pasts.

He suspected that he knew why Finch was hesitant to share his ideas in front of the others. Cal was glad that Hayes had held him back afterward and forced him to speak. Finch's idea could very well buy them much-needed time and save countless lives. It was too bad that Finch's background kept him from reaching his full potential. Unfortunately, that was often the case with brilliant minds.

"Finch is an exceptional individual," Cal told Hayes. "He's a good thinker and tactician. It wouldn't be so bad to recruit him to the spy force. He'd fit well in that position, I think."

"No. Finch may be a good candidate but I hope he doesn't have that kind of life in store for him. He could achieve great things out in the open if not for certain obstacles in his path."

"You seem to have taken a special interest in him," Cal remarked.

Hayes shifted uncomfortably. "I saw his potential from the beginning. I took him under my wing when he started training as a castle archer. Someone needed to look out for him and keep him from being sent to the front lines for no good reason."

"Aw," Cal said, "so, that's why you requested to see the list of those who would be stationed at Outpost Gray. You wanted his name off the list. If I didn't know better, I would call that favoritism sir. Though, it seems God's hand may have been in that decision. If he'd been sent to Gray, he never would have returned."

Hayes huffed in agreement. "I guess somewhere along the way, helping the young man, I seem to have formed an attachment. He reminds me of myself at that age. I wanted to prove myself but I didn't know how to. I didn't come from the best background myself and sometimes I did foolish things in an attempt to break free of what was expected of me. The difference between me and Finch is that, while I was reckless in trying to prove myself, Finch wants anonymity. He would rather sink into obscurity than stand up for himself. I won't allow that kind of life for him. He deserves much more than that."

"It's not all bad," Cal said. "It seems that Finch is already achieving great things under your mentorship. You should be proud of him."

Hayes smiled ever-so-slightly, the scar on his face twisting with the gesture. "I already am."

CHAPTER 30

Will came to inform Corin that morning that his lesson would be delayed. The boy didn't explain why and it was likely Clifton hadn't told him. Corin didn't mind. For some reason, he'd slept poorly. He felt unsettled. He'd tossed and turned with horrible dreams of darkness and death all night. He wasn't eager to train and he took the respite gratefully.

Will scurried off to his own classes without delay, leaving Corin alone to find a way to spend his unexpected free time. He decided that he would use the extra time to try to find Ruena. Life in the castle had started to improve, knowing he had her to talk to. He didn't feel as lonely or out of place. They talked about minor things like Corin's past training as a knight and her own studies. It was a welcome respite from the usual intensity of topics surrounding Corin's training as a mage. He went searching for her but she wasn't in the usual room overlooking the garden. She wasn't in the great hall or library either. The whole castle felt strangely empty. The servants still bustled about and the nobles wandered the hallways as they went from room to room. And there was something else different. Among the nobles' ranks were knights with varying uniforms from all over Ashnah. There were the green surcoats of the Baron of Iverny, the muted yellow of the southern pasturelands, and even the gray of the far north. Knights from all over the kingdom were wandering the hallways of Castille castle. Representatives maybe? Corin was confused at their presence and confident that he hadn't seen them before. Why had they come to Castille Castle? Were they waiting to speak with the king? Despite the strange newcomers, Corin couldn't find any familiar faces. The people Corin knew: Ruena, the king, Clifton, and Sir Hayes, all seemed to be missing. It felt like something was going on and everyone except Corin had been informed of it.

Corin tried to convince himself that they were all just busy. Poor Clifton had been forced to study his books more than usual lately in an attempt to find magic that would challenge Corin while also not overwhelming him with overly complicated concepts. Hayes was probably training the knights. The king no doubt had an endless number of tasks to accomplish. Most of all, Corin was disappointed to not find Ruena.

He wandered the halls, hoping to maybe run into her at random or at least find something else to occupy him. Maybe he would watch the garrison train again and try to pick up a few more sword drills to practice during his free time. As Corin had the thought, he wandered down a hallway and finally caught sight of someone he knew. Dorian stood talking animatedly with another young man. Corin felt that he had seen the young man before, likely in the great hall during a meal. Yes, it was the archer who had glared at him with such intensity a while ago, the same archer he'd seen arguing in the hallway before the ill-fated trip to the town of Castille. Corin was surprised at remembering such an occurrence but the archer's stare had stayed with him, especially after the argument he'd overheard. Corin wondered who the strange young man was. He didn't know his name or his rank among the king's archers.

Corin, having no better use for his time, decided to approach the two young men. He hadn't talked with Dorian in a while and maybe he could make amends with the archer for however he had upset him. However, as Corin came close, a hint of annoyance washed over him. The young man was an archer but if Corin hadn't known before, he may not have been able to tell. The young man was dressed sloppily, showing no pride or respect for his station. Corin had heard about the king's archers, the force of bowmen who possessed uncanny accuracy and were deemed the best archers in the kingdom, perhaps in all of Ademar. Not many in the kingdom achieved such standing. It was a high-ranking and respected position that few could even dream of attaining. The young man didn't seem to care judging by the manner of his appearance. His sloppy state was a disgrace to his king. His clothes were missing almost all distinguishing aspects of the uniform and what he did wear was horribly wrinkled. Even his hair was messy and longer than it should have been.

Corin was tempted to turn around then and there and leave Dorian and the archer. He suddenly didn't want to interact with the shameless young man. But he hesitated. He knew something was going on around the castle that was keeping everyone on edge and busy and bringing knights from all over the kingdom to the castle. He wondered if Dorian would know whatever it was. Corin decided he could manage a conversation with the archer if it would solve some of his questions. Maybe he was jumping to conclusions anyway. He approached the two men.

"I don't see why you're so surprised that I'm back in one piece," Dorian said. "I told you it was only a temporary position. Besides, that outpost is so out of the way, I was probably safer there than here. Why were you so worried? Was it something you heard in those oh-so-secret meetings?"

"I've told you, Dorian. I really can't tell you anything," the archer addressed his companion. "I'm just relieved you're back. That's all."

"I know the state of things, Finch. I'm just worried for the kingdom and for you, my friend."

The young man, Finch, seemed to hesitate, about to say something, when he looked up and spotted Corin. Anything he might have said was cut off.

Dorian followed his companion's gaze and caught sight of Corin as well. Dorian looked disappointed and maybe even a little annoyed at seeing him. Corin took a step back, immediately feeling bad for interrupting the conversation.

"I'm sorry. I didn't mean to interrupt," Corin quickly apologized. "I was just passing by and wanted to say hello."

Dorian waved off the apology and instantly changed his demeanor from disappointment to cheerfulness. Corin wondered if he'd imagined the annoyance on the knight's face.

"It's no problem, Corin. It's good to see you. This is my friend, Finch. Finch, this is Corin."

Finch soured. His face twisted into a grimace. "I'm aware. He's the almighty mage everyone is drooling over."

Corin flushed with embarrassment and anger. He'd definitely been correct in his assumption that Finch was not someone he wanted to interact with. He squared his shoulders and tried to hide his irritation.

"Yes, I'm the mage," Corin stated. "Who are you?"

Finch glanced to the side as if he didn't have the patience for any sort of conversation with Corin. He gestured vaguely to his sloppy, partially dissembled uniform. "Archer," he explained dismissively.

"Could have fooled me," Corin mumbled.

Finch bristled. "What are you doing wandering the halls, mage? Shouldn't you be busy learning your magic? I know you have a fondness for listening in on other people's conversations but there are far better uses for your time. The rest of us are working around the clock trying to prepare for this war but you seem to have plenty of time on your hands."

Something in Finch's words gave Corin pause. He noticed for the first time the dark circles around Finch's eyes. He chose to ignore the obvious signs of exhaustion. It didn't mean anything. As far as Corin knew, Finch may not have been working at all. He might have spent all night in a tavern. Nothing excused his rudeness.

"Finch," Dorian said, trying to calm his friend, "come on, that's not fair."

"I am working hard," Corin defended himself.

"Maybe you should focus on your duties. You obviously don't care much about your position."

"You have no idea how much I've sacrificed by being a castle archer," Finch snarled.

"You don't show much care about the honor you've been shown with that position. Most archers or knights would take better care to present themselves in a worthy manner."

Dorian snorted which only angered Finch further.

"Maybe I didn't have time to 'present myself in a worthy manner' seeing as I haven't slept in two days and I was dragged out of bed after my watch to attend a meeting." Finch looked like he might say more. Dorian looked at him expectantly but Finch stopped speaking.

"What was the meeting about, Finch?" Dorian questioned.

"I've already told you I can't say," Finch snapped. "I can't tell anyone anything and no one bothers to tell me anything either. No one warned me that you would be sent off to Outpost Verin until it was set in stone. I'm sick of all these ridiculous secrets but I can't do anything about them. And now Hayes suddenly expects things from me on top of it all."

A vein pulsed at Finch's forehead after his outburst. He took a deep breath in an attempt to compose himself. Finch glared at Corin and muttered to Dorian, "Maybe you should just hang around your new friend. You'll be *plenty* involved in matters if you stick around the oh-so-important mage." Finch stormed off after the words.

"Finch!" Dorian called after his friend. Dorian

glanced back apologetically at Corin. "I'm sorry, he's not usually like this. He hasn't slept well and he's stressed about something that he won't tell me."

Dorian didn't stick around to talk to Corin but instead rushed after his friend.

Corin huffed in annoyance and crossed his arms over his chest. How had Finch even gained such a sought-after position as a castle archer with an attitude like that? Corin had tried harder than anyone to be a knight and even then he'd failed. Why were people like Finch allowed such lofty positions when Corin hadn't even been able to move past the station of squire?

"Don't let Finch get on your nerves," a voice said behind Corin. "He's hot-tempered on his best days and he's currently under a good deal of pressure. But he doesn't mean you any harm."

Corin turned and found the young man he'd seen speaking with Ruena. He searched his mind for his name; Cal, that was it. Corin wasn't sure how to act around the man whom Ruena had called a friend. Corin couldn't quite meet Cal's gaze. He still didn't know who the man was but he supposed if he was Ruena's friend that was good enough.

"I'm used to people losing their tempers with me anyway," Corin said in answer.

Cal held out his hand. "I'm Cal. I saw you the other day while I was talking with Ruena."

"She said you were her friend, like a brother to her."

"Yes. She's talked about you too, Corin. Though, everyone knows about you."

"So I'm aware."

"Don't let the rumors and whispers get to you. Most of them are meaningless and ill-advised. Ruena is a good friend to have. Stick with her and you'll be fine."

Corin reluctantly shook the proffered hand.

"I don't know if I'm Ruena's friend exactly," Corin murmured.

"Are you something else to her?"

Corin turned crimson. "That's not what I meant!" he protested.

Cal grinned. "Ruena sees you as a friend. I assure you of that. It's good for her to have someone she can relate to. If she likes you, that's good enough for me. Remember that not everyone around the castle is displeased about having another mage. I won't tell you that you're just what we need for this upcoming war because I'm sure you've heard plenty of that already. Instead, I'll say that I'm glad you're here in this castle for Ruena's sake. You seem to fit in well, or at least you will before long. This castle is where you belong, mage or not."

Corin was a little surprised at the words but it felt good for someone to be treating him like a person instead of just a mage. He'd been skeptical about Cal before. He still had no idea what the young man did around the castle. But Corin didn't mind him so much now. He seemed friendly and kind, a good person.

"I'm afraid I should be going," Cal excused himself. "I'm plenty busy. But, I'll see you around, Corin."

Corin waved goodbye to the strange young man. It was time he found Clifton for his lesson anyway. Some people, like Finch, might not be so welcoming but others, like Cal, seemed to be glad Corin was around. Maybe Cal was right, maybe the castle was where Corin belonged.

CHAPTER 31

Clifton stood before the king and Sir Hayes with a feeling of foreboding settled deep in his chest. He knew this would not be a pleasant conversation. Still, it was a necessary one. He'd already spoken to the king about the attack at the market. He'd already been lectured on the foolishness of taking Corin into the town of Castille. Clifton hated that Corin had to experience the same isolation that he had when he'd come to the castle. Perhaps it was even worse for Corin who had arrived during a time of war. The attack had been unexpected but as Clifton had suspected, the king wanted to keep the matter quiet. It meant that both Clifton and Corin were confined to the castle for a time. Clifton wasn't sure if they were any safer within Castille's walls. The enemy spies in their midst could just as easily slip a knife between their ribs or mix poison into their meals.

Clifton had faced danger and disgust all of his life. He was used to it. But he worried about the impact it would have on Corin.

"Your Majesty, you called for me." Clifton addressed the king.

"Clifton, there's no need for formalities. I only

called you here to discuss a few things that have come to my mind."

Clifton bowed his head in acceptance. It still felt strange to speak to the king using any sort of title. He'd known Rupert since he was a boy and had always thought of him as a friend. He'd known Theon, the king's elder brother, too; he'd grieved his departure and later death. The Castilles were the closest thing to family that Clifton had.

"Of course. What is it you wanted to talk about?"

The king exchanged a glance with Hayes, a silent conversation passing between the two men. Clifton felt unsettled. Whenever Hayes was included in a conversation it usually meant there would be talk of the war, talk of battle.

"We're concerned about Corin," King Rupert finally said.

"Corin?"

"How is he faring after the attack?" Hayes cut in.

Clifton took a moment to ponder the question. Corin was somewhat flighty by nature. Sir Burke had warned Clifton of what he could expect from Corin.

"He's never felt quite at home anywhere," Burke had said. "When I pulled him from the streets of Nevara, he was nearly starved to death, dressed in rags, and with the vicious look in his eyes of a feral cat. It took him months to settle into the battle school and even then he wouldn't accept his place. He was constantly trying to prove himself and always suspected he would be thrown out. He might do the same in Castille. I hesitate to let you take him at all."

Clifton hadn't fully taken Burke seriously. When he'd seen Corin, he'd seen a meek and confused boy, not a fierce and defensive one. It wasn't until Corin had skipped his lessons, sneaking off to the garrison that Clifton remembered Burke's warning. He'd feared that Corin had run away when he didn't appear that morning.

After the attack in the town, Clifton had kept a close eye on Corin. He'd even set Will to act as a spy on the young mage. He'd feared Corin would leave for good. Part of Clifton wouldn't blame the boy if he did.

"He's reacted better than I expected," Clifton told Hayes.

"Good. That's good. We can't lose him, Clifton. Corin is our only hope against the enemy mage," the king said.

Clifton swallowed hard. He knew it wasn't meant as an insult, but it still hurt to know he wasn't as strong as he should be. The years had weighed heavily on him. He couldn't fight this battle. Corin had to be the one to face the enemy mage. It pained Clifton to lay that burden on the boy.

"He's not ready," Clifton said simply. "Corin has only been here a short time. He's already learned more than I did in my first year. I'm rushing his training and I fear the long-term effects that will have. You can't expect him to face the mage. Not yet."

"There's no other choice," Hayes replied.

"Difficult decisions must be made in times of war. I take no pleasure in putting Corin in such a position," King Rupert stated.

"But you're right, Clifton. Corin isn't ready. Not yet. He wasn't able to defend himself during the attack in the town. He doesn't possess the skills to defeat another mage. Is there anything you can do to better prepare him for that fight?" Hayes's words sent a chill of fear into Clifton's heart.

There was a way. But he'd sworn to Neos Loch that he would never use it. He would have waited years to even teach the technique to Corin. He may have never passed that skill on. The only reason Loch had shown him was to keep the skill alive for a time of great need.

"You have to promise to never use this technique unless there is no other choice," Loch had warned him.

Neos Loch had developed the skill as a necessity during the great war and he had regretted doing so ever since. Yet, he had shown Clifton, he had kept the skill alive, always holding on to it in case… in case there was no other way. Was this that moment? Was this the dreaded time when all other hopes were lost and that forbidden skill must resurface?

Clifton shook his head. He couldn't tell the king and he certainly couldn't tell Sir Hayes. They wouldn't understand. They would only see it as another weapon in their arsenal. They wouldn't think of the potential repercussions.

"What is it, Clifton? You know of something, don't you?" Hayes pressed.

Clifton shook his head again. "No, it's nothing."

"Clifton Eaves, as your king, I demand that you hold nothing back. We are in a time of war. Secrets can kill. If there is anything that might aid Corin in defeating the mage, you are honor-bound to reveal it. If you don't, you could be withholding information that means the difference between life and death for Corin."

Clifton shuddered at the words. He couldn't. He shouldn't. Loch had made him swear that he would never tell anyone. But what if the king was right? What if this technique was the difference between life and death for Corin?

Corin had come to the castle and offered Clifton hope. There was someone else like him. There was another who was blessed and burdened with the same gifts. The loneliness and despair were gone. Clifton couldn't let Corin die. He had to help him. Even if that meant acknowledging the skill that Loch had warned him about.

"There is one thing," Clifton told the king. "But I have to warn you, this technique is one that is against the very nature of magic. Neos Loch created it out of necessity during the War of Three Kingdoms. He told me that he regretted ever doing so."

"What is it?" Hayes questioned.

"It is a skill used to destroy. Its power is great and the consequences are dire. I hesitate to even tell you about its existence and I fear what would happen if I taught Corin how to use it. He's powerful. I have never seen such strong abilities, even in my mentor, Neos Loch. Corin has already learned more than I did in my first few years as a mage. He's learning fast and I don't want to overburden him. This is complicated magic and dangerous. I don't want to risk corrupting Corin."

"Corrupting him?" King Rupert asked.

"He doesn't fully understand what magic is. He still sees it as a danger more than a gift. I cannot read his mind. I don't know what his relationship with God is. What I do know is that he is young and he has had a hard life. This kind of power is dangerous in anyone's hands. Giving Corin the ability to use his magic to destroy opens a door that cannot be closed. If he starts to think the power is his own and tries to do things with his own skill, he could be corrupted by the very power that is such a blessing. This technique is incredibly powerful and it walks a line that mages should avoid at all costs."

"But we have to prepare him. The battle is swiftly approaching. We must ready Corin for whatever he may face," Hayes put in.

"I..." Clifton got no further. He couldn't adequately put his fears and concerns into words.

"I agree that this is not ideal, Clifton," King Rupert said kindly, "but it's necessary. Hayes is right. Corin needs to know this. If there is even the slightest possibility that this could save Corin in the coming battle, then he needs to know it."

"Teach him and warn him like your mentor did for you to only use it as a last resort. We are desperate, Clifton, more desperate than you realize. The threat this enemy poses is one greater than we've ever faced before. We have to find some way to combat this force or the war is as good as lost already."

Something about Hayes's words unsettled Clifton. He couldn't explain why. He remembered what Loch had told him before demonstrating the dangerous ability for the first time.

"I fear that my creating this technique was because I was weak. I feared the enemy and what they could do to me and the kingdom. I wanted a solution and quickly. So, I took matters into my own hands. Perhaps that was my greatest mistake."

Clifton couldn't help but feel that he too was making a great mistake. Was he leading Corin astray by teaching him this technique? Was he saving the boy or corrupting him? Clifton had no answer and he had no choice. Desperate times called for desperate measures.

CHAPTER 32

Cal knew Finch had a good plan. Good, not perfect. It was true that they were desperate to delay Freiwade's mage and buy Ashnah some much-needed time. Cal knew Finch's plan would work but what would be the cost for Ashnah?

The plan required knights and archers to go into the midst of danger and face the enemy head-on. What if the mage wasn't weakened enough by his attack on the outpost? What if he didn't fall for the dummy knights and archers? They had already lost so many to the mage and Freiwade's army. How many more would they lose before this war was over? How many would die to bring Finch's plan to fruition?

Cal was unsettled by the questions plaguing him. He wasn't made for war. He wasn't cut out for it. He had served the kingdom as a spy for years. During that time there had been many rumors of war and skirmishes aplenty. However, nothing could have prepared Cal for the actual thing. It was horrible to think of all the lives lost and the lives yet to be lost. He could handle gathering information and even the occasional skirmish. He didn't know if he could stand much more of this.

He needed someone to talk to. He needed to find Dusk and Lark. They were his most trusted companions and both of them possessed unique thinking patterns. Dusk was intellectual and strategic. Lark was blessedly practical. The three of them were a unit. They worked best when they worked together. With everything that had happened, there was no one Cal wanted to confide in more. Maybe the three of them together could find any faults in Finch's plan and remedy them to preserve as many lives as possible.

The only problem was that Cal wasn't sure he could trust them anymore. Should he be sharing such critical information with them? How could he lead a group of spies if he was afraid to tell them anything? He hated it. He wanted to discount Hayes and the king's worries entirely but just when he was ready to forget the warning and trust in Lark completely, something happened that made him doubt once again. Earlier that day he had seen her following Corin again even though he'd told her to leave the young mage alone. Cal trusted Ruena's judgment about Corin. If she believed he could be trusted, then Cal was willing to leave the mage to his own devices for now. But Lark had disobeyed his instructions and followed Corin anyway. Was she reporting to someone else about Corin's movements? Was she reporting to Freiwade?

Cal made his way to The Cavern, the spies' headquarters. As he walked, a weight not only from exhaustion but also discouragement weighed heavily on him. He couldn't keep on like this. He couldn't keep doubting those closest to them. He had to talk to Lark and Dusk, even if it was foolish to trust them so readily. Cal hadn't made it far past the war room when he spotted Vesta, Ruena's maid. He sighed in exasperation. She was one of the last people he wanted to see at the moment. It wasn't that he *disliked* Vesta. It was only that she flirted with him incessantly. It was uncomfortable for multiple reasons, not least of which was the fact that Cal had absolutely no interest in her. He'd tried to let her down gently but, no matter what lengths he went to, she didn't seem to get the hint. The way she fluttered her eyelashes at him was almost ridiculous. Cal was in no mood at the moment to fend her advances off.

Fortunately, it seemed he wouldn't have to. Vesta wasn't lying in wait for him as he'd feared. She wasn't alone. She was talking with a knight. Well, not exactly talking. Cal blushed and backed up a few steps to conceal himself around a bend in the wall. He glanced at the pair ahead of him. Vesta and the knight were close, so close their bodies pressed against each other. Cal peered closer and realized he recognized the knight. He had seen him not long ago. Dorian.

The young man was new to the royal force but, as Cal had learned, he was very skilled. He'd been speaking with Corin earlier, though Cal wasn't sure if they were friends or not. He did know that Dorian was Finch's friend. It was Cal's business to know everything about everyone in the castle. He'd kept an eye on Dorian since he was a newcomer. Cal had excluded him from the war council meetings because of his short tenure at the castle. There were times when Cal wished he'd included the young knight in the meetings to serve as a fresh sight of eyes on matters that many of those who'd been at the castle long stagnated on. Maybe Dorian would also encourage Finch to speak out in meetings instead of withholding important information. The knight was certainly a better option than some of the other members of the council. However, one of the criteria for inclusion was a tenure of at least three years.

It seemed the young knight had taken a fancy to Vesta and she obviously returned the sentiment. Dorian had a hand resting on Vesta's arm, almost possessively. Well, good. At least she would finally leave Cal alone. Though it was annoying that neither of them were doing their jobs. Instead, they were hiding in a shadowy alcove together, improper and unproductive. It also hurt just a little that Vesta would shift her affections so easily. Although Cal had never been interested in her, he wondered if he was so undesirable that she could lose interest so quickly. He shook his head, knowing he was being ridiculous and grateful she would stop pursuing him.

He was in no place to start a relationship with anyone even if he did have feelings for them. Cal knew that if he sought a romantic relationship he would only be putting the person he loved in danger. It was one of the drawbacks of being a spy. He'd hardly considered that fact when he joined the king's forces as a young teenager. He'd just lost his sister and romance was the furthest thing from his mind. Besides, if he loved someone, he wouldn't want to keep his secrets from her. As a spy, he couldn't share aspects of his work with others even if that person were a romantic partner or wife. It was hard enough keeping what he was doing for the kingdom secret from his parents. He was doing this for his family. They knew he was serving the king; they just didn't know how.

"I feared you wouldn't come back," Vesta said softly to Dorian, her breath catching on the words.

"I wouldn't leave you, Vesta," Dorian murmured in response.

"But what happened at Verin? Freiwade's army...?"

Dorian brushed a hand down Vesta's cheek. "They never came. We waited and waited at that outpost and the army never came. I don't know what's happening. I feel so in the dark here. I've been trying to get Finch to tell me what's going on but he's so stubborn."

"Don't talk about it. I'm just... it's good that you're back."

"I won't leave you. I know you're afraid of losing me."

"My family..." again Vesta hesitated. "You know how it is. I feel like I should be there with them but I have duties here as well."

Cal felt suddenly guilty, both for eavesdropping on such a private moment and for his negative thoughts about Ruena's maid. He remembered that Vesta's mother was dying miles from the castle and yet Vesta still showed up every day to serve the royal family, even when it must be killing her to do so. Cal knew what it was like to leave family behind to serve. He knew how lonely it could be. He was glad that Vesta had found comfort in someone in the castle. It reminded Cal how important winning this war was. There were lives at stake and, as long as there was fighting, knights like Dorian would be risking their lives, and those who loved them would be waiting and praying for their return.

Cal backtracked a few steps then decided to take a different route to The Cavern. The last thing he wanted to do was cross Vesta and Dorian's path. It was a relief when he finally descended the ladder and jumped the last few rungs. Lark and Dusk were already there waiting for him.

"Lark, Dusk," Cal greeted.

"What happened at the meeting?" Lark jumped right to the point.

Cal studied her. She still appeared upset from what they had seen at Outpost Orion. Her eyes were red-rimmed and her eyebrows were scrunched together in a perpetual frown. She'd apparently told Dusk about everything. He too looked tired and wary. Cal realized not for the first time that his spies, maybe even more than the knights and archers, would be worn to the bone by this war. They would be the ones working around the clock to gather information about the enemy. They would be the ones sneaking around the enemy encampments to count soldiers and attempt to overhear strategies. There would be no rest and no peace until the war was over. Maybe they would win or maybe they would die. Either way, there would be rest eventually. The spies were few in number and they had many responsibilities. They took their positions seriously. They would fight harder than most during the coming battles.

Cal collapsed into a chair at the table. "Well, we might have a plan, though it has some flaws."

"If Sir Hayes came up with it, I'm sure it has

potential," Dusk commented.

"Actually, it was Finch."

"The archer?" Lark asked. She, just as Cal, knew about everyone in the castle.

"Don't sound *so* surprised," Cal teased her. "It's pretty sound. Fortunately, Hayes forced the idea out of him. He almost didn't share it. Finch is smarter than he looks. He has a roundabout way of thinking too. He doesn't miss details and he's not afraid to take risks. I'm somewhat tempted to recruit him."

"Recruit him? Please don't tell me you mean as a spy," Lark said. "He might be smart but he's also incredibly rebellious."

Dusk cleared his throat pointedly and raised an eyebrow at Lark.

"Oh, be quiet, I am not," she responded. She continued, "Besides, isn't he…"

"It doesn't matter," Cal cut her off. "The plan was a good one. That's all that's important."

Cal explained the plan to them then. Lark and Dusk listened in rapt attention. When he had finished, Lark rested her head on the table and released an annoyed breath.

"Okay, fine, it does have potential, I admit it," she stated.

"It's the best plan at the moment," Cal explained. "Hayes thinks it will work. I have no outright reason to disagree but I'm still worried we'll lose good men to carry it out."

"Lives are lost in wars, Cal," Dusk reminded him.

Cal was tired of hearing that. "So, I've been told. But I can't accept it so readily. I know neither of you do either. This loss of life can't be God's plan for us. I only pray this plan will buy us some time and that we'll prevail in the end."

"A wise person once told me that there were times in the Bible when battles ideal for the enemy were won because of God's favor on His people," Lark said quietly.

"Wise words indeed," Dusk added, looking at Cal intensely.

They were right of course. But everything was starting to add up and amount to more than Cal could handle. It was all overwhelming. At times it felt hopeless. He forced himself to take a deep breath.

"I know. It's all according to God's will," Cal said, reminding himself as much as them. It did no good to worry about things he had no control over. There was plenty he could turn his focus to instead. "Lark, what's your report?"

Lark straightened in her seat. "Corin seems to be starting to fit in. It's good that he's made friends with Ruena. She has a positive effect on people. I've watched them a little. She seems to have encouraged him."

"Well, I'm glad you're learning something from watching Corin even though I've directly instructed you not to," Cal said somewhat bitterly.

Lark stiffened. "I'm a spy, Cal. It's my job to keep an eye on potential threats. You may be willing to trust Corin but I'm not. You're too trusting, you always have been. I thought that trust would extend to me."

"Fine!" Cal snapped. "Do as you want. It's not like you listen to orders anyway."

Lark's jaw clenched but she chose to ignore his comment. She addressed the rest of her report to Dusk who looked at Cal like he'd lost his mind.

"Also, the rumors regarding the meeting of the war council and what has been happening at the outposts have mostly been silenced, at least among the nobles. Though, that can't last for long. Lives have been lost and there are too many eyewitnesses. Eventually, word will get out that a mage is responsible for all of this. I don't want to imagine how people will react to that."

Cal winced, neither did he. It certainly wouldn't gain any favor for Clifton and Corin. It also wouldn't instill confidence in Ashnah's ability to win the fight once outright war was declared. At this point, that was only a matter of time. The king was waiting for Freiwade to declare war. King Rupert didn't want to acknowledge the severity of Freiwade's attacks or let the kingdom think that the state of things rattled Ashnah in any way. King Rupert was constantly on shaky ground. When his brother Theon abandoned his role as king, the people lost faith in the Castille family. King Rupert was constantly trying to instill confidence in a people who had lost their loyalty to the crown. However, if Freiwade's attacks grew bold enough, if they reached the capital, the king would have no choice but to be the one to say the dreaded word, war. Cal nodded at Lark's report and looked to Dusk.

"Most of the nobility still side with King Rupert," Dusk explained, "though, an increasing number of them favor Duke Heirson's view of the king's inability to lead the kingdom through conflict.

They're worried about the lack of a male heir should the king die. More troublesome is the fact that some of the knights and archers are gaining similar views. I fear their loyalties will be torn during an actual war."

Cal thought of Commander Terin. Was he one of the dissenters? Cal wasn't sure but after the man's comments about the king needing to be more brutal to win the war, it seemed likely. Terin could make trouble for them.

"What else?" Cal asked.

"The uproar over Corin's arrival seems to have died down a little," Dusk continued. "Life is starting to return to normal in the court. However, the duke's words are bordering on treason, especially regarding Corin. I overheard him saying that Corin should be dealt with before he can fall into the hands of the enemy."

"I don't want to know how he'll react when he hears that Freiwade already has a mage," Lark commented.

Dusk clenched his hands into fists, "However he reacts, I can assure you, it won't be good."

"What about the others in the castle? How do they talk about Corin?" Cal steered them back to the report.

"The nobles are either frightened or uncertain how to react. I'm keeping a special eye on the knights and archers though," Dusk stated. "Some of them might be bitter about Corin's popularity. Those who show loyalty towards the duke will be particularly troublesome if war is declared. I hope their loyalty to Sir Hayes will prevent them from working against the king."

Cal was grateful again for Hayes's good reputation and the respect he'd gained among his knights. It would serve the kingdom well. Even if loyalties to the king were on fragile footing, loyalties to Hayes would stand the test of time. "Keep a special eye on Terin. I don't trust him."

"Do you think he could be sending information to the enemy?" Lark wondered aloud.

Cal shook his head, trying to find a hidden meaning behind such a question coming from Lark. "I'm not sure. I don't think his dissent would go that far. He's more likely to conspire with the duke than anything. However, he's dissatisfied with the king's rule, he's made that much clear. He could be trouble."

"Are you sure his foul demeanor isn't the reason behind your suspicions?" Dusk questioned. "He's troublesome to be sure. But that doesn't mean he's conspiring against the king."

Cal considered his view of Terin. The commander of the archers was always causing trouble for someone with his unpredictable anger, unshakable pride, and bad attitude. Did that make him a traitor? No.

"I won't make assumptions merely because I dislike the man," Cal assured Dusk, "but I'd still like to watch him and make sure he doesn't try anything."

There was no argument against that.

"The duke is still our biggest concern," Cal continued.

"I wish the duke would just go away and cause trouble in his dukedom instead of here," Lark muttered. "That man is a fiend."

"Unfortunately," Cal said, "if the duke catches

wind of what's been happening at the outposts, he's likely to stay in Castille even longer. He'll not want to miss anything. I'm sure he has informants among the knights and servants. If so, he'll be one of the first to hear of what happened when the information leaks."

"Well, maybe it's better if he's here where we can keep a close eye on him," Lark agreed.

Cal and Lark both looked to Dusk who resolutely avoided their gazes and stayed silent.

Cal cleared his throat.

Lark took up the conversation again. "How is Corin's training going? Do you think he'll be ready to face the threat?"

Cal answered truthfully, "I'm not sure. What I do know is that pressure is being put on Clifton to ready Corin and not keep him in the dark about things any longer. He needs to know the danger that's coming so he can be ready for it."

Dusk shook his head with worry. "It doesn't bode well. Rushing Corin and pressuring him with the truth isn't going to help matters. Likely, it will only end in disaster."

CHAPTER 33

As Corin headed for his training with Clifton, all he could think about was seeing Ruena. They had planned to meet again that afternoon in the empty room. She was in the midst of giving Corin a true tour of the castle. Ruena had lived in the castle nearly all her life. She knew all the secrets its walls held. Just yesterday she had shown him a small hallway, a crevice really, that was a shortcut from the great hall to the kitchen.

"In case you don't want to talk to anyone on your way to breakfast," Ruena explained.

His favorite of her tours was when she led him to a room with huge windows that overlooked the castle garrison from a distance. Corin had relished the view, though he hadn't been able to see inside the building. He'd longed to join the knights despite the fighting being well out of his league.

Corin enjoyed every minute with Ruena. He felt like he'd finally found a true friend. He'd never had one of those before. Being with her didn't feel like an effort. He didn't have to put on an act or tiptoe around her. She always asked him how his training was progressing and he was able to talk freely without fear of her judging him. He still wanted to treat her with the utmost respect but he'd become more comfortable around her. She wasn't the type to insist on formalities. He looked forward to seeing her again.

Maybe his lesson would end early again so he could meet up with her sooner. Maybe he would even beat her to their meeting room. Ruena had her own lessons in the mornings focusing on writing, diplomacy, and history. Despite her uncertainty about her position in the court, it seemed obvious to Corin that the king was preparing her to take his place one day.

Corin arrived at Clifton's office and knocked once, waiting for Clifton's invitation to enter. Corin knew that this annoyed Clifton, the fact that Corin wouldn't simply enter the office, but Corin didn't want to impose. He felt more comfortable knowing Clifton might be slightly annoyed than risking entering when he wasn't invited.

"Come in," Clifton called, the sound had a hint of irritation even as it filtered through the door. He must recognize Corin's knock.

Corin entered the small office with the expectation of finding Clifton searching the shelves of books as usual. Instead, Clifton was waiting for him with a serious expression on his face. Corin wondered if he was in trouble. Was the knocking really that bothersome?

"Corin, please, have a seat," Clifton gestured towards the chair in front of him.

Corin warily sat down. Clifton was deadly serious, more serious than Corin had ever seen him. Whatever had happened was bad, really bad. What had he done? Whatever it was, it must have finally convinced the castle to get rid of him once and for all. Corin only regretted that he wouldn't get the chance to tell Ruena goodbye. His eyes darted to Will who was sitting behind Clifton's desk as usual. Corin tried to question the boy with his eyes, desperate for an answer to Clifton's severity. Will only shrugged and returned to his writing.

Clifton started to pace the room. His hands were clasped behind his back. Back and forth, back and forth, Clifton went. His feet beat a steady drum into the floor. Corin's heart followed the sound, thumping wildly with every paced footstep. He sat on his hands to keep them from shaking. Finally, Clifton stopped in front of Corin. Corin leaned forward with anticipation. Clifton took a deep breath, shook his head, and went on pacing. Corin sighed. He wanted to yell at his mentor, 'Just tell me and get it over with!'

Clifton paused again, opened his mouth to say something, then closed it with an audible sound. He seemed to contemplate for a moment and Corin thought maybe, just maybe, he would tell him whatever it was. Clifton loosed a sigh and dragged a hand down his face.

"We should start our lesson," Clifton said at last.

Corin waited for more, thinking, *that's it?* It couldn't be. Clifton was clearly upset. A pale pallor shined on his face. He looked slightly green. Something was weighing on the mage and whatever it was, Corin felt he should know. Clifton could tell him but he'd chosen not to. Corin had felt the strange atmosphere of secrecy and distress in the castle. Maybe this was related to that. Corin had the distinct feeling that something serious was going on and no one was willing to tell him. Even Ruena at times seemed like she was keeping something from him. Corin wanted to demand answers but he couldn't speak so directly, not to Clifton, or even to Ruena. It was incredibly frustrating and it put Corin on edge.

Clifton developed a façade of ease as if nothing strange had occurred. "Today, I finally have a lesson that might challenge you, Corin."

Corin couldn't shake off his uneasiness so quickly. Dread was seeping into him. He pretended to be excited though. Maybe Clifton really would have something to teach him which would pose a challenge. Corin had learned a lot already. He could summon objects to himself, mend broken items, make himself stronger, produce light or fire, make gusts of wind, and even create a blast of energy as he'd done at the battle school. None of those lessons had posed much of a challenge for him. Corin craved a challenge, something that he had to work for as he'd done during training as a squire. Clifton kept suggesting more and more difficult skills but nothing halted Corin's progress for more than a few hours.

"God has truly gifted you," Clifton had said on more than one occasion. "I think He has chosen you for a special calling, Corin, something that I am not capable of and Neos Loch likely wasn't either."

Clifton's words on those occasions only unsettled Corin. If God had called him for a purpose, then what was it? Why couldn't God just tell him? He'd left everything he knew behind; it would be nice to at least know what his future had in store. He was forced to wait instead and keep training. Even the king had come to one of Corin's lessons. It was a mortifying experience to have to attempt magic in front of the ruler of Ashnah. Corin had managed to muster the courage to demonstrate his abilities and the king had been impressed. After the attack in the village from the strange Freiwade man, the king, and Sir Hayes had kept studying Corin with a look like they feared he might disappear. Nothing had been done about the attack. Clifton had been right that the king wanted to keep things quiet. It upset Corin to know that the assassin might still be wandering the streets unchallenged. Even Ruena seemed unaware of what had taken place. Corin could only hope and pray that Clifton's display of magic had scared the man away for good.

If the attack in the town had done anything, it had motivated Corin to keep training. He had felt useless and defenseless during the attack. It was Clifton who had been forced to defend the both of them, weakening himself in the process. Corin kept training and mastering the skills Clifton taught him. In the meantime, Clifton had tried fruitlessly to find something that would pose a challenge for Corin. Maybe he had finally found it.

Clifton retrieved a book from his desk. "I'm going to teach you some magic that took me years to master. Although your gift is strong, don't be discouraged if you don't get this right away. This is a particularly difficult skill because it does not follow the traditional uses of magic. It is a technique used to destroy an object. It is to be used in construction, to break stones or fell trees, or to clear patches of land for agriculture. Sometimes it's necessary to break away the old to build something new. Doing so is more difficult for a mage than creating. It's also more dangerous."

"Dangerous?" Corin questioned.

"This skill was one of the abilities that Neos Loch used in the Great War. It can destroy objects but if used with great force it can also destroy enemies."

Corin swallowed hard. "But I thought destroying something would be going against the nature of magic."

"It's not its intended use, no. However, as I've stated before, sometimes people can get hurt in the process, as was the case when you fought with Phineas York."

Corin leaned back in his chair. No, he didn't want to learn this, whatever it was. He didn't want anyone to get hurt because of him. "I can't do this, Clifton. What if I hurt someone? What if you get hurt while I'm training with it?"

"That won't happen," Clifton reassured him. "You are powerful, Corin, but you are also more than capable of controlling your abilities. You must learn this skill. I will be here to make sure nothing goes wrong. I doubt your abilities will be as strong as usual when using this technique. As I said, it is not natural magic's nature to destroy but to create."

"What do you mean *natural* magic?" Corin asked. He didn't like the way Clifton was phrasing things.

"I've told you before that there are two forms of magic, that which is natural and given as a gift from God to certain chosen individuals, and that which is corrupt and comes from the enemy which men seek to gain power for themselves. I admit I know very little about this second type of magic and unfortunately, it could very well be strong enough to be used against another mage. However, you will not hurt me with your power, Corin, I assure you."

Corin wasn't satisfied. "I don't want to do this, Clifton."

Clifton shook his head. "You must. It is your duty as a mage to better your abilities. I know that you're worried you'll hurt someone but I won't allow that to happen. It's time for you to learn this new type of magic, Corin."

"I don't even understand what this ability does besides destroy. What if it gets out of control? What if I destroy the entire castle on accident?" Corin argued.

"That won't happen," Clifton pressed, growing slightly annoyed. "The force from this technique is difficult to summon but once you master the ability it comes easier. It's true that, like other forms of magic, it can grow out of control. However, even if that happens, it won't be so bad."

"How bad will it be?"

Clifton laughed nervously. "I accidentally destroyed Neos Loch's desk when I finally started to get the hang of the ability. I doubt anything worse would happen, Corin. I'm not overly fond of my desk anyway."

Clifton's words only unsettled Corin.

Clifton grew serious again. "However, I will give you a warning, Corin. Never abuse this ability. Normally, I wouldn't even begin to teach you this kind of magic so early in your training. It's important to fully understand magic and recognize it as a gift on loan instead of a personal power. However..." Clifton hesitated before continuing, "you must be fully trained. You must prepare yourself, Corin." The words were cryptic. There was a long pause before Clifton said more. "There are dangers you cannot understand. The magic I am about to teach you is dangerous but you *must* master it."

Corin again felt the same sense of dread. There was something Clifton wasn't telling him. What was it?

"When you summon this magic," Clifton went on, "you must disperse it quickly. If you do not, it will keep building up and become more destructive. If you let it get too strong, it might become dangerous and it could destroy something you don't want it to. We'll start with a very small object."

Clifton walked back to his desk, set the book down, and retrieved two apples. He handed one apple to Corin and kept the other for himself.

"Watch as I demonstrate," Clifton said. He took a deep breath and focused intently on the apple in his hand. A black glow erupted from Clifton's hand and the apple crumbled to pieces like a log burning to ash. Corin watched with eyes wide in shock. He was both horrified and fascinated at the power demonstrated. The black glow disappeared and Clifton stood facing Corin and watching him very carefully.

"You must understand, Corin, that there is no skill to repair the damage done by this technique. Nothing can undo the effects of this technique."

Corin swallowed past the lump in his throat and nodded.

Clifton gave him a slight smile, "Now, you try."

Corin stood up, almost toppling his chair over in the process. He was shaking with nervousness even though Clifton had assured him he was more than capable of performing the technique. It was just an apple, Corin reminded himself. Still, it was unsettling to destroy something so completely. What if the magic got out of his control? He didn't want to hurt someone. But he couldn't refuse. Clifton had told him this was his duty as a mage. He couldn't disappoint his mentor or the king. Besides, he'd wanted a challenge. Now, he would finally have one. Corin studied the apple in his hand. It was large and red and he was about to destroy it.

"You should feel a tug of sorts in your gut when the skill is working," Clifton explained. "Focus on the apple and imagine it crumbling in your hand."

Corin stared at the shiny, rounded apple. He imagined it crumbling as Clifton's apple had. He imagined the red turning to gray like ash and falling into a heap in his right hand. He reached deep down inside himself and after one last moment of hesitation, summoned the power inside him.

He wasn't sure what went wrong. He felt the tug in his gut that Clifton had mentioned and he released the feeling in his magic. His hand glowed black and the apple started to slowly crumble.

"Good, Corin," Clifton exclaimed proudly. "I knew you could do it! Freiwade's mage won't stand a chance when you fight him." Clifton's words cut off as he realized what he'd said.

Corin's eyes went away from the apple and met his mentor's guilty gaze. The words hit him like a death blow, pierced him like a sword to the chest.

"What?" Corin's voice shook.

The enemy had a mage? Corin was expected to fight him? Corin's chest constricted with panic. He was expected to fight another mage?

The tug in Corin's gut turned into a twisting sensation like his intestines were being moved around. Then there was a sharp, piercing pain. The black glow grew brighter than before. The dull light emanating from the black spread fast, and the apple completely disintegrated. Not even the crumbled remains were left. The blackness kept growing. It enveloped Corin's right hand and then his entire arm up to the elbow. Corin's mind was racing with useless thoughts. What was happening? What was happening to him? The sound around him faded. He was dimly aware of Clifton shouting but Corin could only hear a buzzing in his ears. Everything was happening too fast and the world around him was blurring. He wanted to shout out that something was wrong but he couldn't make his voice work.

Suddenly, Corin couldn't think of anything because his arm started to crumble. It happened as easily as the apple. Bits of flesh turned gray and cracks appeared along his hand and arm. Corin watched with confusion and amazement. He couldn't feel anything. Then the pain came at last and it brought him to his knees. There was absolute, blinding agony. It worked its way from his twisting stomach to his arm and worst of all his hand. It felt like he was dying. The pain was nothing like he'd ever experienced before. Corin couldn't bear it. And he couldn't make it stop. He tried to release the magic as Clifton had said. He tried to force the glow away from himself. He no longer cared if the entire castle crumbled to the ground. He only wanted the power to get away from him. He couldn't turn it off. He couldn't get rid of the eerie black glow. Corin thought that maybe he was screaming. He wasn't sure. If he was, he couldn't hear it. The pain was overwhelmed only by his increasing terror. Corin couldn't take anymore.

Then everything went dark.

CHAPTER 34

Corin awoke in agony.

He couldn't recall what had happened and he was in too much pain to think about it. Everything felt like it was burning. His vision was slightly blurred and his eyes were heavy. He cried out as he shifted his weight, sending pain shooting through him. Worse than the pain was the confusion and above all a mounting sense of horror when he realized he couldn't move his arm. He ground his teeth and squeezed his eyes shut against the pain as a wave of dizziness and nausea swept over him. He thought he might be sick.

There were voices all around him but he couldn't hear what they were saying over the ringing of his ears. The words all blended together into an indecipherable murmur. Somebody touched his arm. Corin might have screamed as pain shot through him at the touch. It hurt, it hurt so terribly that he couldn't bear it. What had happened to him? Was any of this even real? Corin tried to piece together what had taken place but the pain was the only thing his mind could focus on. The voices grew distant like they were at the end of a long tunnel. Corin managed to crack open his eyes and saw the blurred shapes of several heads hovering over him. He wanted to ask what had happened. He wanted to ask them to make the pain go away but before he had a chance, everything went dark again.

◆ ◆ ◆

The next time Corin woke he was able to open his eyes and see what was around him. He was in a dim room. He was lying on his back on a soft bed, cushions pressing in at his sides. He tilted his head a bit to the side to look around him but a pain shot up his arm all the way to his neck. Spots danced in front of his eyes and his stomach clenched with nausea. He quickly laid still and waited for the pain and nausea to ebb. He saw that there were several people in the room. He couldn't make the figures out right away in the dimness. He saw them hovering around the room like specters. Upon noticing that he was awake, the figures sprang into action. There was suddenly a great deal of noise and movement.

Corin hurriedly closed his eyes and willed the noise to quiet. His head pounded with every anxious voice. Eventually, the uproar died down until only a few frantic and worried murmurs remained. Corin opened his eyes again and blinked through the pain. It was excruciating. He had to fight to stay awake when all he wanted was to sleep and pray that the pain would go away. He managed to stay conscious through sheer willpower. He needed to know what had happened. He vaguely remembered a new technique, something dangerous that Clifton had shown him. Corin began to feel a sick sense of dread stirring in the pit of his stomach.

He tried to speak but only got out, "What?" before he had to stop and suck in a few deep breaths to fight the pain and nausea.

"Corin," he heard his name and he recognized the voice immediately.

"Ruena," he managed to respond. He was afraid to move but he used his eyes to search the room for her. He found her worried face hovering beside him. He felt a small sense of peace knowing he wasn't alone. It was terrifying being in such great pain, unable to move or even properly speak. What was happening to him?

Corin realized there was someone else he wanted to be there too.

"Clifton?" Corin ground out through teeth clenched in pain.

"I'm here, Corin," Clifton said.

Corin sensed his mentor's presence somewhere near his right side, the side that hurt so terribly. Corin managed to tilt his head a little to look at Clifton more clearly. He didn't like the expression of guilt and worry that he found clouding Clifton's face. What had happened? What had gone wrong?

Corin did a quick scan of the rest of the room to see who else was there. Will hovered anxiously nearby. King Rupert himself stood some distance away just at the edge of Corin's line of sight. There was also a stranger whom Corin assumed was a physician. Much to Corin's surprise, Cal was also present. Corin immediately felt embarrassed. He had failed as a mage. He had disappointed everyone. He couldn't even remember what had happened to him but he knew it must have been his fault. He'd messed up beyond fixing. He closed his eyes for a moment, trying to block out an entirely different sort of pain. When he opened his eyes again, he instinctively sought out Ruena. She plastered a small, sad smile across her face. Corin knew it was a false one.

Corin glanced at Clifton again. Yes, whatever had happened had been very bad, something irreparable. Corin had a feeling whatever it was had to do with his arm. He couldn't see the limb. It was hidden beneath the blankets on the bed. A more accurate word would be 'buried'. Suddenly, Corin was desperate to see what had happened. He took a deep breath and then, with his left hand, reached for the blanket. A firm hand stopped him before he could pull back the covers. It was Cal.

"Corin," Clifton said solemnly. The dread in Corin's chest grew. "Do you remember what happened?"

"The skill," Corin croaked. He couldn't remember anything else. There were only vague memories at the corners of his mind. He couldn't gather his thoughts, they all felt fragmented.

Clifton nodded gravely. "You lost control. There was too much power. The apple was destroyed but the damage went beyond that."

Corin glanced at his arm under the blankets. He thought about the awful, unbearable pain. Just how much damage had been done? Corin stared at Clifton, uncomprehending.

"Your arm, Corin," Cal gently explained.

Corin tried unsuccessfully to process the

words. No, it didn't make sense. It couldn't be. He was fine, just a little pain, nothing he couldn't manage.

"I'm sorry, Corin," Clifton said. "The physician did all he could but there was nothing we could do to reverse the damage."

Clifton's voice faltered as he choked on the words. There was an undeniable pain and sorrow in his expression. "It's my fault. I never should have shown you that skill."

Corin shook his head, unable to accept anything that had been said. Cal released Corin's arm, allowing him to pull back the blanket if he still wanted to do so. Corin didn't know what to do. He wasn't sure he could bring himself to look at his arm. He glanced at Ruena who had turned away with her eyes shut and her shoulders hunched as if all the joy had been sucked out of her. The king and the physician stood in the corner of the room talking quietly, too quietly. Will was silent, quivering like a leaf in a storm. Clifton had an expression of guilt and pain on his face that he made no effort to hide. Only Cal seemed composed. He watched Corin with a steady expression. There was no pity in that look, only empathy. Corin focused on the blanket, the only barrier between him and the truth of what had happened. He hovered his hand over the cover, not quite ready to pull it away. He mustered all of his courage, took a steadying breath, and then finally pulled back the covering.

He was going to be sick.

Corin gagged and looked away, revulsion and horror overwhelmed him. It should have been a relief that his arm was still there and in one piece. However, it was damaged in a way that Corin never could have foreseen. It was gray with cracks and fissures like a mountainside stretching from the tips of his fingers to just above the crook of his elbow. His fingers were mostly intact. The worst of the cracking was along the hand. On the edge of his hand, an entire chuck of flesh was completely missing as if it had crumbled away. It left only a small indent where it had once been but it was enough to cause a permanent disfigurement. His entire arm was unnatural and lifeless. Corin tore his gaze away.

A gasp of horror and disgust escaped his lips. He tried to yank the blanket back up to hide the wounded appendage from sight but the fingers of his left hand slipped and he refused to look back at *it* to find his grip on the blanket. He fumbled in his haste to cover up the horrid sight. Tears of frustration crept down his cheeks and he let out a pathetic sound as he tried and failed to move the blanket back into place. Cal hurriedly did the task for him, grabbing the blanket in one deft maneuver and yanking it back over Corin's arm. Cal seemed to not hesitate to do so. It was impossible to move the blanket without seeing what was left of Corin's arm but Cal didn't appear bothered by the injury. Corin let out a breath of relief when the blanket had hidden his arm again from view.

Ruena muffled a sob and hurriedly stood from where she had been sitting at the edge of Corin's bed. She clapped a hand over her mouth as if ashamed by the noise which had escaped. She fled the room with tear-stained cheeks. Corin watched her go with a mixture of sadness and concern. She was probably just as disgusted by the wound as he was.

"She isn't bothered by your arm, Corin," Cal

said as if reading Corin's mind. "It's just that you gave us all quite the scare. It was terrifying when we first moved you to the room. You were thrashing and screaming bloody murder. We could hardly keep you from clawing at your arm as if you were going to rip it off. The magic didn't stop at first. It kept growing until your entire body was glowing. We had to wait until you passed out and the magic dissipated before we could do anything to help you."

Corin shuddered, imagining what had happened, and grateful he'd been unconscious through most of it.

"Clifton sent Will to get help," Cal went on to explain. "On his way to find someone, I intercepted him. He was frantic but all he could tell me was that something had gone very wrong. I told Will to find the king but not to tell anyone else what had happened. Then, I went to help. Ruena saw me running towards the office and followed. I tried to warn her to stay away because I didn't know what we would find. She didn't listen of course and followed me straight into that office."

That sounded like Ruena. She was gentle and kind but also determined and not afraid to do what she believed was right. If there was trouble, it seemed fitting that she would rush headlong in to help.

"We were both horrified to find you in such a state," Cal said. "You were obviously in extraordinary pain and the magic was overwhelming you. Clifton and I were able to carry you into this small bedroom. Your room was too far away and we didn't want to attempt to carry you down so many flights of stairs. The magic was all around us. It felt cold but it didn't hurt us. You were in a daze. You were still conscious but you weren't *with* us. Clifton and I had to hold you down until you fully passed out because you were thrashing around so much. Even when you were unconscious, you kept twitching."

Maybe that was why Corin's entire body ached like he'd run a marathon.

"Ruena was afraid for you. She stayed by your side the entire time and refused to leave for even a moment. You've been unconscious off and on for the last two days."

"Two days," Corin murmured. It didn't feel real. How had he been unconscious for two whole days?

"Ruena has lived in this castle almost all her life. She's seen knights come from battle in worse shape than you were in. Then there's what happened to her parents. Although she was too young to remember that, she's told me she's haunted by nightmares of what it must have been like to be burned alive. She isn't upset at the sight of your arm, Corin. She's just afraid for you because you're her friend. She's been brave this whole time just as you're being brave now. But even the most courageous person cracks at some point."

Corin didn't feel very brave. He felt horrified and hopeless. "What will happen to me now?"

Clifton cleared his throat softly. His eyes were filled with deep sadness as he answered. "There are a few options. Nothing can repair your arm to what it was, I'm afraid. You could leave it how it is. It didn't crumble away completely but you'll never be able to move it the same again."

Corin didn't like that answer but he had a

feeling there was a worse option still to come. His suspicions were confirmed when the physician, finished speaking with the king, approached Corin's bedside.

"The other option," the physician spoke, "is to amputate the arm."

Corin swung his gaze to the lump that was his arm hidden beneath the blanket. That was when the realization finally hit him. It was his right arm, his dominant hand. Corin felt all the breath whoosh out of him like he'd been hit. He couldn't breathe. Try as he might, no oxygen made it to his lungs. Cal was the first to notice Corin's panic, he yelled something that Corin couldn't hear over his heartbeat pounding in his ears. Clifton rushed over. He and Cal carefully pulled Corin into a more upright position. Pain shot through Corin's arm, causing his breath to come in even shorter gasps.

It was his *right* arm. He was useless without his right arm. He couldn't write, he couldn't shake someone's hand, he couldn't eat properly. Most importantly, he couldn't use a sword.

"Breathe, Corin. It's going to be okay," Clifton urged him.

But it wasn't going to be okay. He couldn't be a mage without his right hand. He didn't even have his training as a knight to fall back on if he was thrown out of the castle. He'd always held on to the hope that even if he couldn't make it as a mage, he could always go back to being a knight in training. Now he didn't even have that. He wasn't blessed as they all said he was. He wasn't gifted or chosen. He was cursed. He'd always been cursed. If God had a plan for him, if God cared about him, why would He do this to Corin? What did Corin do to deserve such an awful fate?

"Corin," Cal's words were a demand, "breathe."

Cal rested a steady hand on Corin's shoulder until he relaxed a little. He finally sucked in a few deep breaths and his heart settled to a more steady beat. A heavy, persistent exhaustion replaced his panic. Corin's eyes were heavy. His entire body felt weak. His arm throbbed as nausea swelled in his gut.

"Good," Cal praised.

"He should sleep," the physician said. "I might have to sedate him."

"Wait," Clifton told the man. "Corin, listen to me, please. You don't have to make a decision right away about your arm. This injury doesn't have to hinder you though. You can still be a mage. You can still do everything, just with your left hand. It will be difficult but you are one of the strongest people I know, not just because of your gift. With God's help, you may still be able to be a mage. I know that you are more than capable of it. Do you understand?"

Corin nodded absently. Clifton was the one who didn't understand. He never would. Now they had no reason to keep him at the castle. He was useless to them. It was always this way for him. As soon as he started to feel at home someplace, he was thrown to the streets. Corin didn't want to be banished from another home.

Cal, seeming to sense that Corin's feelings ran deeper than just worry about being a mage spoke. "Corin, regardless of whether you can continue as a mage or if you choose to do so, the castle is your home now. We won't be getting rid of you any time soon."

The words were a slight comfort but nothing could give Corin full relief. His mind wandered back to his first panicked thought. This injury was the final blow in his dreams of becoming a knight. Maybe, just maybe, being a mage might still be possible but now he had no hope if he couldn't use his magic. He had no fallback plan. Corin mourned that loss as he started to doze off to sleep. Before he fully closed his eyes, he saw the others in the room exchange a dire look, and just before he fell asleep, he saw the door open to reveal Sir Hayes. At the battle master's appearance, the king, Clifton, Will, and Cal all left the room, leaving Corin alone with his dreams.

CHAPTER 35

It was rare for Dane to actively seek out his father the king. He tried to avoid doing so at all costs. However, he felt that there was no other choice. He had to do something. The sight of the Skellans arriving at the castle to be paraded around like cattle hadn't sat well with Dane. What sat with him worse was the idea that those men, taken from their homes unwillingly, were to be used as pawns in the coming battle. They would be cast to the front lines to die while Freiwade sat back and watched. Perhaps it was foolish for Dane to interfere, but his conscience refused to allow him to sit idly. He had to do *something.*

It took him longer than he cared to admit to work up the courage to address King Corpin on the issue. He knew by the time he did rally himself, the Skellans would likely already be nearing the front lines of Ashnah. They might be in a battle with the enemy kingdom at the very moment Dane was striding purposefully down the castle halls.

He felt a wave of disgust wash over him. He had always been protected in the castle. Even when it felt like his life was at risk at the hands of his brothers, there had been a modicum of safety in his life. Strong walls surrounded him, protecting him but also caging him in. What was his life in the castle worth if he couldn't stand up to defend the defenseless? He knew none of his other brothers would. Dane's primary strategy in life was to go unnoticed and forgotten but how could he continue to do so when people were dying? He had to take a stand.

He tried to cement that ideal in his mind as his legs wavered on the route to his father's office. He tried not to feel as if he were walking onto a battlefield himself at that very moment. He knew what happened to those who disobeyed his father's wishes. Dane also knew that although he shared half of his blood with the man who sat on Freiwade's throne, he would be shown no mercy because of it.

Dane picked up his pace, desperate to avoid detection from his brothers and to reach the office before he could change his mind. As he was approaching the dreaded door, he halted. There were voices coming from inside. Perhaps Dane was foolish but not so foolish to interrupt the king in the midst of business. Dane recognized Claude's voice and Warson's. He thought then of giving up his idea entirely. But as he had the thought, he remembered the face of a young Skellan, no older than Dane, innocent, scared, being led through the castle and still maintaining a brave composure. If the young Skellan could muster his courage in the face of turmoil, then Dane could address his father. He waited off to the side of the office, trying not to eavesdrop on the conversation happening inside. He couldn't help himself though.

"We'll plan another attack," King Histen Corpin announced. "That mage, Nox, proves himself to be a faulty weapon, a cracked sword. We can't rely on him to win this war. He shows his weakness again and again. I should have ordered him killed as soon as he stepped foot in this castle."

"You were wise to delay that decision, my king. Nox may prove to be useful yet," Claude answered decisively.

"Do you have something in mind?" the king queried.

"I have my resources and I am never without a plan. Nox is a distraction to Ashnah. They will keep their focus on him, giving us an opportunity to attack them from another direction."

"Cowards attack from behind," Warson muttered.

"Not cowards, brother, tacticians. Ashnah won't expect the attack, making it all the more brutal. Duke Heirson's dukedom is open, unguarded. It offers the perfect entry point into Ashnah. We will move our strongest fighters through Trestle, the duke's domain then up, conquering Cheston the viscountcy. Cheston is in a unique position, it will provide a vantage point to stage the second phase of our attack, a roundabout strike on Castille."

"A solid plan indeed," King Corpin said. "And the army in Cheston, will it pose a great threat?"

"Cheston's army is a minor obstacle. The viscount is an aging man, never skilled in battle. His forces are small, many of them have inadequate training."

"Good. We will strike Cheston and then

Castille. I won't risk our army on one mage. Nox may continue his planned attack. If we're fortunate, Ashnah will defeat him for us."

"If they do not, then my spies will accomplish that task."

"They'll die trying," Warson scoffed.

"Then so be it. They are expendable. But I wouldn't discount them so quickly. They have something important that many lack, a reason to fight."

Dane swallowed hard and leaned further away from the door. He didn't like the sound of that statement. He wondered what exactly the spies were fighting for and how far they would be willing to go to defend it.

"Very well, that is a challenge for another day. For now, plan the attack, Warson. Gather our strongest fighters and send them to Cheston."

Dane hurriedly ducked into a dark corner to escape the notice of Warson and Claude as they exited the office. Claude paused a moment as he descended the corridor. He stiffened and Dane feared he would glance over his shoulder and catch sight of him but then Claude continued walking, disappearing in the distance.

Dane was tempted to abandon his plan. He was tempted to forget the Skellans and let his father's plan unfold as it would. But his conscience again pricked him like a needle and his legs moved of their own accord. His arm raised and landed, issuing a knock at the office door. There was silence from within for a moment before the king spoke.

"What is it?"

Dane's words caught in his throat. He forced them out with great difficulty. "May I speak with you, my king?"

"Dane?" the king hesitated. "Come in, then."

Dane felt that perhaps this might be the most difficult thing he would ever do. He sucked in a shallow breath and pushed open the door. His father, the king, sat behind his great oaken desk, an expensive piece imported from Ashnah during the time of peace. Its corners were gilded with Freiwade silver. The king sat stoically, studying Dane like he was an insect that had somehow managed to find its way inside.

"Well, what is it?"

Dane tried not to shudder at the harsh tone. He forced himself to stand erect, his shoulders straight and his face pointed towards his father, even if his eyes focused on a point in the distance.

"I apologize for disturbing you, my king. But there was an issue I wished to discuss with you."

"Out with it then."

"It's about the Skellans."

The king jerked in his seat almost imperceptibly. "What do you care about the Skellans?" The king's tone was harsh and brutal. Dane nearly fled then and there. Somehow he found the courage to keep speaking instead.

"Why do you send them to die at the front lines of battle? Surely it would be more beneficial for trained soldiers to take that position?"

Dane instantly regretted his words.

"You would dare question my decision?"

Dane swallowed hard.

"You know nothing of war, boy, nothing of

sacrifice and duty. I have a duty to this kingdom, Freiwade, and I must uphold it. The Skellans are a pitiful people. They are worth no more than the blood they may shed on the fields of battle. Why would I risk my men when I can use the Skellans to achieve my goals? Nox's plan is flawed and he will likely fail. My hope is that he will take many Ashnans including their mages with him. But I do not anticipate Nox taking this victory for Freiwade. If he is to die then it will be Skellans who die alongside him, not Freiwade men."

"But why allow anyone to die at all? Why make this sacrifice when war is unnecessary?"

"Enough!" the king snapped. "War is unnecessary you say? You are a child. Do you not see how necessary this is? Ashnah has trapped us in dependence on them. Freiwade wallows as long as Ashnah rules."

"But we can trade our goods for theirs. We can cooperate and have peace."

"There is no such thing as peace. It is a child's dream, a fool's imagination. There is only power and control. You could not possibly understand the necessity of these things Dane. You are hardly my son."

The words stung in a way that Dane couldn't quite explain. He cowered at his father's insult. He knew it was true. He was barely the king's son. He might share his father's blood but he was illegitimate. He was a mistake.

"Be gone from here, Dane. Do not question my rule again."

Dane felt his chest constrict. He had

accomplished nothing. He had wanted to save the Skellans but he had only drawn a target on his own chest. He bowed to the king and retreated like a dog with its tail between its legs.

"And Dane," the king said before Dane had reached the door, "do not concern yourself with the Skellans. They are a rebellious and troubled people. They are doomed to eternal servitude; it is all they are worth."

Dane felt like he might be sick. He didn't say a word as he closed the office door behind him and sunk against it. He felt fortunate to have escaped the meeting alive but he was not unscathed. His heart felt like it had been crushed under an immeasurable weight. How could he go on as the son of *that* man? How could he justify his existence when he couldn't even stand up for what was right? Dane felt that he was a complete failure and he had no hope that the feeling would ever go away.

CHAPTER 36

Finch had no idea what was going on. He only knew that Sir Hayes had sent a messenger to find him with the instructions to drop everything and come to the war room immediately. So, Finch did as he was told. He was in the middle of his midday meal, eating with Dorian when the messenger came.

"What's going on?" Dorian asked the servant.

"I'm afraid I can't say, sir. I don't know anything except what Sir Hayes told me to instruct Royal Archer Finch."

Dorian turned to Finch. "Finch, I want to help. There are people in this castle I care about. There are people I want to protect. Please, I... I know you can't tell me anything but please ask Sir Hayes to include me in these meetings or at the very least to tell me how I can help. I feel like all I'm doing is sitting around while our kingdom is in danger."

Again, Finch felt a pang of guilt and annoyance that he couldn't include Dorian. He knew it must be killing his friend to be left so in the dark about things. Finch waved off the messenger. Hayes could wait for one minute. This was more important.

"I'm sorry about all of this," Finch said. "I will

talk to Hayes on your behalf. I think this seniority nonsense is nothing but foolishness. The king and Sir Hayes are paranoid, maybe rightly so, but I'll argue for you attending the meetings. I should have done so long ago. I was too much of a coward to speak up at all during the meetings. You know why."

"It's not your fault. I'm sorry for pushing so hard. I know Hayes has his reasons but he doesn't understand. I have family and friends that I have to protect. I feel like I can't do that with all these secrets."

"I hate them too," Finch replied. "I think this kingdom is starting to fissure from the inside. All of the secrecy, all of the conflicting agendas are going to defeat Ashnah before Freiwade can even reach us."

"Not if we can help it," Dorian said with a smirk. "Now, you shouldn't keep Hayes waiting."

Finch nodded and rushed off to the war room, leaving his half-eaten meal and confused friend behind. He was grateful to at least be on better terms with Dorian. He couldn't let the paranoia of others tear his friendship apart. He arrived at the war room and found Hayes, the king, Cal, and Clifton already waiting. Finch noticed immediately that none of the other members of the war council were present. Finch wasn't sure if he should be concerned or relieved at that. He was grateful to not see Terin at least.

"What's going on?" Finch worriedly asked.

The faces of the four most important men in the castle were filled with worry. Finch wondered why *he* of all people had been called to this room. Something had happened, something terrible.

Hayes's words confirmed it. "There's been an incident."

Oh, how Finch detested that word. It could mean any number of things, and almost all of them were bad. It was too innocent a word to convey what always seemed to be a catastrophic occurrence.

"The young mage, Corin, has been in a terrible accident," Hayes continued.

"Accident?" Finch asked. The word seemed too mild. Given the stricken look on everyone's faces, Finch suspected Hayes was sugarcoating things.

"Corin lost control of his magic. It was…bad," Cal filled in. "He's lost the use of his right arm completely."

Finch didn't particularly like the young mage but the news was still troubling. He wondered how Corin had lost control of his power when he was under Clifton's supervision. Then again, Finch didn't know much about how magic worked. He winced in sympathy at learning about Corin's arm. Finch couldn't imagine losing the use of his dominant hand. He wouldn't be able to be an archer. He wouldn't be able to do anything as he used to.

"Will Corin be okay?" Finch asked.

"At the moment his body has stabilized," Hayes explained. "His arm is a wreck but otherwise, he's in good enough health. However, his mental state is in shambles."

Finch could understand that the shock of what had happened was likely even more severe than the injury itself. Finch pitied the young mage but more than that he couldn't help feeling worried that Corin's injury would cause a major setback and put them all in danger during the upcoming battle.

Hayes seemed to be thinking along the same

lines. "We've decided to go along with your plan to stage an attack on the enemy mage. We must do so now. Corin needs time to recover. Hopefully, he'll still be able to fight in the battle when the time comes."

Finch could tell that Hayes's hope was a far-fetched one. None of those present in the room seemed confident that Corin would be in any state to fight. Finch hadn't seen the extent of the injuries but he couldn't help wondering how Corin would manage to use magic if he couldn't use his right arm.

"Quite simply," King Rupert stated, "we need to stall for time."

Time, what a precious and rare commodity it was. It seemed they never had enough time. Now, they were racing against the clock to halt the enemy mage's progress towards Castille. Corin may very well turn the tides of war but in the end, would it be in favor of their enemy? His injury may cost them everything. Finch wanted to be angry about that but he couldn't bring himself to fault Corin for something that he was already suffering plenty for.

"Your plan is a good one," King Rupert stated. "We will follow through with it and pray for God's hand of protection over us."

"Not trusting in God's ability to save us is what has gotten us into this mess, to begin with," Clifton murmured gravely.

Finch realized he had to speak or he would lose his opportunity. He had to ask about Dorian. If his plan was going to work, he needed his friend beside him.

"Sir," Finch addressed Hayes, "about Dorian…"

Finch never got the chance to finish. As the

words were leaving his mouth, the door to the war room was flung open without so much as a knock to announce the presence of the intruder.

"This is a private meeting!" Hayes berated the newcomer.

"I'm sorry, sir," the messenger panted. "News has just come from Cheston. There's been a gruesome attack! Freiwade forces have attacked the viscountcy!"

"Cheston," Cal said. "But that's in the north, a different route than the army was taking before."

Hayes turned pale. "There are two forces. Freiwade has split their army. They're sending some of the soldiers a different route to surround Castille from all sides."

The room hushed as the severity of the situation sunk in on all of them. If Freiwade split their forces and sent some soldiers to attack Castille from the back, Ashnah would be hard-pressed to win the battle.

"What can we do?" King Rupert questioned.

"What is Cheston doing about the attack?" Hayes questioned the messenger.

"They're holed up inside the keep," the man replied. "They are planning to attack and prevent the army from moving forward or die trying. They have called for reinforcements. They can't hold out for long. They have no provisions stocked up and they are a small force. The viscount's son has been holding the enemy back by staging attacks on their camp every night."

Finch's eyes widened. It was a gutsy maneuver but apparently, it had been thus far effective.

"I'll go myself," Hayes said.

"What?" Finch objected. "You can't be serious."

Hayes leveled a serious stare at Finch. "I will take a force of knights to Cheston to reinforce the viscount's men. We'll defeat this threat and prevent the Freiwade soldiers from arriving in Castille. You mentioned Dorian earlier, Finch. I'll take him with me. I suspect you were going to argue for his attending these meetings. I agree. It's time we stop neglecting him. He'll be my lieutenant for this fight. I only pray that Cheston can hold off the enemy until we get there."

"What about the ambush?" Cal asked.

"It will still go on," the king said. "It must. Finch, Cal, you must halt Nox and his forces. Buy us time."

Finch knew they would need a miracle to win the war. They would need a miracle to survive. Everything was resting on his plan working. It couldn't fail. It couldn't! Everything depended on them gaining more time. Finch started to second-guess himself. Had he missed anything? Were there any faults in his plan that would lead to defeat? Surely someone else could come up with a better idea than he had. Maybe if Dorian put in his input...

"It will work, Finch," Hayes reassured him as if he had read the doubt in Finch's eyes. "We'll set the plan in motion immediately. Because it's so important that nothing goes wrong, you'll be joining the group on the front lines. It's your plan, you should be in the lead. But you'll have to leave immediately. The chosen knights and archers are being gathered for departure as we speak."

Finch wondered if Hayes would take no for an

answer. He doubted it. Surely this was how he would die. Worst of all, it would be because of his plan. A wave of unadulterated fear filled Finch's chest. He didn't want to die. He didn't want to go into battle. He wasn't ready. He couldn't lead others. He couldn't be in charge of their lives.

"Everyone, give us a moment," Hayes instructed the others in the room.

The messenger, the king, Clifton, and Cal filtered out of the room, leaving Hayes and Finch alone. Once they were gone, Hayes studied Finch with an unflinching stare.

"Finch, this plan will work because you came up with it. You've thought through everything. You're a good planner. Don't doubt yourself."

Finch scoffed. "I've done nothing to prove I can be trusted with such a great responsibility. Why would you put me in charge? Why are you listening to my plan? I've spent my entire career as a royal archer attempting to lose my position and be forced out of the castle."

"I know why you did that, Finch. I know your reasons for wanting to leave. I've never looked down on you for doing what you thought you had to. I made my own foolish choices in my youth to try to escape. It doesn't prove you can't be trusted. I know you can lead these men and I know your plan will work."

Finch fought back the emotion threatening to show itself on his face. "I'll do my best," he said sincerely.

"God will be with you Finch."

Finch rubbed his arm. "I just... I don't understand how He can care about me. I know He's real and I know He loved the world enough to send His Son to die for us. But sometimes it's hard to believe He did that for me too. When stuff keeps happening and I can't escape the past, sometimes I wonder why He put me here in the first place. Why has everything happened to me that has? Why am I always trapped?"

Hayes approached him and placed a hand on Finch's shoulder. "Finch, listen to me. God cares about you. He loves you. He is your Heavenly Father and He wants what is best for you. Sometimes those He loves are put under trials and tribulations. Sometimes they are hated for being different from the world around them. However, all of the pain you face in this life will be taken away in the next. You won't be trapped forever. Your past does not have to ensnare you."

Finch took a deep breath, trying to fight back the tears that threatened to escape. He nodded.

Hayes gripped his shoulder and then released him. "I'm proud of you, Finch."

Finch choked up and had to turn away to compose himself.

"You should prepare yourself for departure," Hayes instructed him.

Finch swallowed hard and headed for the door. When he reached the corridor, he turned back once to study Hayes. Hayes had looked out for him when no one else did. Maybe Hayes was right. Maybe God did want what was best for him. Because, despite his situation, God had been looking out for him. He'd sent Hayes, after all. Finch squared his shoulders. The plan would work. It had to.

CHAPTER 37

The front lines weren't exactly what Aster had been expecting. Aster had been expecting open conflict right away. Instead, there was mostly a lot of moving around, setting up camp, and dissembling it again. Freiwade's army was slowly making its way towards the capital of Ashnah. When Aster and the other unwilling recruits were brought to the front lines to join forces with the majority of Freiwade's army, Aster was surprised to see how much progress the forces had made inland of Ashnah.

Aster was less surprised to see that a large portion of the army was composed of Skellans, none of whom were willing participants in the war. They were all dissatisfied and reluctant to fight for a kingdom that had done nothing but harm them over the years. They were quiet in their dissatisfaction though. They all knew that it would only cause trouble for themselves if they rebelled; unlike Aster who had spat at the king himself when the Skellans were taken to the castle to be paraded around like sacrificial lambs. He'd pleaded with the king to send Hagan home, to have mercy on the boy and his family. The king had pretended not to hear the request.

He'd deferred to his son to answer. The tall, sinister-looking young man had warned Aster that it wasn't his place to make requests of the king. It was Aster's anger and fear that caused his act of foolishness. He regretted his recklessness, knowing he could have been killed for such rebellion. As it was, he escaped only with a severe beating. He didn't care so much for his own life. But if he died, who would watch out for Hagan?

The thing that most surprised Aster upon arriving at the front lines was the mage. Aster hadn't heard that a mage had presented himself to the king of Freiwade. It should have been a relief to be led by such a strong ally. However, Aster detested the strange mage, Nox. Nox may be an ally but Aster got the feeling that it was a temporary alliance. The mage would likely turn on them all at some point. Aster could see that Nox was an evil force to be reckoned with. There was something inherently sinister about the mage, a dark energy emanating from him, a depthless emptiness in his eyes. However, when Aster had first arrived with the Skellans from Talbrandt, Nox hadn't been so intimidating. He'd been bedridden for several days, only appearing to inspect his new soldiers three days after their arrival. Even then he had appeared pale and lifeless. Aster had ventured to ask one of the Skellans who had been there before whether the mage was ill.

"He's come from a battle," the man hesitantly responded. "He destroyed an entire outpost by himself, slaughtering all of the men inside."

The man's voice was filled with a mixture of horror and awe as he spoke about Nox. It made

Aster nervous. Even after such brutality, the mage had somehow gained the respect and loyalty of the Skellans. Aster worried at the idea that Skellans were submitting to a Freiwade general. Aster refused to trust the mage and he warned Hagan to be equally cautious.

It was bad enough being dragged away from his home and his people to fight in a war he didn't believe in. It was worse to be led by a commander, a powerful mage, whom Aster couldn't trust. Aster tried his best to stay out of sight and mind and go unnoticed by the mage. The last thing he wanted to do was draw attention to himself. However, Nox wasn't the only one Aster had to avoid. He wondered if the mage or the general was worse. General Havoc was an atrocious excuse of a man, brutal and horrid to his soldiers. Aster saw that the recruits from Skellas faced the majority of the man's unwarranted wrath. Aster refused to allow himself to fall victim to the vicious attacks.

Aster's only desire was to survive the war and to protect Hagan, Amery's brother. That was the one consolation of everything. Aster had managed to stay with Hagan. He could look out for the boy. Out of all of the horrible things Freiwade had done to Skellas, to Aster, sending Hagan to the front lines was at the top of the list. It was nearly as despicable as the soldiers killing Aster's mother and stealing his sister away. Hagan, barely more than a child, had been sent straight to the front lines to die. It was a long, drawn-out sentence filled with dreadful anticipation. Aster wouldn't allow it to happen. He would protect Hagan if it was the last thing he did.

Aster missed Skellas. He missed Amery. He spent much of his time thinking of his betrothed. Was she alright? Were any of the villagers of Talbrandt alright? Aster only wanted to get home in one piece and see them all again. He hadn't been with Freiwade's army long but he had already seen Nox in action. About a week after he'd arrived at the army's camp, Aster had watched as the mage attacked one of Ashnah's outposts with absolute brutality, killing everyone inside and even a few of the nearby townspeople. Aster knew he couldn't prevail against such a force. So, he held his peace, despite the terrible things Freiwade had done against Skellas and against him. Aster waited for the war to end. It *would* end and, with Nox as Freiwade's greatest weapon, it would likely end quickly. Then Aster and the other Skellans would pick up the pieces and carry on. What other choice did they have?

Aster listened to the talk of the other soldiers as he sat waiting for the camp to break again. There was discussion of another attack soon. Aster was grateful that they hadn't seen any fighting yet. He was perfectly happy to watch Nox do all of the dangerous work and keep Hagan out of trouble. Most of the soldiers were excited about watching another outpost fall. They respected Nox. Or at least they feared him enough to submit completely. The attacks on the outposts had gained the soldiers' admiration and awe. Aster didn't join them. He knew Nox was dangerous but he didn't fear him. He only detested him and all of Freiwade. He feared what Nox could become, a person to rally behind, a person whom the Skellans bowed to. They had already lost too much of their independence. They couldn't afford to submit to Nox. Aster had always lived by a strong moral code. He had tried all his life to do what was good and just. He knew evil when he saw it and Nox was the embodiment of much evil. Aster couldn't and wouldn't follow him.

Aster yanked the needle and thread in his hand through the fabric of his tunic. It was only during the brief time after setting up camp that he could take a moment to mend the holes in his tunic from travel. Many of the holes had been in his garments before joining the army. In Skellas, they weren't given much downtime. Usually, a sailor's wife or mother would mend torn clothes. But Aster was unmarried and orphaned, he had to find time to patch up his own garments. Fortunately, sewing was a skill all sailors knew well. It was essential to be able to mend sails while at sea.

Aster glanced up from his work to watch Hagan. The boy was training with some of the other soldiers. Fortunately, they were all Skellans, though from different towns than Talbrandt.

"Come on lad, it's not a snake," one of the soldiers called out to Hagan as the boy flinched away from his sword.

"Leave him be, he's little more than an infant," another called out.

Hagan blushed wildly and surged forward with sloppy attacks. It pained Aster to see a sword in the boy's hands. Hagan could barely lift the weapon. He was strong from his work on a ship at sea but he was still weak compared to the other soldiers. He didn't know the first thing about battle and the other men made certain to remind him of that.

They were constantly teasing Amery's brother about his youthful weakness and innocence. All of it made Aster's blood boil. Even fellow Skellans targeted the boy. They were being corrupted by their proximity to Freiwade soldiers. Aster wanted desperately to step in and knock the taunting soldiers upside the head. Let them fight someone their own size. Aster wanted to give them a piece of his mind. But he refrained. He kept his distance, refusing to interfere. Eventually, Hagan would have to stand up for himself and fight back if he ever wanted the teasing and bullying to end. If Aster stepped in and fought the boy's battles for him, it would only make Hagan a bigger target.

Aster yanked the needle and thread, letting his anger sink into his work. He winced and grumbled when the needle pierced his finger instead of the fabric. Aster sucked on his finger as a drip of blood flowed from the pinprick. That's when he noticed a shadow looming in front of him. He lifted his eyes and nearly flinched in surprise. None other than Nox was hovering before him. Aster had to fight to hide the dread and revulsion from his features. What did the mage want? Why had Aster drawn his attention?

Aster waited for Nox to speak, to make a demand or complaint. However, much to Aster's surprise, Nox said nothing. He only lowered himself to sit next to Aster. Aster stiffened but continued his work. He cursed under his breath when he poked himself with the needle again because of his distraction. It was difficult to not be distracted when Nox was sitting so near, only a foot or so away. Aster glanced at Nox out of the corner of his eye. The mage looked worn and weary. His eyes were lined with dark circles and unmistakably bloodshot. His veins stood out dark against his pale skin. He looked thin, especially in the face, and his dark hair hung slack.

Aster wondered why the mage had chosen to sit beside him in the first place. He didn't ask. He just kept stitching his tunic and hoped that the mage would forget he was even there. When Nox spoke, it caused Aster to stab himself in the finger again. He closed his eyes in a grimace but didn't make a sound.

"You're a sailor, from Skellas," Nox stated.

That was it, nothing more. Aster wasn't even sure if it was a statement or a question. He decided it would be safer to answer anyway.

Aster swallowed hard and nodded. "Yes," he murmured.

Nox looked at him but Aster didn't meet his gaze. He focused on his tunic instead. However, he froze when Nox spoke again.

"Rebellion to Freiwade is futile."

The words sent a thrill of panic through Aster. Did Nox think he was going to rebel? Was that why he had approached him?

"I don't know what you heard about my visit to the castle but it was only a reckless impulse. I know I can't fight against Freiwade. I know I wouldn't win."

If it was just him it would be one thing, but Hagan was there. Aster had to protect Hagan. He wanted to deny Nox's words; they felt dangerously close to an accusation. He couldn't bring himself to say anything more, fearing anything he said would be a lie.

Nox continued, "You are not stronger than Freiwade and its king. You are not stronger than me."

Aster couldn't speak. Besides, he didn't know what to say.

"The battle that will decide this war is quickly approaching," Nox said. "Loyalty to this army is not a question of which kingdom you belong to. It is a matter of life and death. You are a proud man. It runs in your blood, I think."

Aster didn't understand what Nox was saying. His family were just poor sailors. His father died at sea and his mother was killed not long after. Aster's father was dedicated to going without notice, not proud by any measure. The Skellans used to be a proud people. Now, they were only worn and abused by Freiwade. Any pride had been beaten out of them after years of hunger and what practically amounted to slave labor.

Nox kept speaking, "If you do not submit to me and this army, you will die on that battlefield and not by the enemy's hand."

Aster shuddered. It was unmistakably a threat. Aster may not come from a proud family or a proud kingdom but it made his mind rage when Nox told him to submit. He would not bow to such a wicked man. Aster would not bow to a foreign kingdom.

"I do not bow to any man," Aster responded.

He gripped his tunic tightly. He could humble himself to stay out of sight and mind. He could make sacrifices to protect Hagan and hopefully return home. However, he could not submit to Nox and he refused to sacrifice his morality to do so.

Nox's next words shook Aster to the core of his being, "I say all this to warn you, Aster Kadesh, from one Skellan to another."

Aster stared at the mage. Nox, the dark mage

who seemed so loyal to Freiwade, was from Skellas? How? What had caused a Skellan to abandon all loyalty to kin and kingdom? Just how had Nox become the horrible creature that he was now? Aster had no answer to the questions but one thing was abundantly clear to him. He had to watch his back. The war was with Ashnah but Aster knew the greater threat came from his supposed allies.

Nox stood to leave but before he did, he gestured with his hand. Aster watched as the hole in his tunic mended itself of its own accord. That, more than anything filled him with dread. This magic that Nox possessed had the power to mend and make whole. What could possess a man with that incredible ability to use it instead for destruction? Who and *what* was Nox?

CHAPTER 38

Cal packed light for the journey ahead. The trip would be a short one, one way or another. Cal needed speed on his side more than anything. Unlike the others sent to enact Finch's plan of ambush, Cal wasn't going to attack the enemy. Cal was only there to supervise and ensure everything went according to plan. He was to report back if things went awry. He prayed they wouldn't. If the worst happened and no one else survived, then it was Cal's duty to report what had happened to the castle. He needed to be able to move quickly without the hindrance of luggage or supplies weighing him down.

Cal was more nervous than he liked to admit as he stuffed only the necessities in his small satchel. His hands shook and he didn't bother attempting to fold his spare set of garments. It was quite possible that something could go wrong, very wrong. Cal didn't like to consider the idea but he had to. He had to be practical and accept the possibility that the plan could fall apart and lives could be lost. He had waited until The Cavern was empty to prepare for departure. There had been a delay in the preparation of the soldiers now that Sir Hayes was taking a separate force to

Cheston to aid the viscountcy. It was late, too late to travel. Instead, they would leave at dawn. Cal could have departed early. He could have gone to scout out the area and prepare. He wasn't technically a part of the main group. He was a solo entity ensuring that his own mission was completed at all costs. It might have been beneficial for him to scout ahead but he wasn't eager to leave.

He hadn't even told the others that he was going. He didn't want to say goodbye to Dusk and Lark for perhaps the last time. He had waited until they were away from The Cavern, so he could gather his supplies without their notice. Dusk had been tasked with quelling rumors about Corin's accident and keeping an eye on the nobility for signs of suspicion. Instead of turning in early after a long day, Dusk had taken it upon himself to look for a solution to Corin's injury. He'd headed for Clifton's office, working with Will to scour Clifton's books for a way to mend the damage done. Cal hoped he was successful.

As for Lark, she'd volunteered to keep an eye on Corin to make sure he continued to recover and didn't take a turn for the worse as well as guard him from potential threats but Cal had denied the request. Despite his own feelings about the matter, which he was still uncertain about, he had to at least acknowledge the king and Hayes's concerns about her. He couldn't leave her solely in charge of looking out for Corin. Ruena and Clifton would do a good enough job of that during their visits to the young mage. Cal had instructed Lark to keep a watchful eye on Duke Heirson instead and make sure he didn't go from mutterings to actual treachery.

Cal didn't want to say goodbye to either of his comrades. He didn't want to consider that it might be the last time he saw them. He hoped to sneak away without their noticing. It was selfish of him, he knew. But he couldn't bear the departure otherwise. However, he wasn't so fortunate in his plan.

As Cal stuffed his clothes into his satchel, a familiar voice cleared their throat behind him. Cal stiffened and straightened. He sighed at the inevitable confrontation that he knew was about to take place.

"Were you planning on leaving without saying goodbye?" Lark asked, not quite able to hide the hurt from her voice.

In times of high emotion, the accent she tried so hard to hide came through a little stronger. It made her voice lilt at the end of words. The huskiness that she used to hide the tone faded away. Cal always enjoyed those brief moments when her act fell away. It gave him a chance to see the real Lark. However, he didn't like the hurt in her tone now. He didn't like that he was the one who had caused that hurt.

Cal slowly turned to face her. "You know I don't like goodbyes. Besides, I won't be gone for long."

Lark walked over to the small table where so many of their plans and strategies had been hatched. She sank onto the edge of the surface. She tilted her head to the side, refusing to look at him. Her arms were crossed over her chest like an obstinate child.

Cal stuffed the last item of clothing into his bag and roughly set it aside. He looked at her fully. Her display of anger was almost petty but he could see the dramatics were only to hide how upset she truly was.

"Lark," he said, "I'm going to come back. I

promise."

She shook her head. "No. Don't promise that. You know the danger. I know the danger. There's no need for us to lie to each other."

Cal could see then that it wasn't his leaving without saying goodbye that had upset her, it was the worry of him going at all. Sitting as she was, she looked very small and young. Cal knew better. He knew she had been through more than anyone. He didn't even know the full extent of what she had faced.

He remembered when she'd first come to the castle, not long after he had joined the spies. She was petite in all meanings of the word but she had been even smaller then. She'd been as thin as a twig, bones jutting out like an emaciated prisoner. She'd been so young too. She was the same age as him but she'd always seemed younger, though not naïve or innocent by any means. There was a hidden terror in her eyes, a brokenness. It was clear she had suffered and persevered. She had appeared out of nowhere. She'd arrived at the castle and begged for a position. She was willing to do anything in exchange for the protection of the crown. Cal had wondered then and he still wondered now what exactly she needed protection from. Whatever it was, he knew it must be bad. She wouldn't even reveal her name to them.

"Call me whatever you want," she'd urged them.

It was Cal who'd thought up the name Lark. It seemed fitting because she flitted around like a nervous bird, determined to never be caged. The other part of the name Cal had never revealed to anyone, not even her. He'd chosen Lark because he knew that her voice under that harsh and rough exterior she hid it behind must be lilting and graceful like that of a songbird.

It was Cal who had persuaded the old spymaster, Barton to take her on and train her. It was Cal who had insisted the king and Hayes give her a chance even when she had done nothing to prove her loyalty. What if he'd been wrong? What if he had let an enemy spy into the castle? Would an enemy spy have appeared in such a state as Lark? Cal wouldn't put it past Freiwade to torture a spy before sending them to the enemy, to make them less suspicious.

Looking at her now, Cal could see that young, broken girl again. How could he leave her? With her head turned as it was, Cal could just barely make out the scar creeping up past the collar of her tunic. The long, thin line had faded with time until it barely stuck out against her pale skin. But it was there and Cal saw it. He remembered years ago when she first came to the castle how fresh that mark had looked. Cal thought it looked an awful lot like whip marks.

Cal suspected a lot of things about Lark but that was all they were, suspicions. Even though he knew her better than anyone, he still didn't really know her at all.

He sat beside her on the edge of the table. She continued to look away from him.

"Lark," he said, reaching for her hand and placing his palm over hers. He waited until she finally met his gaze. "You know I have to go. It's my duty as the spymaster."

She huffed in annoyance but Cal pushed on

before she could say anything. "You should also know that the thing required of me is to survive no matter what. If something goes wrong, I'm the one who must report the news of the battle. If there is any way in this world, I will come back. I'm not abandoning you or anyone else."

Lark stayed silent but she turned her hand under his until it was palm up. Her fingers squeezed his in reply.

Her long, curled hair hung in front of her. The curls were perpetually frizzy as if touched by salt air. The strands shielded her face when she finally spoke, her accent rising to the surface unbidden.

"You and Dusk are my only friends," she said. "No, my only *family*. You've always been there for me even when I was a strange newcomer. You're the only people I trust. I've been abandoned before. I know that you would never do that, not intentionally. You never pressured me to tell you about my past which I am so, so grateful for. But there is one thing you should know, Cal. There's something I know better than anyone. You cannot comprehend the evil that is Freiwade. Its royal family, its army and generals, and the country itself are all tainted."

Cal wondered again how she knew that so well. Many of his suspicions about her, where she'd come from, and what she'd experienced became even more muddled as he pieced things together. It was Freiwade that had hurt her somehow. It had to be.

"What I'm trying to say is, don't underestimate them. And please, please be careful. We... *I* need you here."

Cal felt a lump settle in his throat. Her words

touched him in a way he couldn't describe. He didn't want to distrust her and for the moment he let that distrust fade away. He sat in the moment, looking at her and pretending that there was no obstacle between them. He pretended that things were as they had been before. He had failed people before. He'd failed his sister. In a way, he'd failed his parents. There were others he'd failed, too many to count. He knew he could not fail Lark. He wouldn't fail her or Dusk or the kingdom. He couldn't afford to.

"I'll come back, Lark. I'll come back."

CHAPTER 39

Corin drifted in and out of consciousness, filled with pain, uncertainty, and terror. His dreams, or maybe hallucinations were consumed with images of magic swallowing him whole. He dreamt of black shadows clinging to him and dragging him down, down, down. He was dragged into the depths of a black abyss and try as he might to wake up, to escape, he couldn't. When he was finally able to open his eyes, he gasped for breath, swallowing down mouthfuls of air that never quite reached his lungs. He would thrash around, fighting against the thoughts and aggravating his shoulder and arm in the process. The pain was unlike anything he'd experienced before. Sweat soaked through his clothes and dripped down his face as fever wracked his body. He only wished it would end.

Sometimes he would wake and find Ruena, or Clifton, or Will sitting by his bedside. They would talk to him and try to comfort him. The words fell on unhearing ears. Once Ruena brushed the damp hair away from Corin's forehead, her fingers lingering as she closed her eyes to pray for him. Corin remembered that. It offered him the first moment of peace he'd experienced. He slept mostly, overcome by an exhaustion that seemed insatiable. Sometimes he wished he could sleep forever. When he was asleep, he didn't have to think about the pain or the repercussions this injury would pose.

One of the first moments of awareness that Corin faced came in the middle of the night. It was dark in his sick room when he cracked open his eyes. He was sure everyone must have gone to bed. But he didn't feel alone. His body stiffened of its own accord. He felt eyes fixed on him and a discomfort as if he were in danger. Part of Corin urged him to fall back to sleep and ignore the feeling but instead, he forced his eyes fully open.

He was face to face with another person. The figure's eyes widened, the whites expanding in surprise. The rest of the face was hidden by shadows and cloth. Corin was instantly reminded of the attack in the town of Castille. He scrambled back and winced in pain with the motion. The figure took a step back too. Something metallic gleamed in their hand. A knife. It was the same type of Freiwade knife that the other assassin had possessed. But Corin could tell this was not the same person. This figure was small, feminine. Corin's mind struggled to wrap around the idea. But just because this figure was a woman didn't make her any less dangerous. Corin was completely defenseless. He could hardly move much less fight back.

How had this assassin known what had happened to him? How had she known where to find him? She'd known to attack when Corin would be alone. But now she hesitated in attacking him. She was frightened at his waking up.

"W...who are you?" Corin asked, his throat gravelly from disuse.

The strange figure didn't answer. She turned quickly, flung open the door, and ran. Corin lay still in disbelief. His body shivered with dread. He could have died. She had almost killed him. If he hadn't woken up...

Corin didn't want to consider that idea. The whole affair exhausted him. He settled back into bed, feeling weighted down like chains lay on top of him. Had it even been real? Had he imagined it all in his delirium? Corin couldn't be sure. By the time he drifted back to sleep, he had convinced himself that the strange figure was just another nightmare.

CHAPTER 40

The knights and archers from Ashnah were on the trail, Finch at the lead. Finch could feel himself shaking with pent-up nerves. He tried to hide his anxiety by burying his hands in the folds of his tunic. He had been put in charge of this ambush. He couldn't let the others see his unease and fear. He had to be strong if he wanted to survive the day.

With the sun hardly in the sky, he should have still been asleep. Instead, he was pushing his way ever onward towards Outpost Halliday and presumably the enemy mage. Finch prayed that he was right and that Freiwade's army would attack Halliday next. What if the mage went to a different outpost? Finch didn't want to consider that possibility. Everything could go wrong. They would miss their opportunity to stop Nox. The mage would arrive at the castle unexpectedly and Ashnah's army would be divided between this ambush and the knights sent to aid Cheston. Ashnah would be undefended and with Corin injured they stood no chance. Finch's plan had to work, otherwise all was lost. Finch spent every second pondering the many scenarios of what could happen and dreading the potential answers.

Cal walked beside him, only a step behind, quiet and contemplative. Finch glanced at him and wondered what it meant that the spymaster was going with them. Did Hayes and the king think something was going to go wrong? Finch was smart enough to figure out the contingency plan. If things soured, Cal's job would be to survive and report the news. Finch tried not to dwell on the fact that the king and Hayes were preparing for failure. It made him feel even worse about his plan.

Finch, like most of the knights and archers, traveled light. He carried only a small pack and his bow and quiver slung over his shoulders. For once, he wasn't the only one not wearing his uniform. None of the castle archers wore their trademark clothing. It would stand out too much in such a covert operation. Likewise, the knights didn't wear full armor. They were all dressed in tunics and cloaks of varying shades of green and brown to blend in with the trees. The knights wore light chainmail under their tunics but Finch, Cal, and the other archers were unprotected. Finch knew any armor would only slow him down and inhibit the movement of his shoulders when drawing his bow. Still, he wished he had the extra protection. He knew whatever they faced in this battle, it wouldn't be good. This threat would be the greatest challenge he'd ever encountered and he had only his bow and his wit to protect him.

Worst of all was the fact that Finch was the leader of the group. It was his plan. It made sense for him to carry it out. It also meant that if something went wrong, it would be on his shoulders. He looked at the knights and archers around him. There were one hundred in all, just as in the outposts. Finch didn't want the deaths of so many men on his hands, even when many of those men were archers who had ridiculed him for years. Finch knew they didn't respect his leadership. They still saw him as the rebellious archer who always made trouble somehow. Finch couldn't blame them for doubting his abilities as a leader. He doubted them himself. It took an immeasurable effort to keep up his brave exterior even as his insides twisted with fear and uncertainty.

"It's a good plan," Cal said.

Finch flinched. He hadn't noticed the spy coming up beside him with his head bent to softly murmur so only Finch could hear.

"It's an imperfect plan and there are so many ways it could go wrong," Finch responded quietly. The last thing he wanted was for the others under his command to see him doubting the plan.

"It will work. God will see us through," Cal continued.

Finch had never been great at seeking God before. He'd had many reasons throughout his life to doubt. Hayes often reminded him that God was a Heavenly Father who cared about Finch. That, above all, was most difficult to believe. Hayes had encouraged him to trust in God but Finch still struggled to do so. This battle seemed so big, so impossible, and somehow he had been chosen to lead. Cal's words brought him back to Hayes's encouragement before Finch had left.

At that moment, heading towards the battle, Finch was so terrified that he was desperate like never before to seek God. The problem was that he didn't really know how to.

"Pray," Finch told Cal. "Please."

Somehow, Finch knew Cal would be better at it than he could hope to be. They needed powerful prayers to survive this conflict. Finch wanted more than anything for God to hear and answer their prayers. He didn't know how to phrase things and he was sure he'd make a mess of it all.

As the two walked side by side, Cal spoke quiet prayers and Finch silently agreed.

They passed the rest of the walk like that. Finch saw some of the other knights and archers with heads bowed. He suspected they were saying their own prayers for deliverance. Before Finch was ready, they reached their destination, the location of the ambush. Outpost Halliday towered above, one of the larger outposts in Ashnah. It would be catastrophic for the kingdom if Halliday were destroyed. In many ways, it was the last real stronghold before Castille. Finch stared at the heavy, stone walls. The enemy possessed the power to destroy those immovable stones in an instant. It was an unthinkable power that they were up against. Finch swallowed hard.

The men stationed at Outpost Halliday would join their ranks for the ambush, adding another hundred men to their numbers. Hopefully, it would be enough to face Freiwade's attack force since they had the element of surprise on their sides. In addition, Freiwade's front-line attackers were only footmen. There were no archers or cavalry riders. Ashnah had the advantage, at least that was what Finch told himself.

Before Ashnah's two forces could unite, they

had to set up the mannequins and prepare the cannons to fire at the enemy lines with only one brave person manning them. Finch was grateful Dorian wasn't there because he surely would have volunteered for that dangerous job.

The outpost loomed ahead and Finch readied himself to step into the role of leader and start giving orders. He glanced at the men who would fight with him, men who were quite possibly following Finch to their deaths. He took a deep breath and sent his prayer above. *God, please protect us.* That was all he could find the words to say. He hoped it would be enough.

"Okay," Finch said to the men, "let's get to work."

❖ ❖ ❖

Hours later, after all the mannequins had been assembled along the outpost parapets and all the cannons had been loaded with balls and powder, Finch crouched in the highest limbs of a tree, bow at the ready. The knights and archers from Castille and the men from the outpost were spread out and hidden all around. The ambushers lay in wait for the enemy to arrive. Cal was hidden, nowhere to be seen, located in a position where he could easily watch all that occurred and escape should the need arise. They waited and waited until Finch saw, blowing in the wind, Freiwade's standard. The flags rose above the approaching army, a signal, and a warning. A black-clad man, tall and menacing, led the charge towards the outpost. A shiver ran through Finch at the sight of the enemy mage. It was time for action.

CHAPTER 41

Aster was falling behind. He wasn't sure if it was intentional or not. He couldn't sort through his own mind lately. Were Nox's words really getting to him so much? He couldn't help wondering if he would go into the attack on Outpost Halliday and find himself numbered among the dead enemy. Would Nox turn on him because of suspected disloyalty? Aster wasn't sure. He only knew that he didn't belong with this army. He found it difficult to walk among them as if he had nowhere else he should be. It felt wrong and cruel to be fighting Freiwade's battles for them. Aster wasn't about to make a run for it though, not with Hagan to worry about. Aster kept an eye on Amery's brother. He hadn't always been the best at protecting people but he was determined to protect the boy.

Nox strode ahead at the front of the army. He looked a little better than he had during his conversation with Aster. But his eyes were lifeless. There was no soul behind them. Aster was wary of the mage, the upcoming attack on the outpost, everything. He felt a sensation of anxiety that he couldn't shake. He knew beyond a shadow of a doubt that something was going to go very wrong.

He was concerned about Hagan above all. Aster only wanted to keep the boy out of the fighting. Fortunately, the army hadn't entered any conflict yet. Nox had quickly wiped out the opposing forces on his own. Aster hoped it stayed that way. He didn't want to see Hagan brawling with the sword he could hardly lift. Maybe they would win this war quickly and Freiwade would allow the Skellans to return home. Aster doubted the little town of Talbrandt would ever find real peace again. Even if the war ended, they would still be worked into the ground by Freiwade. Their persecution at the hands of the kingdom which had controlled them for so long would never end.

Aster saw Ashnah's outpost approaching. It was a great structure, tall and built for defense. In ordinary circumstances, it would have been a beast to attack. The enemy had the advantage of a good position and a large number of forces stationed inside. At least, that was how it would appear to an onlooker. But Freiwade was in possession of a mage. This fight, if it could even be called that, would be over soon.

Nox strode confidently forward, approaching the outpost. He surveyed it like it was an annoying boulder blocking his path. A few of the most loyal soldiers of the army followed Nox at a short distance, offering backup that would likely prove unnecessary. However, General Havoc stayed back with the main force. The wicked man was too much of a coward to risk himself in the fight, no matter how mild it may be. Aster doubted there would be much of a fight at all with Nox leading the charge.

Distracted as Aster was, he still took a moment

to look up at the outpost parapets. Men were standing there, eerily still as if they hadn't noticed the approaching army. Aster watched the figures which were indistinct from the ground. They must have heard about Nox and knew there was little they could do to stand against them. Aster wouldn't be surprised if they were saying their last prayers at that very moment. A cannon went off. The cannonball impacted the ground sending tremors through it. Aster turned to Hagan.

"Stay close to me. Don't get any foolish ideas."

"Me? Never," Hagan replied.

The boy sounded nervous. Aster couldn't blame him.

Aster was just grateful that none of the knights from the outpost came out to meet them. Another cannon fired after a short delay. The projectile landed closer than before. Why were they only firing one cannon at a time? Wouldn't it be better to bombard them with attacks upfront? And what about the archers? Why wasn't there a barrage of arrows following the cannon blasts? Aster had a premonition of trouble. Something was strange about all of this. The men weren't moving on the parapets. Then there was the lack of arrows fired down on them and no knights coming to meet them in battle. And finally, the cannons firing one at a time instead of in a melee. It was all strange.

It didn't matter because, without another moment of hesitation, Nox underwent his horrifying change. Darkness gathered in the sky, emanating from the mage. It swept up the sides of the outpost. Then there was a loud booming sound like thunder or the pounding of a drum of war. The outpost collapsed into rubble and ash in an instant. It was in the space of the blink of Aster's eyes. It happened so quickly that the men inside didn't even have the chance to scream. Either that or the sound of their final cries was engulfed by the rumble of Nox's magic.

"Aster," Hagan sounded horrified.

"I know," was the only response Aster could give.

"The men," Hagan's voice shook.

Aster knew immediately what the boy was referring to. The men in the outpost, the hundred or so knights and archers, would all be dead by Nox's attack.

"I'm sure it was quick and painless," Aster reassured the boy.

He was grateful that Hagan didn't have to see the carnage of a sword fight but he certainly wouldn't be letting the boy get close to any remnants of the bodies which may remain. Fortunately, there was no village nearby so the damage only involved those who had been in the outpost. No civilians were harmed. However, Aster couldn't help thinking about the men in the outpost. They all had families who would mourn them. They had hopes and dreams that would never be fulfilled. This was the cost of war. And what a horrific way to die, at the hands of Nox.

Even with the outpost lying in ruins, Nox's magic kept growing. The blackness filled the sky until the clouds were no longer visible. The dark power crept to the edge of the tree line before it finally flickered out and Nox collapsed to his knees.

Hagan surged forward as if he would rush

towards the fallen structure but Aster held out an arm to keep him back. He knew his gesture of restraining Hagan would only highlight the youth of the boy to those who already targeted him but Aster didn't care at that moment. He was wary of Nox's awful power. If it started spreading again, he didn't want Hagan to be caught in the path of destruction.

Nox knelt in the middle of the field with his head hung low, his shoulders hunched, and the life seemingly sucked out of him. He didn't move, only knelt there, completely motionless. No one was brave enough to approach him and offer help. They all lingered back, afraid of his power striking them next. Aster watched the mage. Despite his best efforts, he felt a twinge of pity for the man hidden somewhere inside Nox. However, before Aster could dwell too long on the mage, he realized something was wrong. A glint of something metallic caught his eye. He turned his gaze to the tree line. He tensed with anticipation, though he didn't know why. It was because of his wariness that he saw the arrow flying toward him.

Aster jumped in front of Hagan to shield the boy with his own body.

"Aster, what are you doing?" Hagan asked.

Aster braced for the projectile to hit him but fortunately, the arrow wasn't aimed at his own body. Instead, it targeted the man beside him who, not being aware, wasn't able to defend against the arrow. Aster watched as the shaft of the arrow appeared in the man's chest, the tip buried deep into flesh.

"Archers!" someone cried out in alarm.

More arrows followed the first and there were sickening thuds as they connected with their targets.

Bodies started to fall all over the field. Then, with a cry of battle, a battalion of Ashnan knights surged out of the forest all around them.

"Ambush!" General Havoc yelled. "Fight back, you sorry lot of soldiers!"

Then the general turned tail and ran. Aster noticed that their supposed leader didn't call for retreat. Instead, he had commanded them to stand and fight while he saved his own hide. Aster looked to Nox but the mage wouldn't be of any assistance either. He could barely lift his head, much less issue orders. The soldiers of Freiwade's army were left in a haze of confusion and disorder. They didn't know how to face this unexpected foe and they didn't have any orders to follow. Aster was just as horrified and confused as they were. He watched as his fellow soldiers were struck down on his right and on his left. Ashnah's army surged forward and arrows continued to pelt them from above.

Aster shoved Hagan behind him. "Stay at my back!" he ordered the boy.

"I should fight too!" Hagan argued.

Aster spared the boy a glance and growled out, "No!"

There was no further argument, which was good considering one of the Ashnan knights was suddenly upon Aster. The man looked to be unarmored but when Aster struck the man's torso with his sword, the blade glanced off, ripping his tunic and revealing chainmail. Aster wore only the uniform of Freiwade as did all of the soldiers unwillingly recruited from Skellas. They were not afforded the luxury of armor. It was seen as wasted on them. It might just mean his death in this battle.

Aster deflected the strike of his opponent, trying to keep focused on the threat in front of him and not the boy hopefully still behind him. He would kill Hagan himself if he ran off and picked a fight.

"You Freiwade scum!" the knight growled, thrusting his sword at Aster.

"I'm not from Freiwade!" Aster retorted.

The knight looked confused but he didn't receive further explanation. Aster managed to get through his defenses and slash his blade across the man's stomach. The knight was quickly replaced by another and Aster exchanged more strikes before taking down his opponent once again. Aster was provided a short instant of pause from the battle and he took the time to look around. Hagan was fortunately still behind him looking nervous at the battle around them. Freiwade was losing. Soldiers fell left and right. Some fled, abandoning the fight completely. Many fell from the persistent barrage of arrows. They would be destroyed completely if someone didn't take charge. It was obvious to Aster that Nox was the enemy's next target.

The mage was completely defenseless in his prone position. The enemy knights were moving towards him. Aster was torn for a moment. He couldn't just let them kill Nox in a defenseless state, despite how much he disliked the mage. Or could he? He couldn't let Freiwade's forces be destroyed. Or could he? He could take Hagan and flee, leaving the rest of them to fend for themselves. They'd be branded as traitors and sentenced to death if they were ever caught but they would escape and live to see another day. No. He couldn't do it. If it were just him, then maybe. But he couldn't sentence Hagan to such a fate. Hagan had a long life ahead of him. He shouldn't be forced into a life on the run.

Aster's choice was made for him when, in a moment of distraction, he heard the boy yelp and call out his name. Aster looked frantically around him. Where had Hagan run off to? That foolish, foolish boy!

"Hagan!" Aster called with a mixture of anger and panic.

Aster finally located the boy and his heart sank. With mounting horror, Aster saw Hagan standing frozen with an arrow piercing his shoulder. Aster raced to the boy's side and softly grabbed hold of his arms. One of Hagan's hands was wrapped around the arrow shaft. The arrowhead had pierced through his shoulder and was sticking out at the back.

"A... Aster," Hagan cried, his voice wobbling. "I didn't mean to wander off. I... I don't know what happened."

"It's okay. Everything is going to be okay." Aster didn't know who he was reassuring, himself or Hagan.

Any plans in Aster's head dissolved into sheer panic. If they ran now, they would have to keep on running. Hagan wouldn't receive the medical treatment he needed to survive this wound. He would die. Aster only had a moment to act.

"Hagan, find a place to hide against a piece of rubble from the outpost," Aster instructed.

"But..."

"Just do it. Be brave for a little longer. I won't let you die; I promise."

Hagan did as he was told and ran for a

particularly large piece of rubble. His steps staggered as he endured the incredible pain from his wound. Aster didn't watch him for long before he turned and raced towards Nox. He was a little late. Several carefully placed arrows littered Nox's back, shoulders, and legs. A weak, magical shield had lifted itself to protect Nox's head, neck, and vital organs. Still, the mage was in rough shape. Aster dodged arrow after arrow to reach Nox. He felt like he was a traitor to Skellas as he helped Freiwade's mage. But there was an old saying, 'The enemy of my enemy is my friend.' In that case, the threat of Ashnah's army was a greater enemy than Nox. Besides, he had no choice but to help the mage if he wanted Hagan to stand a chance of surviving.

Aster reached the mage and fell to his knees in front of him, using the man's body as a shield for the arrows.

"Nox?"

There was no answer. Another arrow thudded into Nox's exposed back and the mage only winced. Aster couldn't believe he was about to do this. He wasn't sure if that made him merciful or incredibly foolish.

"I'm sorry. This is going to hurt. Bad," Aster warned the mage. Then he grabbed hold of one of the arrows piercing the mage's shoulder and broke the shaft in the back. Nox groaned but didn't scream or argue. Aster quickly broke a few more of the shafts. It would make it easier to move Nox. However, with every arrow shaft he broke, another seemed to appear. Eventually, Aster was forced to give up. He was wasting time.

"I'm going to get you out of here now," Aster explained.

There was still no response. Aster took that as answer enough. He lifted Nox to his feet with no small effort. It was apparent immediately that Nox wouldn't be able to stand on his own so Aster draped him almost entirely over one shoulder. More arrows came and landed dangerously close to Aster's feet. He had to get out of there. Aster ran, finding Nox surprisingly light. He looked frantically for Hagan but he couldn't find the boy.

"Aster!" Hagan called.

Aster backtracked and found Amery's brother hiding entirely out of sight between two pieces of rubble. Good. The boy was smart. He'd found a good spot out of sight and protected from any incoming arrows.

"Come on, Hagan. Let's go."

Aster grabbed Hagan's arm and helped him up. He kept supporting Nox and he dragged Hagan on, keeping hold of his arm.

"Retreat," Nox murmured so quietly that Aster barely heard him.

So, Aster gathered all his breath and, using the voice he had so often used on ships at sea, he called, "Retreat!"

The Freiwade army readily obeyed the order. Aster suspected they would have listened to anyone who took charge at that point. They beat a hasty retreat with yelling knights and whizzing arrows following after them. A few more of the arrows struck Nox's back as they fled but by some miracle, they survived. They had survived.

CHAPTER 42

Hayes had a sense of foreboding about what they might find when they reached Cheston. For all Castille knew, the place may be nothing more than rubble by the time help came. They could be riding into a massacre. Hayes tried not to dwell on that fear. He'd seen enough massacres and lost battles in his lifetime. His 35 years felt like an eternity. And how many of those years had he wasted on reckless foolishness? He looked at the knights riding alongside him, a meager force of one hundred. It was all Ashnah could spare. Hayes hoped it would be enough.

He'd tried to teach the knights under his command to take their positions seriously, to live for God with honor and chivalry while they were young. Nothing was guaranteed and every moment was fleeting. Hayes wondered how many of them would take heed of his instruction and how many would have to learn the hard way that their actions now had future consequences. The young man riding beside him seemed to have clung fast to Hayes's teaching. Dorian was one of the more responsible of Hayes's knights. It was why he had chosen him as his lieutenant during this mission. Dorian was not only a good fighter but also responsible and competent. He'd demonstrated those qualities from the moment he'd arrived in Castille. It was why Hayes had introduced him to Finch, hoping the two would become fast friends.

He'd hoped that Dorian would be to Finch what Sir Burke had been to Hayes. Eamon Burke had saved Hayes from his foolish and youthful nature more times than Hayes would care to admit. The man had been nearly 10 years his senior and still had adopted Hayes as a friend. Hayes supposed being stationed at Outpost Carmine didn't offer much of a selection. It was the most dreaded position in Ashnah. Most knights would rather walk unarmored and without weapons through Freiwade than be stationed at Carmine. It was far north, cold, windy, miserable, and right on the border, straddling the line between Ashnah and Freiwade. It was known for its danger and low survival rate. Many died in the skirmishes that frequently took place there, others perished due to cold and illness. Hayes had volunteered for the position. Looking back, he would have liked to claim that it was out of a sense of courage and compassion; that he'd wanted to understand the worst of what the knights of Ashnah faced so that he could lead them properly. In reality, it had been an escape. He'd been desperate to escape expectations that he couldn't meet. He'd thought he would either find his own way in the world or die trying.

Sir Burke had been stationed in Carmine because he hailed from the far north, a miserable little town called Nevara. He was used to the cold and expected to fare better than most in it. He did manage well, though not from acclimation to the climate so much as his never-failing optimism. He rubbed some of that goodness off on Hayes, offering a friendship that he would need, especially after news came of his father's death. The very man that Hayes had wanted so desperately to escape had died suddenly, giving Hayes no chance to make amends with the man who had given him life. The bitter grudge he had held against his father for years didn't matter in the end and Hayes would forever regret letting anger and pain keep him from making peace while he still had the chance. There were many adventures in Carmine including the skirmish that left Hayes with the scar running down his cheek. He and Burke worked up in the ranks and eventually parted ways, each accepting a lofty position that neither felt they truly deserved.

 Hayes saw his past as something to be learned from, not something to be particularly proud of. His chief desire was that the young men under his command would learn from his mistakes and not have to endure the hardship he had. As Hayes and his small army neared Cheston, he hoped that they wouldn't find a dire battle waiting for them.

 "Sir?" Dorian questioned, breathless with the exertion of riding long and hard.

 Hayes looked to the young knight, a question on his face.

 Dorian hesitated then spoke. "Is there a reason you haven't allowed me to attend the war councils? Have I done something wrong?"

 Hayes had known the question would be coming. Maybe he had been foolish to exclude Dorian from the meetings. He'd attempted to follow protocol but protocol had led him astray more than once. "You've done nothing wrong Dorian, rest assured. I hope to amend that decision when we return. Your input in the meetings might be helpful. In the meantime, we should focus on the battle ahead."

"Yes, Sir."

Hayes was drifting in his thoughts when he heard one of the knights call out. "Look up ahead! It's Cheston!"

Hayes pulled on the reigns of his horse, jerking to a rough halt. He raised his hand and his men followed, pulling up short on a small knoll overlooking the viscountcy. Hayes wasn't sure what he had been expecting to see but it certainly wasn't the sight that met him. Cheston wasn't in ruins, there was no raging battle going on. At first, Hayes feared the report sent from the viscountcy had been a false one, perhaps to mislead them and distract them from a different attack elsewhere. But when he looked a little closer, he saw that there was a Freiwade camp, positioned not far from Cheston's towering walls. The enemy kingdom's banner billowed in the northern wind; men moved about from tents to fires constructed throughout the makeshift camp. It was all Hayes could see.

"Dorian, you have young eyes, at least younger than mine. What do you see?"

Dorian peered long and hard at the camp. "I see Freiwade soldiers. There are some injured, there are bandages wrapping their heads, and arms, and legs. The tents look like they've been there for a while."

As Dorian was speaking, there arose a great trumpeting sound from within Cheston's walls. The gate of the estate slowly inched open. An uproar sounded from Freiwade's camp. Men leaped to their feet, drawing weapons.

"They look afraid," one of Hayes's knights, Heath said.

Rightly so. At that moment, a force of knights surged out from Cheston's walls, raging savagely towards the Freiwade soldiers. The Cheston knights were scantily clad in armor. Their weapons were varied. Some carried swords, others spears, and yet others only daggers. But the ferocity with which they rushed at the enemy was unparalleled. At the head of the small army was a young man, sword held out in front of him. He called a battle cry, urging the army forward.

"Defend Cheston! Defend your families! Fight! Fight like there's no tomorrow!"

The young knight led his makeshift army into the midst of Freiwade's camp, thrusting weapons into flesh, fighting with all the power they could muster. It was a spectacular sight; unlike anything Hayes had seen since he'd been stationed in Carmine. But it was not enough. It was clear from the beginning that the fight was only meant to attack swiftly and brutally and to injure as much as possible before fleeing back to the safety of Cheston's walls.

"Who's that there in the lead?" Dorian wondered aloud.

Hayes was pondering the same question. Whoever it was must be a knight formally trained. More than that, he possessed a natural talent for fighting that few others could boast. The young man carried the brunt of the fighting himself. His men could hardly keep up with the destruction he wrought on the enemy. Just as quickly as the fighting began, it ended.

"Retreat!" the young man called to his army. "Retreat!"

"Why is he calling for a retreat now?" Heath asked, bewildered. "They're just starting to win."

"No," Dorian answered. "He's right to call for a retreat. Freiwade was surprised, now they've started to rally themselves. If Cheston doesn't retreat now, the fighting will turn against them. They're already outnumbered four to one at least, they were only doing so well because they had the element of surprise."

"I suspect they've been conducting these surprise attacks for some time now, judging by the state of Freiwade's camp," Hayes commented. "It's a wise strategy. Freiwade will have to stay on constant alert. They'll tire and maybe eventually retreat."

Cheston's small army fled and Freiwade didn't bother to give chase. The knights disappeared inside Cheston's walls, leaving the Freiwade soldiers to lick their wounds and fight another day.

"Come, let's go speak with the viscount," Hayes said.

Hayes led his men towards the castle keep. He halted his horse at the gate.

"Who goes there?" A voice called down from the parapets.

"Sir Hayes of Castille! I've come to aid you at the request of a messenger sent from Viscount York."

The man ducked down, disappearing. Hayes waited. Several minutes passed before the gate began to open. Hayes urged his horse forward into the courtyard, his knights following after him. The viscount was waiting for them. Beside the viscount stood a young man in armor covered in grime from battle, the same young man who had led the warriors against Freiwade.

"Sir Hayes," the viscount called, "it's a relief to see you."

"I've heard there's been trouble," Hayes responded, "but from what I saw only a few moments ago, it seems you've been handling the situation well."

"It's a temporary repose," the viscount responded. "We've been doing what we can but we're far outnumbered. I... I was going to surrender but my men were less willing."

"With such fine fighters, it would have been a pity to yield to the enemy so quickly."

The young knight beside the viscount bowed his head either in an attempt to hide his flash of pride or flush of embarrassment at the words.

Hayes dismounted from his horse and a stableboy rushed to take the reins. Hayes nodded to his men. "Go, refresh yourselves from the journey, expect a fight tomorrow at dawn. These Freiwade scum have overstayed their welcome. Dorian, you stay with me. We have much to discuss with the viscount."

The Castille forces ventured into the keep, led by the small group of Cheston warriors, discussing plans of battle as they went. Hayes waited until all of his men had dispersed before he turned to the viscount.

"Is there somewhere we can talk in private."

Viscount York gestured for Hayes and Dorian to

follow him and the young knight into the keep. Hayes studied his host and the young knight as they walked. He noticed a hunch of exhaustion in the viscount's shoulders and a limp in the young knight's gait. The knight walked gingerly as if he were favoring some invisible injury. It served to unsettle Hayes. Things were worse than the viscount was willing to let on in front of Hayes's men. They remained silent until they had reached the viscount's office. The door was closed behind them and then the viscount spoke.

"I am truly glad you came."

"Are things really that bad, it seemed like you were handling yourselves fine?" Dorian asked.

But Dorian hadn't seen what Hayes had. His inexperience had led to an optimism that the situation didn't warrant. Hayes looked to the young knight who seemed to be trying hard to hide an expression of pain.

"Please, sit, rest," Hayes told the young man.

The knight stiffened. "I'm well, Sir."

"No, you're not. Don't stand on my account. I have a feeling this is going to be a long conversation."

The young man hesitated a second longer before succumbing and sinking into a chair.

"Are you hurt?" Dorian asked the knight.

The boy shook his head. "I'm fine."

"This is my son, Phineas," the viscount said.

"Son?" Hayes was caught off guard by the statement. He turned on the viscount, slightly annoyed. "The boy is hurt and you've let him continue fighting. He's your only heir, is he not?"

Viscount York winced. "Yes. But we've had no other choice."

"Tell me everything."

"They arrived about a week ago," Phineas said solemnly. "The first attack was... it was bad. We weren't ready. Cheston is north and inland. We don't usually expect attacks. We suspected immediately that the Freiwade army was planning to hit Castille from behind by taking Cheston quietly then staging an attack using the viscountcy as their base."

"I knew they wouldn't give up if that was truly their plan," the viscount explained. "I was prepared to surrender to save my people. I know it's shameful but I feared there was no other choice. We are a small, mostly untrained force. Most of my men were never formally trained. We didn't stand a chance against Freiwade."

"I wouldn't let him do it," Phineas cut in. "I knew we couldn't let Freiwade take Cheston. It would give them too much of a tactical advantage. Even if we all died trying, we had to keep them from taking the viscountcy and then advancing to Castille."

"And who came up with the plan to stage surprise attacks on the enemy camp."

"It's a flawed idea," Phineas stated self-consciously. "It was the best I could come up with though."

"It's the wisest course of action, nothing to be modest about. I was particularly impressed that you were able to discern when to pull back. Most knights would try to push their advantage until it was too late and then get caught before they can retreat."

"I'm not a knight," Phineas said quietly.

Hayes jolted in surprise. "What?"

"I'm not a knight," Phineas repeated a little

louder. "You said 'most knights.' I'm not a knight though. I never finished my training."

"That's no fault of your own," the viscount assured his son.

"It is my fault," Phineas objected, a little hotly. "I'm the only one to blame, really. At least I know now that I shouldn't underestimate anyone and I certainly shouldn't think so highly of myself."

"I find it difficult to believe that someone so skilled flunked out of battle school," Hayes stated.

"I didn't flunk. Not exactly. I was injured. I had to come home." Phineas gave an ill-humored laugh. "I was supposed to come back here to rest. I was told... I was told I might never fight again."

Hayes studied the young man calculatingly. Yes, he was still injured, though he hid it well. Whatever had happened had been serious and yet he had still staked his life to defend his land, his kingdom.

"I only wish I had been able to learn more before I had to leave. It was an honor to train under Sir Burke, an honor I'll never be offered again."

"Sir Burke," Hayes uttered. That explained much. It explained why such a young man who hadn't even finished his training as a knight had still been able to come up with such a brilliant strategy to hold the enemy off, had been able to lead such a meager force of men into a battle where they were outnumbered at least four to one, and how he had been able to overcome soldiers twice at powerful as he was. But that wasn't only because Sir Burke had trained him. There was something inherently special about Phineas York. And something had changed in him recently, Hayes could tell. There was a newfound humility that Hayes suspected had been missing before. Whatever had caused the young man to leave Nevara's battle school had taught him a lesson more valuable than Burke ever could.

"How can you fight like you do if you're injured?" Dorian asked, genuinely curious.

"I can't explain it," Phineas responded, sounding somewhat awed. "When I'm in a battle, it's like the pain just goes away. I feel strong. I think... maybe it's silly... but I think of what Burke taught me and I wonder if it isn't God who gives me the strength I need. I never listened to Burke's teachings much but my injury gave me time to think. I'm fortunate to even be alive, I don't think that was by mistake. I've been given a second chance and I intend to use it well."

"I believe you will," Hayes said. "And I believe that such a brave soul as yours should possess the title fitting for him. You've proven yourself more than you ever could at any battle school. You've proven your capabilities in the most unyielding testing ground, the battlefield. You've led men into war and held your own in a real battle. You kept the enemy from advancing to Castille Castle. Your bravery may have saved us all. I believe Burke would agree with my decision. Rise Phineas York and be knighted as a knight of Ashnah."

York's eyes widened. He stood shakily from his seat and shook his head. "I can't sir. I never finished my training and I don't deserve such an honor. I may have learned the reality of battle but I doubt I can ever make amends for the lack of chivalry I demonstrated in my past."

"Our past is to learn from, not to dwell on. Do

you wish to serve your kingdom and your king?"

"Yes."

"Do you wish to carry out the will of God? Do you swear to always be charitable to defend the poor and helpless and to be brave?"

"Yes."

"Then kneel."

Phineas dropped to his knees.

Hayes drew his sword. It wasn't a ceremonial blade but one hewn for battle and washed in the blood of enemies. It was the proper tool to knight Phineas York.

Hayes rested the flat of his blade on the young man's left shoulder. "This isn't the proper ceremony nor the one you deserve for your bravery and courage but in times of war, it is sometimes necessary to treat knighthoods with haste. However, if we all survive this war, then you, Phineas York will come to Castille Castle and be knighted again by King Rupert Castille himself. Until then, I Gregori Hayes with the power invested in me as the battle master of the kingdom of Ashnah do so knight you Phineas York a knight official of the kingdom of Ashnah."

York swallowed hard, fighting back his emotion. An errant tear streamed down his cheek.

"Now rise and take up your sword. We have a battle to fight."

CHAPTER 43

Cal didn't know what to make of the stranger who had in many ways thwarted their ambush. It had ultimately been because of one man that the attack hadn't been a complete success. One Freiwade soldier had somehow mustered the courage and willpower to take command of the enemy army, rescue Nox, and retreat. It was a situation that Cal and Finch could never have predicted. Still, the battle had been Ashnah's victory. It just didn't feel like that when Nox was still a threat. Cal knew he should be grateful for the success they'd had. They were heading back to Ashnah with minimal casualties. Only a few of the Ashnan knights and archers were making the journey home on a stretcher.

Finch was at the head of the group looking a little sick. Cal realized it had been the young man's first real battle and a trying one at that. Despite that, Finch had performed well. He'd dealt out considerable damage to the enemy. His arrows took down numerous Freiwade soldiers and it was his bombardment that had so injured Nox. It was only the strange, magical shield that had protected the enemy mage from death. That and the one soldier who'd been brave enough to intervene.

Cal knew that they had been fortunate with the attack. A lot could have gone wrong. Things had proceeded mostly according to plan. They had suffered minimal casualties, they'd dealt a crushing blow to Freiwade's forces, and they had taken Nox out of the fight for now. Cal knew it was unlikely that the enemy mage would be harmed enough to stay out of the war but he could hope. More than anything, they'd gained a lot of useful information from the attack. They'd learned more about the mage's weaknesses and the weaknesses of the enemy army. The soldiers were fearful of the power displayed by their mage. Cal had overheard the Freiwade soldiers call the mage Nox. They kept their distance from Nox after he used his magic, apparently afraid that his power would attack them as well. It was just the sort of information that Ashnah needed. The Freiwade soldiers were loyal to Nox but only to a certain extent.

Cal approached Finch and walked beside him. He kept silent for a few moments before speaking. "What do you make of everything?" he asked the young archer.

Finch studied his feet as he walked. He was very pale. "I can't believe it worked. I mean, it wasn't completely successful but I'm honestly surprised that we're still alive."

"I knew it would work," Cal assured his companion. "But that isn't what I meant. What do you think about the mage?"

Cal wanted another opinion on what had happened. He knew Finch would offer a new perspective to the issue.

"There seems to be a lack of control over the magic," Finch remarked. "I don't think the mage, Nox I think they called him, is capable of fully controlling it."

"I'd noticed that too," Cal admitted. "That lack of control could help Ashnah in the long run."

"Or make it worse."

Cal nodded in agreement. The lack of control could cause Nox to struggle in a drawn-out battle. It could also mean trouble for Ashnah in the form of increased destruction and death.

"What I think is more troublesome is that the magic seems to defend itself," Finch stated.

"How do you mean?"

Finch answered, "I don't think Nox lifted that shield around himself by his own doing. I think the magic inside him acted on its own accord. Clifton says it's a different type of magic. I think it's obvious that Nox and his power are not in agreement on how things should happen."

"In other words," Cal said, "the magic has a mind of its own."

"Exactly."

That was an entirely different problem. Cal wasn't sure what to make of it.

"Then there's the matter of that strange soldier who took charge during the battle," Finch added.

Cal agreed. "What I find strange is that he wasn't a high-ranking soldier. He was dressed in a basic uniform. I don't even think he was wearing armor. He didn't have to take charge. It's strange that he did."

"He hesitated though," Finch commented. "I

saw him. He didn't rush to Nox's aid. He seemed almost annoyed to do so."

"But he didn't appear frightened of Nox either."

"True," Finch agreed. "That set him apart more than anything from the other soldiers. His main goal wasn't to save Nox. I think he just wanted to make a quick retreat without being branded a traitor. He was dragging another comrade, a young man, a boy really, off the field as well."

"Whatever his reasoning," Cal stated, "he did an effective job in rallying the enemy to retreat even during the chaos. He had an authoritative voice and they didn't hesitate to obey him. This newcomer will be one to watch. He might prove himself to be a new threat."

Finch agreed and they sank into silence, walking side by side.

"I wish I had killed him," Finch said. "This ambush may buy us some time but not enough. If I had been able to kill Nox…"

"I'm not sure anyone could have," Cal told the archer. "He's not wholly human. It will take more than a few arrows to end him."

"But with Corin injured, and Clifton… well I think everyone knows at this point that he's not able to use his magic like he used to."

Cal faltered a step. In fact, few people knew about Clifton's ailing abilities. Cal was surprised that Finch had made the connection. It was true that Clifton wouldn't be of much use in the coming battle.

"There's nothing more we can do. It's up to Corin now," Cal said.

"That's not good enough. What if he's not

strong enough to defeat Nox? What if he never recovers?"

"I'm not willing to write him off yet."

Finch shook his head. "I'm not willing to risk all of Ashnah on him."

"Finch," Cal warned, "we've done our part. The rest is up to Corin. Our duty now is to return to Castille and make our report. We've gained a little breathing room in this battle. Nox will be out of commission for a while. I only pray we've gained enough time to ready ourselves for the coming conflict. This isn't the end, not by a long shot."

Finch nodded but Cal could see that he wasn't in agreement. When they stopped to make camp for the night, Cal stayed awake, feeling unsettled though he wasn't sure why. He got his answer when he heard a muted scuffling long after everyone had gone to sleep. When Finch slipped away from the camp, Cal followed after him.

Cal wasn't surprised by Finch's intended destination. He'd been half suspecting it. Still, he'd been hoping Finch wouldn't go through with it. He half wanted to strangle the archer because he had. Instead, Cal followed quietly, keeping a short distance, close enough to stop Finch from doing anything foolish, or at least more foolish than he already had. Cal hoped he wouldn't have to step in. He hoped Finch would realize he wasn't being rational on his own. Cal, like Hayes, had seen potential in Finch but Cal had also seen recklessness and a certain lack of self-preservation. It would do Finch some good to realize he wasn't invincible but Cal wouldn't let him get himself killed in the process.

Finch was surprisingly good at moving quietly. He had a light step. But he wasn't as good at perceiving others doing the same. He showed no signs of noticing Cal's presence. They moved back towards the outpost lying in ruins. Fortunately, they hadn't gone far after the battle. The men had been wearied and with Freiwade seeming to pose no further threat, they had set up camp close by the destroyed outpost.

Freiwade seemed to have a similar idea. Their camp was hastily established a little past the outpost, hidden among the trees. Finch hesitated when the camp came into sight. There were a few unlucky soldiers standing guard around the perimeter. They looked tired, as if they were sleeping on their feet. Finch noticed this just as Cal did. The young archer wasted no time in slipping quietly through an opening in their perimeter. The tired guards didn't notice the two figures who entered the camp. The rest of the camp was silent, almost unnervingly so. There were no fires burning, no men gathered around to talk or enjoy a meal. Every man who hadn't been commanded to stand guard was either asleep or in the medical tent. Finch and Cal passed the large tent used to house the injured and heard a sob of pain that broke the stillness of the night. Cal risked a look inside the tent through a crack in the cloth entrance. There were so many injured, he tried to count them. It must have been at least a fourth of Freiwade's men in varying states of injury. The cry seemed to have come from a young man, almost a boy, who was lying on a cot, his shoulder wrapped heavily with gauze. Another man sat hunched at his bedside whispering reassurances. Nox wasn't in the tent with the other injured men.

Cal moved on. He couldn't lose sight of Finch. The young archer moved at a speedy pace, rushing through the camp like an angel of death. Cal caught sight of the knife Finch grasped in his hand, a small thing. It was the knife the archers carried, used more as decoration than anything else. Finch scanned the camp and seemed to find what he was looking for. He made his way for a tent larger than the rest. Then as he reached the tent instead of stepping inside, he turned to the tent beside it. Cal was confused. It took him a moment to see that Finch had thought one step ahead. Nox wouldn't be in the largest tent. He might be leading the army but not officially. The largest of the tents would belong to no other than General Havoc, Freiwade's most brutal military leader. Cal was tempted to slip into Havoc's tent himself and put an end to the man who had singlehandedly led more skirmishes on Ashnah's borders than any other. He might very well have led the skirmish which had resulted in the death of Cal's sister. Cal's fingers twitched. It would be easy to kill the monster in his sleep. But he wouldn't. His conscience wouldn't allow it. If King David had refrained from killing Saul when he found him sleeping in a cave, then Cal could stay his own anger. Besides, he had to look out for Finch.

Finch parted the entry to the smaller tent and peered inside. A small gasp broke the stillness of the night. Cal felt his heart pounding. He approached closer. He saw through the crack the same thing Finch did. Nox, the mage who had destroyed three outposts, leaving nothing but ruins behind, Nox, Ashnah's greatest enemy, a wicked man who had sacrificed his very soul for his power, lay helpless and weak before them. Nox was wrapped in bandages, head to toe it seemed. The white was seeped through with red. The bandaging was a haphazard job, not done by any surgeon. Cal wondered if one of the soldiers, whoever was brave enough to get close to Nox, had been left with the task. Nox was sleeping, a deep crease between his eyebrows. The veins of his forehead bulged either with physical pain or some mental agony.

Cal knew he should stop Finch then and there. They had seen Nox. They would be able to report his current, weakened state. But he hesitated. Maybe they should end Nox while he lay defenseless before them. Maybe they could in his weakened state. A knife through the heart would surely be enough to kill even him. But would it be right to kill their enemy in such a way? As it was, Nox may still die from his wounds. They looked serious enough. And Cal couldn't let Finch do the deed. It was bad enough having to kill from a distance with bow and arrow. It would be much worse to sink a knife into flesh.

"Finch," Cal hissed.

Finch jolted in surprise. He opened his mouth, probably to yell in surprise but he was quick enough to clamp a hand over his face to keep the noise silent. Finch took a step away from Nox towards Cal. "*What are you doing here?*" he whispered angrily.

"I could ask you the same thing."

"I've come to finish him once and for all."

"Finch..."

"No, there's no other way. Someone is going to have to kill him eventually and now is our best opportunity. The army is weary and unprepared for another attack. Nox is barely alive. I can stick this knife between his ribs and then all of our troubles will be over."

"There will still be war and Ashnah will still be hard pressed to win. Nox isn't the only threat. He might die from his injuries on his own. Do you really want his blood on your hands?"

Finch glanced at the unconscious mage. "Isn't it already? Those wounds are from my arrows. I did that to him. Why not finish the job?"

Cal didn't have an answer at first. Why not? Why not? Nox was their enemy, wasn't he? "We can't kill him in cold blood like this. He is our enemy, yes, but while he is defenseless it would be like murder. There's a difference between killing an enemy in battle and killing them like this."

"Do we have any other choice? This is war, Cal. If we don't kill him now, how many more lives will he take? Wouldn't it be better to mar our own conscious a little then to let this man live even a day longer?"

Cal thought of General Havoc sleeping in the tent only a few feet away. "Do you know, Finch that my younger sister was killed in a Freiwade skirmish."

Finch's face paled. "Why are you telling me this?"

"Most of the skirmishes that took place along Ashnah's border were led by one man. That same man is fast asleep in the tent next to this one. I could easily slit his throat, avenge my sister, and possibly save many others. But by doing so, I would sacrifice a part of myself in the process, a part that I could never get back. Would it be worth it? I don't think so. My mentor, his name was Barton, he used to say that once the line is crossed, you can never go back. Once you kill Nox, you can never undo it. Your hands will be stained, and so will your heart. Are you willing to make that decision?"

Finch swallowed hard, his throat bobbing. He took a deep breath and turned away from Cal. He approached Nox's bedside and looked hard at the mage's sleeping face. Finch's grip tightened around the knife at his side. He reached towards Nox. Cal wanted desperately to reach out and seize hold of Finch's arm to stop him but he restrained himself. This was Finch's decision to make. Finch's fingers gingerly brushed across one of the bandages covering the mage. He slipped his finger under the gauze and lifted it to inspect the wound beneath. Cal looked closer and saw that the wound, so grave only a few hours earlier was almost completely healed. Nox's magic was mending his body, even exhausted as he was. Nox would be delayed, yes, but not for long. Finch sighed heavily and let the bandage fall back into place. He lifted his knife.

"Finch, no!" Cal demanded quietly.

In a flash the knife moved. Finch savagely thrust the blade into the pillow right beside Nox's head.

"Come on, let's get out of here," Finch said, turning and leaving his knife behind. "I hope that monster wakes up and sees how close he came to death at the hands of Ashnah."

CHAPTER 44

Hayes, Dorian, and the Castille knights gathered in Cheston's grand hall to share an evening meal with the keep. It was then that Hayes saw why the men fought so valiantly, why they hadn't been willing to surrender. There were not only warriors gathered in the great hall but also women and children, servants and elderly. All of the people of Cheston were crowded into the small room.

"We got as many of them out of the town as we could," Viscount York explained. "The keep is the safest place for them at the moment. We can provide them safety if not comfort."

Hayes felt guilty for bringing so many of his knights into a space that was already filled to the brim. He prayed that it would all be over tomorrow and these people could return to their homes. He hoped they had homes left to return to.

"I apologize that we can't give you a warmer welcome," Viscount York said. "We truly appreciate your service. If the situation were different, there would be a feast thrown in your honor."

"This is more than enough," Hayes responded. "A warm meal and a place to lay our heads and then we'll drive out the enemy in the morning and be on our way."

The viscount seemed dissatisfied at these words but offered a small smile in return. Hayes understood why before long. When he and Dorian took their seats beside Viscount York and Phineas at the head table, the meal laid before them may have been hot but it was hardly substantial. It was a modest portion of porridge, no more, no less. Dorian looked sadly at the meal, not with distaste but with pity. Hayes shared the feeling. Hayes's pity grew when he looked to Phineas's plate and saw a smaller portion than his own.

"I'm afraid our provisions are low," Viscount York stated as he spooned up some of the gruel. "We weren't expecting a prolonged siege. Our stores were never well-stocked to begin with. We had a small harvest this last year. Grains are about the only thing we have left."

Dorian pushed his plate away. "Please, Viscount York, give my portion to one of the children. I don't need it."

The viscount looked concerned at Dorian's statement.

"Eat, Dorian," Hayes urged the young knight. He appreciated Dorian's generosity and sacrifice but it would only offend the viscount. "You'll need your strength for the battle tomorrow. After that there will be food enough for all. Castille will send some relief provisions to Cheston for the people."

"You would have our great thanks," the viscount replied.

After the meal, Dorian went with the knights

to make camp in the keep's courtyard, there was no room inside for them. Hayes was offered the honor of a guest room inside the castle. He refused.

"I sleep with my men," Hayes responded. "I appreciate your offer but I prefer to be with them. I may be their leader but that doesn't make me any more worthy of a nice bed then they are."

A nice bed didn't matter much anyway. Hayes slept poorly that night. As a knight, he was accustomed to sleeping any chance he got and anywhere he found himself but the situation in Cheston disconcerted him. He laid awake most of the night praying for God's grace in the coming battle. When morning dawned, he roused his men. After another quick meal of porridge, it was time to fight.

Hayes pulled aside Dorian and Phineas York to discuss their plans for the attack.

"You know the area best and arguably the enemy as well," Hayes told Phineas. "You'll take the lead in this fight. Me and my men will support you."

Phineas flushed. "But Sir…"

"We desire victory, do we not?"

"Yes."

"Then you will lead. That gives us our best chance."

Phineas swallowed hard and nodded. "I suggest a direct attack. We've been striking randomly, sometimes in the morning, sometimes at night, sometimes in the afternoon. We've been trying to confuse the enemy and keep them on guard at all times. That way they can never really rest. Sometimes we strike every day, sometimes every other day. They may have seen your forces coming into Cheston but if they haven't then we'll catch them entirely by surprise with our extra fighters. If we take a wedge formation with the strongest fighters positioned in the front, we can cut through their ranks and the weaker of my men will be able to fight the stragglers instead of having to take on Freiwade's best fighters. After the initial attack, the wedge should break and our men will fan out to surround the enemy from the back. Once they're overcome, we'll retreat, allowing them to withdraw and return to Freiwade. Cheston doesn't have the capacity to take prisoners."

"It's a good plan," Hayes praised. He probably couldn't have come up with anything better himself. Phineas York had potential. Once the war with Freiwade was over, Hayes was determined to offer the young man a position as a knight at Castille Castle.

They mustered their forces and as the sun started to crest the horizon, they pressed out from the keep's gate towards the enemy camp. Phineas York took the lead with Hayes and Dorian a half step behind. Hayes watched as York's limp became less noticeable, his back straightened slightly and his shoulders squared.

"For Cheston and for Ashnah!" Phineas rallied the men.

"For Cheston! For Ashnah!" they cried in unison.

The cry of battle was enough to rouse the enemy and thus the battle began. The combined Cheston and Castille forces took a wedge formation with Phineas and Hayes as the driving points. They struck the enemy as a battering ram, clashing swords and yelling with the heat of conflict. Hayes felt alive as he only did in battle. He was no longer a commander, a battle master. He was just another knight. In battle, rank didn't matter, only experience and ability. Hayes demonstrated both with flawless strikes and an impenetrable defense. He saw fear in the eyes of the Freiwade soldiers with whom he crossed swords. They hadn't expected such a formidable adversary. But Hayes wasn't the only fighter they had to be wary of. If anything, Hayes was the least of their worries. Dorian and Phineas may have posed an even greater threat. Dorian was skilled, young, and quick. He was stronger than most. He parried strikes, driving ever forward through the ranks. He didn't kill, only drove the enemy away with a flurry of attacks that they were hard-pressed to defend against. Phineas was perhaps the most savage warrior of the day. He had the greatest desire to destroy the enemy. He was fighting to protect his home and his people. He wouldn't let Freiwade prevail. He slashed and stabbed with a viciousness that made his opponents cower. It was mesmerizing to watch.

In fact, Hayes was so mesmerized that he became distracted. Just as the wedge of the Ashnan forces was breaking to split apart and attack the enemy from behind, a Freiwade soldier got behind Hayes without his noticing.

"Sir Hayes!" Dorian cried out.

Hayes turned just in time to see the soldier raising his sword for a killing strike. There was no time to defend against it. There was no time to raise his sword or even step away from the weapon's downward trajectory. Hayes knew then and there that he wouldn't walk off this battlefield. For more than a decade, he had walked the line between life and death, defending his kingdom. He'd taken lives to protect Ashnah. He'd taken a scar down his cheek as a constant reminder of how dangerous battles could be and how nothing was guaranteed. He'd known all along that he would die fighting. The only question was when and where. Now he finally knew.

But Hayes wasn't fated to die that day. Just as the enemy's sword was a hairsbreadth away, it faltered and dropped to the side along with the man's body. The point of a blade pierced through the man's chest from behind. As the body fell, Dorian was revealed, standing behind the soldier with his sword penetrating through the man's back.

The look on Dorian's face as the Freiwade soldier fell was akin to if the blade had been driven into Dorian's heart instead of the enemy's. He paled, his eyes growing wide and horror-stricken.

"Dorian," Hayes said, raising his hands in a placating gesture. "It's okay."

But Hayes knew that it wasn't okay. He realized then that not only was this Dorian's first real battle but the soldier lying dead at their feet was the first life Dorian had taken. Dorian's face turned from white to green and he turned aside to retch. Dorian dropped to his knees next to the fallen soldier and sobbed. He reached for the Freiwade man's body, weeping bitterly.

"No, no, no," Dorian repeated again and again.

Hayes sheathed his sword, satisfied that Phineas could handle driving the army away on his own. Hayes lowered himself to his knees beside Dorian, resting a hand on the young man's shoulder. Dorian jerked away from the gesture, inconsolable.

"You saved me," Hayes said. "I know it hurts, Dorian. But you did what you had to. I'm sorry that you ever had to experience this but I thank you for the sacrifice you made for my sake."

Dorian shook with another wracking sob. He fell forward, his face pressing to the ground, his tears turning the dust damp. "I... I killed him. I killed him!"

Hayes allowed Dorian a few more moments of grief. His heart bled for the young knight. He remembered his own first battle, his first kill. There had been weeks of pain and confusion after that day and he'd never forgotten the face of the man whose life he had taken nor those of the lives which had come after the first all in the defense of Ashnah. Hayes let Dorian shed his bitter tears and choke out cries of moral agony but then he raised the young knight to his feet and forced him away from the body. Dorian fought against him but Hayes was unyielding. The battle around them had died down. Phineas had successfully driven the Freiwade army away and they were retreating back to their homeland. There was still much to do and Dorian couldn't stay kneeling in the midst of the battlefield forever.

Hayes knew that Dorian wouldn't offer much help in the clean-up so he led him back to Cheston Keep to rest and mourn. Dorian's steps dragged wearily as if he were in a daze. He didn't speak. He was lost to the world around him. Hayes knew it would take time for Dorian to overcome the pain. He would overcome it someday. In the meantime, Hayes would leave him to his tears. There was much still to be done before they could return to Castille and there was no time to waste.

CHAPTER 45

It was late when Dusk finally headed back to The Cavern. It had been a long day. He'd spent most of it in the library trying to help the boy Will find a solution to Corin's injury. It had been an interesting interaction between them. Dusk had explained, without revealing that he was a spy, that he'd been sent to help Will search for answers. Will had been rightly suspicious of him and how he knew about Corin's injury to begin with. Fortunately, Clifton had vouched for Dusk and urged Will to work with him. Dusk was grateful for Will's determination in finding answers and since Will was the scribe's apprentice, the boy had a much more extensive knowledge of the castle library than Dusk did. They'd been searching tirelessly for a way to heal Corin's arm but as of yet they'd found nothing substantial. It was tiring and Dusk was more than ready to retreat to The Cavern at the end of the day. But first, he needed to sort through his thoughts.

He was accustomed to wandering the castle when everyone else was asleep. It was the perfect time to think and he had plenty of thoughts to sort through. His mind was a never-ending maze of ideas, a storm that never calmed. There were so many issues to find solutions to, people and things to decipher, and past conversations to think over and analyze. Sometimes, his mind made it difficult to find rest. Sometimes his body felt like it would burst because of the chaotic state of his head. It helped to move and think, to sort through the problems keeping him awake. Things had only gotten worse with the war approaching, especially now that Duke Heirson and Dresden were at the castle.

Dusk needed space. He needed to control his thoughts so he could get some sleep and be of use to everyone. But somehow, he still found his feet leading him to a part of the castle that he'd sworn to himself he would avoid at all costs. And then he found himself standing before the door to Duke Heirson's rooms. It was late. Everyone should have been asleep but it was evident to Dusk immediately that voices were coming from inside the room. The voices were raised in argument. Dusk took a step closer to the door and listened.

"It's time for you to commit, Terin," Duke Heirson spoke.

Dusk jolted in surprise. Terin? What was the commander of the archers doing talking with Duke Heirson?

"I'll tell you again as I've told you before, my position is important. I cannot act rashly where this is concerned. I'll wait things out," Terin replied.

"The time for waiting is over. The end is approaching. The battle is on Castille's doorstep whether King Rupert chooses to acknowledge it openly or not. If the king doesn't tell the people the truth soon, then I will. I'll announce the true state of things in front of the entire court if I have to. Maybe then the king will finally consider an alliance between my family and his. I won't delay for much longer. With that boy mage injured, it's finally time to act. It's time for you to pick a side, Terin. You must commit or be left behind."

There was a moment of heavy silence. Dusk could only wonder how the duke knew about Corin's injury. How had he found out? They'd worked so hard to keep it secret but the duke had discovered the truth anyway. That could only mean trouble.

Then Terin spoke again, "You know how I feel about the leadership in Ashnah. The Castille family is weak, they have been ever since that girl Ruena's father abandoned his duties, married a commoner, and went to die in the country. Rupert was never meant to rule and he never should have. And I refuse for the heir to this kingdom to be a female. But I am loyal to Ashnah, not Freiwade. Your plan is not the answer, Heirson."

There was a scuffling sound and Dusk craved to be able to see what was happening through the walls.

"Father, don't!" Dresden spoke up for the first time.

"Get your hands off of me you cowardly weakling!" Terin growled. "I won't reveal your plot. I said I can't stand with you, not that I am loyal to the king. I'll wait and see how things play out. I won't risk losing my position. If you swear to me that I will remain commander of the archers if your plan comes to fruition, then I won't expose you. But I can't help you, not directly."

Dusk waited, perched dangerously close to the door, anxious to hear the response.

"Fine," Heirson said. "But you will gain no special privileges either."

"There is only one privilege that I require, the ability to choose the archers who serve Ashnah and expel those I wish to."

"Fair enough, Terin. Corin's injury means he no longer poses a threat. Now that the young mage is out of the way, real change can happen."

"What about Clifton?" Dresden asked.

"He doesn't pose a threat," Duke Heirson replied shortly. "Everyone knows his abilities are useless now. He's nothing more than a weak, old man."

"But he's still a mage."

The duke ignored Dresden. "Our first step will be to eliminate Corin entirely, then gather our forces and make a move to finally start an uprising against King Rupert. I'll be holding you to your support, Terin, weak as it may be. Now, get out of my sight."

Dusk scrambled back from the door, trying to remain silent. His heart was racing as fast as his mind. He looked around frantically and found a dark hallway a few feet away. He ran for it, finding cover in its shadows. What was happening? Terin was conspiring with Duke Heirson? To do what? Dusk knew the answer to that question. He'd been hiding from the truth for too long.

He knew that Cal was starting to have doubts about Lark. He was worried because she was keeping secrets. Little did Cal know that Dusk was keeping a few dark secrets of his own. They were the type of secrets that should have been revealed long ago. Dusk feared the consequences of them now. He should have told Cal. He should have told someone. Things were moving quicker than he'd anticipated. He'd wanted to gain their trust first and establish himself in the castle. But he'd waited too long. He'd kept telling himself 'just a little longer' and 'not quite yet'. Now would he be too late?

He remembered the day when he had revealed his true identity to Cal. He hadn't had much choice. Cal had recognized him for who he truly was, despite his careful disguise. Dusk had anticipated betrayal and banishment, maybe even being turned over to the very place and people he had run from. Instead, Cal had been calm and considerate. He'd demanded an explanation but then he'd heard Dusk out and believed him. He had accepted Dusk's word as truth in a way that surprised Dusk completely. Cal always surprised him with his generosity, care, and trust in others. For a spy, Cal was surprisingly trusting. He accepted people without restraint, even when those people were secretive and damaged. He didn't hesitate even if it meant he would likely get hurt later. Dusk should have told him everything. He'd only told Cal a fraction of the truth. He'd kept the most dangerous secret locked away. Cal hadn't pressed then or since. Cal had believed what Dusk said but Dusk still hadn't been willing to reveal everything.

Terin stepped out of Duke Heirson's room, shaking his head in disgust. It complicated things that someone in a position like Terin's was involved. Terin held power, more power than he should have. He had a whole contingent of archers at his beck and call. Many of them were loyal to Terin above even the king.

They held him in awe and fear. Terin might claim that he would stand back and watch, not aiding Heirson but it still posed a problem for Ashnah. Would Terin persuade the archers to stand back from the battle or not give it their all in the fighting? That alone could turn the tide of the war against them. Dusk's head throbbed with the rush of fears and realizations.

    This was all his fault. He'd let things go on for too long. He'd let it expand into a horrible obstacle that he worried Ashnah wouldn't be able to face. He had no choice now. He had to reveal everything to Cal and the king. He couldn't hold onto his secrets any longer. He only feared that it would be too late. And after staying silent for so long, would anyone believe him now? Would he lose his most precious allies forever? It didn't matter anymore. Dusk no longer had a choice. He knew what he had to do.

CHAPTER 46

Corin practiced raising and lowering his damaged arm with the help of the physician. The doctor did much of the moving. It was painful work and frustrating beyond all measure. Corin could barely move his stiff shoulder. From the elbow down, there was no control at all. No amount of work on Corin's part could cause the appendage to move. He struggled and struggled but he could hardly feel his arm, much less move it. The only sensation he felt at all was pain. From the tips of his fingers to his neck, there was pain. Sometimes it would go away and he would feel nothing at all. Other times it would be excruciating as if every nerve was on fire.

"It's a good sign," the physician told him. "It means the nerves aren't dead."

Corin wished they were. Besides, he didn't believe anything positive the physician told him since it was the same man who had suggested amputation as a better alternative. It didn't particularly matter if the nerves in his arm were alive or dead. He still couldn't move it. He would never be able to move it again.

"Why do we bother with this if I can't use

my arm again?" Corin asked the physician after a frustrating hour of useless exercises.

"There is a slim possibility..." the man began.

"Don't lie to me," Corin interrupted. "I don't want false hope."

"Then, I'll be plain with you, young mage. If you don't amputate the limb, this exercise is important to try to stretch the muscles and tendons. It may help alleviate some of the pain eventually."

Corin didn't like the words 'might' and 'eventually'. Everything was a 'maybe' lately. Maybe the pain would go away. Maybe he would be able to train as a mage again. Maybe he would function somewhat like a human.

Corin refused to even look at the arm. He requested that it be kept wrapped in a bandage to hide the evidence of mutilation from the sight of others and himself. The bandages weren't needed. The flesh was ruined but there was no blood or burns to be covered up. The physician seemed annoyed at having to wrap the bandages for him since Corin couldn't do it with only one hand. Still, Corin refused to remove them. He couldn't look at it. He couldn't. And he didn't want anyone else to either.

His heart twinged every time he even thought about the arm and how useless he'd become. He'd had a few visitors to his sickroom the last few days but life in the castle still went on without him. Everyone was surprisingly busy. Corin worried before long he'd be forgotten completely. Will spent a lot of time with Corin at least. He seemed to be attempting to keep Corin company though it was done awkwardly. The boy was a welcome guest. He usually told Corin about the goings on in the castle and was eager to help make Corin comfortable in any way he could.

"I've been scouring all of Clifton's and Neos Loch's writings," Will explained. "I know there has to be some way to fix this, to make you feel better at least."

Corin's heart was warmed by the effort but he held no hope that Will would find an answer. "Don't waste your time, Will. Clifton told me before that this skill, what caused the accident, can't be undone. I'm... broken. There's no fixing it."

Will shook his head, refusing to take no for an answer. "I won't give up. It's not a waste of my time. If there's any way you can get better, then I'll find it."

Corin didn't point out the fact that if there was a way to heal injuries so severe then someone would have found it by then. Corin was sure Neos Loch and Clifton had searched long and hard to find a way to save the injured. If they weren't able to find anything, then Corin wouldn't either, and certainly not Will.

Clifton was also a regular visitor. He came by to visit at least once a day, always with a look of greater concern than before. Corin knew that Clifton was hiding something from him and he was incredibly angry about it. After everything that had happened, Corin felt he deserved to at least know if something important was going on.

"Do you remember what happened right before you lost control of the magic?" Clifton asked on one occasion.

"I was trying to destroy the apple," Corin responded.

"I mean the conversation, what I said."

Corin remembered bits and pieces of that day but he was forced to shake his head, unsure. His mind was muddled. Clifton refused to say anything further. It was frustrating to Corin to have something he knew must be important kept from him. He knew he couldn't demand that Clifton tell him the truth either. He didn't want to risk angering his mentor and have Clifton stop visiting him. When Corin tried desperately to remember what Clifton might have said, he only felt a sense of impending doom.

As for the strange visitor in the middle of the night, Corin still wasn't sure if he'd actually seen the figure or if he'd imagined it. He didn't voice the event to anyone, afraid they'd think he was losing his mind. It was obvious to Corin that they feared his injury stretched beyond just his arm. They didn't understand magic and they had never treated such a wound before. They worried what the repercussions of the accident might be.

Corin's most frequent visitors were doctors and physicians who all wore pitying, hopeless looks. They gave increasingly terrible reports with every visit. The chances of him being able to use his arm again dwindled. The doctors kept pushing for him to consider amputation.

"This magic could be similar to an infection," the doctors explained gravely. "It could spread through your arm and into the rest of your body. The sacrifice of a limb is a better alternative to the unknown that we face if we leave the injury as it is."

Corin craved any visitor who didn't bring a diagnosis or piece of unwanted advice.

Cal was one person who hadn't visited Corin

yet during his recovery. Corin found it strange since Cal more than anyone seemed to understand what Corin was going through and had been supportive after Corin had woken. Cal's absence hurt. Corin wondered if he'd misread Cal. He finally ventured to ask Clifton about Cal's absence. He was told that his newest acquaintance was busy. Corin was surprised at the quick and dismissive answer. Fortunately, Cal's missing presence was filled by an unexpected visitor.

One evening after Clifton, Will, and the doctors had all gone and Corin was alone, Dorian entered the room. The knight knocked once, softly, then looked behind him into the hallway before entering Corin's sick room and shutting the door.

"Dorian?" Corin asked, surprised.

Dorian looked pale, terribly pale, almost lifeless. There was a distance in Dorian's eyes and a cut across his brow. Corin wondered if the slight injury was from training.

"Corin," Dorian answered then hesitated before speaking further. "Um... my condolences. For your arm, I mean."

Corin nodded. He wasn't sure how to respond. He wanted to point out to Dorian that 'condolences' wasn't a fitting word to use. It wasn't as if Corin had lost a loved one, though sometimes it felt like with the loss of his arm he himself had died a little. He couldn't help noticing that Dorian was acting strange. Had something happened?

"How are you feeling?" Dorian asked, then asked another question without waiting for the first to be answered. "How long do you think you'll take to recover? Will you be able to use your arm again?"

Corin felt unsettled at the quick questions. It felt as if Dorian was eager to be out of the sick room as quickly as possible. Corin didn't want to talk about his arm. He wasn't ready to accept the state of his physical injury. He couldn't manage to hide the hopelessness of his situation from Dorian.

"I don't know. Nothing's certain anymore. I feel okay, I guess, but… things don't look particularly good either."

Corin knew he was skirting around giving any real answer but he didn't know how else to respond.

"Oh," Dorian replied awkwardly. "Well, I'm sorry."

Corin waited for a further comment but there was none. After a long, awkward moment, Dorian bowed his head and reached for the doorknob. "I should… I should go. Goodbye."

Dorian didn't wait for a response before ducking outside, leaving Corin alone once again. Corin wanted to call out and ask if Dorian was alright but he didn't get the chance before the door was shut. Corin wondered if Dorian was acting strange because of Corin's injury. Dorian probably didn't care much for having such a useless and pathetic friend. The strange visit only increased Corin's feelings of hopelessness.

The worst visits were the ones from Ruena. She never stayed for long. That was largely Corin's fault. He didn't talk to her when she was there. He couldn't even meet her gaze. He only answered questions when she asked them.

"How are you feeling today?" she would ask.

"Fine," Corin would mumble in reply.

He never encouraged further discussion. He

was embarrassed at his weakness and he felt very sorry for himself. He knew it was self-pity that he was feeling. He knew it was wrong to dwell on himself so much. But he hated how his life had turned out. He hated how useless and pathetic he'd become. Most of all, he hated for Ruena to see him in such a state.

She was lovely to him despite his unfriendly and brooding nature. She prayed for him every time before she left. She rested her hand on his shoulder and murmured a few words then smiled warmly at him and said she hoped he felt better soon.

Corin started to wonder if he ever would feel better. His progress was slow, painful, and there were no signs of any progress being made. He was told again and again by the doctors that he was only being troublesome in his refusal to concede to an amputation. They said it would be for his own good. They said there was no hope of recovering and he was only suffering out of obstinance. But Corin couldn't bear the idea of losing his arm any more than he already had. He sunk further and further into despair with each day that passed. He couldn't overcome the weight driving him down. He felt unbearably lonely and worthless. And on some dark nights when he lay awake trying to sleep but unable to because of the pain and his racing thoughts, he would wish that the magic had killed him instead.

CHAPTER 47

Dane waited impatiently in the throne room with his father and brothers. He shifted from foot to foot, looking to the door, his only means of escape. He stood in the shadows in an attempt to go unnoticed. If they just didn't look at him he might get out of the room unscathed. He knew it was a useless hope. Eventually, his brothers would corner him. They would probably just wait until his father had left the room to do so. Then again King Histen Corpin enjoyed watching his children fight and everyone in the castle preferred when Dane was the target. Dane knew his brothers were only maintaining a measure of composure because they were on display. Even in the midst of conflict, the nobles still made every effort to attend the king's daily receptions, eager to ingratiate themselves with their ruler. Everyone was on their best behavior, or at least that was how it was supposed to be. Standing *behind* the throne, the Corpin brothers tended to jab and shove each other when they thought no one was looking. Dane was frequently at the center of this negative attention. Dane hoped for once his brothers wouldn't cause a scene with him in the middle of it. He felt that he was already walking on shaky footing after he met with his father. Why was it that Skellas was such a sensitive topic? That question had been bothering Dane for a while now and his curiosity only increased as the war progressed.

If only he could stay out of sight for a while until his father forgot the conversation about Skellas. Dane had been too bold, too demanding. He feared he would regret that momentary courage. It wasn't as if taking part in the reception was doing him any favors. He didn't stand a chance in the competition of succession. His brothers could spend as much time as they wanted battling for their father's favor but Dane knew it was only a game. King Corpin enjoyed the conflict and chaos that the fight for inheritance brought out. Sometimes Dane wondered if the only reason King Corpin had fathered so many potential heirs was to make the fight more interesting.

Dane had never wanted the throne. He detested the ruthlessness required of Freiwade royalty and found himself hating it more and more as bodies piled up as a result of the war. Remembering the Skellans being paraded around made bile rise in Dane's throat. Dane had absolutely no say in how his father ruled. He'd been reminded of that, harshly. He could only hope that whichever of his brothers took the throne next would be a more gracious king. He feared the opposite might prove to be true. None of his brothers were kind or even fair. Only Claude seemed to calculate the well-being of the kingdom, though Dane suspected his second eldest brother would ensure his well-being above all others. Unfortunately, it seemed that, like Dane, Claude had no desire for the crown. Claude supported Warson's attempts for power, content to offer advice from the shadows.

Maybe Dane would be able to do the same. He could help his kingdom by allying with whichever brother took the throne. He could help make decisions that would benefit the kingdom. But ingratiating himself with his brothers was easier said than done. It would almost be easier to be king. All of Dane's brothers hated him. Dane knew he was no threat but he still couldn't trust his brothers. They might use the competition as an excuse to be rid of him. They all had their faults, and heavy ones at that. Warson, the eldest, was brutal, Claude was sinister, Thorin irresponsible, Dion insatiable, Horace bitter and jealous, Scythe proud, and Acedio listless. Even so, Dane was no threat to their positions. The real reason they hated him was because he was illegitimate.

It should have worked in his favor and excluded him from vying for the throne, making him less of a target. But Freiwade's strange and skewed laws made the sons of mistresses acceptable heirs. Dane suspected his father and prior rulers had bent the rules to their benefit. His brothers hated him because of their father's immorality and Dane felt only disgrace. He was a living reminder of his father's disloyalty to his wife and cruelty to others. He wasn't sure if it was a blessing or a further curse that he didn't know his mother. She'd left him in the castle so he wouldn't live a life of total disgrace as she was forced into. Dane tried not to think of it as abandonment.

It would serve Dane well to remember his position. He always had to tread carefully. He never should have sought an audience with his father. He couldn't persuade his father of anything, especially regarding Skellas. The sooner he could escape from the courtroom, the safer he would be from his father's wrath. He hoped his brothers would attack him first. Dane glanced at each of his brothers trying to determine who would strike first. They were surrounding him on all sides. That was just one of the many problems that came with having seven brothers. He might escape one or two of them but there was always another waiting to pounce. Dane contemplated which of them was most likely to make the first move against him. Probably Thorin or Horace.

Dane didn't have long to consider. A messenger burst into the room and Dane immediately knew that something was very wrong. No messenger would dare enter in such a rude manner if something wasn't amiss. They'd be drawing unnecessary attention to themselves and possibly gaining the king's wrath by doing so. Dane's mind flashed back to when Nox had interrupted the court, nearly killing Dane in an attempt to use him as leverage.

"What is the meaning of this interruption?" the king demanded.

The messenger paused for a moment, struggling to catch his breath. "T...there's been an attack on the front lines. The mage, Nox, has been seriously wounded. So many dead. Great delay in the plan of attack."

The man's words were jumbled. It took a moment for the severity of the situation to sink in. There had been an attack and the mage, their best weapon, had been injured. Dane felt sick. There were murmurs throughout the court. Voices rose in panic, confusion, and dismay. The king remained cool and collected.

"Explain," King Histen Corpin said.

The messenger took a deep breath and began, "There was an ambush. Ashnah staged knights and archers in the forest around Outpost Halliday. They put mannequins in the parapets to fool us into thinking it was fully manned. They set up cannons to fire at us from the outpost. Nox struck with his magic as he always does and the outpost collapsed. We thought we'd won. Then the men from Ashnah attacked. It was when Nox was weakest and he was unable to fight back. General Havoc told us to stand and fight but he fled the scene of battle, leaving us without someone to issue orders. There was chaos and many men died. Then a soldier drafted from Skellas stepped in and took charge. He rescued Nox from the onslaught of arrows and issued the order to retreat. His actions saved us all."

The king frowned at the news. Dane noticed how his father's face soured more at the mention of the Skellan soldier than at the news of the attack or Nox being wounded.

"Of course, it had to be a Skellan," Claude murmured under his breath.

Dane glanced at his brother but he knew better than to ask what he meant. Dane could only wonder again if there was something he didn't know about Skellas.

"Those Skellans never lose their will no matter how much we try to break them," the king muttered quietly. "That doesn't make them brave, it makes them dangerous."

Dane wondered how it could be seen as a bad thing that a soldier stepped up when the occasion demanded it. He would have thought that would earn the man praise, not contempt.

"What is the Skellan soldier's name?" the king asked.

"Aster Kadesh, Your Majesty."

King Corpin shook his head and then addressed the messenger. "Tell General Havoc to keep an eye on that man. Mark my words, no good can come from Skellas. This victory should not go to that soldier's head. The last thing we need is for Skellas to stage an uprising."

"Is an uprising a threat we should be worried about?" Warson, the eldest, asked.

The king scoffed. "Skellas must always be worried about. It would be foolish to underestimate them."

"Skellas provides the majority of Freiwade's food," Claude reminded Warson. "Lately they've provided many of our soldiers as well. If the sea nation were to turn against us, the war would be as good as lost."

"Regardless of that foolish soldier and the threat that Skellas persistently poses, they won't retaliate. After all, they have no one to rule them. The Corpin line has made sure of that," the king stated.

Dane wondered what his father meant. He didn't know as much about the history of Freiwade as he would have liked. He was too afraid to ask questions and he hadn't been given the preference in lessons that his brothers had. Besides, the history of the three kingdoms of Ademar was muddled and difficult to understand. Much of the past was forgotten or ignored in favor of establishing a set future. The king's words made Dane curious about the history between the kingdoms of Freiwade and Skellas. Why was Skellas seen as a threat even now when they had no ruler and they were barely managing to stay alive under Freiwade's command? Dane was full of questions but he didn't say anything. Instead, he remained silent as the king finished his conference.

"Report to General Havoc," the king instructed the messenger. "Tell him what I've told you. Instruct him to muster his men and renew the attack on Ashnah. This victory of theirs will not be allowed. We will strike back harder than ever before. The mage is not our only weapon. The soldiers must not rely on him too fully. They are to fight and die if need be. We will win this war."

Then the king turned his head to speak to Claude who stepped forward, bending close to his father's ear. Dane still managed to overhear the words exchanged. "Command your spies to report what is going on in Ashnah. There must be news after this ambush. Reprimand them for not finding out about this attack sooner. This incident must not be repeated."

"Yes, Your Majesty," Claude answered with a bow.

Dane watched his brother wearily. He knew little about Claude's force of spies but he was wary to use such ruthless tactics. He didn't like the idea of endangering their people in Ashnah. It didn't matter what information they gained as a result. Dane was reluctant to resort to such methods.

"This reception is dismissed," the king announced.

The messenger, the nobles, and the sons of the king filtered out of the room. Dane strode out of the room quickly, hoping to avoid his brothers. He was determined to learn more about Skellas. He had let the feeling of uneasiness he experienced about the fallen kingdom sit for too long. He needed answers. There was one place where he might find out what he wanted to know. Dane headed to the library. Why was Skellas such a sensitive subject to the king? Why were they seen as a threat when they were treated as less than human by Freiwade? Dane hoped he would be able to answer those questions and more. However, he had barely stepped inside the library when he saw that Claude was already there, seemingly waiting for him. Dane swallowed hard. Claude's focus on him was penetrating.

"I saw the look on your face," Claude spoke. "I knew you'd come here. You're curious about Skellas."

Dane detested the way Claude said everything in statements. He never asked questions. It was as if he already knew the answers to everything. As such, Dane didn't bother to respond.

"It's only right that you know the truth about how brutal and ruthless Freiwade can be," Claude continued. "Maybe then you can fully comprehend how much you don't belong here."

"I just want to understand," Dane responded quietly, "please."

He hoped begging would put him in Claude's good graces. It wasn't as easy to manipulate Claude as it was some of his other brothers. Dion could be bribed with delicacies, Thorin could be bribed with alcohol, and Scythe could be flattered for his greatness. Claude was more difficult to read. Dane never knew what Claude was thinking.

Claude lifted an eyebrow at him. "I am not so easily fooled," Claude responded. "I know what you're doing, Dane. You've been trying for some time to find favor with anyone you can. You can beg me all you want but it won't sway me. However, I will oblige you this once. The story of Freiwade and Skellas might serve as a warning for you. The Corpin family has a long and esteemed history. The nobility of this family stretches back centuries to a time before history and civilization. It's a pity that legacy has been marred in recent years."

The words were filled with a subtle venom. Dane shifted uncomfortably. It was common for snide and even disgusted remarks to be made towards him. His mother had been a servant in the castle, a commoner. The fact that his father had associated with her at all was reproachful in the eyes of many.

"My great grandfather, Claudius Corpin the First is considered one of the greatest kings in Freiwade's history. It was he who put an end to false doctrines and ridiculous religions in our kingdom. He instilled a separation between nobility and commoners and made the gaining of wisdom something to be earned by birthright not freely given."

Dane thought he sounded like a truly despicable man. It wasn't fair for only the nobility to be given the privilege of an education but that was the way it had been in Freiwade since Claudius Corpin's time. As for religion, Dane didn't care much for it but he didn't think it was ridiculous if it gave people hope. Surely that was worth something. He didn't know as much about his kingdom's history as he should have but he did know one thing that Claude and so many others often left out of their lessons. Claudius Corpin's changes didn't benefit Freiwade at all. Quite the opposite, it sent the kingdom into a dark age of ignorance and fear. Dane wondered if that hadn't been the point from the beginning.

"King Claudius Corpin also was the man who forged the assimilation of Freiwade and Skellas. Claudius was gracious enough to allow Skellas to retain their status as a kingdom but they had no ruler. The old king of Skellas, Alexander Strond, was rebellious. He would have driven his kingdom into the ground. Claudius Corpin made a brutal but necessary decision to take the man from the throne and bring Skellas under Freiwade's control."

"In other words, he was slaughtered by Freiwade," Dane said bitterly.

Claude grinned. "Yes, you could say that. The entire royal family of Skellas was eliminated. Any surviving heirs were killed to ensure Skellas would stay under Freiwade's control. It was a tactical decision and a wise one at that. It discouraged rebellion and quelled any opportunity for an uprising."

"Then why did Father seem concerned about just that?"

Claude pressed his fingers together and studied Dane closely. "The *king*," he emphasized the word as if Dane had no right to use the term 'father', "has every reason to be worried. No matter how hard we try to subdue them and no matter what actions we take, there is always a little fight left in the Skellans. You saw as much when the group from Talbrandt was brought to the castle."

"How did you know... of course you knew I was watching."

Claude gave a sardonic grin, no humor in the expression. "The Skellans are *so* spirited that despite our best efforts to quelch the rumors, there is always talk of a lost heir who will one day come back to save the kingdom from under Freiwade's foot."

Claude scoffed as he spoke the words but Dane felt a spark of something he hadn't felt in a long time, hope. He couldn't explain the feeling. He shouldn't feel that way about something that could cause harm to Freiwade. But when he thought about all the suffering his kingdom and the kingdom of Skellas had endured, he couldn't help but wonder if things would be better if they were two independent kingdoms once again. He wouldn't discount the rumors. All rumors were based on some truth. He determined to learn everything he could about the matter.

"What kind of rumors?" Dane asked, trying to seem casual in his question.

Claude looked at him knowingly, not buying his act. "I hesitate to tell you anything because it seems a foolish notion is brewing in that thick skull of yours. I will only say that a servant and the infant son of King Alexander Strond were rumored to have escaped. The rumors are that the woman raised the boy, the only surviving heir, as her own in secret to protect the royal line. However, rest assured, the royal family of Skellas was destroyed by Freiwade. The Corpin family does not make such foolish mistakes often."

"What do you mean often?" Dane questioned.

Claude didn't answer but Dane thought he detected a certain pallor to his face. Claude finally spoke, "Be cautious Dane. You're already in dangerous territory simply being in this household. I only tell you all of this to remind you how ruthless this family can be. You have no place here. You would be wise to consider departing before Father dies. Once he is gone, there will be no one to protect you."

The words left a bitter taste in Dane's mouth but he nodded respectfully to his brother and waited for him to exit the library. Dane couldn't read Claude but he suspected behind the cold exterior, there might be a small part of his brother that actually cared about him. As soon as Claude was gone, Dane set to work searching the many shelves of the library for further mention of Skellas's lost heir. If Skellas could rise against Freiwade, then maybe Skellas and Freiwade could be saved.

CHAPTER 48

Finch was weary from the ambush. All he wanted to do was collapse with exhaustion but first, he had to speak with Hayes. The battle master and his men had returned to Castille Castle before Finch's group. Finch's little excursion into the camp of the enemy to try to kill Nox had set them back the better part of a day. The ambush forces had woken to find both Finch and Cal missing and without leadership present, they'd remained at camp until the two young men returned. After spending the better part of the night sneaking through the enemy's camp, Finch and Cal hadn't made good pace on the return journey home. They'd been so tired in fact that Cal had made the executive decision to set up camp a few miles after their starting point. None of the men complained, they were all wearied from the previous day's fighting. Still, Finch felt guilty about his actions which had led to such a delay. He felt even guiltier for making Hayes wait for a report. Finch was sure the battle master had worried when he'd arrived back to Castille and found Finch and his men still missing.

A servant went to fetch Finch as soon as he arrived back at the castle. Cal let him report on his own. Finch was sure Cal would be giving his report later. Finch hoped the spymaster wouldn't give too poor a report about Finch's midnight escapade. Finch already dreaded the explanation he'd have to give. He couldn't even soften the blow by telling Hayes that he'd managed to kill Nox. Finch would face the repercussions of his decision. He knew he'd been foolish. It was fortunate that Cal had been there to stop him before he made a decision he couldn't take back.

Finch headed for Hayes's office with a slow step. His feet ached from the long journey. He hoped and prayed he wouldn't run into Terin until later. Finch didn't have the energy to deal with the man. If holding a knife to Nox's throat had been foolish, meeting Terin now would have been disastrous. Fortunately, it was near the lunch hour and the halls of the castle were mostly empty. Finch's stomach growled, reminding him that he would have to eat soon as well. He still felt a little queasy from everything that had happened. He pushed on until he reached the door to Hayes's office. He knocked and entered.

"Finch," Hayes greeted.

The battle master looked more weary than Finch felt. Hayes sat behind his desk, arms propped on the wooden surface and his head resting in his palm.

Hayes sighed heavily. "I'm afraid to ask why you're late."

Finch shifted. "I'm... I have no excuse, Sir. I know Cal will report it later so I want to be the first to explain myself. I got carried away. After the ambush, I thought I could go into the enemy camp and finish things, finish Nox. I wanted him dead so he couldn't create any more trouble for us."

"Please tell me you didn't kill him." There was genuine concern in Hayes's voice.

"I didn't, Sir. Cal stopped me before I could. My actions caused a bit of a delay. I didn't mean to create any trouble."

"I'm just relieved you've returned safely. I'll expect more of a report later but for now, I can see that you're tired. You should get some rest. But first, there's something else you must know."

Finch felt a wave of dread wash over him. He looked around the room and felt his heart leap to his throat. He had the worst premonition of his life at that moment. "Dorian," he said. He could hardly force the word out.

"Dorian's alive. He's uninjured."

The statement was a relief but Finch still felt unsettled at the way Hayes was phrasing things.

"Did something happen in Cheston? Is everything alright? Is Dorian alright?"

"Something did happen and Dorian..." Hayes hesitated.

"What's wrong, Sir?"

"It was Dorian's first battle, Finch. There was a moment when one of the Freiwade soldiers got behind me. I didn't see him. I would have died. Dorian saved me. He killed the man. It was his first kill. He's struggling."

Finch felt pain for his friend as if he'd been stabbed. Dorian had killed a man. Kind, generous, brave Dorian had taken a life. Finch couldn't imagine the agony his friend must be feeling.

"He's not handling it well," Hayes went on, confirming Finch's concerns. "He was inconsolable afterwards. He didn't speak a word the entire ride back to Castille and he's been ill, pale and weak, distant."

"Where is he?" Finch's exhaustion faded. At that moment, he only cared about his friend. He had to help Dorian.

"I'm not sure. Probably outside. He's spent a lot of time outside since we've returned. I think the castle walls are constricting to him."

Finch understood the feeling. "Is there anything else, Sir?"

"The rest can wait until later. Now, go help your friend."

Finch needed no further invitation before he hurried from the room, eager to find Dorian. He hadn't known Dorian for long but during that time Finch had discovered that Dorian was a very compassionate person. He cared deeply about others in a way Finch could never understand. Taking a life would be difficult for anyone. Finch was still overcome with terror at the idea of what he'd done during the ambush. He was sure his arrows had ended more than one Freiwade soldier but he hadn't had to watch the light go out of their eyes. It wasn't until he saw what his arrows had done to Nox that he considered what it might feel like to kill another person. That feeling came to a crest when he held his knife over Nox's head and prepared to strike. In the end, Finch hadn't been able to do it. Dorian hadn't been given a choice in the matter. Finch knew it would be even more difficult for Dorian to come to terms with what had happened because of his compassion towards others.

Finch wasn't sure if he could offer much comfort to his friend but he was determined to try. He found Dorian outside as Hayes told him he would. His friend was sitting against one of the walls of the battle school barracks. His head pressed back into the stone and he stared up at the overcast sky. His open eyes looked red and swollen when Finch approached him but any tears had dried up some time ago. Finch wished again that he hadn't let the foolish idea of killing Nox delay him from returning to Castille. He should have been there when Dorian arrived. He should have been able to comfort his friend sooner.

With a heavy heart, Finch sank to a crouch beside Dorian. He stayed silent for a moment, not wanting to break the quiet before Dorian was ready. The words 'are you alright?' rose in Finch's mouth but he forced them back. He knew the answer to that question already.

"I'm sorry," Finch said instead.

The words opened a floodgate inside Dorian. A sob slipped past his lips and he choked, trying to force it back. His fists clenched at his side. The pain was palpable. Finch's heart clenched seeing his friend in such misery. Finch reached out and laid a hand on Dorian's shoulder. He thought of all the times Dorian had reassured him and been there for him when he struggled. He hoped he could return the favor somehow. This was too heavy a burden for anyone to carry alone.

"I... I..." Dorian couldn't say anything more.

"I know. I heard what happened," Finch replied. "You don't have to talk, not if you don't want to."

And Dorian didn't talk. He just sat there in

silence. He seemed so unlike the Dorian that Finch knew at that moment. He seemed changed in a way that Finch feared he could never understand. It was all because of Freiwade. It was all because of this war, this horrible, unnecessary war. Finch hated Freiwade for the pain that was caused by a meaningless battle. He hated Freiwade for the agony that Dorian must now face because of it.

CHAPTER 49

Corin was starting to feel undeniably anxious at being cooped up in his room for such a long time. There was something about laying around staring at the same walls day after day that made his brain itch. Sometimes he wanted to scream with frustration at being stuck in one place. However, at the same time, he was afraid to go out into the castle again. Things had undeniably changed for him. He was no longer the mage that people were in awe and fear of. Now he was a cripple. His arm was a horrifying sight when it wasn't bandaged and it hung uselessly at his side. He didn't want the judging stares or looks of pity. He didn't want to face the reality that the only reason he was at Castille, his only use, had been stripped from him. He knew he had no hope of being able to do his duty again, despite what Clifton might say.

Corin felt completely alone. His visitors seemed to only be coming out of obligation. He doubted they cared much about how he was feeling. The physicians gave up trying to convince him to amputate his arm. They seemed to give up on him entirely. He made no progress with his rehabilitation. Sometimes it felt like he was regressing instead.

The days passed by both agonizingly slow and too quickly. Lying in bed, Corin quickly lost track of time. His injury still throbbed with pain, making it difficult even to sleep. Sometimes Corin was tempted to inspect the useless, lifeless arm and listen to Will in trying to find a solution but he could never bring himself to look at the injury or raise any hope.

Burke would have told him to get out of his own head and stop being so self-pitying. Corin didn't care what Burke would have thought though. He wasn't there. He wasn't there to help Corin, offer him comfort, and encourage him. Maybe a small part of Corin had hoped Burke would come and be there for him. He knew it had been a silly wish.

It was while Corin was drowning in his thoughts that Cal finally paid him a visit. Cal himself looked a little worse for wear. He was clearly tired with dark circles under his eyes and a slouch to his shoulders. His hair was starting to grow long and a few days of stubble were on his chin. However, he smiled at Corin when he entered the sick room and helped himself to a seat next to Corin's bed.

"Corin, it's good to see you. I'm a little surprised to see you still in here. I thought you'd be running around the castle again with that fighting spirit of yours."

Corin looked away. It was true that he didn't need to be in bed anymore but what would be the point of walking around? What could he do with his arm in such a state? Besides, walking anywhere other than the small sick-room would require him to be seen by others.

"Why are you here?" Corin asked just a little

bitterly.

Why hadn't he come sooner, is what Corin wanted to ask. Cal seemed altogether too happy to be there. Was he pleased at Corin's pathetic state? Corin shook the thoughts from his head. At least he wasn't alone.

"I'm sorry for not visiting sooner. I was away on a bit of an errand," Cal apologized. "How are you feeling?"

Corin shrugged noncommittedly then winced at the pain in his bad arm.

"Well, I can't imagine that lying in bed all day is doing you much good."

"It's not like there's much else I'm capable of," Corin snapped.

"That seems a little pessimistic," Cal remarked. "You could go for a walk outside. The fresh air would be good for you."

"I'm not interested."

Cal looked pointedly at the wrapped arm that Corin refused to even glance at. "I heard those bandages were just for show," Cal stated.

"Show? Show!" Corin leaned forward, anger rising in him. "None of this is for show, Cal. Do you think I want to be like this? It makes me sick to look at it. I… I can't do it."

Cal held up his hands in a placating gesture. "We're all just worried about you, Corin."

"Who are 'we'?"

"Myself, Ruena, Clifton, Will, the king, and Sir Hayes."

Corin laughed bitterly. "They aren't worried about me. They're worried about their mage."

A muscle in Cal's jaw tightened. His eyes turned serious. When he spoke again, his voice was laced with cold. "This self-isolation of yours is doing no one any favors. It's your self-pity that's the real problem, Corin, not the injury itself."

"Where are these people who supposedly care about me, Cal? I haven't had many visitors. Those who do come around only want to see how fast I'm healing. They don't care about me. They just want me to start training again."

"You ask where the people are?" Cal responded. "You've driven them away, Corin. Your pessimism and outright animosity have given the clear signal that you want to be left alone. They're only obliging."

Corin scoffed. "This isn't my fault. Besides, it's not self-pity. I'm tired and in pain and I know that I'm useless to everyone now. I'm broken and there's no hope of ever getting better!"

Corin took a deep breath, feeling like a weight had loosened from his chest. He hated this, all of it.

Cal's face clouded with rage. "That's not true!" he objected angrily. "You're not useless to anyone. This injury isn't the problem. Clifton and the physicians believe you can still be a mage. Even if you couldn't, you would still be welcome in the castle to study magic or simply be a member of the court. People would still want you around even if you weren't a mage. Ruena wants you to stay, Clifton does, and I do too. It's your attitude about all of this that's the real problem."

Corin felt a lump rise in his throat. He felt dreaded hopelessness creep into him again. More than anything, he felt angry. What right did Cal have to say such things? Corin was angry at Cal, at everyone else, and most of all at himself. Why was he like this? Why was he so pathetic? He thought of Ruena who had lost her parents in a horrible fire but remained positive and grateful anyway. He thought of Clifton who still tried to make him feel welcome even when he himself was an outcast. And then there was Cal who barely knew him but had still come to visit him despite his obvious exhaustion. Maybe Corin was the problem after all.

Cal, seeming to sense the change in Corin's mind, spoke again, "Corin, you're allowed to be angry and upset over what happened. This accident is not something to ignore or belittle. I'm not trying to downplay your situation. I know you're in pain and you're feeling hopeless right now. You have a long road to recovery ahead of you. You'll have to learn how to adapt to this new way of life. It will take time and it will be difficult. But what you need to realize is you're not alone through it. You have people who want to help you and support you. Most of all, you can rely on God throughout your recovery. God may not choose to fix everything that's happened but He is still there through the trial. I guarantee that if you depend on Him, you'll come out on the other side of this stronger than ever before."

Corin felt tears come to his eyes. When he tried to wipe them away with his bad hand and was unable to, he grit his teeth in frustration. Through his pain, he spoke. "I don't understand why this had to happen to me. I wish things could just go back to the way they were before I learned I was a mage and before I injured myself. I want this to be over!"

Cal hesitated only a moment before pulling Corin into a brotherly hug and letting Corin's angry tears drip onto his shoulder. Corin realized that it had been a very long time since he'd last had a hug. He never knew his parents, the orphanage wasn't much for displays of affection, and it was far from anyone's mind in battle school. Sir Burke was the closest thing to a father that Corin had and their relationship had never been that of actual family. Cal's hug felt like what it must be like to have an older brother, someone to look out for him and give him advice and encouragement and perhaps most of all to hold him accountable. Corin had never felt that way, even in battle school surrounded by other boys.

Corin's tears subsided and Cal released him with a reassurance, "Things will get better, Corin. There are people who care about you and your well-being no matter what."

Cal paused to wait for Corin's nod of acceptance.

Then Cal spoke again, "Ruena is one of those people. She's been worried about you. Maybe you could try to be more open around her. Stop ignoring her and let her into your life."

Corin looked away, feeling guilty for how he had treated his first friend in the castle. Ruena had been nothing but kind to him and Corin had cast her aside as if he didn't care. He just… he didn't want her to see him in his current condition. It was embarrassing.

"She doesn't think you're weak because of this," Cal said, seemingly reading his mind. "She cares about you and wants to help however she can. But she won't press the issue if you continue to ignore her. Do you want her to go away for good?"

Corin knew Cal was right. He felt ashamed of himself for how he had treated everyone lately. They deserved better.

"Now," Cal changed the subject, "you need to get out of this room, move around, and get some fresh air. This room is suffocating. It's no wonder that you feel so terrible when you're keeping yourself trapped inside."

Corin nodded, reluctantly agreeing that it wouldn't hurt. Cal took the nod as acceptance. "I'll wait outside for you to get ready."

Corin appreciated the privacy and the moment to gather his thoughts. He struggled to change into a fresh tunic with only one arm. His other arm was stiff and difficult to maneuver around. It took him an embarrassingly long amount of time to ready himself. Cal probably thought he'd gone back to sleep or something. Finally, Corin managed to get the tunic on and didn't bother with a cloak. Hopefully, it would be warm outside. When Corin finally stepped outside the room, he paused. He'd been hiding away in the sick room for so long that the change of scenery was a little off-putting. However, Cal led the way before Corin could change his mind and retreat.

Corin realized it felt good to walk. His muscles were sore from prolonged laying around. His joints felt stiff and it was pleasant to stretch himself out. It was also good to have a change of scenery. The hallways were brighter with more natural light. There were paintings, windows, and tapestries to look at. He felt a little more alive again. His arm ached with every step but it wasn't unbearable. Soon Corin was able to ignore the sensation. He managed alright until they arrived at the main part of the castle. Then Corin was reacquainted with the stares he'd forgotten he hated so much. There were servants, nobles, and knights wandering the hallways. They all stopped to stare at Corin. Murmured conversation and rumors rose to meet his ears. They were surprised to see him.

Corin positioned himself so he could hide his bandaged arm behind his back as much as possible. He should have brought a cloak. He felt on full display in front of their prying eyes. He could feel their gazes drifting to the bandages heavily wrapped around his arm to conceal the injury. Cal shot pointed glares at each person, forcing them to look away but Corin already felt increasingly unsettled. He wanted more than anything to flee back to his room.

"Come on," Cal gestured for Corin to follow him.

He led Corin down a few hallways. Corin trailed obediently behind. He couldn't think about anything but the stares. What did they think of him now? Did they think he was weak and useless? Did they think the king should get rid of him for good? After a while, Corin's thoughts returned to the present and he realized he knew where Cal was leading him. It was the empty room where he usually talked with Ruena.

"Cal?" Corin questioned.

There was a slight smirk on Cal's face.

Before Corin could think to retreat, Cal grabbed his good arm and pulled him forward into the room. Ruena was sitting on the windowsill as usual. Corin blinked at the sight of her with the sun reflecting in her honey-colored hair. He felt short of breath. She looked up as they stepped into the room and a broad, genuine smile crossed her face. Then Corin stopped thinking about anything else.

CHAPTER 50

Ruena rushed through the halls of Castille Castle with Cal beside her. There was no time to delay. Worry settled itself in Ruena's chest and she suspected Cal felt the same. Cal's worry stemmed from a note he'd received from Dusk requesting an immediate meeting. Ruena was worried because Cal had specifically sought her out to take part in the meeting. It was an incredibly uncommon occurrence.

Ruena was used to receiving updates about what the spies were up to from Cal. She was the king's niece and he tried to keep her informed of the goings on in the castle to prepare her for when she would take the throne. However, it was rare for him to bring her to a meeting between the spies. Those meetings were kept very secret. Not even Sir Hayes attended them. Ruena suspected that something was going on between Cal and his spies. He'd been silent about them lately and she hadn't missed the dark circles under his eyes from lack of sleep and worry. It might be because of the conflict with Freiwade but she suspected there was something else more personal going on too. She followed after Cal quickly as they headed for The Cavern. Ruena couldn't help but think that it was fortunate Vesta was away visiting her mother. Ruena didn't have to find a way to sneak away from her increasingly protective maid. The girl had stuck close to Ruena's side for the last few weeks. Ruena suspected it was because she'd been spending more time with Corin lately, though it was only the last day that she'd had a good conversation with him after his injury.

Ruena and Cal stayed silent as they moved hurriedly down the hallways and into the cupboard, then down the wooden ladder into The Cavern. Ruena's hands felt sticky with sweat as she released her grip on the last wooden rung and stepped onto the dirt floor. She'd been in The Cavern before. She knew the spies whom Cal worked with. But this time felt different. She felt as if she were intruding. She wanted to ask Cal why he'd brought her to this meeting in the first place. When she turned to survey the cavernous room, she saw the two figures waiting for them. Lark and Dusk looked pale and worried as they waited impatiently for Cal's arrival. Dusk seemed like he might be sick. He was hunched over in a chair, pale to the point of being green. His eyes were wide and bloodshot. Lark watched her companion with concern but the spies both looked up when Cal and Ruena entered the room.

Lark and Dusk both stood and started to bow but Ruena quickly waved them off. "That's not necessary. What happened?"

They knew her, not well, but Cal had told them before that they could trust Ruena explicitly with any news they discovered. It was a mark of how much they trusted Cal that they accepted his words without question and trusted Ruena as if she were one of their own.

Dusk swallowed hard, meeting Cal's gaze. A look crossed Cal's face that told Ruena he knew immediately what had happened. "It's the duke, isn't it?"

Dusk could only nod.

Lark took up the conversation, sharing what she knew. "He's found out about Corin's injury and he's trying to get Terin to turn against the king. There's something more but Dusk wouldn't tell me until you were here."

Ruena knew without them having to tell her that this was bad news. Cal had told her the worries they had of the duke staging a coup. Ruena could have figured that much out without the spy's input. The duke wasn't exactly subtle. Duke Heirson had been nothing if not rebellious towards the crown for as long as Ruena could remember. She recalled when she was a little girl how the duke had visited the castle on occasion. The memories were foggy to Ruena but she could remember the duke's rudeness, especially to her. He'd treated her as if she were another servant to order around. She hadn't known at the time that she should demand the respect owed to her. She despised the duke's treatment looking back. He'd always second-guessed every decision her uncle made and done so in the eyes of the entire court. His position as duke made his comments regarding her uncle's rulings detrimental and cast the king in an unflattering light. Ruena knew even then to be cautious of the man. His knowing about Corin's injury could only mean trouble.

"Dusk, give your report," Cal instructed.

Dusk managed to compose himself a fraction and then spoke, "I've been keeping a close eye on Duke Heirson and his son." He faltered at the word 'son' but quickly masked the slip and continued. "Despite our best efforts, Corin's injury has become common knowledge to several people around the castle."

"It was inevitable," Ruena stated, "especially now that Corin has started to walk around the castle again. With his arm bandaged up and hanging limply at his side, it's obvious something happened to him."

Dusk sucked in a sharp breath. "Somehow the duke knew about the injury even before Corin left his room."

Cal stiffened beside Ruena. "What do you mean?"

"I overheard the duke and his son talking with Commander Terin."

"Terin?" Ruena asked. "Since when has Terin been involved in all of this?"

"We've had suspicions about him for a while now," Cal explained. "Go on, Dusk."

"They were discussing Corin's injury. Dusk Heirson said that Corin being injured meant that he no longer posed a threat. He said that now that Corin was out of the way, real change could happen. That was two days ago. It was before Corin had ever stepped out of his room."

"Why didn't you report the news sooner?" Cal demanded.

Lark came to Dusk's defense. "He did. He told me what he found. Or, at least most of it. You were gone, Cal. We had to deal with it on our own. We did some poking around and we kept an eye on the duke and Terin but we couldn't report to you until you were back. Then you were busy checking on Corin. You didn't even check in with us first."

Lark sounded hurt when she spoke. Cal winced guiltily at her words. "I'm sorry."

"How could the duke have found out?" Ruena asked. "We've all been quiet about what happened. Corin's condition has been hidden from everyone. My uncle reported to anyone who asked that Corin was too busy training to come to meals or wander the castle. Not even Commander Terin knew."

"That's what Dusk and I have been trying to figure out," Lark explained. "We've tried to narrow down everyone who has visited Corin. The only person who might be responsible for the leak has to be the scribe's boy, Will."

"No," Ruena dismissed immediately. "It's not him. I know Will. I know his uncle. That boy is more loyal than anyone."

"He's only a child though," Lark reminded them. "He could have slipped up. It doesn't mean it was intentional."

Cal shook his head. "I personally chose Will to be Corin's aid. I'd gathered background information about the boy. He's responsible and can be trusted. He's been instructed to keep his mouth shut about all matters relating to his job. I even tested him beforehand and he proved to be discreet. His family has proven many times that they're trustworthy and loyal to Ashnah. He wouldn't betray Corin even unintentionally."

"I agree," Dusk stated. "I've been working with him to try to help Corin and he was hesitant to trust me even after Clifton vouched for me. He's cautious. I don't think he'd make a slip to anyone."

"Then what about Finch?" Lark asked. "He was in the meeting with Cal, Hayes, the king, and Clifton. He knew Corin had been injured. And with his past, he could have told…"

"No," Cal cut her off. "He wouldn't do that. Besides, when would he have had the time? Immediately after finding out about Corin's injury, Finch led the knights and archers to ambush Nox."

"There was a short delay before the departure," Lark reminded him. "He could have found time."

"But he had no motive for doing so," Cal argued.

"Then who could it have been?" Lark asked.

None of them had an answer.

"It doesn't matter at the moment," Ruena interjected. "What matters is what's happening with the duke and Terin."

Dusk took that as a cue to finish his report. He seemed a little shaky as he spoke. "The duke mentioned that it was time to make a move and that with Corin incapacitated, they must be quick about it. Dresden, the duke's son, asked about Clifton but Duke Heirson claimed that Clifton didn't pose a threat. He told Terin that it was time to pick a side."

"They've been conspiring together this whole time," Lark said.

"Not exactly," Dusk said. "Terin didn't accept the duke's offer."

"What?" Cal and Ruena said in unison.

"Admittedly, Terin seemed tempted. The duke claimed that Terin would have respect and power if he and his archers sided with him. But Terin refused. He said he would stay out of the conflict and wait to see who prevailed. He said that he wouldn't fight against the duke but he wouldn't aid him either."

"The coward," Ruena said. "He wouldn't even pick a side."

"I suppose that's good news," Cal commented. "It proves his disloyalty to the king. He's not willing to defend this kingdom if he might end up on the losing side of the battle. I'll be speaking to Hayes and King Rupert about him. It's time his power was revoked. This is only the latest sign that he's not fit for such an important position."

"There's more," Dusk said. "Duke Heirson said that the first step would be to completely eliminate Corin from the picture, then gather their forces and make their move to start an uprising and take over."

"That can't be possible," Ruena argued. "The duke wouldn't be so foolish. He doesn't have enough force to strike against Ashnah. I know some nobles, knights, and archers side with him but not enough to stage an uprising. There's no way they would succeed, right?"

The spies were silent. Ruena realized there was something they hadn't shared with her yet. She turned to Cal accusingly. "What? What is it you haven't told me?"

Cal turned to Dusk. Ruena moved her attention to the lanky, dark-haired spy with confusion. He had gone from looking worried and upset to ashamed. Lark and Cal both watched their companion with a soft, concerned gaze.

"What else did you have to report, Dusk?"

Dusk took a deep breath. "The duke has been

gaining supporters loyal to him for the last decade," Dusk began. "The supporters include knights, archers, commoners, and nobles with their loyal retinues. He's kept the threat hidden and subtle enough to prevent the castle from taking action against him. Do not be fooled, the threat is very real. In all reality, we don't know the full extent of his treachery. The castle and the king could be in more trouble than we realize, especially if Corin and Clifton are taken out of the picture."

Ruena glared at Cal. "Why haven't you told me all of this? Does my uncle know? Does Sir Hayes know? What's being done to protect the Castille monarchy?"

Cal was pale. He studied Dusk with an expression of horror.

A realization came to Ruena like a blow. "You've all been hiding this."

Cal shook his head numbly. Ruena glanced at Lark who had taken a step back to lean heavily against the room's table. Dusk sat with his head hung low.

"The information was sensitive," Dusk claimed.

"Sensitive. Sensitive!" Ruena objected. She turned to Cal. "Cal, you're the spymaster. How did you not know? It's your responsibility to share any sensitive information with the king. You have to protect him."

Ruena's voice cracked. She couldn't imagine losing her uncle. He was the only family she had left. She trusted Cal to protect him from the many threats that always encroached on him. Could she trust Cal anymore after he had kept something so important a secret?

Cal sighed heavily. "I was only doing what I thought was best, Ruena."

Ruena felt outraged at the answer. "You had no right to hide such information from leadership!" she exclaimed. "It's your job to report any and all information that might prove a threat to the kingdom, regardless of how doubtful that information is to come to pass."

Cal accepted her rebuke stoically. Ruena was surprised that he didn't argue or try to defend his actions. Why had he kept the secret at all? It was unlike him to lie like that. She knew his loyalty was to the kingdom of Ashnah. So why had he kept the secret? She felt disgusted with him. She turned her head away.

"It wasn't his fault or Lark's," Dusk interrupted angrily. "They didn't know."

"What do you mean they didn't know?" Ruena asked. "They had to have known. Besides, how do you even know so much about the duke's plans? You couldn't possibly have gathered so much information simply from eavesdropping. How would you have any idea of how many men he had at his disposal? Cal would have had to have been at the duke's estate, found the letters gathering dissenters, and personally inspected the duke's forces and allies. It would be impossible for you to do that, Cal. I know for a fact that you haven't visited the duke's estate for years and when you did, you didn't stay long enough to learn all of that."

Cal stiffened almost imperceptibly. He was keeping something from her, something important. Lark and Dusk also shifted uncomfortably. Dusk finally sighed heavily and in a defeated tone spoke. "Cal, tell Ruena the truth."

"No," Lark protested. "We don't have to."

Dusk shook his head. "We've kept it hidden for long enough. It's not right to keep it a secret, it never was. I'm... I'm grateful for the risk you both took to keep it quiet. It means more to me than you'll ever know. I shouldn't have kept the rest of the truth hidden. I'm sorry."

Ruena tilted her head. "What are you talking about?"

Cal ignored her and directed his words to Dusk. "Are you sure?"

Dusk nodded.

Cal hesitated a moment more before turning to Ruena. "I didn't know about the duke gathering forces, Ruena. But there is a reason we've kept the duke's treachery quiet until we knew he'd make a move. There's a reason I didn't tell anyone until I knew it was essential. It's because of the very question you posed. How did we know all of this? We kept it secret, I kept it secret, to keep Dusk safe."

Ruena felt only confusion at the answer. Fortunately, Dusk stepped in to finish the story. "My real name," he stated, "is Everett Heirson and I am the first son of Duke Heirson."

Ruena gaped at the news. "But... I heard that the eldest son of the duke was dead and..." she hesitated and didn't say the rest. The rumors the duke had spread were that his son had lost his mind and had taken his own life.

"I know the rumors my father spread about me," Dusk explained. "They're all false. He wanted to discredit me. That way if I ever revealed myself to be alive no one would trust what I said against him. I've known for a while now that he was gathering forces."

Dusk faltered as if he were going to say more but couldn't.

Cal swallowed hard, an expression of pain crossing his face. "There's more isn't there?"

Dusk looked at Ruena, hesitantly. Ruena knew she should leave. There was more being kept secret and Dusk wasn't comfortable sharing it while she was there. But she couldn't leave, not now. She had to know the truth so she could help protect her uncle. She stood firm, unmoving.

"Yes, there's more," Dusk finally said. "I'm sorry Cal. I should have told you everything from the start. It wasn't right for me to keep it hidden. But I was scared. Being with the spies is the closest thing to safety I've had in a long time. I didn't want to lose my place here. You didn't make me leave when I told you who I was and you didn't force me to tell the king. I should have told you everything. I just knew no one would believe me. And the duke, my father, would have killed me if he found out where I was hiding."

Ruena was horrified by the words. The duke wanted to kill Dusk, Everett, his son. And what was Dusk keeping secret?

"Dusk, you can tell us whatever it is," Cal stated. "I believed you before, didn't I? I trust you. Your word is all the evidence I need."

"Me too," Lark agreed.

Dusk closed his eyes as if pained by the kind words. "The truth is, the letters gathering forces against the king aren't the only things I found in my father's office. If it were just that, he might not have been so intent on finding me and killing me when I ran. It wasn't just a gathering of supporters. I discovered my father's correspondence with the king of Freiwade."

"The king of Freiwade!" Ruena exclaimed.

Cal looked like he might be sick.

"When I discovered the letters, I discovered that my father was secretly assembling an army with the help of the king of Freiwade. There was a deal between them. The dukedom's location on the border of Ashnah and Freiwade allowed soldiers to assemble there unnoticed. I was foolish enough to confront my father about it directly. He gave me the opportunity to work with him. As his heir, he claimed I would inherit the throne of Ashnah after him when he took the crown for himself. The king of Freiwade had promised to make Duke Heirson a figurehead ruler when he attacked Ashnah if my father aided in the war. I refused my father's offer and he and my brother tried to kill me."

Ruena was horrified at what she was learning. How had so much been kept secret for so long? This changed everything. If the duke was working with the king of Freiwade, then Ashnah was in dire straits indeed. She stared at Dusk. Why had he kept all of this hidden? He hadn't even told Cal. Then again, if he had, Cal would have been forced to report it. This changed the duke's empty words of a coup into a very real possibility.

"Why?" was all Ruena could say.

Dusk wasn't finished with his story. "I couldn't tell anyone what I found. My father burned the letters in front of me. There would be no evidence to support my claim if I told the king what I'd uncovered. There would be only my word against my father's. It wasn't enough. But I refused to work with him against my kingdom. I refused to forget what I'd seen and go on as things had been before. I had no choice but to run. My father promised to find me and kill me. He pursued me for years and continues to do so today. I lived in constant terror of my father and brother. I hid for a long time and waited for my face to sharpen with age. I cut my hair and altered how I walked and talked. I started dressing more casually. I put on an act so I would be seen as an entirely different person. It worked. Nobody has recognized me. But I know that if my father or brother ever saw me, they would see through my disguise. With them at the castle, I've had to be even more careful. If not for Lark, I would have been caught by my brother during the feast to celebrate Corin's arrival."

It was true that his disguise had worked. Ruena had seen Everett before when she was young. He'd visited the castle with his father once. She never would have recognized Dusk as the eldest son of the duke now. It was as if he were a different person entirely.

"I originally planned to reveal everything to the king," Dusk explained. "But I knew my claims wouldn't be believed. Not only did I no longer look like Duke Heirson's son, but my father's claims of my insanity and supposed death would have painted me as an imposter. Even if the king did believe I was the duke's son, he would have seen me as a madman, especially with such unbelievable news of betrayal.

Who would believe my word over the duke's?"

Despite her anger at the secrets that had been kept, Ruena could also understand Dusk's reasoning. She'd heard the rumors the duke spread about him. They were awful. Ruena had always found them hard to believe, as had many. She'd liked Everett the few times she saw him. He wasn't exactly outgoing but he was smart and friendly enough. He was also responsible and took his future role as duke seriously. It had been difficult to believe he'd suddenly lost his mind but Duke Heirson and his son Dresden's acts of mourning were so sincere that the story had quickly been accepted as fact. Ruena knew Dusk would have had a difficult time convincing the king and others that he was Everett. It would have been even more difficult for him to claim the duke was staging a coup with the help of the king of Freiwade.

"I had visited the castle often enough to perceive that Cal was a spy," Dusk went on. "I'd even suspected that he was the leader of the spies."

"You say it so casually," Lark mumbled. "Only you would be able to pick that detail out so easily, Dusk."

It was true. Cal's position as spymaster was a closely guarded secret and one that took a genius to pick up on.

"I knew my only chance of warning the king about what my father was planning was to build a reputation for myself, not as Everett but as someone whom the king would trust. I couldn't join the court openly because I knew it would be too risky. I wasn't willing to take the chance of putting myself in the open where someone might recognize me. So,

I decided joining the spies was the only way to gain the king's trust without risking my identity being discovered. I planned on revealing the truth once my position was stable but I didn't count on Cal recognizing me from my earlier visits to the castle and confronting me about being Everett."

Ruena looked at Cal. "Why didn't you say anything to anyone?"

"I never believed the rumors about Everett," Cal explained. "I met him when he visited the castle and I knew he wasn't the type to go insane or hurt anyone. I knew something else was going on. When Dusk came to the castle and wanted to join the spies, I recognized him as Everett. I confronted him and demanded an explanation. I reassured him that I didn't believe he was insane but he needed to tell me the truth if he was going to work as a spy. He told me a little about how he had run from his home with his father and brother trying to kill him. He told me that his father was disloyal to the king. However, he left out all mention of Freiwade."

"I was scared," Dusk admitted. "It wasn't according to my plan. I knew my position in the castle was still fragile. I couldn't reveal something so unbelievable until I had proven myself trustworthy. I begged Cal to let me take on a false name and not tell anyone even the king who I was."

"I agreed," Cal explained. "I knew that Everett was a good man and I didn't believe the duke's rumors. I also knew that if Dusk was found out to be Everett, the king would never let him work as a spy. He would report Dusk's presence to the duke and it would put Dusk in danger. I agreed to keep his identity secret. He revealed the threat the duke posed to us and it allowed us to keep a close eye on the duke."

"But you said nothing about his alliance with the king of Freiwade?" Ruena asked.

"I had no proof," Dusk said softly. "It was only when the duke's plans to move against the kingdom became very real that I knew I had to reveal everything. I'm sure the attack on Cheston was possible because the Freiwade army entered Ashnah through Trestle, my father's dukedom."

"That's why we've been careful in our dealings with the duke," Cal revealed. "Though, if I had known how serious the situation was, I might have taken action against the duke sooner."

Ruena didn't know what to make of the news. She could understand in a way why Cal had kept Dusk's identity secret. He was loyal to the kingdom but he was even more loyal to his friends. Ruena looked at Dusk in a new light. She could see a slight resemblance to the Everett she remembered. His mannerisms were so different that he was almost indistinguishable as the duke's son. But the dark hair and tall figure undeniably belonged to Everett. How had she never noticed before? She believed what he said. She knew him well enough to know that he couldn't be insane. He was telling the truth; she was sure of it. It was a frightening truth too. Duke Heirson was conspiring with the enemy. He must be stopped.

Ruena was willing to look past the deception for now. There were bigger problems to deal with. "What are we going to do about the duke?"

Cal answered, "Our priority is to report to Sir Hayes and gain his insight on the matter. Then we'll strengthen our defenses, monitor the duke's mail, and ensure that he stays in the castle where we'll keep a close eye on him. Ruena, please keep what you've learned about Dusk quiet. His life is on the line as long as the duke is in this castle."

"I will," Ruena agreed. She didn't envy Cal having to keep the fact secret from Sir Hayes. "But you can't hide this for long, Cal. You need to tell Hayes and the king everything. Dusk isn't the only one whose life is at stake anymore."

"I know but we won't let the duke succeed," Cal assured her. "We'll keep a close eye on him and we'll eliminate him from the equation before he can cause any severe damage."

Ruena certainly hoped so.

Lark stiffened, having thought of something. "If Dusk overheard the duke talking about taking Corin and Clifton out of the situation, shouldn't we be worried?"

"What do you mean?" Cal asked.

"Clifton might be busy in meetings guarded by any number of knights who could help defend him and his power is fully functioning even though it's weak, but Corin can't use his magic and he's isolated in his room. Is anyone with him or is he alone?"

Ruena felt a jolt of panic pierce her chest as she realized Lark was right. She suddenly felt like something very bad was about to happen. She and Cal exchanged a look of alarm.

"We'll handle the situation with the duke but first we need to check on Corin," Cal stated.

There was no need for further conversation as Ruena and Cal rushed from The Cavern towards

Corin's room. Ruena prayed they wouldn't be too late.

CHAPTER 51

Things were getting better. Corin knew it was true because one morning he woke up and found that he was able to think of his situation in a more positive light. The bitter despair had dissipated, though it had not completely vanished. There was an undercurrent of worry dwelling in the pit of Corin's stomach that he couldn't quite shake. He couldn't ignore the feeling that everyone was keeping something from him. Whatever was causing their worry seemed to be escalating. They all stared at him with concern and anticipation. Corin desperately wanted to ask questions but he didn't want to overstep. He wasn't even sure if he wanted to know the answer to why they were so uneasy.

He was thinking over the possibilities behind everyone's worry when his tray of food was delivered to his room. He'd finally been able to move back to his old room and the window which let in more natural light was a welcome change of pace from the dreary sick room. He had wanted to eat with Ruena that day but he couldn't find her. Then again, he hadn't searched very hard. He wasn't comfortable leaving his room without someone accompanying him. He couldn't stand the stares. He hoped that Ruena and maybe even Cal would come to see him later. He wouldn't mind a visit from Will as well. Maybe, just maybe, the boy would find something to help. Corin felt unbearably lonely, especially after such pleasant company yesterday. With the quiet emptiness of his room penetrating his thoughts, Corin couldn't bring himself to eat. He was trying to think more positively as Cal urged him but there were still moments when he lost himself in despair and the horrible self-pity that Cal had warned him about.

Corin picked at his plate, knowing he needed to eat to strengthen his body and aid in his recovery. But the meals at the castle had already lost their novelty. The feasts were no longer pleasantly rich and enticing. Not when Corin's mind was in such a chaotic state. He was just lifting his fork to his mouth, a difficult task with his left hand, when the door to his room slammed open and both Cal and Ruena barged in dramatically.

Corin dropped his fork.

Cal looked hurriedly around the room and seemed surprised at the lack of danger. Ruena rushed to Corin's side.

"Are you alright?" Ruena asked.

"Y...yes," Corin responded uncertainly. "Why shouldn't I be?"

Ruena exchanged a look with Cal that Corin didn't like one bit. He frowned at the two of them. "Okay, what's going on?" he asked.

"We were both just worried about you being alone," Cal answered.

Corin, frustrated, sat up a little straighter. "I'm

fine," he stated again. "But I wish everyone would just come out and say what's bothering them. I may be crippled but I'm not blind. I can see that something's been upsetting everyone lately and no one's bothered to tell me about it."

From the look on Cal and Ruena's faces, Corin knew he wouldn't be getting an answer any time soon.

"Fine," he huffed, "if that's the case, then you can leave."

"It's not that we're trying to hide things from you, Corin," Ruena explained. "We just can't tell you everything. It's not important anyway."

Corin highly doubted that. He glared long and hard at Cal. "Why exactly can't *you* tell me anything? I still don't even know what you do in this castle."

Cal visibly swallowed, caught off guard by the question. Corin pressed his advantage.

"I don't think you're here just to be Ruena's friend. You're not a noble and you're not a knight. I don't think you're an advisor and I know you're not an archer. So, who *are* you, Cal?"

Cal hesitated and for a second Corin thought he might tell him the truth before his mouth closed with a click.

Corin huffed in annoyance at the both of them and waved a hand in dismissal. "It's fine, I know I'm useless here anyway. It's not like I can expect to be let in on anything, not anymore anyway."

"Corin," Ruena said placatingly but he didn't want to hear it.

"Maybe we should leave," Cal suggested.

"Okay," Ruena agreed. "Corin, we aren't trying to keep things from you. We want to tell you everything. We just can't."

Corin ignored her, feeling guilty as he did so. He looked at her and tried to convey with his eyes that he understood. He didn't blame her, not really. But he couldn't hide the hurt from his expression.

Ruena offered a soft smile, showing that she wasn't upset at his behavior. He just needed some space to let out his frustrations without taking things out on her. Corin awkwardly picked up his fork again and stabbed at a piece of potato on his plate. However, as Ruena and Cal were passing by him to leave, Cal paused and pivoted to look at Corin.

"Don't eat that!" Cal suddenly snapped.

Again, Corin dropped his fork. He stared at Cal like he'd lost his mind but Ruena's eyes widened in an expression of understanding. Cal stepped to the bed in an instant and snatched up Corin's plate of food.

"Hey!" Corin objected.

Using the fork, Cal poked around the plate and then took a long sniff. His eyes widened with alarm. "Poison!" he exclaimed.

Corin stared, uncomprehending.

"Corin," Cal demanded, his voice harsh, "did you eat any of the food yet? Answer me!"

Corin shook his head. "Um, no. I didn't."

Cal's shoulders sank with relief.

A few tears dropped from Ruena's eyes and Corin could practically hear her and Cal's hearts beating at a rapid pace. Or maybe that was his own heart he was hearing. He felt a sense of urgency, excitement, and worry even though he didn't know what was going on. Ruena sank onto the edge of his bed. Her hand patted his knee through the blanket.

It was then that Cal's words sank in. Corin looked at the tray of food in Cal's hands with growing apprehension. Only by God's grace had he not eaten any of it. If he had, he could have died. He felt himself shaking a little from the brush with death. *Poison*, the word echoed through his mind. He felt sick to the stomach as a wave of dizziness washed over him. Cal set the tray down and approached Corin's other side, resting a hand on his shoulder.

"It's okay, Corin. Everything is alright. You're alright."

Corin could only wonder who would want to poison him. Who could have done it? Who was trying to kill him? The questions made him realize that it must be related to whatever was worrying everyone. If he had only known what was going on, he could have been on guard for danger. If Cal hadn't stepped in, he would have been dead all because they were keeping secrets from him. Corin shifted so Ruena's hand fell from his knee and Cal's hand slipped from his shoulder. His fear turned to anger. He looked up, eyes bright with intensity.

"I want to know what's going on," Corin demanded. "I deserve to know. No more secrets. No more lies. I want the truth. All of it."

Cal didn't argue. All he said was, "Okay."

CHAPTER 52

It turned out that it wasn't so easy for Corin to learn the truth. First, Cal had to call for a meeting to be held. Clifton, Sir Hayes, the king, Cal, Ruena, and Corin were all in attendance. They gathered in Clifton's office and it was immediately clear to Corin that everyone was on edge. He fixed them all with a weary, distrustful gaze. Just what was it that they had been keeping from him? He was suddenly nervous to know the truth. Corin hadn't ventured into Clifton's office since the accident so he was even more on edge being surrounded by such uncomfortable memories. He had to muster his courage to step foot into the office and finally demand the answers he so desperately needed.

Fortunately, Corin wasn't forced to speak right away. Cal started the meeting by explaining why they'd all been gathered together. "Someone, we suspect it was Duke Heirson or one of his accomplices, tried to assassinate Corin. Ruena and I discovered evidence of poison in his food and barely stopped the attack in time. We believe that Duke Heirson was behind the attack and that he might make a future attempt on Clifton's life as well. He is planning to take action against the king now that Corin is injured and not seen as a threat."

The comment stung but Corin knew it was true. He couldn't fight back, not now. He was worthless in defending the king and kingdom. Cal's words were directed to the others in attendance and Corin had the feeling there was much more left unsaid which would soon come to light. But first, there was something else Cal wanted to say.

"In light of this attempt on Corin's life, he's demanded information about what is being kept from him. It's a fair demand given the fact that he could have been better prepared for danger if he hadn't been kept in the dark for so long. I for one intend to tell him the full truth."

"It's time," the king agreed.

"But..." Clifton objected.

"No," Sir Hayes said, "this secrecy has gone on for too long, Clifton. It's not doing Corin or anyone else any good. He needs to know the truth of the threat we're facing. He's in more danger than any of us. He should prepare himself for the danger he will face."

Clifton looked uncertain but finally nodded.

Cal continued. "Corin," he said, "the first thing you should know that we've been keeping from you is my position in the castle. I am Ashnah's spymaster."

Corin was surprised at the news. It was something he had never previously considered even when his mind went over all the possibilities of what Cal did in the castle. However, it made sense. It explained Cal's comings and goings, how he didn't seem to have a specific task in the castle, why he was always lurking in the shadows, and how he knew so much. It also explained his strange relationship with

Ruena a little better. Cal was close to Ruena because he held such an important position in the castle. He probably kept her informed as well since she would be queen someday. It hurt more than Corin liked to admit that he hadn't known the truth about Cal. He wondered if the reason Cal had been following him and watching out for him wasn't because he was Corin's friend and confidant but because he was assigned to keep an eye on him and report news to the king.

Cal seemed to sense the questions plaguing Corin and see the feelings flashing in Corin's eyes. "While it was my duty as a spy to keep an eye on you when you first arrived at the castle, you've more than proven yourself trustworthy. I had started to hope recently that I might act as more of a friend to you instead of a spy. However, with my line of duty, I understand how difficult it can be to accept a friendship with me."

Corin could only nod. He felt conflicted and uncertain. He was hurt at being lied to even if only by omission. It felt like he didn't know Cal at all. He hoped what he had learned about the young man whom he'd started to see as a friend wasn't all a lie.

"Cal," Sir Hayes spoke, "where did you gain the information about Duke Heirson finally making a move against the king and his planned attack on Corin?"

Cal easily shifted back to his role as spymaster. "We've been keeping an eye on the duke for some time, listening to conversations between him and his son, keeping a watch on his estate and how he manages it, and other areas. There wasn't much to report in that regard for some time but some information that has recently been revealed makes the duke's intentions certain. However, that can be discussed some other time in more detail. For the time being, the important thing is that Corin and Clifton be wary of the threat against them and be prepared for any other attempts on their lives."

Corin didn't want to think about another attempt on his life. The last one had nearly ended him. Then there had been the attack in the town and he was seriously beginning to think he hadn't imagined the strange woman who'd tried to kill him in his delirious sleep. Would he always have to be on guard? Would he eat each bite of food with worry that it would be his last? His stomach churched thinking of the seemingly innocent meal that could have killed him and how close he'd come to death. He realized that he needed to reevaluate his entire life. Sir Burke's talk of eternity seemed more important and pressing now than ever before.

"The attempt on Corin's life very nearly came to fruition. That's why Corin is so desperate to learn the entire truth now," Cal stated.

Corin stood from his chair and stepped forward. "I want to know the truth. All of it. I nearly died today because you've all been keeping things from me. And this wasn't even the first attempt on my life. What is going on? Do you all think I haven't noticed the worry and panic in the air? I know something is happening and I'm tired of being kept in the dark. If I really am the important mage... the weapon, that you claim I am, then shouldn't I know the truth?"

Corin immediately felt embarrassed at his speech but he refused to back down. He knew he needed to know the truth, no matter how painful that truth might be. For once in his life, he would accept the important position he had been placed in and use that position to demand the information he deserved to know. The others in the room exchanged a weighted look.

The king himself nodded. "He's right. It hasn't been fair of us to hide so much from him, especially when it personally involves him. He deserves to know the truth."

Sir Hayes took the lead. "The truth, Corin, is that the war with Freiwade has been increasing in severity while you've been at the castle. Things are progressing more rapidly than we ever expected. New threats have arisen that drastically change things. There have been numerous attacks at outposts along the border and even inland. Entire outposts have been destroyed, leaving nothing but rubble and bodies behind."

Corin felt a thread of panic weave into his chest. He knew the news would only get worse. He dreaded what he was about to hear.

"Duke Heirson is hardly the worst threat we face," Hayes continued. "We suspect that there are Freiwade spies in the castle, though we have no idea who those spies could be. One of Cal's greatest tasks is to discover who they are."

"The worry is that the spies, whoever they are, have been reporting to the king of Freiwade and telling him what attacks will hurt Ashnah the most," Cal cut in. "The spy or spies must be in positions where they can learn about the army and the efforts Ashnah is making to prepare for war. The attacks so far have been strategic and planned to cause the most damage in a short time. My spies and I also suspect that the Freiwade spies are conspiring with the duke. Somehow, Duke Heirson knew about your injury before you ever stepped foot out of your room. He knew when you would be alone and vulnerable to the attack with the poison. The spies are a serious threat and one that I hope to quickly put an end to."

Corin wracked his brain to try to discover who could have reported his injury to the duke. Who had been watching him? He felt like eyes were focused on the back of his neck even then. Was there anyone he could truly trust? "I thought it was a dream but when I was still delirious I woke up in the middle of the night and I thought a woman was standing near my bed with a knife in her hand. I couldn't see her face but I could tell it was a woman. She ran when I woke up."

Cal's face paled. All of the color fled and he looked like he might pass out.

"Cal?" Ruena asked, concerned.

He swallowed hard. The king and Sir Hayes both looked to Cal, a silent conversation passing between the three of them.

Cal shook his head, warding off questions. The strange moment passed and the conversation continued as if nothing had happened at all.

"The greatest threat we face comes from Freiwade," Sir Hayes continued. "We've kept the knowledge of it hidden from almost everyone to keep panic and fear from spreading. It's something we should have warned you about long ago."

All eyes shifted to Clifton who looked incredibly weary. Corin felt an absolute sense of betrayal. He knew instinctively that it was Clifton who had been hiding this secret, whatever it was, from him. Corin felt incredibly hurt that his mentor, one of the few people who should have understood his situation and presumably been on his side, had betrayed him in such a way. Ruena was watching him carefully but Corin didn't look at her. He was upset at her too. She had been part of the betrayal. She had kept quiet as well. Still, Corin was grateful she was there because he took a small sense of comfort from her presence. It was comfort he was sure he'd need as he readied himself for what was sure to be terrible news.

Clifton took a deep breath and met Corin's gaze, an apology in his eyes. "I am truly sorry, Corin. But you should know that we've only kept this from you because we wanted to protect you from it until you were ready. I didn't want to upset you during such an important and delicate time in your training as a mage. And after the accident... I couldn't bring myself to worry you with the news. I slipped up then and what I said is part of the reason you panicked and lost control of your magic."

Corin searched his mind. "I don't remember," he admitted. "What did you say?"

Clifton shook his head. "After everything, I'm not surprised you forgot. It was such a small thing that I accidentally revealed. I didn't want to remind you afterward. I only wanted you to be at peace so you could heal. Maybe I should have told you sooner."

Corin's mouth was dry with worry but he pushed words past the lump in his throat, expecting the absolute worst. "What is it? Please, tell me."

Clifton sighed and then revealed everything. "The attacks on the outposts demonstrated that Freiwade has a great weapon at their disposal. Freiwade has a mage in their service, a powerful mage, more powerful than any before. The mage can use magic that was previously impossible and by all accounts still should be. He has a wicked power. And this mage is heading for Castille Castle as we speak. He is expected to reach us long before we're prepared to face him. When that happens, if we cannot fight back, Ashnah is doomed. With his power, Freiwade could win the war and kill us all in the process."

Corin stared in horror at his mentor. The words came as blows, knocking the breath from his lungs and sending his mind reeling. But Clifton's next words made Corin nearly catatonic with panic. "The plan was for you to face him and fight him. You are incredibly talented, a natural with magic, and far more powerful than I am. You are our only hope, Corin. You can face this mage and win."

Corin's heart picked up its pace until it was beating an erratic rhythm against his chest. He felt dizzy and sick. Long moments passed and he felt the wood of a chair pressed against his legs from behind. Hands pushed him down into the chair and another hand pressed between his shoulders, a steady weight.

"Breathe," Cal instructed. Corin realized that it was Cal's hand on his shoulder.

He blinked and saw Ruena bent at his side, watching him carefully. Sir Hayes had taken several steps forward as well. Corin managed to suck in several breaths, realizing he had stopped breathing altogether for a moment. His mind raced as he realized with horror that he had been, and he still was, expected to face the powerful enemy mage. He couldn't. It wasn't possible. He hadn't been ready before. He hadn't been powerful enough before. Now, he couldn't even use his arm. He hadn't attempted magic since the accident. It was impossible. They would all die and Freiwade would win the war and it was all his fault because he wasn't strong enough.

"Relax Corin," Sir Hayes instructed him. "You have time. You're not expected to face the threat alone. You're not merely a soldier. You're a person, a human being, and you're not going to carry the weight of this war on your shoulders alone."

Somehow the firm, definite words relieved some of the pressure in Corin's chest. He managed to look up at Sir Hayes. He nodded in gratitude. It was something Sir Burke would have said.

Corin noticed then that Clifton hadn't approached to offer him reassurances. Clifton hesitated in a corner, seemingly ashamed at revealing the secret and sending Corin into such a panic. Corin couldn't bring himself to look at his mentor. It hadn't been right for him to keep such an important thing from Corin, despite the good intentions he'd had.

Sir Hayes clasped his shoulder to get his attention again. "You should know that a promising young archer has already devised a plan to delay the enemy mage who we now know is called Nox. It has been discovered that, although Nox is powerful, when he uses his magic in an attack, he is exhausted and helpless for a time afterward. The magic seems out of his control. It turns on him as well as his target. The young archer and a group from the castle staged an ambush a few days ago outside one of the outposts. When Nox was weakened after he attacked the abandoned outpost, the men from Ashnah struck, killing and wounding many of Freiwade's troops and incapacitating Nox. They nearly succeeded in killing the enemy mage and it will likely cause a long delay for Freiwade's forces. So, although the threat is still severe, we have gained some time, time that can be used to ready ourselves for battle. You can train, Corin. The army of Ashnah can prepare to face the threat. You won't face this danger alone and you're not expected to."

The words should have been more comforting than they came across as. Corin felt the pressure again weighing down on him. He still had to face the mage. He still wasn't ready. To prepare himself for the coming battle, he would have to practice magic, the same magic that had nearly destroyed him. Maybe this time he wouldn't escape it alive.

CHAPTER 53

Cal wasn't in the best of moods. Telling Corin the truth, revealing that they had all been keeping secrets from him, had been even more challenging than Cal had anticipated. He hoped it hadn't ruined any chance of friendship between him and Corin. Cal liked the young mage. He hoped Corin would eventually come to forgive him. What had been even more difficult had come after the meeting. Sir Hayes had cornered Cal in the hall before he left.

"Are you making any progress with the enemy spies?" Hayes asked.

Cal had known it was coming sooner or later. The king and Sir Hayes had every right to be worried. Unfortunately, Cal had nothing good to report.

"Nothing," he admitted tiredly.

"Cal, I know that it's not something you want to consider but..."

"No, I haven't talked with Lark. I haven't looked into it any further. I know I can't dismiss yours and the king's suspicions, Hayes, but I can't turn on her so easily. She's my friend. I trust her."

Hayes studied Cal long and hard. It was left unspoken that the assassin who'd tried to attack Corin was a woman.

"Do you know why I never married and started a family," Hayes said softly.

Cal was thrown off guard by the sudden change in subject. He shook his head, staring at Hayes with incomprehension.

"When I became battle master for King Rupert and all of Ashnah, I knew that duty would surpass all of my other responsibilities. I knew that I couldn't serve my kingdom to the best of my abilities by forming attachments just as I couldn't serve a wife or family to the best of my abilities because of my work for the king. I made a choice. It was no easy choice and there are days where I still regret the loneliness I've subjected myself to. But that detachment has allowed me to fulfill my duty. Do you understand what I'm saying?"

Cal thought he had a good idea. He sighed heavily. He knew he was the spymaster and he had a duty, a crucial duty, to uphold. He didn't have time for distraction. Sometimes he wondered how such an important role could have fallen to him. Sometimes he regretted that it had. The truth was that being spymaster meant he had to put his duty to his kingdom above almost all else in his life. His primary duty was to catch the enemy spies.

Cal nodded to Hayes. "I understand, Sir."

"I'm sorry, Cal. Sometimes I wish things were different for all of us."

"Me too."

Cal left Hayes and headed for The Cavern. He descended the ladder, feeling so weary that he didn't bother skipping the last two rungs. He clung onto the ladder for a moment, resting his forehead against it, not willing to fully enter The Cavern just yet. He took a deep breath. He hated that he had to do this, to question her like she was a criminal.

He finally mustered the courage to enter the cavernous room. He found Lark as he suspected he would. She was reclining at the room's table. A half-empty mug of coffee sat before her as she leaned forward. She rested her face in the palm of her hand, dozing. They were all tired, bone-weary from everything that had happened. But a small, traitorous part of Cal's mind wondered if her exhaustion was from something else. Was she sneaking out of the castle in the dead of night to report to messengers from Freiwade? Was she at work during every off hour looking for information for the enemy? Cal shook his head to clear it and approached the table. He took a seat across from her. Lark lifted her head and blinked to awareness.

"Cal?" she asked. "Is something wrong?"

Cal shook his head, unable to find words. He rested his elbows on the table and ran his fingers through his hair in frustration.

"Something's wrong," Lark said, sitting up straighter.

"I'm just tired," Cal told her. "I just came from a meeting. The king, Hayes, and Clifton finally told Corin the truth about everything."

"Oh."

"It's hard to keep friends in this line of work."

"You have me and Dusk at least."

Cal swallowed hard. "Yeah."

Lark stood and moved to the room's small

fireplace. She grabbed a kettle that was sitting on the hearth and brought it to the table, grabbing a spare mug on her way. She poured Cal a cup of coffee. It was dark and bitter, the way all of the spies took it. They consumed it more as a necessity than an enjoyment. Cal gratefully accepted the proffered drink and took a deep sip, scalding his tongue in the process.

He took a moment to simply sit there before he set the mug aside, forcing himself to confront the task at hand. "With everything happening, it's nice to sit down for a moment and just talk."

Lark smiled softly. "You look like you would rather sleep than talk, Cal."

He shook his head. "No, I don't want to sleep. I... don't think I could. But talk to me, Lark. Tell me about yourself. Please."

Lark raised a quizzical eyebrow. "Tell you about myself? What do you want to know?"

Cal gestured vaguely and tried to act casual. "Where are you from?"

Lark immediately stiffened. She reached forward and clutched her mug of coffee like it was a lifeline. "Does it matter?"

"I want to know more about you Lark. You've been here as a spy for a long time but I still don't feel like I really know you."

"Of course, you know me. Don't be ridiculous. You know that I like to climb and squeeze into tight spaces. You know that my favorite meal is fish stew and that I detest venison. You know that I hate wearing dresses because the hems are always too long and cumbersome. You know me, Cal, in all the ways that matter."

Cal sighed heavily. He had always thought the same. It was why he hadn't questioned her further in the past. He knew her as a person. He knew her likes and dislikes. He understood her. The rest didn't matter, or at least so he had thought.

"But I don't even know your real name."

"It's Lark," she said, annoyed. "My name is Lark. That's the name you gave me when I joined the spies. That's the name that I claim. Why are you asking these questions? You've never pressed me like this before."

"I'm not pressing you," Cal argued. "I just want to know more about you, Lark. You're my friend. Why won't you tell me anything?"

"Because maybe I don't want to live in the past, Cal. Maybe I don't want to go back to the way things were before I came here. I came to Castille to start a new life. I always thought you respected that."

She was angry and hurt. He could tell because her voice changed from the carefully masked roughness that it usually was to a lilting, odd accent. It only unsettled Cal further.

"What happened to you? What are you hiding from that you can't tell me about?"

Lark bristled like a cornered animal then she stilled. She pushed back her chair and stood, gaping at him with shock. A multitude of hurt was evident in her eyes.

"You're wondering if I'm one of the enemy spies, aren't you?" The accusation in her words pierced Cal's heart.

"Lark," he started.

"No. I can't believe that after everything, after

I've proven myself loyal through my actions more than my words, you would still doubt me and think I could be an enemy spy."

Cal stood up from his seat, a hint of anger working its way into his chest. "You haven't given me much option, Lark," he said, an accusation in his own words. "You're so secretive. I know nothing about you. I have to consider the possibility even though it makes me sick to do so."

"Do you truly believe I'm working with the enemy?"

"No. My heart tells me you're not."

"That isn't enough."

"In our line of work, it isn't," Cal agreed.

He could see the hurt on her face and in every line of her body. She looked like a wounded animal, eyeing him with distrust and betrayal. She had trusted him and he'd hurt her by not returning that trust. But what choice did he have? Hayes was right, relationships in their line of work only led to hurt and distraction.

"I'm sorry for not telling you more," Lark said. "But I can't, Cal. I can't."

Cal felt like the worst kind of criminal. "If it was just me, if I didn't have my duties as spymaster to consider, I would trust you without hesitation," he told her.

Lark closed her eyes. "I know. But our positions make that kind of trust impossible."

"I'm sorry, Lark."

"Me too."

With that, she turned and left. Cal could feel the tension that had been built between them, taut as a string on the verge of snapping. Before there had been trust, absolute trust. Now, there was doubt and suspicion. Cal couldn't discount that Lark might be an enemy spy and now she knew of his suspicions. Cal didn't know what to believe anymore. He was afraid his heart might be lying to him as it always seemed to do where she was concerned. He watched Lark's retreating back with a painful ache in his chest. When she reached the exit, he noticed another figure, standing silently at the base of the ladder, Dusk. How long had he been there? How much had he heard?

Lark ignored him as she ascended the ladder out of The Cavern.

Dusk slowly moved into the room, not looking at Cal. Cal knew that Dusk wouldn't comment on the conversation, or rather argument, that he had walked in on. However, it was clear that Dusk had heard it.

"How much did you hear?" Cal asked, sighing heavily and leaning back against the table.

Dusk shrugged. "As much or as little as you want me to have."

So, he'd heard all of it then. Or, at least, most of it. *Great.*

"You don't have to pretend like you didn't hear it," Cal said. "In fact, I could use your advice on the matter."

Dusk was silent, waiting for Cal to continue. Cal sought for the right words to explain everything, not just his conversation with Lark, but the king and Sir Hayes's suspicions, and now his own.

"I don't know what to do or think," Cal admitted. "The truth is I know so little about Lark and she refuses to reveal anything about herself or her past. With the enemy spies in our midst, it's becoming hard to overlook those secrets. The king and Sir Hayes suspect her. I don't know how to feel but I certainly can't discount it so quickly. You know her as well as I do, what do you think?"

Dusk considered for a moment. Cal could practically see his friend's analytical mind working.

"You're right to have suspicions," Dusk said. "You have to have the facts in order to make the right decision. If it makes you feel any better, I've kept an eye on her all along."

"What!"

"As you said, we don't know anything about her. I learned long ago, Cal, that I couldn't fully trust anyone. People are unpredictable and we all have that evil called sin within us. Even those you trust are capable of terrible things you could never imagine. So, yes, I've been keeping an eye on Lark. I can tell that she's sensitive about her past. I can respect that. However, that doesn't mean I have to blindly trust her."

Cal was surprised at Dusk's words. He'd been keeping an eye on Lark all along? Cal had only started to suspect her after his conversation with the king and Sir Hayes.

"Do you think she could be one of the enemy spies?" Cal asked, fearing the answer.

"I don't know. I've tried to discreetly find out more about her but there's nothing. It's difficult with Lark because she's so secretive but also because she's my friend. I've tried to respect her boundaries, even though it's difficult to not understand."

"I'm starting to think I'll never fully

understand her," Cal said. "And now I fear I might have ruined everything."

"You were right to question her. And you're right to be cautious. I'm concerned about what you would do if she did prove to be an enemy spy."

Cal straightened. "What do you mean?"

"Well, because you have feelings for her. That might get in the way of you making a logical decision about how much to trust her."

Cal startled. "W...what!"

He felt a blush creep up his cheeks which he couldn't control. He wanted to hide his face. Dusk's gaze was steady, unfazed. There was no emotion in Dusk's expression. His words hadn't carried any implications. It was a statement; nothing more, nothing less.

"What do you mean feelings?" Cal demanded.

Dusk crossed his arms. "Exactly that. Love. Adoration. Passion. Desire."

"Okay, enough!" Cal waved his hand through the air to cut Dusk off. "I know what you mean. I just... why would you say that?"

"It's true, isn't it? I've watched you with Lark. You look at her differently. I don't understand why you're upset that I said so."

Cal grimaced. Dusk wasn't one to beat around the bush. He was always straight to the point. He wouldn't understand why Cal didn't act on his feelings or even fully acknowledge them.

"You're worried about your position as a spy. You don't want to hurt her and you don't want her to hurt you," Dusk said, surprising Cal.

"Yes. How?"

"I may not understand the passion of emotions as well as some," Dusk said, "but I do understand reason and logic. I understand why you would stay away from any sort of relationship as a spy."

"Maybe it's a good thing I've never tried to go beyond friendship. I can't trust her, after all."

"That's your problem, Cal. You trust her anyway. You say that you don't but I can see in your eyes that in your heart, you still trust her. You don't think she's one of the spies. Just don't let your heart become a stumbling block for you."

Cal was unable to find words. His throat felt constricted with emotions that he couldn't describe. Dusk was right. He couldn't outright suspect Lark. Even if all of the evidence pointed towards her, he would need a confession or irrefutable proof in order to accept that she was an enemy spy. Not yet. He wouldn't accept it yet. For now, he would continue to cautiously trust her. He was glad he had talked with Dusk. He hoped he could follow his friend's instructions and use logic to make the right decision. He only prayed that it would never come to a decision between Lark and the kingdom because he honestly wasn't sure which he would pick.

CHAPTER 54

Finch, sloppily dressed as usual, reported to duty on the castle parapets. It wasn't uncommon for him to skip his post altogether to annoy the commander but after the battle at the outpost, Finch had started to take his position a little more seriously. That didn't mean he had to take as much care in his uniform as the other archers though. His clothes were still wrinkled and untidy but at least he had most of the components of his uniform. He felt more optimistic about his position as an archer after the successful mission to ambush Nox and the Freiwade army. If he were honest with himself, he was just grateful to be alive and that the men he'd been leading had faced minimal casualties. He wasn't sure what he would have done with himself if the attack had been unsuccessful and there had been a great loss of life on his account.

He was proud of himself for managing to lead the group and for coming up with the plan in the first place. He had never once in his life felt like he had accomplished something so meaningful. He knew he was talented with the bow but he had accomplished that out of spite more than anything else. He'd trained and trained. It had taken blood, sweat, and tears to master archery and prove himself. His motives had soured the achievement. He hadn't done it for himself or to do good, but to cause anger and resentment in others. The plan for the ambush was different. For once, Finch felt like he had done something to help others and he was proud of the fact. He was proud of the accomplishment. Hayes was proud of Finch too. That meant more than anything.

Finch walked with a slight bounce to his step up the long staircase to the parapet where the archers met for patrols. He felt ridiculous with his archer's cape over one shoulder and the silly little feathered hat resting atop his head. But, for the first time he could remember, Finch felt pleased to display his position.

Finch didn't think anything could sour his mood until he reached the top of the stairs. That was when he immediately knew his day was about to take a turn for the worse. A feeling of dread settled over him when he took the last step. Commander Terin was waiting for him right at the head of the stairs. His arms were crossed over his broad chest and the foulest expression Finch had ever seen was on the man's face.

Finch felt vaguely ill. He wasn't angry that Terin was blocking his path. Instead, Finch was more afraid of the man than anything. Despite himself, he cowered from the commander's brutal look. Finch was at least allowed to step onto the parapet before the commander paced towards him, forcing Finch to retreat until his back was pressed against the battlements. Finch swallowed hard, half-expecting the man to hit him. He glanced behind himself and saw the massive drop down to the courtyard. If he fell from such a height, he would die. His hands dug into the stone battlements to steady himself.

"I'm sure you're very proud of yourself," Commander Terin said, dampening Finch's mood in a heartbeat. "Oh, wise, resourceful Finch Caraway. Am I even worthy to be in your great presence?"

Each word hit Finch like a slap. The stone of the wall bit into his back as he pressed closer and closer to it.

"What exactly possessed you to think you could rise to such a lofty perch? If I didn't know better, I would say you were lucky, but I know you and there isn't an ounce of luck in your miserable body. The fact that your plan was even remotely successful was just as much of a mistake as you are. Don't expect for one moment that this success will change anything. I will make certain that this small victory doesn't go to your head. You don't deserve any recognition or pride for what you've done. The fact that Hayes trusted you enough to follow the plan in the first place is a mark against him."

Those words, the insult against Hayes, snapped something in Finch. "What did you say?"

The commander scoffed. "Hayes is a fool for putting any faith in you. He doesn't deserve the position he's in. He's too soft, too sentimental, and too willing to trust any common soldier that comes his way."

Finch felt hot anger spark in him. He could accept the comments against himself, even though they felt like a mortar dragging him to the bottom of the ocean, but he wouldn't listen to the commander saying anything against Hayes. Hayes had been more of a father to Finch than his real father ever was. Hayes had looked after a nobody archer from the start even though Finch didn't technically report to him at all. Hayes had told him the truth about God's love and the possibility of salvation.

"You've always resented Sir Hayes," Finch responded. "It's not because of his humanity, it's because he's respected by everyone. He's respected by his subordinates, his peers, and the king himself. You resent him because you know you are inferior in every meaning of the word."

The commander's fist connected with Finch's face, hard and fast. It surprised Finch even though he knew he should have seen it coming. The pain hit him in an instant. His heart hammered wildly in his chest with fear that he resented much more than the stinging of his cheek and eye. He knew there would be a bruise. He hated that the mark would serve as a reminder of the strike for days after. He glared at Commander Terin. Terin yanked Finch's collar and shoved him hard against the battlements.

"You better get rid of that rebellious look in your eyes, boy. You don't know the beginning of how miserable I can make your life. There is no escape, not from me. You'll regret your words and your disrespect." With that, the commander shoved Finch one more time hard into the stone, then released him and stalked away.

Finch leaned heavily against the wall for a moment, struggling to catch his breath. His whole body ached. His legs felt weak with his racing heart. His face stung from the punch. He felt himself shaking with anger and fear. He watched the commander's retreating back and hated how helpless he was to stand against the man. He hated the commander with every fiber of his being and knew that it was wrong to do so. He despised how powerless he was against the man.

Finch knew he would be punished for it later but he couldn't bring himself to go about his duties. Not now. Instead, he headed back to the lower levels of the castle. He had to use the wall to balance himself as he descended the many stairs. He huffed through the pain that enveloped him. There was no bounce to his step anymore, no joy or sense of pride at his accomplishments. There was only a heaviness that he doubted he would ever be able to shake. He stared at the steps and frowned when he noticed a red splotch on the step below him. He watched another drop of red land next to the first. He brought a hand up to his face. His nose was bleeding. Finch sighed in annoyance and pressed the back of his hand to his aching nose. He knew it wasn't broken at least, there would surely be a lot more pain if it was.

He was tempted to stop on the blood-splattered step and rest a while but he forced himself to keep moving. He wanted to find Dorian. He hated to bring his own problems to his friend when he was suffering himself but Finch was desperate for a listening ear. His friend would offer him some comfort. Finch didn't want to be alone. He somehow made it down the stairs, one difficult step after another. He was exhausted and felt on the brink of collapse when he reached the bottom step but he mustered the strength to search for Dorian. As he looked, Finch thought how he hadn't seen much of his friend lately. They'd both been busy and Dorian hadn't made much effort to seek him out. Finch had given Dorian space, knowing he'd need time to sort through his thoughts after what had happened at Cheston.

Finch found himself hating the ambush that he had been so proud of only an hour earlier. He hated that he was involved in the matter at all. He wished he could just disappear. He didn't want to be at the castle, he never had. He wanted to be far, far away, a nobody. Finch kept searching for Dorian but after no success in finding him and with exhaustion weighing on him, Finch finally asked the first knight he saw if he knew where Dorian was. The knight looked concerned at the blood caked on Finch's face and the bruise already starting to bloom at his eye and cheek.

"No, I haven't seen Dorian," the knight answered. "The last time I saw him though he was with a maid, hidden away in some dark hallway. Lucky fool."

Finch shook his head, "No, you must be mistaken. That wouldn't have been Dorian."

"I know who I saw. He and that maid were pressed so close together I had to look closer than I would have liked to see his face."

Finch felt a wave of annoyance at the news. Why would Dorian act that way? It wasn't like him. At least, Finch didn't think it was. Dorian hadn't said anything about seeing someone. Why hadn't he told him? Finch supposed he should be happy for his friend but he worried Dorian might be seeking comfort in the wrong places after what had happened.

Finch was too tired to look any further. He

knew it was selfish but he wished Dorian was there. He stumbled along the corridors until he found a deserted hallway to hide in. He leaned heavily against the wall and sank to a sitting position with his legs stretched out in front of him. He leaned his head back and felt utterly, miserably alone.

CHAPTER 55

It wasn't long after Corin learned the truth about Freiwade and Nox that he was urged to begin training again. He was still weak and recovering but he had to be ready to face Nox when the enemy inevitably arrived at the castle. It was good to know the truth, Corin decided, but now he had to deal with the fact that there would be no taking things easy on him anymore. Clifton, Sir Hayes, and the king told him plainly that he had to return to training. He had to ready himself for Nox. In Corin's mind, if he never had to use magic again, it would be too soon. A new, dangerous fear surrounded his skills. However, he was given no choice in the matter. He had to return to training.

He found himself praying as he walked to Clifton's office. Will followed quietly behind him, a silent but welcome companion. Corin had been doing a lot of thinking lately. He wanted to be in the right place spiritually. He wanted to have a relationship with God more like what Sir Burke had. Corin had nearly died, first from his magic and then from the poison and the other attempts on his life. He wanted to know where he was going when he did die. He also wanted to understand the magic that everyone called a God-given gift.

It wasn't so easy to seek God after years of doubt and thinking God wouldn't want him in any way. Corin knew he was completely unworthy of any of God's mercy but he also knew that he had to try to seek God. He had to have faith that his prayers would be answered and that God would hear and see him. It was no easy task for Corin. The best he could do was practice praying. Maybe, like swordplay, he would get better the more he trained. Though, maybe that wasn't the best example. He hadn't improved much as a knight even after years of struggle.

God, I have no idea what I'm doing, Corin admitted. *I feel lost and confused. I'm terrified to try using magic again. I nearly died the last time. I still don't understand how any of this works and I don't want to make a mistake again. If this is a gift that comes from You like everyone says it is, then please help me use it. I know I'm not good at much and I know I can't do this alone. Thank You for protecting me from the magic and the poison. I know I could have died but for some reason You let me live. Thank You for those who've helped me through all of this, Cal and Ruena especially. And Will. I just hope I don't disappoint them all. I don't know how I'm going to face Nox. I'm afraid of that too. I'm sorry I haven't sought You more. I'm trying now. Please give me the courage and strength to do what I have to do.*

Corin cut off his prayer when he reached the door to Clifton's office. He took a deep breath. With a thrill of fear and unease in his chest, Corin automatically went to knock with his injured right hand. When he couldn't lift the bandaged arm, frustration and discouragement surged through his chest. He still found himself forgetting about his injury on occasion. He sighed and knocked with his left hand instead. He felt something inside him crack a little as he thought of how his life would be from then on. Clifton met him at the door and offered a warm welcome. He had been on edge around Corin ever since the accident but particularly since Corin now knew the truth about the enemy mage, the approaching army, and that Clifton had intentionally kept it from him.

"Corin, have a seat," Clifton instructed.

Corin gladly sat down. He worried his legs wouldn't support him much longer. He was scared and weak from so long lying in bed.

"Thank you, Will. That will be all," Clifton dismissed the boy.

"No," Corin said, "stay Will. Please." He didn't want to be alone with Clifton. Corin wanted Will nearby. For once, Corin didn't ask for Clifton's permission on the matter. He needed Will there, strange as it may be. Will looked to Clifton for permission anyway. Clifton nodded his assent and gestured for Will to take a seat in the corner of the room. There was no notebook for Will to record in this time. None of them had any idea how this lesson would turn out.

"This first lesson back will be an easy one, I assure you," Clifton explained. "Our only goal today will be to get you reconditioned to magic and find a way to adapt your magic without your right arm. It will take time."

There was a strain around the word, 'time'.

They didn't have time, not anymore. Corin swallowed hard and nodded. He watched Clifton warily. He was still a little angry at the secrets his mentor had kept from him. He couldn't believe that Clifton had kept so much hidden. Clifton hadn't thought Corin was capable of handling the news. He hadn't trusted Corin enough to share the truth with him. Corin was upset at everyone but at Clifton most of all. He understood that Cal had to keep the secret because he was ordered to. Cal had confessed to Corin after the meeting that he had long disagreed with the plan to keep Corin in the dark.

"If it had been up to me," Cal had told him, "I would have trusted you with the news right away instead of keeping it quiet."

Corin understood that Ruena didn't have much of a say in the matter either. She had to do what her uncle wanted. But Clifton had known everything and still wanted to keep it hidden from Corin. Corin knew he had to put his feelings aside for the moment. He needed all of his concentration to get through the lesson. There was an urgency to his training now that there hadn't been before. He would have to push himself past his limits. Clifton couldn't coddle him anymore.

The pressure of time running out only made Corin more anxious. He couldn't help remembering the pain of the magic turning on him as he lost control of it. His arm still throbbed with every step he took as if it remembered too. There was always that tingling pain in his arm along with an uncomfortable numbness. Sometimes the muscles would spasm as if they were trying to work but unable to. That was the worst pain. Still, Corin wouldn't regret his decision to keep the arm. Even if it caused him more pain, he couldn't bear the idea of losing his arm completely.

As Clifton readied for the lesson, Corin kept himself from voicing his concern that this lesson would end just as terribly as the last one had. He wanted nothing more than to turn and run from the office but he knew he couldn't. At least Will was close by, looking equally nervous but trying to put on a brave face for Corin's sake. Will had been acting differently lately, more serious. He seemed protective of Corin, following him around like a guard dog. Corin knew that Will had been there when the accident happened. Will had been the one sent to fetch help. Corin could only imagine how terrifying the experience must have been. He appreciated Will. Life at the castle would have been a lot colder without the young boy's presence.

Clifton pushed past the tension in the room and spoke. "We'll try an easy skill first. Let's start with the first thing I taught you, how to summon light."

That at least was a comfort to Corin. It was something extremely familiar to him. The decision to start with the simple ability filled Corin with relief. He could do it, he hoped. It would still be more difficult than before because he would have to use only his left hand. However, when he'd first learned the skill, Clifton had shown him how to do it with either hand for convenience. He prayed it would work now.

"Well, let's give it a try, shall we?" Clifton gestured for Corin to begin and Corin stood from his chair.

Suddenly Corin's mouth felt unbearably dry.

Fear pierced him. Somehow, he hadn't imagined having to do magic again. He knew he would have to but now that the moment was there, he was filled with fear. He silently prayed that everything would be okay. But what if it wasn't? What if everything went wrong again? Even though magic had come naturally to him, now he struggled to force himself to even try. He had never craved the ease before. Instead, he'd been upset at how easy magic came when his real passion, swordplay, was so difficult. Now, he wished any of the acts of magic came easily. Clifton watched him closely, almost impatiently, waiting for Corin to make a move. Corin felt frozen.

"You can do it Corin," Will encouraged him.

Corin knew his fear was ridiculous, especially with such a harmless act of magic. There was nothing that could go wrong. He knew he had to try. He raised his left hand to summon the light. Corin's hand shook. Nothing happened. He straightened, trying to summon the power with more confidence. Still, nothing. Corin took a deep breath. He pulled from deep inside himself and brought forth as much power as he could muster.

The magic came in a flash. The spark of light startled Corin. He flinched hard and immediately dropped the magic. He took a step back as if trying to escape it but he knew he couldn't because the power came from inside him. He could never escape. His mind flashed back to the accident and he started to shake. He felt like he was suffocating. His arm throbbed with pain as he remembered the power surging up and overtaking him. He remembered his arm crumbling away from the magic. He gasped loud and hard and felt panic creeping over him. Somehow, he found himself backed up against a wall and leaning heavily against it.

"Corin, are you okay?" Will asked.

Corin could hardly hear the noise over the ringing in his ears. Clifton's hand rested on Corin's shoulder but he flinched away from the touch.

"I'm alright. I'm alright. I'm alright," Corin muttered over and over again. But he felt far from it.

Clifton's worried face swam blurrily above him. Corin waved off his mentor with his good arm. He just needed a minute to breathe. Just one minute. Clifton took the hint and backed off, pulling Will back with him. Once Corin had the space, he managed to settle his breathing. He looked up, feeling exhausted and pathetic.

"I think I'm done for the day," he murmured.

"That's probably a good idea," Clifton readily agreed.

Corin pushed himself away from the wall with difficulty and with hunched shoulders, headed for the door. At that moment, he felt that he would never be ready to face Nox. He might never be able to use his gift again.

CHAPTER 56

Dane had kept himself busy studying every book he could find about the royal family of Skellas. He searched the castle records, the library, and even a few of the offices. In the process, he discovered that many of the documents that should exist to prove what Claude had said were carefully hidden or missing altogether. It wasn't just information regarding Skellas that was mysteriously absent. There were many historical documents, accounts of the Great War, and relics from The Three Kingdoms Period which had taken place before the war that were missing. Dane suspected they'd been destroyed.

The castle archives were dismal and incomplete already because so much knowledge had been destroyed over the years by Dane's conquering ancestors. The castle was one of the few places in the kingdom, in all of Ademar, that had any books and scrolls in the first place. Dane knew he was fortunate to be able to study them. He was fortunate to be able to read. So many of the people of Freiwade and Skellas were illiterate. As Claude had said, there was a separation between nobility and commoners. Only Ashnah allowed its lower classes to obtain proper schooling. Dane wondered if that was part of the reason Ashnah flourished while Freiwade struggled to maintain its power.

Not for the first time, Dane wondered where the knowledge had gone. Surely with so many years of history, there would have been thousands of books and scrolls. Instead, there was a pathetic pittance of material. Dane wished he could read the books in Ashnah. He suspected that any texts he did find in Freiwade's library were biased and meant to fit within the Corpin family's narrative of a necessary war and their right to kingship. Dane started to lose hope that he would find anything relating to Skellas's lost heir. It seemed likely that any records would have been destroyed to quell rumors. Indeed, Dane didn't find anything about a secret runaway heir of Skellas. But he did find something interesting.

He discovered the document among the prison records which detailed any and all prisoners who'd been kept in the castle dungeons. It was an account from several years ago. Dane studied the document with intrigue. The account read:

A Skellan child was brought to the dungeons for suspicion of coming from the Strond royal family of Skellas. The child, age fourteen, was sickly. The child's location was revealed by the father, also suspected to be a descendant of Alexander Strond. The man was captured at sea in his sailing vessel, tortured until he revealed the information, and then killed and thrown overboard. It is suspected the family was living in secret for some time. The father and child both possessed a remarkable resemblance to the late king of Freiwade. Soldiers entered the family's home, killed the mother, and brought the child back to Freiwade to be imprisoned and used as leverage if the need arose. The king suggested the need for a figurehead ruler if the Skellan people attempted to rebel and so tried to train the child to obey his commands.

Dane kept reading and was horrified to discover that the child had been kept in Freiwade's dungeons for years, mentally and physically abused in an attempt to break the spirit. However, it seemed the king's plan backfired. The account explained that the child grew physically stronger after being taken from the harsh climate of Skellas. The child's health improved and resilience set in. The king worsened the conditions as the child rebelled. There were accounts of the types of punishment used which made Dane's skin crawl. Finally, he came to the last section of the document:

The child refused to submit to Freiwade ideals and to obey the king. It was decided that the risk of maintaining the child was too great. The king determined that death was the only option.

The account ended abruptly. Dane had the feeling that it had been left unfinished. But why? It didn't matter, he supposed. It was obvious how things ended. Dane wondered how there could be rumors of a surviving heir if it was clear that all of the descendants of King Alexander Strond had been killed by Freiwade. Something didn't add up. Knowing his family, Dane suspected that the majority of the truth was being concealed. It only made him determined to learn more.

Unfortunately, Dane couldn't spend all of his time searching the archives. Reports had been coming in from the front lines. All efforts to proceed further into Ashnah had been halted until Nox was recovered. The mage's injuries were severe and his magic had not risen to heal him as quickly as usual. Dane suspected because Nox had used all of his reserves of strength in the battle, he would have to heal like normal mortals. Dane knew Nox was hated. He knew King Corpin detested the mage. Dane himself saw only evil behind Nox's dark eyes. However, Nox was also Freiwade's best weapon. He was their best chance to win the war against Ashnah. Dane knew his father was conflicted about Nox and his injuries. Dane had overhead a few interesting conversations between the king and his two eldest sons, Warson and Claude.

"It's a pity the injuries didn't take place after we defeated Ashnah," the king remarked. "We could have ended the mage when he was weak. Now, we'll have to wait until after he's regained his strength and defeated the enemy."

"I don't understand," Warson responded. "Wouldn't it be better to keep using him as a weapon even after the war is over? He would force our people to submit."

"No," Claude answered. "Father is right. The mage is too great a threat. Think for a moment, Warson, how easily he could turn on us next. If Nox decided he wanted to be king, his power would be difficult to combat. He must be eliminated once the war is over."

Dane thought the treachery was disdainful. He supposed he shouldn't be surprised that the king and his sons would so quickly turn on someone who was currently fighting their war for them. However, Dane also had to agree that Nox was a dangerous enemy to have. It might be for the best to ensure he didn't turn against them. Maybe Dane didn't have a mind for war and tactics. He still didn't know what to make of the conflict with Ashnah. He could only see the harm the war was causing the people of Freiwade and Skellas. Men went into battle to die, women were left widowed and children orphaned, all for a needless war that was driven by pride and a want for power. The war was a mistake. Dane didn't want Ashnah to win but he didn't see a problem with the treaty the three kingdoms had shared before. Certainly, Ashnah had an advantage in the treaty but it had still provided Freiwade with more than enough. There had been food provided for them when their barren lands produced little to no provision. They had sent metals and jewels to Ashnah and paid a small reparation for the trouble caused by the Great War. They were provided for and there was peace between the three kingdoms, or at least between Freiwade and Ashnah. However, King Histen Corpin was a proud man like his ancestors before him. He wouldn't allow Ashnah to keep their advantage. Was war the answer?

Dane wondered, as he often did, what life was like in Ashnah. Was it more peaceful? If there was a lost heir to Skellas, the heir would have the greatest chance of surviving if they escaped to Ashnah and hid there. So, Dane looked into any records of Ashnah. He doubted he would find anything. As expected, there was nothing written about a lost heir, but Dane found something even better. There was a document buried among the accounts of Ashnan history that was intriguing. It was written by a spy who had been stationed in Ashnah soon after the War of Three Kingdoms, the Great War. The spy wrote that Ashnah was a powerful kingdom that shouldn't be underestimated and that the most danger they posed wasn't from their armies but from their willpower and their faith. Dane hesitated at that word.

"Faith," he murmured aloud.

Dane had heard of the heresy of Ashnah's religion before. He knew how much his father detested the Ashnan belief in a God who offered salvation from sin and eternal life if a person repented and believed in Him. That faith had driven Ashnah's need for independence. The Ashnan people refused to submit to Freiwade if only because they refused to sacrifice their religion and their belief in God. Dane read the spy's document. The spy's report revealed that he was stationed in Castille Castle at the heart of the kingdom of Ashnah. A book was brought to the king of Ashnah, a religious text that changed the kingdom altogether. The spy wrote about the content of the text and that while he knew Freiwade had come to see the book as heresy, the spy couldn't help but be overcome by the wonder of it. He was amazed by the account of a powerful, vengeful, but also merciful God who bestowed gifts on His people and offered them salvation through the sacrifice of His Son. The spy wrote:

> It is a far more optimistic view than what the people of Freiwade and Skellas have come to accept.

Dane read on:

> This religion is so much more than just a religion. It might very well be true. Freiwade should

consider the content of the text more closely and listen to what Ashnah has come to accept as factual. The book, which they call a Bible, was brought to Ashnah by a scribe who escaped from the fire which destroyed the great library connecting the three kingdoms and killed most of the scribes and mages studying at the library. Although the history of Ademar and the books that gave the three kingdoms their knowledge were destroyed, this Bible survived the blaze. I believe the words written in the book can endure both fire and war, pestilence and peace. I believe in the God of Ashnah.

Dane was amazed by the account, written so long ago. There had been a great library. That was where the knowledge had been held and it had been destroyed. There were mages who had studied there. Dane was shocked that such ground-shaking information had been hidden away and not spread. Even a spy of Freiwade had seen the book, the Bible, and accepted it. Why had the king of Freiwade, who would have been Dane's grandfather at the time, still not listened and attempted to look into the matter further?

Then Dane realized that he shouldn't be surprised at all. He knew his family. He knew their pride and their beliefs. He knew how wicked they were. They would never cave and ask for anything from Ashnah. They would detest and deny the religion only because Ashnah accepted and valued it. Dane wondered just what was in the Bible. He wanted to see it for himself. If it offered a different view from that of Freiwade, then he was even more interested to see exactly what was in it and to see if it offered what he needed so much, hope.

CHAPTER 57

Ruena was beyond busy trying to keep everything together and functioning. She was furious that she had been kept in the dark over things for so long. She feared the consequences of what they had kept from Corin. She feared the things her uncle had been denying for so long, the war, the threat of the duke, the spies in their midst, and the murmurings of the court. The danger of Duke Heirson was particularly troubling. Ruena couldn't believe he was conspiring with the king of Freiwade. She was still in shock over the fact that Dusk was the duke's supposedly dead son, Everett. The danger that Nox posed was even more terrifying. Ruena knew he was approaching the castle. Even if he had been delayed for a moment, he would still arrive long before they were ready to face him.

Lingering in their midst was a further danger that no one else had recognized, a danger that Ruena couldn't ignore. She refused to voice her concerns aloud but they were heavy in her heart. Corin.

Corin was a mage as well. He was a powerful mage with a natural gift for the talents God had given him. With the way they had treated Corin after his arrival at the castle, the way they had kept him in the dark, Ruena worried he would run. He was a flight risk. He had always been a flight risk. He had never wanted to be a mage and now he was expected to face off against a powerful enemy. More than that, his injury and the attempts on his life had been debilitating to both his physical and mental well-being. Corin had always had trust issues, that much had been obvious from the start. Now, he had every reason to distrust them all further.

They needed Corin on their side if they wanted to win the war. Ruena wouldn't blame him if he denied his duty and refused to fight for them. The secrets they'd kept from him were terrible and wrong. She should have told him everything, even if she had been instructed not to. Ruena feared she would lose Corin's friendship. She knew it was a selfish desire amid the trouble they faced but she had grown to value Corin's company more than almost anything else.

She had always been lonely in the castle, even with Cal's companionship. She didn't regret that time of loneliness because it had drawn her closer to God and taught her to seek Him and find her worth in Him. However, she still craved friendship with someone her age, someone like-minded. Then Corin came along and filled that gap with a new friendship. Ruena worried that Corin wouldn't trust her anymore and she knew he had reason not to. She didn't want to lose his friendship. She didn't want to lose him. She worried that he had been forever changed in more than just a physical way after the accident. He was more withdrawn and serious than ever before. Now, with the news of Nox, it was like he was a completely different person. She was worried about him. She worried at the fact that he wouldn't even look at his arm. She worried when he picked at his food and ate so little, as if afraid it was poisoned or tampered with. She grew even more worried after hearing Cal's report from Clifton of Corin's breakdown after trying to practice magic again. She was concerned with the strain he was facing and the walls he had built around himself.

She wanted to help and she tried to but Cal had warned her to be careful.

"He's embarrassed at any perceived weakness," Cal told her. "Give him some space to come to terms with everything that has happened in his life. It'll take time."

They didn't have time.

Not only was Nox quickly approaching but there was also the threat of the duke. King Rupert had decided to confine the duke and his son Dresden to the castle. They were discreetly encouraged to stay when in reality, if they tried, they would not be permitted to leave. Their correspondence was watched closely. Still, King Rupert was not willing to confront the duke, not yet. There was no solid proof, only Everett's word and Cal backing him up. They needed an outright confession.

Ruena had said as much to Cal but she knew there was little he could do without risking Dusk's identity.

"The spies might be too conspicuous if we paid the duke a visit," Cal told her. "He's already starting to get suspicious."

Ruena could see that much for herself. She saw the duke that morning at breakfast. He sat at the head table with Dresden.

"Where is our young mage?" Duke Heirson casually asked. "We haven't seen much of him lately. I hear there was a ghastly injury. How is the boy's recovery progressing?"

The king dodged the questions as much as he could. "I'm afraid I'm not in the loop about such matters. I've been too busy with other things to keep constant track of Corin. But, I've heard that the boy is doing better. I'm sure all accounts of his injury have been exaggerated. You know how rumors are."

"Yes," the duke smiled around his fork, "rumors can be dangerous things. But they can work to one's advantage if used correctly."

Ruena glared at her plate as she thought about Everett, Dusk, whose life had been destroyed by the rumors his father had spread.

At the end of the meal, the duke spoke again. "I'm afraid Dresden and I really must be getting back to our estate to oversee a few important matters. I fear we've overstayed our welcome."

The king waved off the duke's concerns. "Nonsense Heirson. Whatever it is can wait. We are enjoying your company too much to allow you to leave so soon. Besides, wouldn't it be wonderful to find young Dresden a wife here at court? There are plenty of eligible ladies. You are sadly short of those back in your dukedom."

The duke didn't seem pleased at this comment but his eyes sparked with some idea that Ruena was sure none of them would like.

It was Ruena who finally placated him. "We would so miss your company, Duke Heirson. You can always manage things from the castle, that way you won't miss out on any important matters that might come up."

The duke considered Ruena's words. "Well, I suppose a few more days wouldn't hurt."

"But father," Dresden protested.

"Silence, Dresden," the duke murmured, leaving no room for objection.

Ruena knew they were running out of time. The duke would demand to leave before long and they would have to decide whether it was worth the risk to imprison him on words alone or let him go and risk his plan succeeding. Ruena knew something had to be done. If Cal wasn't able to do anything, then she would.

She would simply pay the duke a little visit. It wasn't as if her presence would be as suspicious as Cal's might be. She was only a noblewoman visiting a nobleman. Nothing would be amiss. Ruena found the duke's quarters after the midday meal and knocked politely. Vesta stood beside her, acting as a chaperone, as befitting such a visit.

"Are you sure you want to talk to him?" Vesta asked. "He's a foul man."

Vesta was nothing if not blunt. Although she was a servant in the castle, she wasn't afraid to say what was on her mind.

"I'll be fine," Ruena assured her friend. "I can handle Heirson."

Vesta sank into silence. The door opened and Ruena was met by Dresden. Ruena forced a smile to her face.

"I would like very much to meet with you and your father, Dresden. Would it be amiss for me to join you for tea?"

Dresden seemed confused and a little flustered but he invited her inside and brought her to the duke.

"Duke Heirson," Ruena greeted, using the greatest composure and manners she could.

"Ruena, what a pleasure. However, I am admittedly a little confused at your presence," the duke responded.

Ruena fingered the strands of her hair, trying to appear casual as if the idea of visiting had struck her on the spur of the moment and she'd decided to follow the whim. "Your words at breakfast this morning got me thinking. I feel that I haven't visited you often enough during your stay at the castle. You've been unjustly overlooked because of my uncle's busy schedule. That is a crime which must be remedied."

The duke puffed out his chest. "I appreciate your dedication to the castle's guests. It is befitting for a young woman of your station. I'm sure that kindness will serve you well when you marry. It would be a pleasure if you would take afternoon tea with us."

Ruena readily accepted the invitation and found a seat at the small table in the room, waiting for Dresden to pull out the chair for her. Vesta took on the task of pouring tea for them all. The duke watched the maid as she worked. Vesta stiffened under his gaze. Ruena felt nausea creep up her throat. Vesta was undoubtedly pretty and she was also at least 30 years younger than the duke. When Vesta had finished filling their cups and taken up a position discreetly in the corner, Ruena spoke.

"You mentioned your estate this morning, my liege. Are there truly pressing matters you must attend to?"

The duke waved off her concern. "There is always something that must be done in my position. It's nothing to fret about, however. There were only a few missives that should be sent."

"We have close ties with several neighboring nobles and updates are sent back and forth as a social obligation more than anything," Dresden put in.

Ruena let out a soft, forced laugh. "You no doubt have many allies and friends, my liege."

The duke shrugged but his shoulders were set with pride as he responded. "A few notables."

"It's for the best that you should have allies," Ruena went on to say. "With your estate so near the border, it must be awfully dangerous and troublesome for you to live in such a place."

"Yes, there are a few dangers and worries but my army is well prepared to face any threats. We have a solid plan of defense. And I am convinced this war will be over before it has fully started. There is no need to worry yourself over Dresden and I."

"But I will worry, my liege. I can't help it. Your loyalty to this kingdom has long been treasured. Your dukedom will be of great tactical importance if the war ever should spread. It's a relief to know that you're prepared for trouble."

The duke laughed. "It sounds like you've been listening to the men talk about war. Do not concern yourself with such things, dear Ruena."

Ruena fought down the urge to say something she was sure she would regret. She had to act the foolish woman in front of the duke if she wanted him to accidentally reveal something to her. Vesta made a gagging gesture in the corner. Ruena tried not to laugh.

The duke laid a hand on hers and Ruena fought back a shiver of repulsion at his touch. The duke studied her carefully, more carefully than he ever had before. Ruena worried that he was starting to grow suspicious at her line of questioning but his next words completely caught her off guard.

"My loyalty to the kingdom of Ashnah is indeed beyond question. I want what is best for the kingdom. I believe this war must end quickly and that we must all step up to the task and do whatever it takes to end this conflict with Freiwade. A powerful leader is necessary to do that."

Ruena noticed that he said nothing about King Rupert in his talk of a leader. He probably meant himself, Ruena thought. Ruena forced herself not to comment.

"You are right about my land being in a good tactical position and my private army is one of the most capable in Ashnah. I'm not attempting to boast when I say that my dukedom is essential to winning this war. In truth, I have been considering proving my loyalty to the kingdom even further by making a more official alliance between my family and the Castille royal line."

Ruena shivered at the word 'alliance'. She didn't like the sound of it. She felt dread settle deep in her bones. She swallowed hard and spoke, though her voice faltered.

"What kind of alliance?"

The duke looked at her and then at Dresden. Ruena felt her heart drop.

"Your uncle's words this morning caused me great thought. It is high time that Dresden has found a suitable wife, a woman of worthy rank. Moreover, it is always important to strengthen ties between powerful families. That is why I propose a marriage between you Ruena, and Dresden for the benefit of the kingdom as a display of unity and power."

Ruena dared a look at the duke's son who appeared almost as shocked as she was. Apparently, the duke had not mentioned the idea to Dresden either. Ruena had the horrible notion that the duke may have come up with the plan just then on the spot. Would her future be decided by a spur-of-the-moment decision? But no, there was a calculating look in his eyes. He'd been planning this for some time now. Ruena cleared her throat and then realized it was an unladylike gesture. She carefully withdrew her hand from under the duke's.

"That would indeed be a powerful alliance," Ruena remarked. The duke brightened but his face darkened again when Ruena continued, "and one my uncle and I would have to consider carefully."

"That is a very diplomatic answer," the duke said. "I will of course offer you and your uncle time to consider. However, do not disregard the impact that such a choice might have on the kingdom and all of us individually as well."

Ruena felt the color draining from her face but

she forced a smile. "I understand."

She felt sick at the idea of marrying the duke's son, the same son who so quickly turned on his brother. The same family who had tried to kill Everett for standing up to them when they were betraying their entire kingdom. Ruena felt sick even looking at them and thinking of the pain they had put Dusk through. How would Dresden treat the wife of an arranged marriage?

Ruena had always known that her position practically guaranteed that she would be married off for an alliance. She had hoped that her uncle would disregard that rule as he and his brother had done with their wives. Still, Ruena had accepted that it might very well be her duty to step into that necessary position. She felt sick at the idea of this particular alliance. She wondered if it would make any difference. Would the power and eventual position of the prince consort be enough for the duke's son? Ruena doubted it. She knew the duke was ruthless. If she married Dresden, he would take over the position of king even though Ruena was destined to rule, not her eventual husband. She feared that the duke would speed along her uncle's death as well, to guarantee the throne much sooner.

Ruena knew she couldn't extract any more information from the duke. She only wanted to get away. She forced herself to sit still and finish her tea, then, as if only just remembering, she admitted that she had forgotten an important meeting and must unfortunately excuse herself.

"Of course," Duke Heirson agreed. "Dresden, escort her to the door."

Ruena said her goodbyes as calmly as she could and then walked a few feet down the hall before dismissing Vesta. Vesta gave her a pitying stare.

"If you want to talk about it…"

Ruena shook her head. She just wanted to be alone. Vesta retreated down the hall, casting one last glance back at Ruena. Ruena felt her heart pounding and nausea creeping up her throat. She was so dazed that she bumped right into Cal who caught her and held her at arms-length. He must have noticed the look on her face because his first words to her were, "What's wrong?"

Ruena choked out a sob and explained. "I talked with Duke Heirson."

"What!" Cal exclaimed. "Ruena, why did you do it behind my back? It's dangerous. He's dangerous."

Ruena could tell he wanted to say more but he backed off when he realized how upset she was.

"What happened?" he asked.

"I was trying to get information from him and I managed to vaguely get him to confirm some of what we already knew."

"Why are you upset then? The meeting sounds like it was successful. Did the duke or Dresden hurt you?"

Ruena forced herself to calm down, brush away her tears, and put on a composed face. "He didn't hurt me." Then she told Cal about the proposed alliance.

He blanched. When she finished explaining, he spoke. "I would never let that happen, Ruena, and neither would your uncle."

Ruena nodded, knowing it was the truth. She clasped Cal's arms anyway. She was shaken from the conversation with the duke. It reminded her that their situation was dire. She voiced her concerns to Cal.

"Cal, we have to do something. Things can't go on like this. The duke must be stopped. Who knows the ties he's already established in this castle? The roots of his betrayal run deep. He has the support of Terin, of some of the nobles, and now he's tried to arrange an alliance with me. He has to be stopped before it's too late before loyalties shift and it becomes impossible to uproot him."

CHAPTER 58

Finch couldn't help but be worried when he received notice that the war council was to meet again. It was another urgent meeting which no doubt meant more bad news. Finch knew immediately that something was happening, probably nothing good. A messenger was sent to rouse him from bed at an incredibly early hour. Finch listened to what the servant had to say and then sent him away while he forced himself out of bed. He was filled with aches and pains from the beating he'd taken from Commander Terin. A few days had passed but he was still bruised and battered. A giant, purplish-green splotch covered his cheekbone and surrounded his swollen eye. His nose was bruised as well and was sensitive to the touch. Fortunately, it hadn't shown any signs of fracture or break. Finch's fellow archers hadn't commented during any meals. They knew where the bruises came from. Some of them had been on the receiving end of Terin's fury in the past. They winced in sympathy but Finch suspected many of them believed he deserved any punishment from the commander. It was only during meals when they saw him. Finch kept shirking his other duties. He knew he would face punishment sooner rather than later, but he couldn't drag himself to the parapets, not when he knew he would find Terin waiting for him again.

The one time when Finch ran into Dorian, the day after his encounter with Commander Terin, Finch didn't stick around to chat with his old friend or to answer any questions.

"What happened?" Dorian had asked with concern.

Finch had ignored him and walked on. He was hurt that Dorian hadn't been there when he needed him but he didn't want a confrontation with his friend. He knew Dorian was hurting in his own way and he knew it was selfish of him to be so upset that he couldn't find Dorian after the run-in with Terin. He wasn't sure what was going on with Dorian and the maid but Finch was not in the mood to deal with it. He was upset but he knew it would pass.

Finch forced himself to dress. He didn't care about being tidy. What did it matter? He didn't want to attend the meeting at all. He didn't want to be involved with the group or draw any sort of attention to himself. He just wanted to disappear. However, he knew if he didn't show up, Hayes would be angry and either send someone after him or come drag him to the meeting himself. Finch knew he would only be humiliated and then forced to explain himself. That was something he wanted to avoid at all costs. So, he headed to the meeting on his own.

When he arrived, the others had already gathered. Because of his delay, the meeting had commenced without him. Conversation halted for a moment as Finch entered. Hayes's eyes widened at the state of Finch's face but he thankfully continued the discussion as if nothing had happened, quickly drawing attention away from Finch once again. Finch found a spot in the corner of the room, partially hidden in shadows to better obscure himself and his bruised face.

Commander Terin smirked, seeing the destruction he'd caused. Finch refused to meet the animosity in the commander's gaze. He tried to act as if nothing had happened. He forced himself not to touch his aching nose and cheekbone. He forced his eyes wide open even though his right eye was nearly swollen shut.

Finch commanded himself to focus on the meeting and was dismayed at what he heard.

"There have been reports of Nox and the army of Freiwade moving towards Castille once again," Sir Hayes announced. "The scout we stationed to keep an eye on the camp reports that the camp packed up and the army is moving onwards towards Castille with Nox at the lead."

Finch's heart dropped to his feet. They'd run out of time and much sooner than they'd anticipated.

"Is there any report on Mage Corin's progress and physical state?" one of the knights asked.

"He's training once again but his injury inhibits him greatly. It's not hopeful that he'll be ready to face Nox," Hayes reported honestly. "We have to prepare for the worst."

There were murmurs among those gathered. Finch heard Commander Terin softly say, "This is the cause of poor leadership. We never should have rested so much on that boy."

"Our main objective," Hayes called them back to attention, "will be to defend the castle and the people within it." Sir Hayes hesitated as if he might say more but decided against it.

Finch noticed that the king and Clifton were both absent from the meeting. Everyone was busy making preparations and readying themselves for the horrible clash which would soon take place. Only Cal was standing in the corner unobtrusively as usual.

Hayes continued, "We must make the castle as stable as possible for an attack from both the outside and the inside."

That comment caused silence to fill the room. Finally, Remus, the archer, spoke the question they were all thinking about. "What do you mean from the inside?"

Hayes sighed. "There are other threats in our midst besides Nox and Freiwade's army. There are enemy spies in the castle. We have long suspected it and now we believe it is fact. We're not sure who those spies are but we must discover their identities. They've already leaked valuable information to the enemy and threatened our mages. We can't afford our plans for this final conflict to reach the enemy's ears. We must all be on guard around all of the nobles in the castle as well. Several nobles are suspected to be conspiring with the King of Freiwade to overtake King Rupert. We can't trust anyone. Even those in leadership positions must be watched carefully." Hayes looked directly at Terin as he said those words.

Finch's eyes went unwillingly to his commander. Had Terin done something? Had he shown disloyalty to the king? He was a cruel, unforgiving beast of a man but Finch hadn't expected him to betray Ashnah.

"Our main goal is to fortify the castle and keep a lookout for suspicious activity. More instructions will be given soon."

Finch noticed that Sir Hayes looked incredibly tired. There was a lot that he wasn't telling them at the current time. Finch wondered how much worse things could get. Hayes had been discreet in what he'd revealed during the meeting. Perhaps he didn't trust Commander Terin and didn't want to risk revealing anything potentially damaging.

"The ambush against Nox was a tremendous success," Hayes stated, changing the topic. "It bought us some valuable time. But we are still at war and must treat every day as such. We must ready ourselves and prepare for the worst. There are a lot of pieces moving into place. I hope to divulge more information soon. In the meantime, be on guard and do what you can to ready yourselves. You're dismissed."

Finch hurriedly headed for the exit but Hayes was too fast. He grabbed onto Finch's arm, forcing him to stay behind. Finch whipped around, at first terrified that it was Commander Terin who had a hold of him. He relaxed when he saw that it was only Hayes even though he didn't want the conversation and questions he knew were coming.

Hayes waited for everyone to leave, keeping a loose hold on Finch's arm to keep him from running away. It wasn't painful by any means and Finch knew that Hayes would never hurt him. He also understood why the man was holding him in place. It was the only thing that prevented the escape that Finch so desperately desired. The room emptied except for Cal who stood uncertainly nearby. Hayes gestured for him to go and Cal readily obliged, leaving Finch and Hayes alone. Hayes released Finch as soon as the door closed behind Cal.

"What happened?" Hayes asked immediately.

At least, Finch thought, Hayes always got straight to the point.

"I ran into a door," Finch deadpanned.

Hayes sighed heavily. "Was it Commander Terin?"

Finch shrugged. There was no need for an answer. An expression of anger flashed across Hayes's face but he quickly masked it. Hayes looked to the door and for a moment Finch thought the man would storm out and find the commander to confront him.

"Please don't," Finch said brokenly. "It will only make things worse."

Hayes's expression turned to sadness. He knew that Finch was right. He knew he couldn't interfere.

"I've tried to talk to King Rupert about him," Hayes said. "He's a brute and a liability. He shouldn't be in such a position of power. And now... it's quite possible he's working with the enemy."

"But he's talented and effective," Finch muttered, knowing why the king had overlooked the commander's violent tendencies. The man was a prodigy with his bow. The only archer who could come close to surpassing him was Finch himself. But he was too young and much too irresponsible to ever be put in such a position of leadership. Besides, most of the archers respected and admired Terin. Finch was the exception to that rule.

Hayes looked at Finch long and hard. "This can't go on. He could have broken your nose."

"It isn't broken though," Finch responded.

Hayes shook his head. "He could have. He *would* have."

Finch looked away. "You could suggest the king reassign me to the ranger's division."

Hayes appeared disgusted at the suggestion. "I would sooner kill the commander myself than waste your potential with the rangers. Besides, it wouldn't be right to punish you for his wrongdoing."

Finch stepped close to Hayes. "It wouldn't be punishing me. It would be an escape."

Hayes's expression soured further.

Finch pressed on, pleading, "Please, just let me disappear. It would be better for everyone if I did."

Hayes planted a firm hand on Finch's shoulder. "It wouldn't be better for everyone. Trust me when I say *he* is the only one who would benefit from you disappearing."

"Then let him! He's won anyway." Finch choked out the last sentence, feeling emotion rise fast in his chest.

Hayes's eyes were filled with compassion that only added to the ache behind Finch's ribs.

"With this war, we need you at the castle. We need your strategy, bravery, and ingenuity. More than that, I refuse to lose you because of what the commander has done. I refuse to let Terin win."

"He already has," Finch repeated.

"No!" Hayes objected, raising his voice. "He hasn't won and he never will. As long as you keep fighting, he won't win. Even if he doesn't face justice in this life, he'll face it in the next. Be sure of that."

Finch brushed away Hayes's hand, desperate to change the subject. "I know you weren't telling us everything during the meeting. What were you hiding? What's going on?"

Hayes stepped away and sunk into a nearby chair, weary and accepting the change in conversation. "It's Duke Heirson. We suspect that he's making his move against the king. Corin was nearly poisoned. We think Heirson was behind it. And Terin has been caught conspiring with the duke, though he hasn't committed to turn against the king. Corin is struggling to perform magic at all with his injury and he's hopelessly far from being able to face Nox. The spies are becoming an even greater threat too. We think the spies might be working for the duke as well as the king of Freiwade because Heirson always seems to know when something's happened before anyone else does. Cal thinks that Heirson is conspiring directly with the king of Freiwade. Either way, it's obvious he's planning to rebel against King Rupert. He's being subtle about it. He's trying to forge an alliance between Ruena and his son, Dresden. With everything going on and the threat that the duke poses, King Rupert is considering negotiating with Freiwade. He may even sign a treaty which would be detrimental to Ashnah to end the war before it goes any further."

Finch was shocked at the information and how much worse things were than what he'd expected. "The king of Freiwade would never accept a treaty unless King Rupert forfeited all of Ashnah," Finch objected.

Hayes nodded in agreement. "I know that King Rupert's primary goal is to save the people of Ashnah and he refuses to fight a war that we are sure to lose. I've tried to talk him out of it but if worse comes to worse and the situation seems hopeless, I doubt I can convince him to fight."

Finch was horrified that the outcome seemed so determined. "Is there any chance of victory?"

Hayes looked weary as he answered, "For us to win this war, we need a miracle. Corin will have to be able to win against Nox. Everything rests on him."

CHAPTER 59

Corin continued to attend his lessons with Clifton despite how much it terrified him to do so. He had to keep training, no matter how he felt about magic and the power coursing through his veins. It was a gift, he kept reminding himself. He had to trust in God to help him use it. Corin managed to quell his fear enough to do basic magic. He was able to use the skill to produce light, though the light still startled him every time it appeared. He still worried he would lose control of his ability again. He couldn't help but flinch every time the magic came to the surface. He also knew there was no helping it. He had to use the magic whether he liked it or feared it. Corin found himself dissatisfied after every lesson. He wasn't doing enough. He was letting his fear control him. He would never be ready to face Nox. But at least Clifton seemed pleased with his progress. Though, Corin wondered if it was just an act. He knew he was moving too slowly. He knew he was nowhere near close enough to be ready to face Nox. He never would be. The magic that once came so easily to him was now terrifying and difficult. Corin found himself sweating at even the simplest acts of magic both from difficulty, pain, and anxiety. His arm ached continually and the herbal teas and foul-smelling salves that the physicians gave him made little impact on the injury.

Despite the achingly slow progress, he was improving and, more importantly, he was getting better at hiding the fear he felt whenever he used magic. However, any magic that required the use of both hands was impossible. He could only move the shoulder of his right arm and he was unable to perform any difficult magic because of it. He couldn't fight back against a threat at the rate he was learning. He could hardly defend himself. Clifton's concern at Corin's failing abilities was evident.

"You'll get there," Clifton kept saying as if to reassure himself as much as Corin. Corin didn't believe it and he doubted Clifton did either.

Sir Hayes had come to watch him train one day to try to find a solution to make up for his inability to use his right arm. It was to no avail. Corin felt like an animal on display at a circus who was ill-performing and disappointing to all who had paid to attend.

He knew he had to do something, anything, to better prepare for what was coming. He prayed and prayed for a solution but none presented itself. He was busy attempting to strengthen his shielding ability when Cal knocked twice at the door to Clifton's office and then entered the room. The spy's face was grim and Corin and Clifton both stopped what they were doing when they saw him. Corin knew instantly that something was wrong. His fears were confirmed when Cal spoke.

"We've received a report that Nox is moving

again and heading for Castille," Cal reported.

Corin was glad that he was in the loop of information now but this particular information felt like a rock lodged in his stomach.

With a lump in his throat, Corin forced out the dreaded question, "How long do we have?"

"Weeks, days, we're not sure. We're trying to slow him down but it's only stalling for time."

The rest of the statement hung silently in the air. Corin wasn't ready. He wouldn't be ready in time.

"We're trying to find a way to face Nox when he arrives at the castle," Cal explained. "The king is preparing for all eventualities."

Corin didn't like the sound of that. "What does that mean?"

"A treaty," Clifton answered for Cal.

"A surrender," Cal reiterated.

If they had any hope of winning the war, or even surviving it, it depended on Corin. They were doomed.

Clifton, seeming to sense Corin's growing dread spoke, "What about Duke Heirson?"

Cal's look turned even more dour. "We'll have to confront him sooner rather than later. He's made an ultimatum of sorts."

"What sort of ultimatum?" Corin asked, dreading the answer.

"Duke Heirson has proposed a marriage between Ruena and his son, Dresden."

Corin felt sick. Not Ruena. Not a marriage to the son of that monster who'd tried to have him killed and wanted to overthrow the king.

"We won't let it happen," Cal assured him. "But

if we refuse outright, it will cause the duke to move against us even quicker. He might not wait for aid from Freiwade."

Corin didn't care about the duke anymore. "What about Ruena? Is she alright?"

Cal's expression softened. "She was in shock at the duke's idea. She was alone with him and Dresden when he suggested it. But she's alright. She's avoiding Heirson and Dresden at all costs so she can stall in giving them an answer. One way or another, it will all be over soon."

Corin's mind raced at all of the new revelations. He wanted desperately to see Ruena and talk to her. And he wanted to sort through his thoughts.

"Clifton, can I be excused to have some time to think?" Corin asked.

Clifton hesitated then nodded.

Corin didn't waste any time before heading straight for the empty room where he so often met Ruena. He found her there, sitting on the window sill and looking out at the gardens as she always did. Corin cleared his throat awkwardly and she startled. She spun to face him and offered a weak smile.

"Corin, I'm surprised to see you."

"Is it true that the duke wants you to marry his son?" Corin jumped right to the point.

Ruena cringed and Corin had his answer. He moved to sit next to her. She didn't quite look at him.

"Yeah," she finally said.

Corin took a deep breath and mustered his courage before reaching for her hand with his good arm. She flinched, having not expected the gesture. Corin felt his heart thundering in his chest. Never had he been so bold with anyone, especially a girl. Tears started to gather in Ruena's eyes and Corin started to pull back his hand, worrying that he had overstepped. Ruena latched onto his hand and held tight. She brushed the tears away from her eyes with her other hand.

"Are you alright?" Corin asked.

She nodded. "I always expected something like this to happen. It's part of my position as the king's niece. I accepted it. It just caught me off guard how direct and demanding Duke Heirson was. It made me feel like I didn't have a say in the matter."

Corin felt a lump lodge in his throat. His heart was filled with sympathy for her. He wished she hadn't been alone to face such a question, more a demand than anything.

"I know I won't have to go through with it," she said, "but I've heard terrible things about the duke and after what he tried to do to you, it made me afraid to have his attention fixed on me."

"I'm sorry you had to face it alone," Corin told her.

"I'm not alone now," Ruena answered. She took a deep breath. "Did you come just to see me?"

"I was worried about you."

She smiled. "I've been worried about you too."

Corin frowned. "Why?"

"A lot's happened. I didn't want you to lose yourself amid all the chaos we're facing. I didn't want you to be overwhelmed or discouraged."

"I'm trying not to be."

"Something's wrong though. What is it?" Ruena asked.

"Cal just came to Clifton's office. He told us that Nox is moving towards Ashnah again. That was when I heard about the duke's conversation with you. I'm not even close to being ready to face Nox. I never will be. I might have managed it before, even that is a big 'might', but now with my injury, I could never win. I can hardly defend myself."

Ruena squeezed his hand again, tighter than before. "We'll find a way. This injury isn't going to stop you. You're too smart for that."

Corin appreciated her words of reassurance but he knew that it was useless to hope. "I can't win. Not without my right arm. I can't even do the simplest kinds of magic because I need both hands to do it. Maybe... maybe I could come up with something if I could only use my right hand."

Ruena was silent and Corin's head whirled. He glanced at his limp, useless hand, filled with frustration. He repeated his earlier words, "If only I could use my right hand."

From somewhere deep in the back of his mind came a thought. It seemed to appear out of nowhere and Corin was thrown completely off-kilter by it. If he could use his right hand? Maybe... no... but maybe.

Corin leapt to his feet.

"What's wrong?" Ruena asked him frantically.

A crazed smile crossed Corin's face. "Nothing's wrong!" Corin practically shouted. "For the first time in a long time, something might be right. I have to go but I'll see you again soon, Ruena."

He didn't wait for a response before he raced off, a flash of hope in his heart that hadn't been there for a very long time.

CHAPTER 60

Corin hurried to Clifton's office with a purpose in mind. He rushed inside without even thinking to knock. Corin instantly felt embarrassed when he saw Clifton's shocked face at his sudden entrance.

"Corin, is something wrong?" Clifton asked, surprised that Corin hadn't knocked as he always did.

Corin's mind was racing. He couldn't stop to explain himself. He ignored Clifton and headed straight for the bookshelf. There was a specific book, one of the first that Corin had seen during his training, one that Clifton had shown him after he'd caught him running across the castle grounds.

"What are you doing?" Clifton asked again.

With his heart racing with excitement, Corin couldn't find the book. Fortunately, Will was there, looking for answers as he had so diligently been doing ever since Corin's injury.

"Will, where is volume IV of Neos Loch's journals?"

Will leaped up from his seat, eager to be of help. He immediately found the book and handed it to Corin. Corin's fingers brushed against the worn spine and he clumsily reached for it with his still-awkward left hand. He couldn't open the book and look through it right then and there which frustrated him, but he was too excited for the frustration to last. He might have finally found a way to practice the more complicated magic again. All hope might not be lost. Corin flung the book on the nearest free surface, Clifton's desk, and flipped it open, hurriedly rifling through the pages and struggling to do so with his less adept hand. He felt Clifton's curious stare and sensed his mentor moving closer, confused and enthralled by Corin's behavior. Will hovered just over his shoulder.

Corin focused on the task at hand. He found the page he was looking for. The enhancing ability. It was the skill that had allowed Corin perseverance and speed when he ran. It was the magic he had been unintentionally using for some time before he even knew he was a mage. Corin read the instructions for the skill once again:

> The enhancing ability is used to give a mage the strength or endurance to perform tasks they would normally be incapable of. It enhances the mage's natural abilities to make them stronger, faster, or more resilient. The mage should concentrate on the part of their body that they wish to enhance. A bit of uncomfortable tingling is common with this magic.

Yes, surely it could be used for what he intended it for. He wanted to make sure he did everything right. Clifton's eyes lit up with understanding. He must have recognized the thought running through Corin's mind. There was hope in Clifton's eyes, just as there was in Corin's. Will shifted eagerly from foot to foot.

"It could work," Clifton voiced in awe. "I can't

believe I never thought of it."

"Me too," Will agreed.

Corin took a step away from the book, readying himself to start the magic. Corin closed his eyes for a moment and focused. He was almost afraid to hope. What if it didn't work? Corin didn't think he could accept that. He would lose all hope. Nox would win. Ashnah would lose the war. And Corin would have no chance of ever being able to practice complicated magic or use his arm again. It had to work. It had to.

Corin took a steadying breath. The only thing he could do was try. He summoned everything within himself. *Please, God, let this work,* he prayed. Then Corin focused on his injured arm.

Nothing. Corin was frozen in shock. Nothing happened. He steadied himself and tried again with more certainty.

The pain was instant. The magic was supposed to be accompanied by an uncomfortable tingling at worst. However, the pain Corin felt was far worse than that. Corin doubled over with the force of it. It felt like his arm was being swallowed by the magic again. It felt like it was crumbling away. All of the pain of the initial injury returned in a rush. Corin collapsed to his knees, releasing the magic. He knelt on the ground panting, not sure if it had even worked. Clifton and Will knelt beside him.

"Are you alright?" Clifton asked.

Corin felt like he might sob with hopelessness.

"What happened?" Will questioned.

Corin shook his head. He didn't know. "It should have worked," he said as despair swallowed him up. Why hadn't it worked?

But Clifton had the opposite reaction. The mage's eyes widened and he smiled broadly. "It did work. It had to have worked. The pain is a sign that you regained feeling in your arm."

Corin pushed himself back to sit instead of kneel. He spoke through his continuing agony, "It doesn't matter. I still can't use my arm because of the pain."

Will stood and started pacing, deep in thought. "Not necessarily," he said. He didn't say anything further for a moment, thinking deeply.

Corin and Clifton watched the boy. Corin had to fight back the tears from the pain that still faintly throbbed in his arm and the failure that weighed heavily in his heart.

Will moved to the bookcase and pulled down several books, flipping through them and then putting them back until he finally seemed to find what he was looking for. "Here it is!" He pulled down an old volume and rifled through the pages until he found a certain section then brought it over to show Corin.

Will offered the book to Corin who set it on his lap and confusedly studied the pages.

"I knew Neos Loch had written it somewhere," Will explained. "I remembered it because it seemed strange to me that although a mage couldn't heal themselves, there were certain uses of magic to ease pain. I found this while I was looking for something to heal your arm but I discounted it at first because the fisherman still had use of his arm to some extent."

Corin read the pages that detailed the story of a fisherman in Skellas who had mutilated his arm in an accident at sea. The man had been in severe pain to the point where he couldn't work. Many in his village thought it would be best to amputate his arm although he could still use the limb. Then suddenly the man began to recover, or at least, partially so. He was able to go back to work, use his arm, and provide for his family. However, when he wasn't working, he had to keep his arm in a sling to ease his pain. The story explained that the man had told Loch when questioned that it was magic that he was using and that he had found a way to alleviate his pain for short periods so he could work and provide for his family. It was a difficult skill and he swore Loch to secrecy to not reveal him as a mage to the king. But he allowed Loch to record the account in his writings in case it might be used in the future for good. The book then detailed the instructions for the magic and warned that the effects were temporary. If a mage relied on magic to quell the pain, the intensity would build up. Once the magic was released, the pain would be worse than it was before.

Corin finished reading and felt amazed and hopeful. This could be the way to fix his arm, at least temporarily so he could use his magic again to fight Nox. But a thought occurred to him. "Wait, this would mean I would have to use two different abilities at once, three if I want to fight back. Is that even possible?"

Clifton hesitated. "I'm not sure," he admitted. "To my knowledge, it's never been done before. But if it can be done, you would be the one to be able to accomplish it, Corin."

Corin wasn't so sure about that but he knew that if he didn't try, the hopelessness would overtake him. He could only pray that it would work. It *had* to work, for all of their sakes. Corin readied himself, worried that the pain would return and fearful that the magic would expand out of his control once again. He was so, so scared. But it was the only chance he had. He took a deep breath, knowing he only had one shot to get it right and the pain would come, he just had to cut it off as quickly as possible.

He summoned the magic that allowed him to use his arm again.

The pain was instant and overpowering. He fought through it and followed the second instruction to quell the pain. The pain was still terrible. Corin grit his teeth and tried again, forcing his willpower to greater strength than ever before. The pain vanished.

One moment it was there and the next it was gone. Corin froze, breathing heavily, and completely shocked. He did it. It worked. Clifton and Will stared at him as Corin lifted his right arm and, for the first time since the accident, flexed his fingers. Corin gasped and did it again. There was no pain. The movement was easy and fluid like the injury had never happened in the first place. Corin sobbed in relief. His chest was filled with the throbbing of relief and surprise. *Thank you, God. Thank you!* Corin silently exclaimed. Will let out a shout of excitement. Clifton laughed and pulled Corin into a hug. Corin hung on with both hands.

Just then there was a knock at the door.

"Who is it?" Clifton asked.

"It's me, Ruena."

Corin smiled broadly. His eyes lit up.

"Come in, Ruena," he called.

Ruena opened the door. "Corin, I've been looking everywhere for you. I was worried since you ran off so quickly."

Corin didn't let her finish. His heart pounded with relief so great that he thought he might burst. He rushed towards Ruena and pulled her into a hug. Ruena froze in shock. It took her a second before she realized what was happening and pushed him away. She stared at him with her mouth agape and her eyes wide. Her eyes glistened as she saw his arm lifted and his fingers grasping her own hand.

She cried out in surprise and joy. "Your arm!"

Corin grinned so wide his cheeks hurt. "We found a way," he told her. "It's only temporary but it's enough."

Then it was Ruena's turn to pull him into an embrace. She held him tight and Corin held her with equal intensity, relishing the feeling of wrapping both of his arms around her. Ruena rested her head on his shoulder and tears soaked through the fabric of his tunic. Corin didn't mind. He was so relieved he felt dizzy. He eventually pulled away from Ruena, blushing a little and realizing that the rules of friendship might have classified that hug as too long. Besides, Clifton and Will were still standing there watching him. But Ruena smiled at him and he smiled back. Corin felt for the first time like everything would be alright.

"Remember, Corin," Clifton stepped in, "there's another part of the magic. You still need to try to conduct a third skill of offense. You should try levitation, the ability I taught you during one of your first lessons."

Corin nodded, joy still surging in his chest. He raised both hands and with only a little difficulty he levitated a book towards him. He laughed with delight and relief. Ruena and Clifton smiled alongside him.

"I believe we've accomplished enough for the day," Clifton announced happily. "You shouldn't overdo it, Corin. Release the magic and get some rest."

Corin reluctantly agreed. Half of him didn't want to stop the progress of the day but he knew that Clifton was right and he was feeling tired like he hadn't felt since his days of training with Sir Burke and the squires of Nevara. Corin stretched the fingers of his right hand one more time, relishing the movement, and then he released the magic.

In an instant, he was overcome with an intense pain that drove him to his knees. Corin gasped in agony and clutched his arm. Ruena and Clifton rushed to his side.

"What's happening?" Ruena demanded anxiously.

"Corin!" Will cried out.

Corin's vision went blurry with the intensity of the pain. It was like nothing he'd ever felt before. He could hear Ruena calling his name and then the world went black.

CHAPTER 61

Cal called the spies to gather for a meeting. It was time they discussed the latest developments and came up with a new plan of action. Cal only prayed that whatever they came up with it would work. He had a headache that refused to go away and his mind was elsewhere. He was busy thinking of Ruena and Corin and the trials both of them faced. He had heard news immediately before coming to the meeting that Corin had found a way to use his arm again but that the pain which came after the magic was released was so excruciating that it had rendered the young man unconscious. Cal had gone to see Corin himself and although he'd been pale and a little shaky, he was awake again and seemed to only be in a little remaining pain. It probably improved his mood that Ruena hadn't left his side.

"I did it, Cal," Corin had said with too much optimism. "I can face Nox. I can fulfill my duty and save us."

Cal felt only pain at seeing his new friend in such a state and knowing that Corin would be forced to endure the pain again. Cal wished they could tell him he didn't have to risk himself against the enemy mage but they were desperate. There was no other choice.

Clifton had pulled Cal aside, out of Corin's hearing afterwards. "Although this new magic is a great breakthrough, it's only a crutch. Corin will be able to use it to face Nox but he'll have to be careful. The longer he uses the magic, the greater the pain that will follow. If Corin isn't careful, I'm afraid he could build up so much pain that when it's released, his heart will stop."

Cal had looked back into the room at the young man, the boy, recovering. Ruena sat at his side watching him with concern-filled eyes.

They were all too young for this. The last thing Cal wanted was for Corin to sacrifice himself to win the war. Would it come to that? Was there any other choice? Cal wished he could take Corin's place but he knew he couldn't face Nox head-on. He would if he could. Finch's ambush had been the closest any of them could get to taking out the enemy mage. Maybe it would have been better to kill Nox in his sleep. In the end, it would be up to Corin and Clifton to face Nox and stop him. All Cal could do was eliminate any other threats that might stand in the way.

Cal voiced this to the other spies, "We need to take care of the duke."

There was no argument to that.

Lark cracked her knuckles. "Just say when."

Cal shook his head, knowing it was only an act, though they all carried a little resentment towards Duke Heirson, especially after learning how he had treated Dusk. Cal wasn't thrilled with the man's conversation with Ruena either. Cal hoped that Lark meant what she said. He still had to find time to apologize for doubting her. Dusk was right, he had to be cautious but he had to go on trusting for now until there was actual proof that she was working for the enemy. But there wasn't time for an apology and Cal hadn't been able to come up with the right words to face her.

Lark turned more serious. "How do we stop Heirson? He's not likely to admit that he's conspiring with the enemy and if the king accuses him and imprisons him but he denies it, it will only cause distrust and alienation of the other nobility. The duke is highly respected. He has too many allies."

Cal knew that she was right. Accusing the duke without sufficient evidence would only lead the nobility to rebel. The letters that proved him guilty had been destroyed years ago. They couldn't find a solid connection between him amassing a private army and wanting to overthrow the king. It would make sense for Duke Heirson to be building his forces to protect his land since it rested on the border of Freiwade and Ashnah. The same could be said for the alliances he was creating with other nobles. But there had to be something they could do.

Dusk stepped forward. "I can get him to confess to his crimes."

Cal and Lark stood from their chairs.

"You'd be putting your life at risk by facing him," Lark said.

"He'll try to kill you," Cal agreed. "You would be revealing your identity if you did face him. There would be no turning back."

"I've already thought through every outcome.

It's the only way. It's not logical for me to hide away while Corin, Clifton, and King Rupert's lives are on the line as well as the entire kingdom being at stake. For a while, hiding was the best way I could serve. I was able to survive and preserve the information that has now become useful to the kingdom. However, it's time I step into the light. The duke will be surprised to see that his son is still alive. He'll be more surprised to see that I have a position in the castle, as a spy no less. By revealing myself to him, I'll put him off balance. That will offer the perfect opportunity to strike."

"It will be your word against his," Lark reminded him. "He's accused you of insanity already. Are you sure you want to take that risk?"

Dusk responded somberly. "That's why I'll have to speak to the king first. I'll admit to everything and apologize for the secrets I've kept. Hopefully, I've proven myself over the years and he'll trust my word. I believe having the kingdom's spymaster vouch for me will help matters."

Cal nodded, a silent agreement that he would do so readily. "It's time the duke was knocked off his high horse. It's time he faces the judgment he deserves."

Those words rang through Cal's ears as he walked closely behind Lark and Dusk. The king, Sir Hayes, and Ruena followed closely. They approached the duke's door and an ominous air settled around them. At least the conversation with the king had gone better than expected. The man was rightfully surprised at Dusk's confession of being Everett Heirson, the first son of Duke Heirson, previously believed to have died from insanity. However, it was obvious that Dusk didn't fit the description of the rumors his father had spread. He seemed the most sane of the spies in many regards. The king listened quietly as he shared his story and Cal vouched for him. Then the ruler spoke.

"This is quite the surprise, Everett. I believe you. I've never trusted the duke and I knew you as a child. I always found it hard to believe that you went insane. I'm only amazed that I didn't recognize who you were sooner. But if Cal assures me that you're telling the truth, then that's good enough for me. I can't condone your secrecy and it would have been beneficial to everyone if you had shared what you knew sooner. However, I can understand the fear you felt and I'm sorry that you ever felt the need to hide who you were. I believe it's a gift in disguise that you've revealed this now and that you came to this castle in the first place, risking yourself when you could have stayed hidden and started a new life. God led you here for a purpose such as this, it seems."

Dusk seemed amazed at the king's words. There was more emotion on his face than Cal was accustomed to seeing. He bowed his head in gratitude. His next words seemed to be a declaration less directed to the king than to himself.

"I've always struggled to find my place, Your Majesty. I never fit in the courts. I grew talented at putting on an act. I enjoyed my studies more than the socialization required for my position. I felt out of place in my family and then abandoned by them altogether. I never fully felt like a member of the spies because I knew I was keeping things from them and I could never truly be myself. However, I've come to learn that what you've said is true, God has led me here. He's led me everywhere I've gone in life. No matter what troubles I've faced, He's been there. Coming to this castle taught me that. Cal taught me that. More than anything, I am grateful to the people of Castille for that truth being imprinted on my heart. I am grateful for the salvation I found here. I know I've done wrong, but I hope from now on to do right in the eyes of you King Rupert, and most importantly, in the eyes of God."

Cal had never heard such heartfelt words from Dusk before. He smiled a little at his friend. He was grateful that Dusk had found his way to the castle, despite the challenges that had led him there.

It didn't take long for the king to agree to their plan of confronting Duke Heirson and before long they were all heading for the duke's chambers.

Cal stepped closer to his friend and murmured in Dusk's ear, "It's not too late to change your mind."

Dusk shook his head. The movement was almost imperceptible. His mind was set. There was only one thing left to say.

"I'm proud to call you my friend," Cal told Dusk.

Dusk didn't have a chance to answer because the king moved forward to knock on the duke's door. Dusk took a position in the back of the group, hiding himself until the right moment. He pulled the hood of his cloak over his face, casting it in shadow. Duke Heirson answered the door and stood in surprise, seeing the king as well as Sir Hayes and all the others standing there.

"Your Majesty," the duke said, a note of uncertainty and unease creeping into his voice.

King Rupert offered a hard smile. "May we come in?"

The duke hesitantly stepped aside and allowed them to move into the room. Dresden stood from where he had been sitting at the room's small table and hastily bowed.

The king strode purposefully into the room. Duke Heirson and Dresden both stiffened, expecting trouble.

King Rupert cleared his throat and folded his hands together. "I believe we are overdue for a talk, duke," the king stated.

"I'm not sure I understand what you are referring to, Your Majesty?"

The king hummed. "As you know, the war is quickly approaching. It seems that the threats posed are not only from outside our borders but also creeping within like a slow-spreading *poison*." The king emphasized the last word.

Duke Heirson flinched almost imperceptibly but quickly masked the movement.

The king went on, "You've made quite the proposal to my niece, Duke Heirson."

The duke visibly relaxed, interpreting the visit as a response to the proposal. "Yes, Your Majesty. As I'm sure you can see, an alliance between your niece and my son would be a wise connection, a connection of strength and power as well as a tactical advantage to the kingdom."

The king looked to Ruena before facing the duke once again. "Yes, I'm sure it would be. That is if I could trust you, Duke Heirson."

"Whatever do you mean?" the duke

questioned.

"Rumors have been circulating for some time now that certain members of the nobility plan to conspire with the enemy, King Histen Corpin of Freiwade, to overthrow the kingdom of Ashnah and the Castille lineage."

"Your Majesty!" the duke exclaimed in horror.

The king waved him off and continued, "Certain… unexpected sources have come forth and declared that you are one of those nobles. In fact, you are the leader of the coup. You are accused of treachery, Duke Heirson. What say you to that accusation?"

"I object vehemently, Your Majesty! The accuser is a traitor himself and a fool for spreading such rumors."

Dusk stepped forward, letting the hood shadowing his face fall. "Is that what I am, father, a fool?"

The duke froze, horror seeping into every inch of his body. "Impossible!" he exclaimed. "G…ghost!"

"Everett," Dresden stammered.

Dusk strode forward but Cal could see that his confidence was only an act. He could see the slight tremble of fear in his friend's stature. "I am very much alive, Father, despite your best efforts and the rumors you have been spreading to the contrary."

Duke Heirson looked to the king, pleading, "Your Majesty, you cannot believe anything this man says. He is not my son. My son is dead. He was a madman, driven to insanity. He died in a horrible accident."

"Do I look insane to you?" Dusk asked the duke.

"Father, brother, look at me. Is it madness to confront a monster? Is it madness to take a stand when I had discovered the most horrifying truths about someone I had once trusted?"

The duke looked stricken, Dresden even more so.

"If what he says is true, Your Majesty, why wouldn't he come forward with such information sooner?" the duke objected.

"You know why," Dusk stated. "You threatened me. You drove me out of my own home and sent men to kill me. You discredited any claims I may have made by declaring me mad. It was my word against yours. I knew I would have to prove myself as trustworthy before I could make my claim against you. I started in the castle as a nobody and worked my way up, proving my loyalty and my sanity. It killed me to keep the secret of your treachery for so long but I had no other choice. When your actions against the king started to be revealed even without my testimony, I knew it was time to step forth. I have no sufficient proof except that I am alive and sane, discrediting that aspect of your story."

"He's lying. He's a fraud, a fraud I tell you!" the duke pleaded with the king. "My son is dead! This man has no proof against me."

"He's telling the truth," Dresden spoke. "That is my brother. That is the brother I tried to kill at my father's command. Everett, my brother."

The duke turned on his son, angry beyond measure. "What are you saying? Why would you admit to such a thing?"

Beads of sweat were forming on Dresden's

forehead but he spoke, "I can't stand any more of the lies. Everett was right to be angry at you for betraying the kingdom. It's all a lie. All of it! The king of Freiwade won't honor our alliance. King Rupert may be weak but so are you, father. The truth can't be hidden any longer. Everett is alive. He's told them everything. We have to accept the consequences of our actions." Dresden turned to the king and the others. "It's all true. We have been associating with the king of Freiwade. He offered us the throne if we helped overthrow you from the inside. We built an army at our dukedom; we gathered support from the other nobles who believed the king was incapable of leading Ashnah through war and dissatisfied with Ruena as an heir. We planned to overthrow King Rupert by eliminating the mages. My father came up with the idea of arranging a marriage between myself and Ruena to better establish our position once the king was gone."

Cal stepped forward. "How did you stay in contact with the king of Freiwade?"

"We were never in direct contact with him. There were spies stationed at the castle. They reported to us and the king. They sent word from us to Freiwade as needed and vice versa," Dresden explained.

Cal felt a thrill of excitement surge through his chest. Finally. Finally, they would find out the identity of the spies. "Who are they? Who are the spies? As spymaster of Ashnah, I will grant you a lighter sentence, Dresden, if you reveal their identities."

The duke grabbed hold of his son. "No! Don't tell them anymore. You've done enough damage."

Dresden jerked his arm free from his father's grasp. "I've had enough lies and deceit. I will tell them everything and maybe they'll let me spend the rest of my days in a dungeon instead of hanging me for my crimes. The spies are…" his words were cut off, ending in a gurgle as a knife appeared sticking out from his throat. His eyes widened as a river of blood silenced his confession.

Everyone jumped in surprise as Dresden fell to the ground. Cal jerked his head to look in the direction the knife had come from. There was a vent in the corner of the room. It was one of the same vents that Lark used when she was spying.

"Lark, go after them!" Cal called.

The young woman ran towards him without hesitation. Cal offered his hands for her to use as a springboard and she leaped into the vent, taking off after the assassin. Cal said a silent prayer that she would be okay. He turned his attention back to the scene unfolding in front of him. Dresden lay on the ground, dying. They wouldn't be getting any answers out of him. He gasped for breath through his ragged throat, gurgling on blood. The duke looked on with disgust and a hint of sadness but Dusk knelt at his brother's side. He cradled Dresden's body and rocked him gently, his little brother. Tears seeped from Dusk's eyes and silent sobs wracked his body.

"Dresden, listen to me," Dusk said with a thick voice. His brother was barely hanging on. He would be gone in a matter of moments. "I don't blame you for any of this. I love you. I'm so, so sorry things turned out this way. But this is important. There is a God and He cares about you. He sent His Son to die for you, that Son's name is Jesus. Repent and believe in Him and you will be saved. You won't suffer any longer, I promise. Please, please do it. I love you Dresden and I'm sorry."

Cal approached his friend, feeling his heart throb with sympathy. Dresden may have betrayed Dusk but he was still his brother. Dresden's eyes were pleading, a silent apology of his own held in the depths of his gaze. He couldn't speak but his eyes expressed plenty. His gaze grew distant then blank as he breathed his last. Dusk's shoulders slumped and Cal rested a hand on his shoulder in silent support.

"Do you think he heard me?" Dusk asked quietly.

Cal answered, "I think in the end, God gives everyone a chance to turn to Him. Think of the thief on the cross. You did what you could, Dusk. The rest was up to Dresden and God."

Dusk nodded.

King Rupert turned to the duke. "Duke Heirson, you are under arrest for your crimes against the kingdom of Ashnah. You are sentenced to hang for your treachery. Sir Hayes, please take him to the dungeons. He'll be extensively questioned later."

As Sir Hayes led the duke away, Duke Heirson leaned towards Dusk. "You deserve to die, you traitor. This is all your doing. All of this is your fault."

Dusk flinched but didn't look at his father. He kept his gaze on his brother's motionless body. The king approached and addressed Dusk. "Arise, Duke Heirson, you've done your kingdom a great service today."

Dusk gently laid his brother aside, closing his

blank eyes and saying a silent prayer over him. Then he rose to face the king. "Your Majesty, Duke Heirson is a traitor and his heir lies dead. My name is Dusk."

CHAPTER 62

Hayes was always in a foul mood when he had to deal with Terin but now so more than ever before. He could hardly stand the thought of the man on a good day. He'd petitioned time and again for the king to dismiss Terin from his command of the archers. But King Rupert had insisted that Terin may be rough around the edges, but his talent with the bow outweighed his lesser qualities. Hayes wasn't so sure. It was important to be skilled, yes. However, it was more important to be able to instill confidence in your men. Hayes had watched Terin as he commanded his archers. Terin wore the men down and demoralized them. He'd stripped them down with insults and outrage until they feared him and followed his every command for fear of the consequences if they didn't. Only a few stayed strong despite Terin's cruelty. The others followed orders blindly and without any passion for their work. They were loyal but they held little respect for their commander. Hayes had warned the king about Terin but King Rupert hadn't listened. Now, things had escalated. Terin was conspiring with Duke Heirson against Ashnah. It was time for Hayes to take matters into his own hands.

He approached Terin's office, a fair-sized room at the base of the stairs that led to the castle parapets. It was rare for Terin to be in his office. He usually hovered among the men stationed on the parapets, criticizing every little thing they did. However, Hayes was willing to wait if he had to. He refused to confront the commander in front of his men. Hayes might dislike Terin but the things he was going to say should not be uttered in front of subordinates. He would disgrace the commander if he did so, which would only make the situation worse. Fortunately, Hayes wouldn't have to wait. Terin was in his office. He seemed to be in the process of leaving, likely to return to the parapets. He looked up at Hayes's entrance and grimaced.

"What?" Terin demanded.

Hayes crossed his arms over his chest and tried to cool his temper. He didn't want to lose his composure. He took a deep breath. "Have a seat, Terin. We need to talk."

Terin continued to stand, obstinate. He went so far as to lean against his desk as if he was bored. He had no qualms of demonstrating absolute disrespect for Hayes. Hayes didn't particularly care if Terin respected him. He certainly wouldn't find himself in the commander's good graces after what he was about to say.

"I'm a busy man, Hayes. If you have something to say, be quick about it."

"Oh, I have plenty I'd *like* to say to you, Terin, but this is a professional discussion."

"Did the king send his pet on an errand for him?" Terin asked petulantly.

Inwardly, Hayes bristled. Outwardly, he stayed calm and immovable. He was used to those types of insults. He was a young battle master, the youngest in the kingdom, perhaps the youngest in the kingdom's history. Few of the other battle masters and commanders of the kingdom thought he had rightfully earned the position. His father had been a respected knight in the kingdom and some believed that had bought Hayes the title of battle master. They couldn't be more wrong. They looked down on someone who they saw as young and inexperienced. However, Hayes was far from inexperienced. He'd seen more battles than most others in the kingdom. The scar on his face was a stark reminder to anyone who dared question his skill.

"It sounds to me like Duke Heirson gave *his* pet a beating," Hayes responded, watching Terin's face for a reaction.

Terin's eyes widened but he quickly masked his surprise. He turned to his desk and started to shuffle a few papers into a pile with one hand while still reclining lazily. "Don't talk nonsense, Hayes, and don't waste my time. What did you come here for?"

"I feel that I've made it abundantly clear in the past that I don't approve of your position as commander of the archers."

Terin scoffed.

Hayes pressed on. "I've tried to convince King Rupert several times to have you removed from your position. I feel that you treat your men poorly. You may be skilled but you are not a fit commander."

Terin grit his teeth. When he spoke, it was with anger and impatience lacing his words. "If you've come to insult me, you can leave. Get to the point, Hayes."

"A trusted source overheard you speaking with Duke Heirson," Hayes said. That finally got the reaction he'd been hoping for.

Terin stiffened, dropping his act of organizing papers. He didn't look at Hayes but his body betrayed his tension and unease.

"Trusted source... rubbish. You're making this up to try to get a rise out of me, aren't you?"

"Is it working?" Hayes asked, trying to hide his pleasure at making Terin squirm.

Terin stood and moved to push past Hayes. Hayes caught Terin's arm, preventing his escape.

"Unhand me!" Terin objected, trying to jerk his arm free of Hayes's grasp.

Hayes's hand held firm, unyielding. He thought of bruises he'd seen on Finch's arms on more than one occasion. He thought of the nearly broken nose, swollen face, and black eyes that the boy almost constantly sported. Hayes tightened his grip until he saw Terin wince with discomfort.

"I've always known you were cruel and callous, Terin, but even I never suspected you were a traitor to the kingdom."

There was fear in Terin's eyes. Hayes was sure it was the first time he had seen such a feeling on Terin's face. He thought of Finch and the other archers who showed that fear whenever they were around Terin. They hunched in on themselves, wavering in their beliefs, and sacrificing their confidence and surety to avoid the possible repercussions. Hayes wanted to see that fear and much more on Terin's face. It was only what the commander deserved.

"I don't know what you heard, Hayes, but you know I would never betray Ashnah." Terin's voice had lost its insult. It became pandering, pleading.

"Why should I believe you?"

Terin looked unsteady as if he was struggling to support his weight. His position was everything to him. If he lost it...

"My source tells me that Duke Heirson tried to persuade you to turn on King Rupert and Ashnah. You hesitated in your answer, Terin. You were considering it. You've been considering it for a long while now."

"Hayes, please."

"What did you tell him, Terin? What did you tell Duke Heirson?"

"I... I said no. I would never betray my kingdom."

"No, not quite. You said you wouldn't put your position in jeopardy. But you were willing to step back and let things unfold as they would as long as Heirson guaranteed your position would be safe if he sat on the throne."

"I wasn't going to work with him. I wasn't going to betray Ashnah."

"Quiet!" Hayes's voice rose, effectively silencing Terin's objections and pleas. "I know what you were doing, Terin. You were being a coward. You wouldn't have reported the duke's treachery. You would have sat back and watched. You might have even ordered your archers to do the same. I promise you that as soon as this war is over, you will face your due rewards for *everything*."

Hayes laid so much emphasis on that last word

that Terin's legs quaked. Because there was so much more than his actions against the kingdom that Hayes would make Terin pay for. Hayes wasn't often one for revenge or wrath. He'd warned his knights to avoid such things at all costs. But for once, Hayes was willing to give in to his lesser impulses.

"You never should have gotten away with so much for so long," Hayes said with disgust. "The only reason I'm not dragging you to the stockades now is because we have a war to fight. Your position protects you for now because this kingdom needs you as the commander of the archers. Your punishment will wait until after the battle. But it will come. You won't escape it this time."

"I did nothing wrong!" Terin objected. "I didn't accept the duke's offer."

"You are far from innocent. You may not have actively worked with Duke Heirson but you did nothing to stop him even when you knew his deceit. There is betrayal by omission too, Terin. You should be punished for far more than just your actions against the king."

Terin straightened, and he managed to jerk his arm free from Hayes's iron grasp. "You've gone soft, Hayes. You went soft long ago. This isn't about a perceived betrayal. This is still about my actions towards *my* archers. You have no business telling me how I should treat my men. Everything I've done is to prepare them for the realities of battle. This isn't a pretty world we live in. That hideous mark on your face should be reminder enough of it to you. But you still want to coddle our soldiers. You try to father your pawns. They are here to serve their kingdom even if it means losing their lives in the process. You would be wise to remember that, Hayes. You would be wise to let me toughen them up."

"What you're doing is not 'toughening' them up. You're abusing them. You hit them and insult them and call them names. That doesn't strengthen them. It demoralizes them. You're brutal and heartless."

"Some of those archers *deserve* punishment and cruelty."

The resulting blow could have been heard across the castle.

Hayes's fist connected with Terin's jaw, snapping the commander's head back. Hayes felt the satisfying pain in his knuckles and relished knowing that Terin fared much, much worse. Hayes had been careful in his strike, even though it was an unplanned impulse. He'd hit Terin in a spot that would bruise and swell but not incapacitate. Terin stumbled back with a cry of pain, surprise, and outrage.

Hayes didn't wait for the objection that was sure to come. With a wave of disgust towards the commander and a hint of satisfaction at his stinging hand, Hayes left the room, leaving Terin cursing behind him.

CHAPTER 63

Cal spent the night walking the halls of Castille Castle in solitude. He was relieved at capturing the duke but also disappointed at how things had turned out. Dusk was mourning the loss of his brother. Dresden may have conspired with his father and tried to kill Dusk, but the loss still impacted the spy. Cal and Lark had given their friend some space to sort through his thoughts and mixed emotions. The duke hadn't revealed who Freiwade's spies were yet. He'd refused to speak at all. Cal could only hope a few nights in the dungeons would loosen the man's tongue. Lark had been unable to capture the assassin whom they suspected was one of the spies. She'd chased down the trail through the network of vents and passages in the castle but there had been no sign of the murderer.

Cal wasn't sure what to make of things. Had the assassin gotten away because Lark was working with them? Duke Heirson had shown no sign of recognition with Lark in the room. Unfortunately, that could just mean he had never directly dealt with her. It seemed increasingly obvious that there was more than one spy in their midst. Cal knew he should be relieved at the progress they'd made but he was also disappointed at how much had gone wrong and how much still needed to be done. Cal's thoughts were tumultuous. He left The Cavern, giving Dusk the space he needed and leaving Lark to her duty of keeping an eye on the nobility to see if news of the duke's arrest had spread. He would have to talk with her later and he dreaded that conversation. It was peaceful in the hallways at night and Cal needed a little peace to sort through the chaos of the day. He stumbled along the halls, tracing his hands against the cold stone walls as he walked. He had practically grown up in the castle. It was his home. But things were changing. War was at their doorstep, secrets were coming to light, and allies were being found untrustworthy. Who could they trust? Who were the spies?

Cal thought about his allies. Dusk had been lying to him for years. He couldn't deny that it hurt. He'd known that Dusk was Everett Heirson but Dusk had said nothing about his father conspiring with the king of Freiwade. Cal understood Dusk's reasons but he still felt betrayed. Why hadn't Dusk trusted him? It made Cal wonder what other secrets were being kept. Cal was in the business of secrets. He hated being left in the dark.

He thought about Lark. How much did he know about her? There was still so much about the girl that he didn't understand. Could he trust her? His gut told him he could but his mind questioned the fact. She was hiding things from him too. He had always known that. Now he wondered how dangerous those secrets might be.

His mind was clouded as he walked the halls of the castle. After a few hours of wandering, Cal was nearly ready to call it a night. He was tired. The day's events, the events of the last few months, had taken a lot out of him. He doubted he'd get much rest anytime soon, not with the war. He had to admit he was discouraged too. He had expected to feel better after dealing with the duke's rebellion but the truth was the spies were still a threat and they still had the much larger issue of Nox and the army of Freiwade quickly approaching.

The hallways of Castille Castle which Cal wandered were unlit by torches and completely dark at night. The only light came from the moon illuminating certain sections through the windows. Cal watched his shadow move along the walls. It bent and transformed, then disappeared altogether, only to reappear a moment later. He felt his eyes growing heavy with exhaustion.

Because of his distraction, it took him a moment to notice that a second shadow had joined his. Cal blinked a few times in confusion before looking up. Ruena's maid, Vesta, was standing in the hallway ahead of him. She seemed to be waiting for someone.

"Cal," she said quietly, "I was hoping I would find you."

She had a lilt to her voice that sounded strange, Cal thought. He didn't remember noticing it before. Then again, he had tried to avoid Vesta for so long that he hadn't talked with her often. At first, Cal worried that something had happened to Ruena. Why else would Vesta seek him out? After all, Cal had seen her with a knight previously. She had clearly moved past any attraction towards him. When Cal reached Vesta, he voiced his concerns.

"Is something wrong?"

"No," she smiled pleasantly at him. "Nothing's wrong. But I'm happy I ran into you." She batted her eyelashes and took a step closer to him. Cal took a step back, his hand brushing against the wall.

Why was she doing this when he'd seen her with someone else? It wasn't the first time Vesta had approached him in such a manner but Cal thought she'd finally taken the hint that he had no interest in her. She was beautiful, yes, but she was too forward and he felt nothing for her.

Cal cleared his throat and raised a hand in warning. "Vesta."

She didn't listen. She kept moving forward until Cal's back was to the wall.

"What do you want?" Cal asked, though he thought he knew the answer.

She didn't say anything. Instead, she leaned towards him and pressed her mouth to his almost aggressively. Cal tried to push her away gently, not wanting to hurt her but she was surprisingly strong. Then in an instant, Vesta backed away. It happened so quickly that Cal didn't realize what was happening. In Vesta's place stepped a man, a tall, well-muscled knight. It took Cal a moment to recognize the newcomer in the darkness.

"Dorian?" Cal asked in confusion.

Before Cal could do anything, Dorian pressed a cloth to his face, covering his mouth and nose. Dorian pushed Cal hard against the wall. Cal gasped at the impact and inhaled a pungent odor from the cloth. He struggled but the drugged cloth remained steady. A wave of weakness washed over him. His legs quaked, unable to support his weight. His limbs felt like they were weighted with stone. His vision swam but somehow he remained conscious. Cal sank to the floor and Dorian scooped him up, carrying him like a child.

"Let's go," Dorian said to Vesta and suddenly they were moving.

Cal blinked and then they were past the castle walls and in the courtyard. He wasn't sure how much time had elapsed. There was a carriage waiting for them there. It was one of Duke Heirson's carriages. Cal barely managed to stay conscious but through the haze, he could make out Vesta and Dorian's conversation.

"Take the spymaster to King Corpin. He'll want to interrogate him. Then stay in Freiwade, Vesta. It's too dangerous here now. The duke has been captured and he's likely to talk. I'll try to slip some poison into his food in the dungeons but if I can't manage it, our covers will be blown. I won't put you at risk for that."

"Dorian," Vesta responded, "what about you? I won't leave you here. I love you."

Cal was jostled as Dorian shifted to lift a hand to Vesta's face. "And I you. But someone has to stay. The duke knows too much. He has to be killed like his son before he can reveal everything. Besides, there's still work to be done here. Promise me you'll stay in Freiwade and not return."

"I can't leave you."

"You must. I can't go back now."

Vesta sighed heavily with defeat. "Be careful."

Dorian didn't answer her. Cal was thrown into the back of the carriage and Vesta slipped inside. She sat across from him with a dagger pointed loosely at his throat. The driver of the carriage whipped the horses and they began to move forward. Cal sunk into oblivion.

CHAPTER 64

It took an immense effort for Dorian to return to his duties once he had seen Vesta off. His heart followed her to Freiwade. Dorian tried not to think of it as a final goodbye but he couldn't help being fatalistic. They had lost their edge. The secrecy of their positions as spies in Ashnah was in jeopardy. It was why he had insisted she go and not return. Besides, outright war was quickly approaching. Ashnah had never been a safe place for them but now Dorian feared for Vesta's life if she stayed. He feared for his own life too but he didn't value it nearly as much. Vesta would be safe, or as least as safe as possible for a spy, once she returned to Freiwade. The king would treat her fairly, especially now that she had Cal in tow as an offering. King Corpin would be greatly pleased to finally have the spymaster of Ashnah in his grasp. But Dorian knew that Cal had more to fear from the king's son Claude than he would the king himself.

That was one good aspect of acting as a spy in Ashnah. Dorian and Vesta had been free from the dangers that Claude posed. Despite his best efforts, Dorian had grown to like Ashnah. It was a beautiful kingdom with a kind people, people like Finch and Sir Hayes. It made his role as a spy more difficult to uphold. He'd made a mistake during the battle of Cheston. He'd killed one of his own, a fellow Freiwade soldier, in defense of Sir Hayes. He hadn't thought and before he'd fully realized what he was doing, his sword was piercing the man's chest and there was blood on his hands. It was his first kill and it wasn't even the enemy whom he'd struck. He wished he had time to sort through all of his conflicting thoughts but time was a commodity he had never possessed, not as a poor child of Freiwade, not as a spy, and certainly not as a knight. As usual, his duties prevented him from claiming even a single moment for himself. But with Vesta finally gone, heading towards safety, Dorian knew that he had an especially important duty to perform. It hadn't been too difficult to persuade his fellow knights to relegate the task of keeping watch on Duke Heirson to Dorian. The dungeons were dark and damp, an unpleasant place to stand guard. When Dorian volunteered for the task, his offer was quickly accepted.

He headed for the dungeons, still thinking about Vesta and hoping she would make it back to Freiwade safely. He wasn't sure what he would do if she were captured. All of this was for her and the family he had left behind. He would never see them again. He took the stairs to the dungeon two at a time and dismissed the guard on watch, taking up his position with his back to the cell that housed the disgraced duke.

"Knight," Duke Heirson said in a disgruntled voice, "how long does His Majesty plan on keeping me in this cell? The other nobles will rage at my treatment when they hear about this. I have allies and supporters. They will not allow this demeaning behavior for long."

Dorian turned so the duke could see his face. A flash of recognition crossed the man's features. It was true that Vesta had been the one to primarily report to the duke but the man still knew who Dorian was and the role he played. His knowledge of the spies' identities was one of the reasons he was so dangerous. It was one of the reasons he had to be dealt with before the king could extract any information from him. The duke flinched in surprise as he saw Dorian.

"Allies?" Dorian questioned. "Where are your allies now, Duke Heirson? They seem to have abandoned you."

"Nonsense," Heirson scoffed. "Your king will not let me, his figurehead for Ashnah, rot in these dungeons."

Dorian had to refrain from rolling his eyes. The duke knew so little about the king of Freiwade. King Corpin would abandon Heirson in an instant now that he had lost his use. The duke was a fool to think otherwise.

"Why would the king of Freiwade want anything to do with you after your foolishness caused the plan to fail? It was your actions that led to your capture. You never knew the meaning of subtlety, Duke. If you had only kept quiet about your dissatisfaction with King Rupert, you never would have been such a suspect for Ashnah's spies. King Corpin won't save you now. You're worthless to him."

"What do you know about it, *spy*?" the duke

spat out the word.

Dorian hid his wince. He hated that word. He hated what he had been reduced to, a spy. It was debase, cowardly, and deceitful. But it was necessary. Dorian had always done what he'd had to do. This role as a spy was no different. He was at least able to serve his kingdom, his family, and the woman he loved. Dorian didn't grace the duke's insult with a response. The man could think what he wanted but the king of Freiwade would never save him. In fact, Dorian's orders for a scenario like the one they had found themselves in were quite the opposite of what the duke expected.

"What do you care about all of this?" the duke questioned. For the first time, the man's voice lost its crass edge. He sounded genuinely curious. "What stake do you have?"

Dorian suddenly remembered that the duke hadn't just lost his freedom. It wasn't only that he had been caught in his lies and deception. He had also lost his son. Dorian and Vesta were instructed to protect their identities at all costs. They were forced to tie up any loose ends and eliminate any threats to their covers. When Vesta had heard about the meeting from Ruena it had made sense for her to hide in the vent to supervise. It had to be her. Dorian never would have fit in such a tight space. She hadn't hesitated to throw the knife that had killed Dresden when it became clear the duke's son would betray them.

Dorian swallowed hard. He hated to feel any sympathy for the duke but he couldn't help feeling sorry that Dresden had to die. It was necessary, Dorian told himself. It was all necessary.

"I have a greater stake in this than you could ever understand," Dorian told the man. "You have lived a life of privilege, Duke Heirson. I grew up in Freiwade, a poor child who had to struggle to survive. I had to provide for my family somehow. I've done what I had to. This was what my king demanded of me; this was how I was to serve my kingdom. I have much at stake. I have a family to provide for and protect."

"And the maid."

Dorian flinched and looked hard at the man. Even wallowing in the dungeons, he held onto his pride and arrogance. "Don't speak of what you don't understand."

The duke gave a derisive laugh. "That girl doesn't truly care for you. She is too cold and heartless to care for anyone."

"That's not true," Dorian argued, feeling heat fill his chest as he defended Vesta. "It may seem that way to some but I know her coldness is a necessity. You don't know what it's like in Freiwade, Duke. It's a constant fight for survival. Emotions are a weakness that many cannot afford. Besides, even if Vesta did not love me, it wouldn't matter because I love her more than anything. I would die for her in an instant. Sometimes sacrifice is necessary. I do not fear it. If you had learned about humility and sacrifice maybe you wouldn't have ended up here."

"I won't be here for long," the duke reasserted.

"You will be hung for your actions. You won't be able to worm your way out of this. King Corpin won't save you."

"I assure you, spy, that King Corpin would not

sacrifice someone so essential to his plans so willingly. Besides, I have plenty of supporters in the court of Ashnah. They will not leave me here to die."

"We will see," Dorian replied simply.

Dorian knew there was nothing more to be said. It was time to act. His heart lurched into his throat. Again, he told himself it was all necessary for the kingdom of Freiwade, for his family, and Vesta. Dorian slid the tray he had carried to the dungeons through the opening in the bars of the cell. The duke's rations were meager but sufficient. It was still finer fare than Dorian had grown up on as a child in Freiwade. The duke reached for the tray without hesitation. Dorian retreated to stand guard a few steps away from the cell. He listened as the duke chewed, his teeth ripping into the stale bread. He grumbled at the distasteful food but ate it anyway. A few moments later there was the sound of choking as the poison started to take effect. The bars of the cell rattled as the duke thrashed, his limbs spasming. He screamed obscenities at Dorian, the words choking and fragmented. Dorian ignored the curses and the clamor of the dying man. He refused to turn and look at the work of his hands. Deep down Dorian's heart started to ache at what he had done.

The duke was a despicable man and Dorian's actions had been necessary to protect himself and Vesta. It was his duty. Still, despite his work as a spy, Dorian had never and would never quite be able to stomach the violence. His hands started to shake as he listened to the duke's convulsions and cries of agony. He tried to refrain from looking, from thinking about what he had done. But at the last moment,

Dorian turned back. Maybe it wasn't too late to save the duke. Maybe he could undo the damage. Surely the man didn't need to die. Surely there was another way. Dorian approached the cell but before he could reach it, the door leading to the dungeons swung open. A knight started down the stairs and then broke into a run when he heard the duke's cries of hate and fear. The knight had probably been sent to question the duke. It was something Dorian hadn't stopped to consider.

"What's going on?" the knight demanded as he rushed to the cell. "What's happening to him?"

Dorian didn't answer.

"Do something!"

Dorian did nothing. "It's too late."

The knight froze. He straightened and turned slowly to look at Dorian. "It was you. You did this didn't you?" The knight called loudly up the stairs for reinforcements. He turned again to Dorian. "Traitor!" he spat the word.

Dorian knew it was the truth. He was a traitor to so many but what choice did he have? He only hoped it would all be worth it. He'd done his part, he'd done all he could, now it was up to Vesta to do the rest.

CHAPTER 65

Ruena, Lark, and Dusk rushed down the corridor to Sir Hayes's office. Ruena's heart was pounding in her chest. She felt like she couldn't breathe. How could so much have happened in so short a time? In a matter of hours, it seemed that everything had fallen apart.

She'd received a letter that morning delivered by a discreet servant no doubt sent directly from Sir Hayes. Ruena had been instructed to open the letter immediately and she was surprised at what she had found written on the page. It had been a request, no, a command, from her uncle the king for her to attend a crucial meeting. It was to take place immediately and Ruena was to tell no one about it. Ruena's mind had tumbled through the possibilities of such a meeting as she quickly prepared herself. On her way to the war room, she had run into a distraught Lark and Dusk. Knowing from their expressions that something was terribly wrong, Ruena had asked them what was going on. They hadn't been able to answer her but Lark had admitted that all they knew was that Cal was gone.

"Gone?" Ruena had asked.

Lark choked as she tried to smother a sob and Dusk had to take over the account.

"Cal disappeared last night. We expect the worst, especially after what happened with Duke Heirson and the assassin killing Dresden," Dusk blanched at the remembrance.

Ruena couldn't believe her ears. Cal was gone! How? She wanted to ask a million questions but she saw the pain on the faces of her companions and she knew it could wait a few more minutes until they reached the meeting. However, Ruena worried there was more going on than only Cal's disappearance.

When they reached Hayes's office, she became sure of the fact. Not only were Sir Hayes and the king waiting for them but also Clifton, Corin, and the young archer, Finch. Everyone's expressions were somber. Ruena looked across the room at Corin. Their eyes met but there was no reassurance in either of their gazes. Corin still looked to be in pain from using his magic. The ability he had discovered to use his arm again had taken a lot out of him. Ruena was glad to see him. At least he was alright. But Cal...

"Now that everyone is present and accounted for, we should begin the meeting," King Rupert announced.

Sir Hayes stepped forward to speak. "Much has been revealed in the past 24 hours. First of all, for all those not privy to the news earlier, Duke Heirson has been arrested for conspiring with the king of Freiwade to overthrow King Rupert and take the throne for himself. During the confrontation, Duke Heirson's son, Dresden, was killed by an assassin before he could reveal the identity of the spies within our midst."

Corin, Clifton, and Finch shared a look before Hayes continued. "The more troubling news is that Cal, our spymaster, went missing sometime during the night."

"How do we know he's missing and not just gone to spy out the area without telling anyone?" Finch asked.

"Will, the scribe's apprentice reported it directly to me," Hayes explained. "The boy saw Cal thrown into one of Duke Heirson's carriages as it was leaving the castle, presumably towards the duke's estate."

"And towards the border to Freiwade," the king added.

Ruena's heart twisted.

"Not Cal," Corin murmured.

"Has anyone been sent after him?" Finch questioned.

"We've sent a few knights after the carriage," Hayes explained. "However, if it crosses into Freiwade, we will be unable to follow."

"It won't matter," Finch said glumly. "The knights are hours behind. They won't catch up in time."

"There's more, isn't there," Dusk said, seeming to sense that Hayes hadn't finished.

Hayes nodded sadly. "Yes, unfortunately. Something else happened in the middle of the night. Duke Heirson was poisoned."

Dusk let out a barely perceptible gasp. His eyes widened before his expression shuttered into a mask of calm. The battling emotions were clear for an instant on his face but he said nothing about the news.

Hayes continued, "The guard stationed outside

his cell must have slipped poison into his meal. He was found dead this morning. The guard was arrested as the only suspect. He confessed to being the spy from Freiwade. However, he couldn't have worked alone and he most definitely would not have fit in the vent leading to Duke Heirson's room that the assassin utilized to kill Dresden."

"He wouldn't have admitted to being the spy so quickly if he wasn't trying to protect someone," Finch commented.

"The question is who?" Ruena wondered aloud.

"Who was the guard who confessed to being a spy?" Finch asked.

Hayes hesitated a long moment before answering. "It was Dorian."

A shudder swept over Finch's body and he made a sound like that of an injured animal. His eyes were wide with disbelief as he shook his head. "No. No, that's not true! It couldn't have been Dorian. Dorian would never betray this kingdom. He's too loyal, too kind, too good. You must be wrong!"

"Dorian confessed to everything," Hayes gently insisted.

Finch swallowed hard and fell into silence. His gaze held a roiling storm that was far from quiet. A mixture of anger, confusion, and above all betrayal was caught in his eyes.

"It was Dorian," Corin murmured in horror.

"Then who is the other spy?" Dusk asked.

"There was a maid," Finch said through gritted teeth. "Some of the knights said that Dorian was seen *fraternizing* with a maid."

"Vesta," Lark said.

"Vesta!" Ruena exclaimed.

"Cal told me he saw her with Dorian. He was relieved because she used to follow him around, flirting with him incessantly. She must have been trying to get information out of him."

"Vesta," Ruena said again, numbly. Her own maid. Her trusted friend.

Ruena stood frozen, horrified at the admission. But she could connect the dots. Vesta left the castle often to visit family. She was around Ruena and she could have overheard conversations between Ruena and Cal. She was known to flirt with Cal, perhaps in an attempt to extract information. Ruena paled and had to steady herself against the room's table. It was her fault, at least partially, that Cal had been taken. She'd never suspected Vesta of being one of the spies.

"So, the two spies we've been looking for all this time have been right under our noses, acting as our friends and confidants while they secretly conspired against us," Ruena stated.

"I don't believe it," Finch said angrily. "Dorian would never... he would never." Finch swallowed hard, unable to continue.

"We should have suspected sooner," Lark said.

"If we had, then Dresden..." Dusk didn't continue.

"Cal..." Corin added.

"We can't dwell on the things we've done wrong and the tricks we've fallen victim to," Hayes addressed them. "We have to focus on what comes next and how to save Cal."

Before Hayes could say anything else, a frantic knocking sounded at the door.

"Enter," Hayes called.

A knight rushed into the room; his face was deathly pale.

"What is it?" Hayes demanded.

"There's news from the frontlines," the knight explained. "Nox is on the move. He'll arrive in Castille in a matter of days."

Horrified silence filled the room. Then Ruena was lost in a bustle of frantic talk of gathering reinforcements. They would bring in soldiers from Nevara, the squires of Sir Burke. They would gather knights from other towns which held militias. There was talk of raising defenses, opening the castle as a refuge, and evacuating civilians further inland. All of the talk passed in a blur. Ruena looked around the room at the ill, shocked faces, the heartbreak, the fear, and the loss etched into everyone's expressions. She looked at Lark and Dusk who had lost their leader, she looked at Finch who had felt the betrayal of his only friend, and finally, she looked to Corin who was shaking at the news of Nox's quick approach.

Everything was falling apart. Just like her parents in the fire, Ruena was suddenly afraid that they were all trapped in a burning house and all their best-laid plans were going up in flames. She knew they wouldn't win this fight. They couldn't win this fight. Not unless God intervened. To prevail against Nox, to win the war, and to survive, they didn't just need magic, they needed a miracle.

S.G.MORAND

Attention!

If you've made it this far, first of all thank you! I truly hope you've enjoyed this book.

Want to read more of my stories? Check out the *Forest Dwellers* series and *Eden's Last Stand* also available on Amazon.

Also, please consider leaving a review of this book. Reviews help independently published authors like me more than you can imagine.

If you would like to learn more about me and my writing, please check out my website https://sgmorand.com or follow me on social media at sgmorand or S. G. Morand.

If you would like to receive newsletters and updates about future publications as well as a free Ebook, please subscribe to my email list by following this link: https://sgmorand.com/contact-me/

ACKNOWLEDGEMENT

This book is written for all of the fantasy lovers, who want an escape into a world grander and more adventurous than our own. As a child I always liked stories of magic but as a Christian there is often a stigma around those types of stories. However, I knew from reading Narnia and The Lord of the Rings that didn't always have to be the case. This is my attempt to write a Christian-centered story with all of the knights, princesses, and mages I had come to love in other stories. My main goal in all of my writing and in this story was to glorify God and to acknowledge Him openly. I am only human and possess a human understanding. Any faults in theology or scripture are a result of my own limited knowledge. I owe a great deal of gratitude to all of those who have helped me bring this world to life. Thanks to my mother who urged me to keep working away until the story was the best it could be, even when I felt discouraged and lost. Thanks to my dad who is always willing to talk through theology and scripture with me and who designs all of my amazing book covers. Thanks to all of my readers including: Anabel Moore, Kenlei Reese, Joel James, Nick Smith, and my aunt Jeanne, and all of the others.

ABOUT THE AUTHOR

S. G. Morand

Sarah Morand lives in Montana where she loves archer, collecting sarcastic t-shirts, and her obnoxious rat terrier, Ivan. She has an eclectic taste in books and her ideal house would be a Victorian library. Sarah started writing in middle school and after writing a plethora of short stories, finished her first novel by her senior year of high school. She is the author of the Forest Dwellers series and Eden's Last Stand available on Amazon.

Find more information:
sgmorand.com
And follow on social media at:
Instagram and Tiktok: sgmorand
Facebook: S.G. Morand - Author
Goodreads: S. G. Morand

BOOKS BY THIS AUTHOR

Forest Dwellers: The Exile

Traitors, Banished, Exiled...
After her father and many others are unjustly banished from the dukedom of Mac'tire, Brier's life changes forever. The hardships of exile force the outcasts to plead with the duke to allow them to return. Along with four other teenagers, Brier is tasked with journeying back to Mac'tire. Brier's trust in God is put to the test. She must overcome her fear of past failures to guide her friends. But the journey back to Mac'tire won't be as easy as they thought.

Forest Dwellers: The Battle Of Mac'tire

Brier and her friends have barely survived the grueling journey to their old home, the dukedom of Mac'tire. Their faith in God and each other has been put to the test. Now they'll face their greatest challenge, gaining an audience with the duke and clearing their names. Beneath the surface are undercurrents of corruption, misplaced trust, and an impending coup. The teens not only must prove their parents' innocence, they must navigate the palace intrigue to save the dukedom. But, their worst enemy might prove to be each other.

Forest Dwellers: The Wolves Of Lupus

Abducted...
After completing their training as foresters, Brier and Reid return to Mac'tire for some much-needed rest. Unfortunately, leisure will have to wait. Soon after they arrive, Flint goes missing. The prime suspect behind his disappearance is a dead man. Brier and her friends must hasten to the Dukedom of Lupus in order to rescue Flint and confront an unexpected threat. Opposition encroaches from all sides as they battle not only present foes but the past as well. They will have to rely on God and each other to save their friend and themselves.

Forest Dwellers: Trials Of The Trade Route

Pressure, Perseverance, Penance...
The young outcasts have finally settled into their new lives, but their trials are far from over. Brier and Reid are sent to investigate a strange cabin in the forest that might hold the key to resolving current trouble and uncovering secrets of the past.
Meanwhile, Flint and Erin deal with their own troubles in Lupus. Duke William wants to give Corvus's son, Lyall, a second chance. But can he be trusted?
Lance has his own adventures as he works with

a group of vigilantes to resolve a series of vicious attacks on Mac'tire's newly established trade route with Lupus. A new threat has arisen that might prove more dangerous than Corvus himself.

The former outcasts are drawn into a series of mysteries and perils as they strive to uncover the secrets of the past, protect the present, and ensure a bright future for the dukedoms. Will the new challenges they face prove too much for them, or will it bring them closer to God and each other?

Forest Dwellers: A Poisonous Past

Past... Present... Future

Brier and her friends have come far since they returned from exile. As they've settled into their new lives, they thought they had put their past behind them. With Tan wreaking havoc on the trade route, Lyall's motives in question, and the discovery of a long-lost document hiding a shocking truth, they are all forced to look back before they can move forward. They won't have long to dwell on their troubles. Danger lurks just around the corner and the consequences could be disastrous. Will they overcome the past in time to save their futures?

Eden's Last Stand

On an island ruled by a corrupt regime, a series of dangerous and immoral experiments force an underground group of Christians to make a desperate stand. Kidnapped on their way home from school, Lynn and Lex are thrown into the middle of a battle between the forces of tyranny and Eden, a group of rebels who operate in the shadows. When Lynn becomes the target of sinister experiments conducted by the forces controlling the island's precious resources, the once-distant struggle becomes personal. Eden's warriors are former victims, each just as determined as Lynn to expose the evil around them and put an end to their suffering. Equipped with unique abilities, Eden's outcasts struggle to control their powers and harness them for the good of all. Will this ragtag group be able to put the past aside, follow God's will, and bring about a brighter future, or will they succumb to the dark forces arrayed against them?

Made in the USA
Monee, IL
13 March 2025